ALSO BY LEONARDO PADURA

THE TRANSPARENCY
OF TIME

THE TRANSPARENCY OF TIME

LEONARDO PADURA

Translated from the Spanish by Anna Kushner

FARRAR, STRAUS AND GIROUX | NEW YORK

Farrar, Straus and Giroux
120 Broadway, New York 10271

Printed in the United States of America
Originally published in Spanish in 2018 by Tusquets Editores, Spain,
as *La transparencia del tiempo*
English translation published in the United States by Farrar, Straus and Giroux
First American edition, 2021

Library of Congress Cataloging-in-Publication Data
Names: Padura, Leonardo, author. | Kushner, Anna, translator.
Title: The transparency of time / Leonardo Padura; translated from the
    Spanish by Anna Kushner.
Other titles: Transparencia del tiempo. English
Description: First American edition. | New York : Farrar, Straus and Giroux, 2021. |
    Originally published in Spanish in 2018 by Tusquets Editores, Spain, as
    La transparencia del tiempo.
Identifiers: LCCN 2020058352 | ISBN 9780374277956 (hardcover)
Subjects: LCSH: Conde, Mario—Fiction. | Private investigators—Cuba—
    Havana—Fiction.
Classification: LCC PQ7390.P32 T713 2021 | DDC 863/.64—dc23
LC record available at https://lccn.loc.gov/2020058352

Designed by Gretchen Achilles

Our books may be purchased in bulk for promotional, educational, or
business use. Please contact your local bookseller or the Macmillan Corporate
and Premium Sales Department at 1-800-221-7945, extension 5442,
or by email at MacmillanSpecialMarkets@macmillan.com.

www.fsgbooks.com
www.twitter.com/fsgbooks • www.facebook.com/fsgbooks

10 9 8 7 6 5 4 3 2 1

To Lucía, we already know how and why

Now he tells, whosoever will listen, that he returns from where he never was.

—Alejo Carpentier, *El camino de Santiago*

CONTENTS

THE TRANSPARENCY
OF TIME

1.

SEPTEMBER 4, 2014

The emphatic first light of dawn in the tropics filtered through the window, projecting dramatically against the wall where the calendar hung, with its perfect grid of twelve squares divided into four rows. The spaces had originally been colored in distinctive tones ranging from spring's youthful green to winter's deep gray, a scheme that only a very imaginative designer could associate with something as contrived as the four seasons on a Caribbean island. With the passing months, fly droppings had decorated the board's motifs with erratic ellipses. Several stains and its ever-fading colors testified to the paper's constant use and the blinding light that beat down on it every day. A variety of capricious shapes were doodled all over the thing—around the edges, even over some of the numbers, hinting at past reminders that were perhaps later forgotten and never acted upon. Signs of the passage of time and proof of a mind suffering sclerosis.

The year at the top of the calendar had received special attention and was covered with a variety of cryptic signs. Those numbers specifically tasked with representing the ninth day of October were surrounded by further perplexing sigils, which had been scratched in (more in rage than approval) with a pen just a bit lighter than the original black printer's ink. And alongside several exclamation points, the digits that—as the doodler only now noticed—resonated with magical, numerological power, the power of perfect recurrence: 9-9-9.

Ever since that slow, grim, slippery year had begun, Mario Conde maintained a tormented relationship with the dates at hand. Throughout his life and despite his historically good memory and general obsessiveness, he'd paid little attention to the effect of time's speed and its implications for his own life and the lives of those around him. Regrettably and all too often, he forgot ages and birthdays, wedding anniversaries, the dates of trivial or major events—from the celebratory to those that evoked grief or commemorated simpler moments—that were or would be important to other people. But the alarming evidence persisted that, among those 365 days squared off by the grid of that cheap calendar, a day lay waiting to pounce that was as yet inconceivable, but threateningly definite and real. The proximity of the day Mario Conde would turn sixty years old caused in him a persistent shock exacerbated by the approach of those notable numbers: 9-9-9. It even *sounded* indecent (*sixty* . . . *sixty* . . . something that lets out air and explodes, *sssix-tttty* . . .), and this milestone presented itself as the incontestable confirmation of what his physical (creaky knees, waist, and shoulders; a fatty liver; an ever-lazier penis) and spiritual (dreams, projects, diminished or completely abandoned desires) selves had already been feeling for some time: the obscene arrival of old age . . .

Was he really an Old Man? In order to confirm it, as he stood before the blurry landscape of the calendar that hung from a pair of nails on his bedroom wall, Conde responded to this question with new ones: Wasn't his grandfather Rufino an Old Man when, at the age of sixty, he took Conde around the city and surrounding areas to cockfighting rings and taught him the ins and outs of noble combat? Didn't they start calling Hemingway "Old Man" a few years before his suicide at sixty-one? What about Trotsky? Wasn't he, at sixty, known as the Old Man when Ramón Mercader split his head in two with a Stalinist and proletarian blow from an ice ax? For starters, Conde knew his limits and understood (owing to well-founded or spurious reasons) that he was a far cry from being his pragmatic grandfather, or Hemingway, or Trotsky, or any other famous old codger. As such, he felt that he had reason enough to avoid so much as aspiring to the category of *Old Man*, capital letters and all, even as he careened toward that painful number, round and decadent . . . No, he was, at best, going to become an old fart. The term was more apt in his case—in the category of possible decrepitude as classified with academic zeal by serious geriatric science and the empirical wisdom of an everyman's street-smart philosophy.

On mornings like this one, suffocatingly hot from the get-go and already inaugurated with his lingering attention to the calendar, those perverse intersections of arithmetic, statistics, memory, and biology invaded him and increased his anguish. Their interconnectedness gave way to a resounding certainty in Conde's mind. Because even in the best of cases (and the best-case scenario here meant simply staying alive, meant his liver and lungs not letting him down), right in front of him was the numerical evidence of his already having wasted three-quarters (maybe more, no one knows for sure) of the maximum amount of time he would spend on this earth, and the firm conviction that the last part of his allotted span probably wouldn't turn out any better. Mario Conde knew perfectly well that being old—even being old without being an old fart—is a horrifying condition, due to all it entails, but especially because it carries with it an incontrovertible threat: the statistical and physiological approach of death. Because two plus two is four. Or rather four minus three is one . . . just one, one-quarter of life left, Mario Conde.

Aches and pains and existential frustrations aside, the presence of that red flag visible on the horizon, near or far, but never entirely gone, had threatened him with greater vigor than ever that morning. Urged by the need to urinate, the need to survive, Conde grappled with the decision to abandon his bed, set aside the desire to burrow into a good book (he still had so many to read, and always less time in which to conquer them!), and resisted even the persistent appeal of throwing himself into his own writing. After expelling his abundant and fetid morning urine, he began the increasingly arduous process of gathering the strength to make his best effort to prevent his own inertia from letting death get ahead of him. In sum: he had to hit the damned streets, the pavement, to make the most of what was left of his life, to avoid the fatal call for as long as possible, and to forget about his pseudophilosophical or literary mental masturbation.

As he drank his coffee and stared hatefully at the damned cigarettes he'd never wanted or been able to give up, he watched his dog's peaceful sleep: Garbage II, the former living hurricane who, like Conde, had also

become slower and more of a homebody as a result of all the pavements he'd
pounded. At heart Garbage II was more of a peripatetic gigolo, but lately
he'd taken to longer naps and smaller meals, telegraphing his own decrepitude, already visible in the graying of his snout, in the opaqueness of his
demanding stare, and in the darkening of his teeth . . . "What a disaster!" Conde said to himself, caressing the dog's head and ears, and trying,
without much enthusiasm, to plan the coming day. This exercise turned
out to be so easy for him that he had enough time left over to continue
philosophizing after all, as he absorbed his drags of the day's first dose
of nicotine. Because he knew that, like every other morning, he would
hit the pavements in search of old books for sale; then he would eat some
ingestible street food, or get a full meal if he let himself swing by the house
of Yoyi the Pigeon, his business partner. Later, full of rum, or even sober,
he would stop by his friend Skinny Carlos's house and then end the day
by sleeping over at Tamara's, from whom he'd unjustly absented himself
for two days. The panorama ahead of him was nothing new, but it wasn't
unwelcome, either: work, friendship, love, all of it a bit worn, a bit old
but still solid and real. The screwed-up part, he admitted to himself,
was his state of mind, which was more and more marked by sadness and
melancholy, and not just due to the burden of his physical age or the
much-feared approach of a terrifying birthday and whatever inevitable
consequences would pertain thereto, but because of the certainty of having failed abysmally at life. On the cusp of sixty, what did he have? What
was his legacy? Nothing at all. And what awaited him? The same nothing squared—or something worse. These were the only responses within
reach of his very simple yet sticky questions. And, to his great dismay,
they were likewise the only available responses to so many people, both
strangers and friends, of the same age, asking the same questions, inhabiting the same time and space.

Once he was dressed, after giving Garbage II some leftovers and another round of expedient caresses in order to remove a couple of ticks,
just as Conde's mood was improving a bit as he emptied the third and last
cup of the infusion that dripped out of his Italian coffeepot, he was startled by the ringing of the telephone. For some time now, calls first thing
in the morning or late at night set off all of his alarm bells. Since he was

surrounded by so many old people like himself, any incoming call could announce the end—or at least be a harbinger of it.

"Yes?" he asked, expecting the worst.

"Is this Mario Conde's residence?" A slow, questioning voice. *Undefinable, unknown,* Conde thought.

He grunted his confirmation, growing more expectant still, before demanding: "Speak."

"What, you don't recognize me?"

That sort of question, posed over the telephone, always managed to scramble Conde's nerves so badly that it sometimes put him into an almost murderous rage. And on this day, of all days, after having enjoyed such a Sartrean morning, the absurdity of it charged at him like a Miura bull. He broke the tension with an explosion of expletives.

"How in the fuck do you expect me to recognize you, shithead?"

"Hey, man, sorry," the voice came back, now quick and decisive as it hurried on to add, "It's Bobby, Bobby Roque, from high school . . . Remember?"

And yes, Conde closed his eyes, nodded, smiled, and shook his head as he detected the distinct fluttering among his neurons of a distant nostalgia, almost vanished, cloaked in the simultaneously grim and pleasant scent of the past—yes, of course he remembered.

Roberto Roque Rosell, Ro-Ro-Ro . . . The confluence of his two surnames had been enhanced by his given name, Roberto, so that with all of those *R*s and *O*s, rotund, robust, roaring, virile, refulgent with the appellation that would accompany him his whole life, under the precarious precept that the name makes the man. Perhaps because of this, or—better still—in order to better manifest it, his parents refused to call him Robertico, Robert, or Robby, but rather, ever since he was a boisterous baby in his crib, dubbed him Robertón, trusting that, with that extraordinary face, he would make his way through life honoring this epithet and fulfilling all of his progenitors' dreams . . . Fifteen years after his baptism, when Conde happened to meet this Roberto Roque Rosell in one of his classes at La Víbora High School—the same classes where he met Skinny

Carlos, Andrés, Rabbit, Candito the Red, Tamara (of course), and even Rafael Morín—the boy was indeed two or three inches taller than the rest of Conde's friends, but delicate and emaciated, lacking the poundage that would have made him a daunting figure, and already known not as Robertón, much to his parents' dismay, but simply as Bobby. And not because *Bobby* was one of the most Anglophilic diminutives possible, so in vogue in those years, and not even due to the fact that this was at the height of Bobby Fischer's eccentric fame. No, Bobby had to be *Bobby* because the nickname had the semantic quality that best went with its owner's most notable characteristics: at fifteen, sixteen years old, the former Robertón of grand ambitions was just kind of dopey and a little too languid—or rather, kind of a fairy, according to the rough linguistic and cultural codes of Conde and his crowd.

Despite never having been what you could call friends, the fact of having been in the same class for a couple of years created a certain closeness between the evanescent Bobby—with whom the others really didn't have much in common—and Conde, Carlos, Rabbit, and Andrés. Bobby didn't even like to talk about baseball; in social studies classes, he acted like an ideological Cerberus, barking out slogans; and when it came to music, he was weird enough to prefer Maria Callas to the Beatles and even Creedence. Nevertheless, the kid's aptitude for matters scientific turned him into a precious jewel his classmates repeatedly clung to when cramming for those difficult subjects on the day before exams. In that context, Conde and his friends had welcomed him as a sort of tutor, in exchange for which they offered Bobby a little protection from the looming, frequent cruelties of their other classmates, generally given to crushing any display of weakness, or the least hint of a predilection for Maria Callas.

Around that time, Conde and his friends discussed the subject often, analyzed it collectively, and came to this conclusion: Bobby was not yet a homosexual, but he would get himself impaled the first chance he got. And it wouldn't be on an arrow shot by Paris or Pandarus, the Trojan heroes of the *Iliad*, about whom Bobby spoke as if he'd known them in person. "Doesn't it seem strange that he likes Achilles so much, huh?" Rabbit used to ask, more a devotee of the Trojans than of the cuckolded Achaeans. Meanwhile, Skinny Carlos, who at the time was even skinnier but just as much of a Good Samaritan as he would remain for the rest of his life, decided to rescue Bobby from the fatal transgression. He assigned himself the task of finding Bobby a female savior among Dulcita's friends (Dulcita was his girlfriend back then—back then, and later too), but his efforts proved unsuccessful: neither the girls nor Bobby himself seemed too willing to go in for that carnal solution. Soon Bobby and his putative saviors ended up being "just friends," even confidants—the kind who go around whispering to each other, laughing and holding hands.

When their cohort finished high school and scattered itself through different departments at the university, Conde kept seeing Bobby from time to time, although less frequently. Sometimes they ran into each other at the dining hall, other times they both ended up at one of the recurring required political meetings organized by the Student Federation. Occasionally they rode the same bus. At each encounter, they greeted each other warmly, almost with joy on Bobby's side, albeit without too much chatter, perhaps because they'd grown apart, each entering their particular milieu, and both felt they had less to say. And then, one afternoon, to Conde's surprise—a surprise that prompted him to relay the gossip to his friends later that very night—the future detective had run into Bobby at a bar by the university where it was sometimes possible to achieve the Havana miracle of procuring beer. There Bobby was, not only there drinking one of those much-pined-for lagers, but doing so in the presence of a woman whom he introduced as his girlfriend. And though in Conde's view the woman was no great catch—she was much shorter than Bobby, a little heavyset, with a demeanor that seemed to Conde, perhaps due to his already firmly set opinions, a little crude—Roberto Roque Rosell's old buddies were happy to hear about Bobby's conquest. Only Rabbit, who always opted for a dialectical and historical approach, opined that the incident didn't really signify anything definitive: old Bobby could go both ways, right? Like Achilles, who was light in his loafers!

During Conde's meeting with the young couple, which proved quite memorable, Bobby had seemed exultant and happy, since he was celebrating his entry to the selective and honorable Young Communist League. As such, he invited his former high school classmate to have a few beers with him, with his red membership ID—*¡Estudio, Trabajo, Fusil!* (Study, Work,

Rifle!)—and his girlfriend (Yumilka? Katiuska? Matrioska?), whom he kissed too frequently and too wetly . . . And then the guy disappeared, like the Phantom of the Opera . . . That was probably around 1978, the same year that Conde, at the end of his third year of college, was forced to abandon his studies and, as an alternative to starving to death, surprised himself by accepting a place at the police academy, thus turning (he would always think) the life he could have had upside down. From then on Bobby practically vanished from Conde's mind, only ever conjured up again during one of those gatherings at which he and his friends might indulge in a little nostalgia and so raise the specter of that obscure character once more. What the hell had become of Bobby? Had he gone North like so many, many other people? No, not Bobby, not Bobby of the Red Guard! Unless he too—was it possible?—had strayed from Party orthodoxy. It wasn't unheard of.

Which was why, when an androgynous being with dyed ash-blond hair, an earring in his left earlobe, perfectly trimmed eyebrows, and a sparkling smile lighting up a face with a few rogue wrinkles impressed itself upon Conde's retinas, his brain wasn't capable of reconciling the vision with his last warehoused image of Bobby: a beer in one hand, eyes overflowing with joy and manly, militant pride, an arm around the shoulders of . . . Yumilka? Svetlana? Conde knew it had to be him, however— had to be Bobby because after speaking on the phone they'd agreed to meet now ("Perfect, five p.m.") and here, at Conde's house ("Yes, the same house as always . . . older and more fucked-up, like everything else, like all of us.").

"*Ay*, but look at you, you're exactly the same!" his guest said as Conde, wearing a stunned expression, held tight to the doorknob.

"Don't screw with me, Bobby," Conde said once he'd recovered from his shock. "If I had this same face forty years ago . . . then I would have been well and truly fucked. But you, you don't look anything like you used to . . ."

"Right? Tell me, what do you think of my look?" Bobby asked, adding in a whisper, "Made in Miami, my friend! The truth is I dye my hair to hide the gray. Old age, *vade retro*!"

But Conde felt that there hadn't been a big change in just Bobby's look, so outlandish and yet so right. His personality had also changed—the two sentences they'd exchanged, and his guest's effeminate gestures announced it clearly. Conde couldn't help but think that Bobby now carrying himself in such a way so as to express his true nature (or, anyway, his preferred nature) seemed to have freed him from his tightly wound shyness, since the person he had become displayed an ease that was completely divorced from the lingering image in Conde's mind of a repressed, not to say *compressed*, young man: as if Bobby had broken through the chains of selfhood and had actually fashioned himself anew. The benefits of freedom.

"You look good," Conde admitted, still feeling the effects of his initial shock. He stepped to one side so his visitor could pass. "Come in. So now you live in Miami?"

"No, no," the other man said. "The clothes and the hair dye are from Miami . . . The rest, one-hundred-percent Cuban . . . And speaking of hair dye, you look like you could use some yourself . . . Check out all that gray! What you need is a little dark chestnut brown!"

Before closing the door, Conde looked up and down the street. He didn't like the idea too much of people in the neighborhood seeing him let a character like this into his house, although at this age, no one could think any worse of him than they already did. He headed for the kitchen, offered a chair to Bobby, and went over to the stove to light the burner on which the moka pot rested.

"You want some water?" he asked Bobby, who looked his own age for a moment as he wiped away some sweat.

"Is it mineral water? Is it boiled?"

"Mineral? Boiled? The water?" Conde asked.

"Never mind, never mind . . . I brought my own." Bobby opened the multicolored bag he had draped across his front to extract a store-bought bottle of water and a manila envelope, which he placed on the table. "You have to be careful—bugs, viruses, all of that garbage polluting the environment. Cholera! Ebola! Chikungunya! Even the names are fucking horrifying. An assault on my brain."

"You're right," Conde said. "Next year, I'll start boiling my water . . ."

"Oh, man, you haven't changed . . . though maybe you're a bit more . . ."

"More what?"

Bobby thought about it before replying.

"More *machista* . . ."

"Damn, Bobby, I'm not even that anymore . . . I've got hypertension and must have a death wish since I don't boil my water . . ."

Back at the stove, he confirmed that the coffee was almost ready.

"Make mine without sugar!" Bobby requested when Conde took the ancient moka pot off the flames.

"Black coffee now?"

"You have to take care of yourself . . . We're getting old . . ."

"Don't even start," Conde said and handed a cup to his health-conscious visitor before putting sugar in his own. As they drank their coffee, he dared to examine his former classmate more closely. He was and was not Bobby. He had gained some weight, not too much, just enough to look more proportional, although his face had softened, in part because of the years, but also, Conde supposed, because it was seemingly animated by a different sort of spirit. And another surprise: besides the earring, the bleached and tinted hair, and the shaped eyebrows, Bobby was sporting a bracelet of blue beads and translucent glass that could only be a proclamation of his initiation into Santería, that tenacious African religion capable of resisting any and all attacks by colonial Christianity, by the bourgeois morality of the Republic, and, indeed, in more recent years (the last fifty?), by the Marxist-atheist offensive. So Bobby, the fervent militant communist, had become a Santero . . .

"Tell me something about your life," Conde said and lit a cigarette, surely violating another of his visitor's rules for healthy living.

"So many things have happened, Conde!" Bobby said and waved a hand delicately. "I don't even know where to start, man . . ."

"Wherever the hell you want. Start with the earring and the hair, maybe . . ."

Bobby smiled sadly. "Ash blond . . . That's a long, loooong story, but I'll try to give you the short version. I got married, okay? Had two sons, who are men already, real men now, by the way . . ."

"How nice!" Conde was bowled over. "Did you marry that girl from the university? Yumilka?"

"Katiuska!" Bobby exclaimed and immediately added, "That bitch Katiuska! How do you even remember her?"

"So what did Katiuska ever do to you? She got uglier, or something? She cheated on you?" Conde asked, to avoid responding.

Bobby looked at him with a helplessness in his eyes that, for the first time, allowed the former cop to find in the sight of the man before him the ghost of the vulnerable boy he had met so many years before: an air of distress with a hint of sadness, a lot of frailty, and far too much fear.

"No, she didn't cheat on me. And I didn't marry her anyway. Katiuska just fucked up my life . . . or saved it, I don't know . . . But that's not the story I wanted to tell you. Look, I'll give you the quick lowdown, okay? After university, I married Estela, Estelita, the mother of my two sons. And everything was smooth sailing until, through some business dealings, I met Israel and . . . I cracked! I fell in love like a dog, no, like a goddamn bitch!"

And Conde thought, *Maybe Bobby's whole amazing story is just one long, liberating escape from the closet?*

Bobby drained his cup of coffee and pointed at Conde's pack of cigarettes.

Conde grinned. "Smoking is hazardous for your health, or didn't you hear?"

"It sure is," Bobby said, "but I want one real bad!"

He lit the cigarette Conde gave him and exhaled smoke with evident pleasure.

"Listen, Conde . . . did you ever end up writing anything?"

"Writing? Sure. I've done a few things," he said, which was true—but without knowing why, he felt the need to dress up his response, as if he needed to excuse himself before the world. "I'm thinking of putting a book together . . . but let's leave that aside for now . . . Go on with your story."

"Well, so . . . I got separated from Estelita, I moved in with Israel, and we were together for about ten years, until he left for Miami because he couldn't stand the heat anymore . . . ."

"They say in Miami it's also hot as hell, no?"

"Oh, come on, man, that thing about the heat is just an excuse . . . Israel couldn't take it anymore . . . You know, the situation, the thing . . ." And he made a gesture as if to include everything around them.

"Ah, yes, the thing," Conde said. "And?"

"And nothing. The usual . . . I've had a lot of partners, until about two years ago, I met Raydel and . . . I fell in love like a goddamn rabid bitch again, and an old one too, this time!"

"It's good to be in love," Conde said. He too was prone to falling into that state of grace and vulnerability. Although in his case, it had only involved women, and, for many years now, the same woman.

"But it's dangerous, very dangerous . . . That's why I'm here."

"Because you're in love?"

"Because of the consequences . . ."

"You lost me."

Bobby crushed his half-smoked cigarette in the ashtray after taking one last, gluttonous drag, just as Conde slid out another for himself and lit it.

"Let's see, let's see, how do I explain this to you . . ." Bobby ran his hand through his faded hair and blinked several times. "It's just that this is terrible, man! I met Raydel at my *Padrino*'s house," he began and touched the bracelet of brilliantly colored beads around his wrist before leaning to one side and placing his fingertips on the floor and then lifting them back to his lips. "It's been eighteen years already since I was initiated into Santería . . . receiving Yemayá at my ceremony . . ."

"Wait, wait. The way I remember it, you were a dialectical material-ist, no?" Conde said after taking in Bobby's ritual in inquisitive silence while fighting to repress thoughts of roughing up (just a bit!) this former slogan-spouting Marxist zealot who'd ended up a devotee of something so primitive, so Afro-Cuban—and which, of course, was no less an opiate than any other religion, as Karl himself would put it.

"Conde, look, that was just a mask I had to wear . . . like almost everyone does at one time or another, right? My entire life, I had to hide that I was gay, hide that I believed in God and in the most Holy Virgin Mother . . . So I spent my first forty years pretending, repressing, tor-turing myself, so that my parents, so that all of you, my friends, so that everyone in our macho-socialist homeland would believe that I was what I should have been and wouldn't take everything away from me. I had to be an exemplary young man, virile and politically engaged, an atheist, obedient . . . You can't imagine what my life was like, not a chance . . ."

Conde didn't dare comment. He knew all about the masks and the hiding and the pressures that so many people had needed to withstand to live in a society so focused on regimenting ethical, political, and social behaviors, and in repressing—rigorously, even wrathfully—any display of difference. And Bobby must have been the perfect victim.

"Anyway, as I was saying . . . I met Raydel at my *Padrino*'s house. Raydel had just arrived from Palma Soriano, out there near Santiago de Cuba, and he was in the business of selling animals to Santeros . . . I wish you could've seen him: olive-skinned with these big eyes, lush lashes, a mouth like—"

"Don't," Conde cut him off. "That's enough. I get it, you fell in love. And?"

"I gave him a good bath to get rid of his goat stink and then I got together with that precious thing. I took him to my house. We lived together for two years, it was like a dream . . . And well, then Israel invited me to visit Miami and those American imperialist gentlemen were crazy enough to give me a visa. I went over there for two months, to see Israel and to try to arrange some things for my business while I was at it . . ."

"You have a business?" Conde arched an eyebrow: his former classmate was simply unfathomable. Now he was a capitalist, too?

"Sure, I deal in objets d'art, jewelry, expensive things like that . . ."

"And when you got home, you found out that Raydel had disappeared along with everything he could carry . . ."

Bobby's amazement was tangible. He blinked several times, as if Conde must have read his mind.

"Christ, Bobby," Conde came to his rescue, "I may not be a Santero, but try and remember that I was a cop for ten years . . . If you came looking for me, of all people, I had to figure it's because something fucked-up happened, right . . . ?"

Bobby nodded, his face settling into an expression of great sadness.

"Yeah, he took it all, Conde, every damn bit of it . . . Jewelry, the TV, even the light bulbs and pots and pans!"

"Shit."

"Luckily, before leaving, I sold lots of things to get dollars to take to Miami to invest in some businesses I set up over there . . . But, even still, Raydel brought a truck around and just cleaned me out . . . He took everything. The mattress! The kettle for boiling water to kill bugs!"

"Did you go to the cops?"

Bobby shook his head no as if the very idea struck him as impossibly arcane.

"I'm still in love, man! If I file a report, they'll throw him in jail . . ."

Conde threw the butt of his cigarette out the window. He resolved not to judge Bobby and his lovesick weaknesses, since he himself had done some crazy things for love. Perhaps it was more accurate to say that he had done *every* crazy thing . . . although always for the love of women, he told himself. *Machista*, he thought.

"So, when was it that you returned from Miami?"

"About . . . eight days ago," Bobby calculated.

"Oof, eight days is like a century when it comes to this shit. So, what? You want me to . . . ?" Conde began, but stopped himself, alarmed when he finally understood what was going on, and changed his tack. "Damn, Bobby, how did you find me?"

"Through Yoyi the Pigeon, of course . . . I asked him not to say anything to you, so I could surprise you . . ."

Conde now sized up his old classmate as though he weren't a dyed and waxed gay man, a believer in Santería, or even a businessman with tentacles in both Havana and Miami, but rather as though he were an extraterrestrial.

"How do you know the Pigeon?"

"Business . . ."

Now it was Conde who was shaking his head. He understood less and less. Or perhaps he understood even more?

"Listen, Conde," Bobby tried. "I've done business with Yoyi two or three times, picked up some valuable books and some works by Cuban painters. And when he found out what happened to me, since he knew that you and I went to high school together, that we had been friends . . . he recommended that I come and see you . . . And since of course I trust you completely . . ."

Conde could only smile: about how small the world was for Bobby to end up being, by way of his partner the Pigeon, the buyer for some valuable books that he himself had tracked down in his hunting expeditions around Havana; because apparently his commercial partner was also working as his promotional agent for his private detective work and because, in honor of old times, it flattered him to hear Bobby confirm that they were still friends, and that he still trusted him.

"Damn, Bobby, you've gotta be crazy for listening to the Pigeon . . ."

"Oh, my friend, you have to help me," Bobby said, taking one of Conde's hands in both of his. "I don't want to denounce Raydel, I'm not even holding out hope he'll return some of the more valuable things . . . but my Lady of Regla . . ."

"This guy took your saints?"

"I told you, he took everything, Conde, everything . . . Except Yemayá's necklaces and mantles . . . I guess he got scared—he didn't even touch that stuff . . . But the statue of Our Lady of Regla, that he took!"

"And now you want to recover a Madonna that you could buy at any store . . ."

"It's not just *any* Madonna, Conde! It's mine, mine! It's my Mother!" Bobby was—or seemed—quite moved. "Imagine. That Lady of Regla belonged to my grandmother, and she got it as a gift from her father when she was very little. And when I was about to be initiated into Santería, and it turned out I was to receive Yemayá—who, as you are aware is known as Our Lady of Regla in the Catholic faith—she gave it to me . . . No, man, it's not just any statue . . . Look, look how beautiful She is."

Bobby, with a light tremor in his hands, patted the manila envelope he'd placed on the table and took out two 5 × 7 color photographs. In one, he himself appeared, a few years younger, dressed in white, with his neck loaded with ritual necklaces, standing in front of a small altar on which an effigy of the Madonna sat, with a black face and limbs, on a chair reminiscent of a throne, in a majestic posture, adorned with a blue cape with silver-white trim. On Her head rested a little gold crown, imposed upon what appeared to be a royal-looking toque. Standing on Her right thigh, with Her arm around Him, was a baby Jesus, as black as She was, who appeared to be leaning toward His mother's chest as He held up a globe in His left hand and lifted His right. The Blessed Virgin's right arm, meanwhile, was extended forward, but the hand seemed to have gone missing. Taking Bobby's body as a reference point, Conde calculated that the statue must be about a foot and a quarter to a foot and a half tall, making Her a bit larger than many of the icons that were produced en masse for home altars.

"The Virgin was missing Her right hand?"

"Yes, it must have broken off at some point. I always remember Her like this, without that hand . . . But tell me, my dear, isn't She beautiful?"

The other photo was one of the Madonna in three-quarter profile: now Conde could better examine Her features—without a doubt more Mediterranean than African, despite Her blackness, with a rather pale green or bluish reflection in the eyes, which were perhaps a bit slanted. Her expression was of a deep and peaceful beauty that, from within the shiny black wood, managed to transmit a palpable feeling of kindness and, at the same time, power, enhanced by Her regal posture.

"Yes, She's pretty, it's true . . . And kind of strange, too, isn't She?" Conde said, readjusting the glasses he'd resorted to in order to take a detailed look at the photographs—and, even so, squinting a bit as well, to help his worn-out old pupils make a proper assessment of the images. "I don't know much about this sort of thing, but I don't think I've ever seen an Our Lady of Regla like this, seated . . . Besides which, there's just something about Her . . ."

"Well, that's why I'm here, *viejo*. Because there *is* something about Her . . . This Madonna is an actual holy relic, She's been with my family for I don't know how many years . . . And She's powerful! Truly powerful! Conde, I need you to help me find Raydel and get him to return my little Virgin to me. You're my only hope. And you have to help me, right? For old times' sake?"

Bobby was just out of sight when Conde phoned his friend Carlos and told him about his recent and extraordinary encounter. Bobby Roque in person! Bobby unveiled! A Santero and a businessman! Robbed of everything he held dear by an Adonis from Santiago! And Carlos made Conde promise that, as soon as he had a chance, he would stop by to see him and share all the details of the fabulous reappearance of Bobby Roque Rosell. And he should bring a bottle of rum, of course, while he was at it. And he shouldn't forget that there was only a month left until his birthday, so they—Conde hung up.

In need of answers and some relief from his amazement, he took a private taxi down the neighborhood's main drag. On the way to Yoyi the Pigeon's house, he thought through all he'd learned. His former classmate wanted to hire him: friendship was friendship, but business was business, as Bobby had said; he'd offered to pay Conde sixty dollars a day (the word *sixty* was starting to sound better phonetically and, especially, semantically), and then a bonus of a thousand if he recovered the Madonna. Why was his devotion to this specific icon so strong? Wasn't it, like so many other such idols, just a piece of carved wood or plaster whose external attributes (clothing, crown, paint) gave it its definitive physical form? Was the fact that it was a sort of family relic really that important to the new and more authentic Bobby? And what did the declaration that She was "powerful" mean? Conde, who, despite his latent mysticism, considered himself a mix of agnostic and atheist, didn't feel capable of understanding a relationship of supernatural, almost amorous, dependency on a small figurine whose significance was entirely religious, and therefore imaginary, existing only in the minds of its devotees; and, as such, he defaulted to believing it must be the family relationship that gave it such an aura—that sort of thing was far more tangible and endearing.

Yoyi was waiting for him on the porch of his house, dressed in white linen pants and a cleanly pressed shirt against which his pigeon chest strained. On his breastbone shone a heavy medallion, hanging from a thick gold chain . . . a medallion with the image of the Virgin, in Her incarnation as Our Lady of Charity, patroness of Cuba. At the curb, its hood pointing toward the city center, his 1957 convertible Chevrolet Bel Air was parked, shinier than ever thanks to the recent coat of lacquer that (only the Madonna knew how!) had reached Yoyi from the Ferrari factory itself.

The men shook hands and the visitor allowed himself to fall into one of the porch chairs, moving it to seat himself in front of his host.

"So, a client came to see you, eh?" Yoyi asked, feigning naïveté.

"Left my house an hour ago . . ."

"So, what did you think of Bobby? He's a character . . . And when he told me what happened to him, I said to myself: 'Business for Conde!'"

"But why didn't you tell me about it first, man?"

"Damn, brother, because Bobby told me that you were a friend of his and because I know that you're still fascinated with everything about high school in La Víbora, and . . . Oh, of course, since I'm your agent, I know you could stand to earn that hundred dollars a day . . ."

Conde raised a hand. "I'm sorry. *How* much a day?"

Yoyi stared Conde down, as though watching prey. Something was up. If Yoyi had one notable quality, it was his professional intuition. And if he had any others, despite behaving like an animal in business, it was that he managed to act on it with honesty and transparency. And if he had one major failing, it was his attachment to Conde himself, to Conde's mind— because despite being about twenty-five years younger than his business partner, Yoyi professed that his friendship with the former policeman was permanent and incorruptible. Not only because Conde once saved him from a robbery that had devolved into a potentially fatal beating, but also because they simply felt comfortable doing business with each other, without any fear of possible betrayal. For years, Yoyi had shown his soft spot by protecting Conde: since he earned so much money with his diverse commercial enterprises—his reach wasn't so much wide as practically un-limited—he tried to keep his less skilled friend both occupied and "liquid," and, beyond that, every once in a while, even saved him—not that this took much effort for someone like Yoyi—from outright squalor. From the *fuácata*, as they called the broke-as-hell state in which the former police-man nearly always existed.

"I said a *hundred*, man," Yoyi said, narrowing his eyes as if he needed to bring Conde, who was shaking his head, into better focus.

"I get sixty dollars a day and a thousand for recovering the Madonna . . ."

Yoyi jumped. "That son of a bitch! We settled on a hundred per day, plus expenses, and two thousand for the Madonna . . ."

Conde felt rage surge in his chest.

"But, Yoyi, so much! Just for Our Lady of Regla?"

"What do you mean 'so much,' Conde? That Virgin of Regla is a nineteenth-century carving brought from Andalucía and is surely worth a pretty sum . . . And Bobby is rotten with cash! Do you know how much he got out of two Portocarrero paintings, an Amelia Peláez, a Montoto, and some Bedia sketches he took to Miami? . . . After the initial investment, and after paying everyone he had to pay to get the paintings out of here, he was left with seventy large, free and clear, man. Seventy thousand dollars! You can't even imagine who some of his clients here in Cuba are, and the things that Bobby's sold! Didn't you hear about those fake Tomás Sánchez landscapes making the rounds in Miami?"

Now Conde really lost it. Seventy thousand dollars in profit, and now counterfeiting too? And meanwhile, they all used to think that Bobby was a dumbass?

"Leave the money thing to me. Your thing will be looking for that little *bugarrón* and figuring out where on earth this Virgin got to . . . and earning that cold, hard cash."

Under the influence of his astonishment, Conde nodded several times, rummaging around in each of his pockets in search of his pack of cigarettes, without remembering that he had placed it, along with a lighter, on the porch's little wrought iron glass-top table. When he finally tracked down the pack, he lit up and took solace in nicotine.

"In high school, we always thought the guy was stupid . . . Stupid and kind of gay."

The Pigeon smiled at last.

"Well, if he was stupid, he's completely cured of that, because now he's a tiger when it comes to buying and selling paintings and getting them out of Cuba when necessary . . . As for the other business, well, you guys clearly underestimated him there too—because he's *super* gay, right? And he's really living it up!"

Conde barely listened to Yoyi's excited analysis, since his mind was caught up in calculations. One hundred dollars a day! Four or five years had already passed since the painter Elias Kaminsky showed up in Havana in need of help with fleshing out the story of his father, a Jewish man named Daniel. Kaminsky compensated Conde quite well for his services, but since then, Conde had spiraled down a dark tunnel as dealing in used books became ever less profitable—to the extent that he was even think-ing about repurposing himself and finding another way to survive, like some of his colleagues were doing.

"Well, man, don't worry about the money . . . Because you're going to take the job, right?"

Conde was busy calculating to himself: What in the hell could he do to find, in Havana or God only knew where, a guy who didn't want to be found? . . . *I'll have to get some help from the police*, he answered himself.

"It won't be easy," Conde admitted and finished his cigarette.

"That's what they pay you for, man . . . Well, allow me to invite you in for supper . . . I have a hot date in El Vedado at nine," he said and pointed at his Bel Air.

"And what's on today's menu?" Conde asked, always ready to be daz-zled by the dishes his partner served him. To satisfy his gourmet tastes, the former engineer Jorge Reutillo Casamayor Riquelmes, aka Yoyi the Pigeon, had hired himself a chef (the woman even dressed in white and wore a chef's toque!) who could prepare all the exquisite dishes he craved, and who (because she had a soft spot for Yoyi) also ironed his pants, lin-ens, and fine shirts. She did so exquisitely, with a touch she'd apparently inherited from her Filipino grandfather, who'd been in the dry-cleaning business.

"I told Esther to make something light, because if I'm going to see this chick later . . . well, you know . . . Anyway, she threw together some rice with vegetables, a very leafy salad, and some gazpacho. It's good in this heat . . ."

With that anticlimactic menu, Conde was crestfallen. That was it? Rice and greens? Were these damn diets following him everywhere? Conspir-ing against his appetite? The Pigeon saw the look on Conde's face and smiled.

"And two full steaks, Conde . . . Dutch-style, with lots of green pepper . . . Because I knew you were coming over! Look, man, it was a premonition, and I felt it here." Yoyi jabbed his fingers below his left collarbone, anchored in the slope of his pigeon chest.

"Yoyi, stop fucking around. I'm the one who gets the nasty premonitions," Conde said. "By the way, do cows still exist? Can you still get filets?"

With growing alarm, Conde felt surrounded, attacked even—everyone was trying to break him down. It was all very well and good to want to save themselves, but the most dangerous thing was that they were also trying to save him in the process. Chamomile tea instead of coffee! And without any sugar to boot! Did they really think he was so old and so fucked-up as that!

Conde watched as Tamara, cradling the porcelain teapot, poured the steaming liquid into her gold-rimmed cups. As always, he marveled at the elegance and precision of her gestures, so harmonious and aristocratic, a far cry from his own barbaric frustrated-ball-player mannerisms. *Why does this woman put up with me . . . even sleep with me?*

At fifty-seven, Tamara looked about ten years younger. Her diet, exercise, hair dyes, and creams (Italian, expensive, and efficient, sent from far away by her twin sister, Aymara) had as strong a positive effect on her as the negative effect of Conde's own habits had on him—his haphazard eating, cigarette and alcohol consumption, and his constant exposure to the island's dog-day sun during his daily book-trade pilgrimages. Furthermore, that night, as if to highlight what he'd been missing during his absences, Tamara was waiting for him dressed in a practically see-through nightgown, no bra, and a black thong that barely covered the small valley of her ever-protruding behind, firm and immune to the passage of time. When he arrived, he had looked her up and down, front and back, and congratulated himself as he felt a slight lift in his scrotum and delightful anticipation in his penis.

As they drank the chamomile tea—he refused to drink it without sugar—Conde relayed the big news of the day: Bobby emerging from oblivion. She found it incredible that their former classmate had become a Santero and a businessman, although she wasn't too surprised by the confirmation of his sexual preferences, and smiled widely at the photo Conde showed her.

"You don't break out in hives anymore when you have to deal with a gay man?" Tamara needled, since she knew each and every one of her lover's prejudices.

"You know I was cured of that a long time ago . . . or at least, improved significantly."

She nodded. *Yes*, Conde thought, watching: *she is still beautiful.*

"So, what are you going to do to find this Raydel?" she asked, and at that moment, Conde was positive that his skills as a detective had endured the same monstrously rapid decline and decrepitude as his body.

"I'm fucking clueless . . . I didn't even ask Bobby if he had a picture of the guy. I hope he does . . ."

"So, if he went back to Santiago, what are you going to do, Mario?"

Tamara seemed truly intrigued. She knew that Conde was capable of going out to Santiago de Cuba and staying there for weeks and months, lost in a forest of rum bottles.

"Bobby thinks Raydel is here in Havana. The better to sell the loot. In Santiago, well, it seems people there are all in the *fuácata*, broke as hell. Worse than here . . ."

Conde carefully finished his tea and lit a cigarette. It took great effort to concentrate, faced with Tamara's transparent apparel. Despite being on the verge of old age, or perhaps because of it, aggravated by its approach, his attraction to the females of the species was not only as vivid as ever, but seemed sometimes to have radically increased: to be more powerful than in the days of his greater vigor. Nowadays, Conde tended to swivel around, as though magnetized, every time a well-proportioned woman passed by (in his aesthetic and geometric canon, a pleasing appearance included an ample ass), and his eyes went running after every open blouse button, delighted in every pretty face. Throughout his life, the enjoyment of the contemplation of female beauty—assuming objective, material enjoyment wasn't possible—was a constant, but rather than diminishing with age, it had developed along with his detective skills, gotten sharp like a bloodhound's sense of smell: when Conde boarded a bus, his eyes zeroed in instantly on the most beautiful girl there; when he crossed paths with a well-endowed, well-proportioned woman, he felt his hormones rampage; when he watched a movie, he was driven into a frenzy by the promise, or actual display, of an actor's feminine charms (how he admired Stefania Sandrelli in *We All Loved Each Other So Much*, Candice Bergen in *Live for Life*, or the number of times he masturbated recalling Sônia Braga's nudity in *Dona Flor and Her Two Husbands . . .* How skinny and terrible the stars of today were, by God!). And despite knowing that his impulses were more physical than aesthetic, he couldn't control them and tended to indulge himself at every appropriate opportunity. Even if only visual, his enjoyment of the female form was a source of nourishment to Conde: he took in the beauty and sexuality of women, and he savored his own curious desire to peer into every woman's infinite physical and mental mysteries; like a vampire, when he plunged his fangs into them he was rejuvenated. Because of that, he'd never been able—nor would he ever be able!—to understand Bobby and his brethren: How was it possible to be attracted to a hairy, rough creature with one of those ugly things hanging between his legs, when there was another option out there, a being made up of delicate, perfect, inviting valleys, mountains, grottoes . . . ? The great prize of Conde's erotic life, and above all, the object of his utterly carnal creative drive, had arrived with the possibility of his taking Tamara to bed—Tamara, the most beautiful girl at La Víbora's high school. The same Tamara who, when they were very young, made Conde and his classmates trip over themselves at the mere sight of her, and who looked down at the future detective as if he were little more than an insect. Years later, he reestablished contact with her, when, as luck would have it, he ran into her again in his capacity as a cop, working the case of her missing husband, who disappeared on the last day of 1988 (that son of a bitch Rafael Morín, a corrupt opportunist). He'd crowned it all by sleeping with her, and Conde entered a different phase of his existence: that of not believing what he had and held, that of asking himself over and over again how it was possible for that magnificent creature to feel any attraction to a disaster like him. Many years later, his relationship with this woman was so firmly established that they didn't feel the need to legally formalize it, since they were satisfied living a kind of eternal courtship, a pleasant state of being that helped them enjoy each other's company all the more by virtue of never dealing with the exhausting burden of cohabitation. Even so, Mario Conde looked at Tamara on nights like this one and asked himself, could it be true?

Aloud, he asked, "By the way, who gave you that pretty engagement ring you're wearing?" He liked this little ritual so much that he started it up on every propitious occasion. Tamara humored him with the expected response.

She whispered, "My husband gave it to me." Sounding very pleased with herself.

"Oh, you're married?"

"No, just engaged," she said, keeping to the script.

Conde felt he might as well accelerate the action.

"So, where's the party?" he asked.

Tamara smiled. "Oh, I think it's somewhere around here."

"But did you really have to dress like that?" He ran his eyes all over her—his eyes, as well as the tip of his finger.

"Don't you like it?"

"I love it."

"Still?"

"More than ever."

"But you haven't come by for days . . ."

"I was exercising . . . To get strong . . . You have to keep in shape . . . At my age . . ."

"And did you get strong?"

Conde acted as if he were thinking the question over.

"Shall we find out?" And he stood up, crossed behind her and began kissing her neck, caressing her breasts, letting her feel his muscle, awake now, in the cleft between her buttocks—that it was willing to test its mettle: against gravity, against the years, with the aid of her beauty, the clean scent of her skin, and the taste of sweet fruit that always, always lingered in her saliva and on her breath.

2.

ANTONI BARRAL, 1989–1936

The sound of a door closing pulls him out of a deep sleep, as empty and prolonged as it is painless, timeless . . . He wants to call out to his wife, to know that he isn't alone, to mock that abysmal and overwhelming solitude and the fear of greater solitudes, but he can't manage to turn his thoughts into words. He feels abandoned, perceives his own etherealness; he knows he is almost at the end. He will go no farther than this. With the slowness of defeat, he opens his eyes and looks at his feet: it's the best he can do, perhaps the only thing he can do. Whenever he's been at a crossroads, he has, at some point, looked at his feet, conscious or not of why he's doing it, pushed by some hidden impulse, as if responding to forces greater than him. He knows that other people have preferred to look at their own faces, their eyes, the shapes of their lips, to discover in those features, or at least try to, vestiges of joy, anguish, expectation: to find answers, even. Others look to their hands: hands that have done glorious, repugnant, irreversible things. And there are also those who like to contemplate their genitals, conscious of what drives human decisions, toward joy or ruin. Many times, he's taken refuge there himself, shyly or shamelessly. But ever since he was a teenager in the mountains, it's been his feet, his eyes pulled there by a strange attraction in which feelings of familiarity and strangeness, of proximity and distance, have mixed in varying doses. Those extremities, now deformed and useless, are in many senses the sum of what his life has and has not been, because it was with those feet, of course, that he walked down paths both chosen and imposed, that led him to the existence he was allowed to create for himself. His feet have led the way: from innocence to blame, from ignorance to knowledge, from peace to death, from a pleasant walk to hauling loads across the mountains to fleeing without a backward look, driven by fear. His feet first set him in motion and now, exhausted at last, they're taking him down the final path. Antoni Barral knows he will soon take an irrevocable step, the step that will bring him closer to his mother, Paula; to his father, Carles; to his sad fool of a brother, l'Andreu, a useless and confused martyr of the war, his death the most terrible aspect of war. Yes, he will go no farther with his feet. Everything else will be silence.

Oozing blood from the bedsores covering his back and behind, inhaling and exhaling with an alarming consciousness of breath, exhausted by a battle he knows is lost, laid out forever, he insists on looking, well aware that this is perhaps his last consultation with his feet and their twisted nails, so prone to growing into his flesh, his last time examining those toes with their protruding joints, all the more evident now that they're little more than bone and weathered hide. His feet, once a wanderer's, are now the impotent extremities of a near-corpse. A sense of alienation ends up defeating whatever sense of continuity he was hoping to find, since he's overcome by the impression that these feet are no longer his. Nothing is his anymore. Wait, yes, She is still his, as She will never cease to be, now and before and forever, and with this thought he at last abandons the contemplation of his feet.

He barely raises his eyes and finds Her on Her pedestal, the mistress of time, of all time, and the mistress of time's ineffable power. Majestic, black, and powerful, illuminated by the scented candle that his wife lit before quitting the room, hoping to leave not only a little light behind but also a smell that might—but couldn't—do combat with the sour smell of death. And She is his because She guided him all the way here, to the foreseeable end of his unforeseeable life, a life cobbled together bit by bit. And She will accompany him to the great beyond, when his feet stumble for the last time and arrive before the Creator to be judged and sentenced for the sins he's committed. Including the greatest, the mortal sin that the commandments warn against and for which there is no forgiveness, even with his mitigating circumstances. The murder that for years he'd been claiming he committed for Her, to save Her.

Overwhelmed by the pressure of the guilt he'd never managed to forget, pursued for over fifty years by the expression on the face of the dead man who didn't understand why he had to die, and overwhelmed too by the pain of not even having been able to dig the graves of those closest to him, he studies his feet once more. He recalls the diffuse light of the damp in the pestilent hold of the trade ship where he'd sat facing Her brilliantly black form, just before putting on his dirty and tattered espadrilles and preparing to leap into the unknown. At that moment too he'd stopped to stare at his feet. On that occasion, the feet he contemplated were filthy, infected with oozing fungus, but young and capable all the same, the only thing, he'd thought, that had always (and would always) be his. And he'd trusted in them and in Her to get him out of that bind, same as they'd gotten him out of others.

They had been at sea for sixteen days since, like a surreptitious rat, he had snuck onto that ship flying a French flag in the Basque port of Saint-Jean-de-Luz. Without the least idea where in the world it would take him, assuming he survived the passage, he had chosen it by the simple virtue of its being the most practical, among the vessels about to set sail, for him to board. The young man knew only that any destination was preferable to the ones haunting his horizon since History entered his life and begun to march him to its own beat, by way of war. It was he, of all people—or so he'd thought—who had lived in a corner of the world forgotten by time, or in a timeless time that, for centuries and centuries, had swallowed up the lives of his ancestors. A passage that didn't even merit the sense of movement implied in the word, since, if anything, it had been a state of continual paralysis plagued by a brief cycle of life and death—the time on earth grudgingly granted by the Creator.

Upon boarding, he had found his stowaway's refuge in the ship's remotest hold, behind the barrels of fat, emanating their greasy stench. He thought he knew what he was risking if he were to be discovered. He had read and heard stories of stowaways who were whipped, even thrown overboard, and he was quite certain that if the trip were prolonged and provisions ran out, the risks would only grow. Prepared for the worst, he carried with him, in the same coal sack with which he'd made his entire pilgrimage, two bottles of water, two loaves of dark bread, a brown paper package of three dozen olives he'd bought with his last coins, the handful of goat cheese—too smelly for his liking—that he'd stolen at the city market, and, lastly, the dark effigy of Our Lady of la Vall. From his waist hung the coarse knife that had proven good for everything: peeling, cutting, sawing, and, if necessary, shaving. Even for killing. But Antoni Barral was also counting on tools that seemed much more important: his years spent navigating the mountains like a goat; his youth, having just turned sixteen; and his feet. And the undeniable power of the Black Virgin.

The day after he'd slipped onto the ship, he felt the metallic murmur of the anchors lifting, followed by the deep tremor of the engine starting up. He placed himself in Her care as he made the sign of the cross over himself. Comforted by the knowledge that he was moving, he slept for several hours, he didn't know how many, until a change in noise and rhythm woke him. Why were they stopping? Where? Antoni Barral dragged himself to the farthest corner of the hold and curled into a ball. From there, he saw several men come down carrying sacks that they piled up on wooden platforms until they formed a mountain. From what the stevedores were saying, he gathered that they'd dropped anchor in Bordeaux and, as soon as some cargo was unloaded, the ship would continue its journey, this time across the Atlantic.

When the vessel was moving again, the young man breathed a sigh of relief, but he remained in his damp corner where he patiently waited for what he calculated to be a single day. Then he decided that the time had come to safeguard the effigy of the Virgin he carried in his leather pouch. As carefully as possible, he used his knife to pry open the cover on one of the barrels of fat and, after kissing the stump of Her hand, whose fingers were lost because of him, he dunked the icon in the white paste where, he hoped, no one would think to look for Her. He marked the lid of the barrel with a barely visible cross and closed it again, lining it up with the floorboards in its original position.

Later, he would learn that he had been navigating through his dark refuge for four days before he was discovered. Trapped by the impossibility of leaving the hold, Antoni hadn't counted on the capacity of his own body to betray him. The fetidness of his bowel movements and the stink of his urine, in addition to the emanations from his skin, created a noxious air that he got used to, but which alerted a sailor sent in search of salt. Accompanied by another seafarer, each armed with a dim lantern, the sailors demanded that whoever was back there emerge from his hiding place before they removed him by force. The young stowaway, convinced that there was no possible escape, at last abandoned his refuge and made his way toward the two men, who stared him down hard and long, as if they'd discovered nothing more than a thief: because, after all, having taken a journey for which he'd paid with neither money nor labor, that's precisely what he was.

Antoni Barral always believed that his relationship with luck was problematic at best. Nevertheless, at the most critical points, the capricious fickleness of fortune tended to favor him. On that occasion as well, one of the diciest in which he would find himself, his lucky star shone down on him (or was it the work of the Virgin?); the captain of the *Saint Martin*, as the French ship was named, saw that his furtive passenger was practically a child, and so decided to hear his story before choosing his punishment. Captain Rogelio Flores was from Cádiz but had spent more years at sea than on land: a man whom Antoni would soon learn was proud to be the grandson of Pedro Blanco, one of the last mercenary slave traders who'd once devastated the Atlantic (and perhaps himself the descendant of that mythical medieval pirate and Knight Templar, the captain of the famous ship the *Falcon of the Temple*, Roger de Flor), and who had also begun his life on the sea as a stowaway. Antoni Barral, laying all his cards on the table, told the captain that he was Spanish, Catalan, from the Pyrenees of Girona known as the Alta Garrotxa, and that he had fled his village when the war began, after some violent anarchists arrested his father, Carles, and his brother, l'Andreu, accusing them of being bourgeois counterrevolutionaries simply because they refused to let their goats be "socialized" in the name of the libertarian revolution. Spurred on more by fear than by any practical considerations or plans, Antoni crossed the sierra through a pass in the mountains known only to contraband runners, shepherds, and mule drivers, where he knew there was no danger of being found. Once he was on French soil, he wandered westward, following a path marked in the sky by the Milky Way. He knew that was the course by which, they said, if he walked far enough, he would someday reach the ocean of Finisterre, the door to America. And thus, he had arrived at that city bejeweled by a river and a seaport. There he heard someone say that the *Saint Martin* would depart in a few hours from the port of Saint-Jean-de-Luz to cross the Atlantic, and confirmed that it wouldn't be too complicated to get on board. Captain Flores, despite his years of wandering the seas, was well aware of the difficulties caused by the ongoing war on the other side of the Pyrenees from his home. He was amused by the idea of socializing goats, fishing boats, and chicken coops in order to foster change in the world. But he considered the obsessive, almost religious way his compatriots liked to kill one another, again and again throughout history, to be pathetic. Perhaps moved by such feelings, the old Cádiz-born captain decided that, to earn some leftover food and, above all, the right to his passage, at least till they stopped over in Havana, the young man could brush and shine the ship's less noble areas, beginning with the foul-smelling hold, and each and every one of the officers' latrines and showers. When it was time to sleep, he would go down to the same vault where he had initially hidden. As a basic measure of security, his rustic knife would be confiscated, without any right of return—in other words, it would be socialized.

They sailed for fourteen days before arriving at their first transatlantic stop, the mythical city named Havana, which the boy had heard Padre Joan speak of as a place where everything and anything could happen, good and bad, that legendarily torrid town mentioned so often in those old and nostalgic Catalan songs known as *habaneras*. For their part, the sailors and Captain Rogelio Flores assured him that the city was one of the world's most entertaining and frenetic, a beloved nexus of freedom, damnation, music, and the most triumphant examples of feminine beauty ever forged by the sun, air, and that mixture of bloodlines particular to the tropics. As they sailed toward port and the boy devoted himself to cleaning floors and toilets, young Antoni invested every spare moment in planning his escape from the vessel as soon as they docked. He knew, or thought he knew, that leaving the ship with his Black Virgin in hand entailed risking further "socialization," in the form of the crew's confiscating the statue as payment for his journey. The sight of it might even cast doubt on his story of escape and his claim of being a war refugee. Who runs for his life carrying such a hunk of heavy wood? And what if the Virgin was actually as valuable as Padre Joan had assured him? Every time he thought about it, the only viable option his mind returned to was that of throwing himself into the sea as soon as the ship was anchored— except Antoni was pretty certain the sea wouldn't be as forgiving as those mountain creek tide pools, where, from boyhood, he had splashed around on summer days, flapping wildly to keep himself afloat when he lost his footing.

The sun was barely up on his fourteenth day at sea when the rumble of the engines changed intensity: the *Saint Martin*'s much-anticipated first port of call was in view and, in the depths of the hold, Antoni Barral stood up, searching for his worn espadrilles and looking, as ever, at his feet: once again, they were about to be on the move. Except that on this occasion, his arrival somewhere didn't depend on him, but rather, on the buoyancy of his image of the Virgin whom, the previous night, he had extracted from the barrel of fat, wiped down, rinsed off, and hidden in his pilgrim's coal sack.

Trusting that the crew and Captain Flores must surely have forgotten him amid the greater responsibilities and attractions of landfall, the young man remained in the hold, like an animal lying in wait, until he heard the three whistles of the merchant's siren announcing their imminent arrival. After delivering himself over to the care of God and all the saints, and after invoking the power of the Black Virgin (so many tales of miracles surrounded Her!), Antoni Barral went up on deck where he found such commotion as befitted the docking of a ship and the expectations of its sailors, the two days of bawdy fun they'd promised themselves before continuing their journey on to Veracruz and Recife. On one side of the ship the boy could make out the city, its domes, towers, and scattered crosses. On the other side, a rocky outcrop, sparsely populated by mangroves, jutted out from a rough coast dotted with small wooden docks. Near the summit, the steep precipice was crowned by the impenetrable wall of an unending rampart behind which rose an old fortress. So, which was it to be? Would Antoni Barral choose the city or the rock? Instinctively he knew he could only choose the outcrop, throw himself off that side of the ship, and flounder for one of the protruding docks. He looked into the dark waters. His icon's ability to float meant life or death. But what else was there to do other than, again, and forever, entrust his life to Her? Antoni tied the sack to his waist, hugging and kissing it before throwing himself at the sea and the unknown.

As he sunk into the bay's murky waters, the young Catalan peasant had time to be surprised: in contrast to the mountain's tide pools, this sea was as warm as soup and so dense that, just as his lungs began to clamor for oxygen, the sack with the Virgin bobbed toward the surface, and he followed Her back into the air a dozen feet from some greenish planks that had to be the remains of a dock. Swept into the *Saint Martin*'s wake, the boy swam and kicked with all of his energy, as he had seen dogs do, and he came to brush against the slippery wood jutting out of the sea. Just when his strength was abandoning him and he began to sink, a wave buoyed him up and he managed to grab onto an old piling. Panting, his arms wrapped around this dark stalk, he looked at the ship, which continued its march toward a small motorized barge. Antoni Barral thought he saw, peering over the railing, the face of Captain Rogelio Flores. Antoni would swear, for the rest of his days, that the Cádizian was smiling and, more mysterious still, that they had somehow met long before their first journey together.

He hopped from stump to stump until he reached the rocky coast and there collapsed, exhausted. Only then did he confirm that he had lost his espadrilles—good for walking, not so good for swimming. He looked at his still-grimy feet and knew they would suffer from the sharp edges of the reefs, but he also reminded himself that it wouldn't be the first time they'd faced such a challenge. In the distance, on the coast, he could see other piers, some houses, humble-looking, although he had no basis for comparison, since he didn't know anything about the place where he'd just arrived. And without having the least possibility of gauging what awaited him onshore or indeed from now on, he felt a warm certainty that he was safe.

It was on that same magical afternoon—after entering the small village church he'd found after crossing a fishermen's hamlet—when Antoni Barral, fugitive, stateless, and a killer, knew for sure that the oft-mentioned miraculous capacities of the icon he'd carried from his hometown were indeed powerful, unstoppable, universal. Because on the great altar of the shrine rising on the banks of the ocean of those distant tropics, dressed in finery and surrounded by votive candles, another Black Virgin looked down on him from Her perch, as if She were there to receive him, as if She had been waiting for him—or for Her. OUR LADY OF REGLA, he read on a small wall card announcing ordinary masses and masses for the dead, weddings, and baptisms. From that moment on, the boy had the conviction that his salvation and that of his Virgin had and would always depend on the extraordinary coincidence of color between She who'd recently arrived from a hamlet deep in Catalonia, and Her hostess in the Americas, mistress of a chapel filled with the smell of the sea, looking out at that city of dreams and songs: Havana, in which Antoni Barral would settle, and where he would find out six years later that his father, Carles, and his brother, l'Andreu, had been killed by some faux revolutionaries back home, and where Antoni would reinvent himself in a way he could never have imagined. The place in which he would turn invisible, become someone else, and live out the rest of his years until at last losing himself, in a final delirium, a final somnolence, in the evocation of his great adventure on the seas—and let out his last breath.

He died early in the morning, old Antoni Barral, sans regrets, eyes on his feet, and the black icon of Our Lady of la Vall illuminated by a funerary candle infused with the lavender essence he had always associated with the remote valley from which History's excesses had expelled him.

3.

B obby was the only possible source. As soon as he was sure of that, he got to work on a preliminary plan, surprised at how automatic and routine it felt. Mario Conde almost began to enjoy his return to the anticipation of the hunt, the reawakening of his hibernating police instincts.

The process came naturally to him, yet gave him a sort of déjà vu, like a memory from another life, perhaps a previous incarnation—it was twenty-five years since he'd quit the force. But as Conde knew only too well, the past tends to be tenacious. The instincts and habits he'd formed were there to stay, for better or worse. As such, when he left Tamara's house and plotted out the best course to Bobby's, his brain was already organizing the information he'd amassed, was already identifying the gaps he needed to fill in order to find the clue that would lead him to the whereabouts of one Raydel Rojas Dubois and a clunky old effigy of the Virgin of Regla.

When the cab dropped him on Miramar's Séptima Avenida, he knew he was equidistant from the coast and Bobby's house. As if fulfilling some rite, instinctively he went down the gentle hill that would take him to the rocky coast and contemplated the ocean's surface, peaceful at that time of day on a fiery and clear September morning.

The sea had always pulled at him like a magnet: to see the ocean, enjoy its color and scent, its unknowability, gave him a powerful feeling of compassion and peace. A sense of freedom, rather than limits and boundaries. For many years, for too long now, whenever he dreamed—as he did quite frequently—of giving himself over to writing squalid and moving stories like Salinger's, using words as sharp as knives like Hemingway, the backdrop for the fantasy was always a modest and breezy house facing the sea. Writing in the morning, bathing at the beach in the afternoons, fishing at night, making love to a beautiful woman in the wee hours, breathing in the salt air, intoxicated by the murmur of the ocean. An idyllic and unsurpassable vision. But his personal life and his country's life, each moving to its own beat (although in painful convergence), had dispelled that fading aspiration, relegating it to that corner of memory where such nagging chimeras pile up—some of them already definitively unrealizable.

Shrouded in that dour mood, Conde walked back up the hill to find his former classmate's dwelling. Bobby now lived in the heart of one of the city's most privileged areas and enjoyed the kind of attractive two-story house that was typical of the 1950s. No, fate had not been completely unkind to his old friend. Not with a house like that.

When Bobby opened the door, dressed in shorts and a long shirt that fell like a smock to his thighs, Conde regained his connection to reality and his mission. He immediately noted that the interior of the dwelling was unbalanced: the sparse furniture seemed arranged any which way, not in harmony with the spaces around them, while bright spots were visible on the walls where missing paintings had hung, and light entered unopposed through a window over which the rods of vanished curtains were plainly visible.

Conde took a seat in one of the wrought iron chairs on the open terrace. From his spot he contemplated the tree-lined garden where some very green malanga trees and some delicate ferns of Jurassic proportions reigned over an English lawn that had recently been mowed.

Bobby reappeared with the promised coffee, its aroma already tormenting Conde. When he tasted the brewed delicacy he was immediately certain that the magic beans had to have come from the great beyond: this coffee was from Italy or from Miami, not from one of the Havana stores that sold the infamous brew now dispensed on the island. He savored the beverage and waited for its flavor to settle in his taste buds and his emotional memory before capping off his pleasure by smoking one of his cigarettes, which, fortunately, were still made from good Cuban tobacco. With a drawn-out sigh, his host had sat down facing him and begun to sip his own cup delicately.

"Bobby, you and I have known each other for many years," Conde opened fire, finally prepared to talk, wanting to clarify their positions. "When we met yesterday, I even felt like we'd been friends, back then, and that I was under some kind of obligation to help you out . . . But you came looking for me because you needed to hire me to do a job; you didn't come asking for a favor . . . So, before we talk about anything else, let's make it clear that we're doing business."

Bobby raised the hand with the coffee cup to cut off the ex-cop's spiel.

"I know, I know . . . Yoyi called me and really worked me over . . . Forgive me, Conde: a hundred a day and two thousand when you find the Madonna. I wasn't trying to fuck you over . . . I just can't help it. You spend time with thieves, you act like a thief. I'm sorry, I'm sorry . . . Look, I'm going to advance you five hundred dollars today . . . And if you find it before five days are up, keep the change, okay?"

Conde took a breath. Halfway between relief and shock. Talking about money was always complicated for him. It felt like a sin. But the night before, Yoyi made the situation very clear: Bobby had money, a lot of it even, and Conde was starving to death. Bobby wanted to recover his Virgin and Conde was his best chance. In Yoyi's words: "good work for good pay." That was how the global economy worked. Or, anyway, how it was supposed to work.

"Thanks, Bobby . . . Now, to get started, I need several things. The first is a photo, or several, of Raydel. Do you have any?"

"I have only one on hand . . . the one in my wallet. He took the rest. The ones I printed out and the ones on the computer . . . along with the computer and everything else, as you can see."

"I also need a list of the most important things he took . . . the paintings that were in the living room, for example. Were they valuable?"

"No, they really weren't . . . Almost all of them were engravings . . . I would sell the valuable ones as soon as I could. I'd already exported a bunch, and then I took everything left that could be sold with me to Miami."

"Any jewelry or peculiar ornaments?"

Bobby put a hand to his chest and sighed.

"Don't make me talk about that, I'll cry . . . My mother's engagement ring and . . . Enough, I'll make a list for you," Bobby concluded, in torment.

"Uh-huh . . . I'd also like the names and numbers of people Raydel could have had any relationship with."

"As far as I know, he didn't have any family here . . . Two or three friends. I know one of them lives around Centro Habana, and I think the other one lives around San Miguel del Padrón, in a neighborhood where lots of people from the eastern part of the island go when they get here. There was another one who lived in El Cerro, or around there . . . They're all criminals, like him . . . They made, or make, a living as con men. I'll put what I know on the list . . ."

"Maybe they helped him empty out your house. I don't think he could have done this on his own."

"Yes, maybe . . ."

"I need those details now . . ." Conde said. Bobby nodded and Conde looked into the yard. The sun made the green of the malangas shine. "Do you have any idea where Raydel could have sold the paintings and the valuable ornaments? Did he know your contacts in the art world?"

Bobby thought for a few moments before replying.

"He knew some . . . because he lived with me, of course. But I don't think he'd have gone to see those people, it would have been like a confession . . . In this business, everyone knows what everyone else has, because that's how it works. I sell what I have, and if I don't, I try to sell what the other guy has and charge him a percentage . . . It's an unwritten rule. One almost everyone respects because it's convenient for us all . . . I asked a couple of people who know everything that moves in this business and they haven't seen or heard anything . . . Although, you know what, there's this one guy, a real rat. He's capable of buying things from Raydel, and the better dealers wouldn't necessarily catch wind of it. Sure, he'd buy whatever Raydel wants to sell . . ."

"Fine. What's this character's name?"

"René Águila . . . a real son of a bitch, a scavenging *mulato* . . . I'll give you his address in a minute."

"But I assume that among the 'better' people you know, Raydel's a ghost."

"As if he was swallowed up by the earth."

"And could he have sold everything to this rat, who's still sitting on it all, and then taken the money and gotten the hell off the island? If it's been more than ten days since he ripped you off . . ."

"I've thought of that, but . . ."

"But what?"

"It wouldn't have been easy to sell all the things he took. Unless he sold it at a loss . . . Yeah, you better go see that son of a bitch René Águila . . ."

"But if what Raydel wanted was to leave with some money . . . Come on, think about it: he wouldn't have needed some expert to sell a mattress, a computer, some furniture, your pots and pans. Anyone will buy that stuff if it's cheap. It's different with the jewelry and the more valuable stuff, he might have hidden those in order to off-load them when he can. Or maybe he plans on smuggling them out of Cuba to get a better price, like he knows you were often doing . . ."

"That's what Eli says—Elizardo, one of my business associates. But Raydel's like a little animal, he doesn't use logic. Like all kids these days in this shitty country, all he cares about is showing off his flashy clothes and that huge fake chain around his neck, mixing pills with alcohol and getting high as a kite with his friends to the beat of reggaeton . . . He makes a living by hustling with that pretty face and that huge cock . . . Man, I tell you, he's hung like a horse!" Bobby touched a spot under his left breast and lowered his gaze. "No, I think Raydel is here in Cuba, Conde. I have a feeling."

Conde was surprised to learn that others also suffered from premonitions, and that they emanated from that same place in the chest as they did for him. But listening to this description of Raydel's finer traits, he had to chase away the image of Bobby receiving his hired horse's member *per angustum viam*.

"That kid really broke my heart."

Among other things, Conde thought, watching Bobby dry a few tears and shake his head, trying to compose himself. Conde felt bad for him and regretted having started out their meeting that morning so insensitive and businesslike. He remembered the old Bobby so often reviled by his high school classmates; how repressed he'd been, forced to wear a mask. Now, Bobby had sought Conde out as his only hope in recovering a priceless spiritual relic and family heirloom, all without wishing any harm to the villain who had stolen from him and broken his heart. Compassion and solidarity overtook Conde, reducing him from a lofty detective to a mere mortal, just wanting to help his friend in need.

Bobby gave him the list of contacts, which Conde folded and tucked away in his shirt pocket.

"When did you discover that Raydel had cleaned you out?"

"When I returned . . . I knew something was up because I'd been calling him from Miami, and he wasn't answering."

"So, it could have been quite a few more than ten days," Conde calculated and looked around the bare room again. "And how did you end up living in this house? It's very pleasant . . . What about your parents?"

Bobby sighed with that exaggerated affectation that he seemed to like so much.

"My father still lives where he always did. In the Sports Casino, remember?"

"Of course. We used to come over to study physics and chemistry with you . . . He always insisted on calling you Robertón."

"And my mother died about ten years ago . . ."

"I'm sorry."

"My grandmother Consuelo, my mother's mother, lived here with her second husband, a Spaniard who'd fled the Spanish Civil War . . . He was posted here at the beginning of the Revolution—nothing important—although *he* believed he was quite important. Back then, it was a free-for-all, and in the middle of all that, they gave him this house when the owners left for Miami . . . I came to live here with my grandmother when I was kicked out of university. After she and her husband died, I inherited the house . . ."

Conde tried to process all this information.

"And how did that one go, again? You were kicked out of the university for . . . ?" he probed, trailing off.

"You know . . . it's another long story . . . and I don't like talking about it . . . It was in '78, when we were finishing up our third year there . . . The Process to Deepen Revolutionary Conscience, remember?"

"I remember," he said encouragingly.

"Anyway, I was accused of being homosexual . . . and it was true, obviously. I'd slept with a guy . . ."

"From the university?"

"No, he wasn't from the university. But they found out . . . Do you know the worst part?"

"There's something worse?"

"Well, the worst part is that I'd never even slept with anyone before that. Girl or boy . . . At twenty-three, I was still a total virgin. Then, a group of us went to a beach house . . . and it was there that I fell from grace."

Conde gulped. Sex, a fall from grace. A crime that warrants a punishment. Is that really what they'd come to? He knew the answer, of course, but still, he could not help but be surprised and indignant by the unnecessary suffering caused by prejudice and repression in this so-called land of freedom and socialism.

"Anyway, they already knew everything, so I could not and did not want to defend myself . . . Losing my v-card to a guy had made me an ideological and social pariah, practically a criminal, an enemy . . . I was kicked out of the Young Communists and removed from the university . . . They wanted to fuck up my life. But I resolved not to give them the satisfaction. I vowed to redeem myself . . . In those days, that's how I used to think. I lived in a state of constant war, amid camouflage, defenses and offenses, drills . . . I believed in redemption. Then I left home, ended up here with my grandmother, and still, I was trying to be a man. I mean, 'a real man' . . . In '81, I was able to go back to the university, to a program specifically for workers. No one asked if I'd been expelled before or anything, so I registered again and finished my degree. That was when I met Estelita, who was so pretty and an absolute angel. We started dating, got married . . . I swear, Conde, I was happy, even more so once my children were born. I thought I was finally a real man, cured of my weakness . . . Even though it all went against my nature, against my true self, I knew I couldn't give up if I wanted to redeem myself. I had to be what I was supposed to be. So, I repressed myself, controlled myself, watched myself, consoled myself by fooling myself. And, like a drug addict who abstains from using, congratulated myself."

Bobby paused and dried the sweat that had accumulated on his upper lip. Conde waited for him to continue.

"I swear, I'd convinced myself that I'd finally done it," Bobby said and shook his head, smiling. "Until Israel showed up and I couldn't go on . . . Thanks to him, I knew that my feigned happiness was not even close to the real thing. I was just a coward, complacent with his surroundings . . . But with Israel everything fell into place . . . Then I really *was* happy, because I started to be myself all the time, without being on guard. Without fear, Conde . . . Or with less fear, anyway . . . My parents were furious, but my grandmother supported me. And Estelita didn't make a tragedy out of my decision to come out, although you could tell she was sad . . . Life started to smile down on me, even Yemayá showered me with Her blessings . . ." Bobby leaned down again to touch the tiles, then kissed his fingertips. "But now, in my old age, I've overshot it with that son of a bitch Raydel and here I am, in an empty house, weeping all over the place like an overflowing bathtub."

Conde swallowed again. He couldn't possibly have a good response to a speech like that. He felt even pettier now for having begun the day's conversation by talking about money.

"I'm going to go get your money," Bobby announced and stood up. He seemed tired. "Do you want me to brew you more coffee?"

"If you're not going to deduct it from my wages . . ."

Conde was trying to lighten the mood but Bobby just sighed, seemingly ashamed. Sighing again, he went to the kitchen to fill the moka pot and place it on the burner. From there, he asked, "You know that the day after tomorrow is the feast day of Our Lady of Regla, right?"

Conde thought for a moment. He pictured his faded calendar again.

"Of course, September seventh," he recalled. When he was a boy, his mother used to go to Mass on September seventh and eighth, to honor the feast days of Our Lady of Regla and of Our Lady of Charity, respectively, two of the most important dates in the Cuban book of saints.

Bobby returned from the kitchen continuing.

"Usually, I invite some friends over to celebrate . . . I'd buy wine, make food . . . But with what's happened . . ."

Bobby seemed too emotional to finish. He turned and headed upstairs to the second floor, where he must have kept his money. *He still keeps money in this house?* Conde thought, when he heard what sounded like the doorbell.

From where he was sitting on the terrace, he could see Bobby come down the stairs, nearly at a run, and open the door. Bobby immediately held out his arms to the visitor and kissed him on the cheek.

"Well, look who's here!" the host exclaimed, making way for the new arrival.

"Stop fucking with me, Bobby, I live the same distance from your house as you live from mine." His visitor responded in a tone of amicable reproach. "And we just saw each other two days ago."

"Come in, come in, here's the friend I told you about on the phone." Bobby ushered the man to Conde to make the introductions. "Well," he gestured exaggeratedly, looking from one visitor to the other. "Conde, this is my friend Elizardo Soler . . . Eli, this is my friend Conde, the one I told you about, who used to be a cop . . ."

The two men shook hands, though Conde felt that Elizardo Soler held his for a few moments longer than necessary.

"There are some things that one never stops being . . ." quipped Elizardo.

"That's true. But not true of everything: Michael Jackson was Black and then he became . . . white-ish. And as for cops, you're mistaken. You either are a cop or you're not," Conde retorted, not willing to cede.

"I rather think it's a chronic illness," Elizardo assured him. "Lifelong . . ."

"With treatment, it gets better. Much better," Conde replied, admitting to himself that his opponent had a certain agility for banter.

Bobby asked them to sit down and went back to the kitchen, announcing that the coffee was done brewing. Conde looked at the recently arrived visitor and smiled to alleviate the tension. The other man imitated him.

Conde took that opportunity to confirm: yes, as Elizardo Soler very well knew, he had indeed been a cop once. And that would never change, just as Elizardo Soler had declared—Elizardo Soler, who must have been about fifty years old and exuded an aura of self-assuredness. He knew a lot of gays without feminine mannerisms, but immediately he sensed that Bobby's friend was just that, a friend. Perhaps there was something else between them, but nothing sexual. Elizardo's hair was very black and curly, without any gray at all. His casual clothing belied the savviness of someone who knows what to wear and how to wear it, at all times. Quality clothing. He wore brown loafers that piqued Conde's envy: they practically shouted softness and comfort, sure to make their wearer's life more pleasant. *For shoes likes those, even I'd be willing to steal a Madonna of Regla*, he thought to himself.

Bobby returned with a tray of cups, cookies, and glasses of water. He seemed somewhat nervous in the presence of his friend Eli, and he was being loquacious. Conde attributed Bobby's state of mind to his previous blunder: having greeted Elizardo like a prodigal friend, when in reality he had seen him very recently. Or could there be something else?

"Like I said, Eli, this man and I are old friends . . . We go way back . . . very way back." He tried to sound cheery.

"Tell him how we know each other," Conde insisted.

"From ancient history . . . And since he's my prehistoric friend, he's going to help me find the Madonna, and the rest of my things, if they show up . . . See if you can get my computer back, Conde . . ."

"But how are you going to do that if you're no longer a cop?" Elizardo Soler asked after having his first sip of coffee.

Conde waited to finish his own espresso before responding.

"I've learned some things. I have a nose for it, and a method . . ."

"I knew it, a chronic condition," Elizardo said triumphantly. "I know quite well what that's like."

"Why, were you also a cop?" Conde asked.

"Cop? Me? No, never a cop," Elizardo responded, and Conde was left waiting for an explanation that never came, thanks to Bobby's untimely interruption.

"Look, Conde, Eli is the person in Cuba who knows the most about the art market. This man is practically a corporation! With his specialists, he represents several Cuban painters, he has his own gallery, he knows a bunch of *marchands* from around the world . . . And he can get you whatever you want from who-knows-where. Anything you ask for . . ."

"And I do it all legally," Elizardo Soler insisted, with sarcasm. "I'm also doing some research for Bobby, to see if we can find that darned Virgin of Regla that is causing him so much trouble."

"But . . ." Conde hesitated, unsure how to address him.

"Eli, call me Eli," the other man said, demonstrating his ability to read minds. That, or his superior intellect.

"In sum, you both think that the Virgin is valuable, right?" Conde asked, avoiding the use of his antagonist's name. Why the hell did this guy make him feel so guarded?

"Yes, it is . . . but it's not worth that much and it's not something that the thief himself would know. That's what's so complicated about this. If it was worth a lot and Raydel knew, then it would be easier to figure out what he's planning. Who could buy it, who would want it, who would prefer to take it out of Cuba. I'd say that could be tracked down, in that case."

"You're right," Conde admitted. "That's why I think the jewels are our best lead."

"Don't underestimate my little Virgin, gentlemen," Bobby protested. "She's a relic . . ."

Conde smiled and realized that, dragged along by the verbal torrent of his former classmate, he still had not voiced the most essential question—the response to which would determine his strategy going forward.

"Bobby, why are you so convinced that Raydel was the one who robbed you? You weren't in Cuba, the police haven't done an investigation . . . Raydel could have disappeared for lots of reasons."

Bobby nodded as Conde enumerated the various possibilities. He took a few moments to respond.

"It must have been him because any old burglar wouldn't have taken the things that he did. Raydel had the house all to himself . . . Things are missing from hiding places that only he knew about."

"Like what things?"

"Private things," Bobby answered, halfway between embarrassed and annoyed. Conde imagined that they had to do with the homeowner's sexual habits. And those of his boyfriend, the one hung like a horse. Weren't his lover's natural endowments enough for eco-conscious Bobby?

Conde nodded and put out the cigarette he had lit after drinking his coffee. He smacked his thighs with the palms of his hands, indicating his imminent departure.

"Well, I've got to go . . . I have work to do." He said goodbye to Elizardo Soler with another shake of the hand, which he cut short this time. "Incidentally, Elizardo, what have you found out so far by asking around?"

Elizardo sat down again.

"Very little. Or nothing, actually . . . but I've spoken to people in the know. Since Raydel also stole some engravings, the first person I went to see was Karla Choy and I put her on alert . . . She hadn't heard about the robbery yet. And if that Chinese woman doesn't know about a missing item in this country, nobody does!"

"Who is this Chinese woman? Is she really from China?" While unlikely, Conde would not have been surprised.

Elizardo laughed. Bobby briefly sneered.

"No, she's more Cuban than purslane. Her grandfather was Chinese. Chinese from China . . . But she has that Chinese hair, and eyes that are a little Chinese . . . And when it comes to business, she knows more than the Chinese do! She's a real devil dressed up as . . . a Chinese-Cuban woman." Elizardo smiled, enjoying his own brilliant description. "She wears clothes that really show off her tits, and that ass . . ."

"She's so vulgar," Bobby declared. "With that tight spandex . . ."

"She's hot," Elizardo retorted. And Conde, who knew something of the beauty of Chinese-Cuban women, wanted to hear more. "And she's got class. She's not vulgar, not at all."

"So, she also buys and sells art?"

"And planes and submarines, too!" Bobby added. "Among her many businesses, she runs a gallery out of her house."

"Envy kills," Elizardo declared. "Karla Choy is educated, competent, persistent . . . The best in this business. And since she has a . . . Chinese intuition . . . well, she knows where to go. She never enters land-mined territory."

"I'll have to meet her," Conde noted and gestured goodbye to Elizardo so as to avoid another hand-squeezing.

Bobby, meanwhile, excused himself in order to see Conde out. At the threshold he handed over an envelope.

"Here's what I promised. And a picture of Raydel."

"Thanks, Bobby . . . I'm going to do everything I can."

"I know, Conde. You're the real thing."

"What about Eli?"

"What do you mean, what about Eli?"

"Is he the real thing?"

Bobby's eyes widened.

"Super real, Conde . . . We've been doing business together for years and he has always been very serious . . . And he's a phenomenon: every time Israel asks me for something from Miami and it's difficult to find, he gets it, just like that!"

"So, is he gay?"

Bobby raised his eyebrows.

"I wish . . . but no, he's like you: a Macho-Leninist. Didn't you hear him talking about Karla? He practically drools when he sees her. And he says she's not, but that Chinese woman is a lynx . . ."

Conde thought for a moment.

"Bobby, if Eli is helping you with all of this, why didn't you say anything to me?"

"But I did. I told you he was someone who knows a lot about how art moves in this country," Bobby said, defensively.

"Those are two different things and you know it. This man has all of your trust and . . . I think he has more chance than I do of finding what was stolen from you. He knows things that I can't even fathom . . . He knows people . . . But you sought me out and you didn't tell me about him . . ."

Bobby finally looked up at him. He seemed at a loss.

"I'm just sure he's not in cahoots with Raydel . . ."

"Bobby, don't answer me if you don't want to . . . But, please, don't play games with me. That's twice now already . . . that I'm aware of. And that complicates my life and makes me uncomfortable. Anyway, I'll call you if I find anything or if there's anything I need to ask you," Conde said, turning away. He now felt like he had one up on Bobby. During his years as a cop, another thing he'd learned was how to leave his prey wounded . . . without killing it.

Calm down, buddy. You're looking even uglier than usual."

Major Manuel Palacios glared at Conde so intently he grew cross-eyed.

"You think I'm playing, man?" the policeman protested.

Conde held out his hand and the other man took it but remained seated. They had agreed to meet at eleven, at a cafeteria close to the police headquarters, but he had arrived fifteen minutes late, sweaty and agitated.

"The car I was taking here broke down and I had to get another one and . . . Do you want a beer?"

"Do you have dollars to buy beer today?"

"I'm a man of means, Manolo, not a starved-to-death cop like you . . ."

"I'm working. Or I should be working, and not here, bullshitting around . . . Get me a juice . . . But you owe me the beer. Beers," Manolo clarified, with an emphasis on the *s*. "So, come on, what the hell is going on with you now?"

Conde called over the waitress and ordered a mango juice for Manolo and a very cold beer for himself.

"I'm looking for a guy . . . I need you to help me," he started to explain and stopped when the young waitress came back with their order. Manolo greedily watched him pour the ice-cold beer into his glass.

"Who's the guy? What did he do to you?"

"To me? Nothing. To a friend. And maybe to other people. That's why I'm coming to see you."

Twenty-five years earlier, Lieutenant Mario Conde and Sergeant

Manuel Palacios had been the most efficient duo in the Criminal Investigation Unit. Manolo, some ten years younger than his partner, was obsessive, possessed implacable logic, and enjoyed his work as a policeman, which is why he was the perfect complement to Lieutenant Conde's heterodox method of trusting his gut.

After Conde left the force, Manolo had remained active. He had received a well-deserved promotion in rank and responsibilities, and now he was the head of the Serious Crimes Division, which covered murders, grand theft, and drug trafficking, among other activities. Through the years, Manolo had ceased to be the thin, practically squalid, young man who the lieutenant had taken in like a godson, and had turned into a forty-something-year-old with narrow shoulders, a bit of a belly, and a face like a pancake: a masterpiece of incongruity. But he had continued to be a good friend. So, on several occasions, Conde had served Manolo as a consultant, even assistant investigator, on the odd case or two. In exchange, Major Palacios, from his position within the headquarters, often got him what he needed whenever Conde found himself caught in the middle of an investigation, sometimes against his will.

Conde had lit a cigarette and Manolo, as usual, had stolen another from him, which he held now between his fingers, playing with it, while his former colleague talked about the tribulations of his old friend Bobby Roque Rosell and his missing Virgin.

"I need you to look in your files to see what you have on this Raydel Rojas Dubois."

"Has he had other problems with us?"

"I don't know, but I wouldn't doubt it. Though he's very young . . . At the very least, I need his address, if he has one."

"Many of the people who come from over there," Manolo gestured toward the eastern part of the island, "don't have a permanent address here. They can't be legal residents . . ."

"Like Palestinians," Conde added, which is exactly what people in Havana called those who emigrated from the east of the country.

"Like Palestinians . . . Every now and again, we have problems with one of them and it's a bitch to track them down."

"And what you do find there isn't always great, I'm guessing?"

"Are you telling me or asking me? Well, there's a little bit of everything, to be honest. But some of these people are a headache . . . They arrive desperate and will get involved in anything . . . And every day, there are more of them. Sometimes we do a roundup, we pick up the ones who fall into our trap, we take them back to Oriente Province and within a month . . . they show up in another neighborhood, in another town, doing the same thing, or something like it . . . There are towns around Havana where there are hundreds of them. They're so desperate that they work as day laborers for peasants who need the labor. The peasants pay them shit and let them sleep on their farms and the Easterners steal everything they can from them. And if they can, they stay around here, living in neighborhoods they can assemble from cardboard and zinc boards . . . They're like the wetbacks of Cuba . . . Oh, and some even become policemen . . . Well, I have to go, this is a hot mess."

"When is it not, Manolo?"

Major Palacios stood up and left his cigarette on the table.

"Aren't you going to smoke it?"

"I don't smoke anymore, Conde, I just like having a cigarette in my hand . . ."

"How long has it been since you smoked, Manolo?" Conde's question was cloaked in envy. He hated, admired, praised those who could give up that sticky vice.

"Since yesterday . . ."

"Go to hell, asshole!" He sighed with relief. Manolo wasn't better than him: Conde had stopped smoking three or four hundred times.

Manolo smiled and leaned across the table toward his friend.

"Listen to this: one day, a guy, here in Havana, ran into a cop from the eastern provinces and the cop stopped him, searched him, and in the process took a Swiss watch that the man was wearing . . . The poor guy went running to the police station to file a complaint against the officer who had stolen his watch, and when he spoke to the officer on guard, he realized that he was also from the eastern provinces. And the officer asked him, "Let'th thee, thitizen, what'th your complaint?" And the man had to think quickly, "You see, officer, I was coming down the street and a Swiss cop stole my Eastern watch . . ."

Manolo laughed as if the joke were a good one and Conde shook his head.

"Manolo, besides being tedious, that joke is regionalist and *politically incorrect*, as they say these days . . ."

"That's why it's a joke, dammit! Forget it, I'll call you when I have something," Major Palacios said, still smiling, and he held out his hand. Then he picked up the cigarette and placed it in the vest pocket of his officer's uniform.

"Manolo." Conde stopped him and took out a piece of paper he'd been carrying in his pocket. "While you're at it, see if you can track down these people. They're Raydel's friends . . . I think they're also Swiss . . . And come see me tonight at Skinny Carlos's house . . . Be my guest for dinner."

Manolo took the piece of paper and looked at Conde with more scorn than scrutiny.

"You're also giving me dinner? How much are they paying you to look for this little bugger, my friend?"

"That's confidential information . . . You take what you're given. I'll see you tonight. There will be beers, plural."

Manolo gestured goodbye. He seemed exhausted, almost defeated. Conde saw him head off toward headquarters, which he could make out in the distance. Against his will, he felt a stab of nostalgia for the times when he used to work there, alongside Manolo and under Major Antonio Rangel. But immediately, he told himself, *No: none of this nostalgia*. How in the hell could a guy like him have stood being a cop for ten years? Even Bobby had asked him as much that morning!

He called over the waitress, ordered another beer, and asked for the check. He couldn't help it: he felt like a kid when he saw the look on the young woman's face as he held out a one-hundred-convertible-peso bill, one of the five Bobby had given him. In one fell swoop, it had made him powerful.

After he got home and before allowing himself a nap and relief from the murderous midday heat, Conde had called his friend Carlos. Now that he was rich, he declared, they were going to live like it: it was the same spiel every time he received some money. This was also the main reason why, on every other such occasion, his "wealth" had disappeared in little to no time. Sometimes just hours.

On the way to Carlos's neighborhood, he stopped by the clandestine home business of a retired doctor who now quietly devoted herself to catering homemade meals. He ordered a banquet, which he'd be back to pick up at 7:00 p.m.: five rotisserie chickens, comparable portions of yuca with mojo and black beans and rice, a decent helping of a mixed-vegetable salad, and a container of shredded-coconut pastry in honey. Next, he ducked into an apartment in the building next door where one could acquire goods with foreign currency. Here he bought a box of Heineken beer and three bottles of the kind of rum that was supposed to be discounted in stores—but not here, not since this was the private business of the warehouse who stocked the store's stolen "quality" products. The rum was not watered down and the beer was not that ignoble beverage bought in bulk and repackaged by illicit entrepreneurs who did the same with the neighborhood restaurants' sodas. Having taken these detours, Conde had liquidated the first installment of the one-hundred-peso bills that he had received that morning but not yet earned. The provisions squared away, he asked Carlos to track down Rabbit and order old Josefina not to put on her apron that night: his friend Carlos's mother would get a vacation, all of them would eat like kings, and then he and Rabbit would wash up like Cinderella.

"You see why I love you so much, Beast?" Carlos said and added, "Rabbit was going to come over anyway because he wants to talk to you about I-don't-know-what."

"You-don't-know-what? *You* don't know *what?*"

"I swear on my mother . . ."

"Don't swear in vain, you son of a bitch."

That night, as planned, they dined like kings. Before sitting down at the table, as the beer was chilling, the three old friends drained the first bottle of rum. While they waited for Manolo to arrive, they talked about Bobby: the old Bobby that all three of them had known, a pitiful guy who was doomed to an inauthentic existence because of the social and political prejudices that would lead him to ostracism anyway, and the new liberated, actualized Bobby, sanctified by the Catholic Church and the Yoruba powers of Orula and Yemayá; a businessman; and now, the victim of a crime, which Conde described to Carlos and Rabbit, who were both having a hard time overcoming their surprise.

When he showed them the photo of a reborn Bobby, posing next to the missing Blessed Virgin, Carlos saw only the man in the picture and, like Conde, didn't recognize him. But Rabbit, always with his historian's curiosity, was more interested in studying the Virgin and asked Conde for a photo that focused solely on the effigy.

"Where does Bobby say that Virgin came from?" Rabbit asked, his eyes fixed on the image.

"It was his grandmother's Virgin of Regla," Conde said. "The family has had Her for a long time."

"The Virgin of Regla? Seated?"

"Why can't She be sitting down, man?" Carlos interrupted. "Don't Virgins get tired?"

"The Cuban Virgin of Regla is not traditionally seated. I don't know about the one from Spain, but definitely not the Cuban one."

"I had noticed there was something different about Her," Conde admitted. "But I thought it could be a different version. There must be thousands, right? Like figures of Christ . . . Although it seems that this one was brought from Andalucía, so . . ."

"Is She wooden or plaster?" Rabbit continued.

"Black wood. The cape She's wearing over Her shoulders was tailor-made at Bobby's request, but the clothing carved into the wood was painted years ago. That's why it's peeling so much . . . and the eyes, too. The truth is that She seems rather old."

"All the more reason for Her to be sitting," Carlos confirmed and took a generous slug of rum.

"Green eyes, green eyes . . ." Rabbit whispered, almost to himself. "This Virgin is strange, gentlemen . . . I don't know . . ."

"Oh, Rabbit, stop screwing around," Carlos intervened. "In Cuba, there are blondes with asses like Black women and Black women with eyes in whatever color they want! The important thing is that Conde finds

Her . . . Well, better if he takes a little while so he makes more dough. I love having a rich friend." He downed the remainder of his drink in one gulp and used the edge of his shirt to wipe his lips and mop the sweat off his forehead. "Rabbit, why did you want to see Conde?"

"No, Bobby didn't say anything to me about Andalucía," Conde muttered, so focused on the Virgin's posture that he barely heard Skinny Carlos's question. "It was Yoyi who told me She was from Andalucía . . . Strange, right?"

Since opening the first bottle, they'd livened up the conversation by playing Creedence Clearwater Revival's greatest hits, listening to their version of "Proud Mary" on repeat, as was their ritual. They even toasted their friend Andrés, who was no longer with them but who was always present in their collective memories and nostalgias. They hummed along to the song and praised Tom Fogerty's divine voice . . . He sang like a Black man! No, like God Himself! Though the three of them knew quite well that it was not Tom Fogerty who sang "Proud Mary," but his brother John, ultimately, they couldn't give a damn: they were merely focused on enjoying this particular recording, over and over again, day after day, for years and years, perhaps until eternity.

Josefina, with her invincible octogenarian agility, interrupted the conversation with orders to come and eat, since it was eight thirty and she wanted to watch her telenovela. The old woman had set the table with her finest tablecloth and her best plates. Besides, she added, she had heated up the food once and wasn't going to do it twice or else she'd dry out the chicken. Manolo could join them when he arrived. The old woman still knew quite well how to wrangle this riotous group. Before taking their places at the table, Conde was fetching the chilled beer and Rabbit signaled to Carlos to forget about the ongoing conversation. Carlos agreed, for now, sealing his lips, though he gestured with his hand to say: tomorrow.

The diners ecstatically beheld the impressive spread that Conde's sudden windfall had provided: the shiny-skinned smoked chicken, the already-peeled yuca, the black beans and rice, all had a powerful magnetic pull. Many times over many years, they had eaten well thanks to the underrated art of Josefina's cooking, but they'd never managed to decimate their endemic anxiety over the void they'd suffered throughout their lives. Like millions of Cubans, their stomachs had been controlled by the ration books which prevented them from starving to death while condemning them all to a life of never-ending hunger. And so, having finished feasting with their eyes, they launched into battle. To the slaughter!

When he arrived, Manolo was all apologies. He was bone-tired, he said. Only Josefina acknowledged him verbally; Conde and the others merely pointed to his place at the table, ensconced as they were in the process of sucking chicken bones and savoring the very tender yucas covered in garlic, diced onions, and a drizzling of sour orange juice. Josefina ate only half of her chicken (redeeming Conde from an unforgivable oversight, she would send the rest to Tamara), but the four men devoured theirs, down to the very bone (and beyond: Rabbit was chewing even the cartilage), Viking-style (using both hands, grease dripping from their chins), aided by the cold beer.

The second bottle of rum on the table, they were determined to pile on the shaved-coconut pastry, which Josefina had complemented with a bit of cream cheese. Manolo, a cigarette in his lips and more relaxed, finally spoke to Conde about his request.

"You're always the same, brother. You make your life complicated and complicate my own in the process," he said.

"What happened, Manolo?"

Before he replied, the policeman took a sip of rum and lit his cigarette, perhaps the very one he had stolen from Conde that morning.

"Simple: Raydel Rojas Dubois does not exist . . ."

"What do you mean he doesn't exist, Manolo? Who the hell is in the photo I gave you? A ghost?"

"Yes, a ghost, who existed once but is no more . . . as Raydel died in a motorcycle accident four years ago . . ."

"So, does he exist? Or did he exist? Or does he not exist?" Carlos struggled to understand. "Was he or wasn't he Bobby's husband?"

"It's obvious, Carlos. Your friend's boyfriend assumed an identity. Or at least, a name. That of a dead person . . . the real Raydel Rojas, who, in truth, looked a lot like him."

"But Bobby saw his ID card," Conde began to think. "Did he make a fake?"

"Maybe not," Manolo countered. "Somehow, he got the ID belonging to the real Raydel . . . after Raydel was killed. I already told you they look a lot alike. I saw the photo of the deceased Raydel Rojas . . ."

"So," Conde thought aloud, "he was someone he knew. His brother?"

"That's what we thought, but we confirmed that the real Raydel didn't have any blood siblings," Manolo informed them. "At least, no registered ones."

"So then, who the hell is the guy who robbed Bobby?" Carlos asked, really worried now.

"That's a job for Super Conde." Manolo smiled and finished his drink in one go. "Pour me some more, brother. I earned it, right? After all, I've brought you the address of Yuniesky Bonilla, a friend of the guy who passed himself off as Raydel, the ghost . . . Be careful, Conde, God knows what that swindler did to end up wanting to change his name."

Conde sighed at this last bit of information and took back the same piece of paper he had given to Manolo that morning, where there was now an address noted. Then he looked at Manolo, at Carlos, at Rabbit, at the half bottle of rum and finally said, "This right here is all I need to be happy, why in the hell do I get myself involved in these messes?"

4.

He shook off the weight of his nostalgia and allowed himself to be led by his recollections, sentenced to an unbreakable physical and emotional sense of belonging, an ever-tormented feeling of love, which was seasoned with hate, as is all love that is real. Every time he wandered the streets of central Havana, increasingly run down by poverty and neglect, Conde was determined to find, beneath the layers of dirt, age, and precariousness of all kinds, the possibility (or impossibility) that any of its charms had survived, even flourished, after the old colonial walls had become incapable of containing the growth of a powerful and ambitious town.

To begin, he liked to savor the names of the streets: Virtudes (Virtues), Lealtad (Loyalty), Concordia (Harmony), and Amistad (Friendship)—places with ethical nomenclature; Águila (Eagle) and Dragones (Dragons)—with exotic resonance; San Miguel, San Rafael, Ángeles, and Neptuno—offerings to Catholic saints, biblical figures, and pagan gods; all mixed together in close cohabitation, like the souls of so many Cubans. These now sclerotic arteries on which several generations of Havana dwellers and transplants, the bourgeoisie and proletarians, builders and predators, had lived. However difficult the present landscape made it to imagine or believe, the city's most important commercial center had once been there, with successful businesses and stores as exclusive as those in

New York, Paris, and Milan. Along with them, Chinatown, with its pungent aromas and transplanted Asians, silent neighbors of the red-light district with its "ladies of the night," as they used to call them, public servants of a variety of nationalities, specializations, and price ranges. Bourgeois palaces, theaters, and markets had also been erected there, along with eclectic, modernist, and art deco masterpieces, in proximity to proletarian tenement houses and collective outdoor areas for bathing and cooking. But now what reigned in that territory, devastatingly and invasively, practically with impunity, was poverty and physical ruin: a neighborhood that had once been so integral to the city that those living on the outskirts, like Conde's family, would say only "going to Havana" when journeying there, as if central Havana spoke for the whole city. Now, that essential "Havana" functioned as a mirror image of a country whose foundation was also cracking, conquered by the weight of time, apathy, and a history of exhaustion.

To wander "Havana" awakened in Conde other, more recent memories: of those who had passed. The father of his former classmate Patricia, Old Juan Chion, a smart-alecky but kind Cantonese man, his guide whenever his investigations brought him to Chinatown, capable of putting together the most unexpected dishes, inviting Conde to try them; or Juan el Africano, a Black man unlucky in life and in death, who was besieged by chronic poverty, armed with rigid ethics, and whose most valuable material possession had been a baseball signed by his childhood idol. There was also the ghost of Daniel Kaminsky, wandering about—the Polish Jew who, in the middle of eating pork cracklings, playing ball, listening to music, and losing his mind over an endless procession of enormous asses, thick thighs, and bouncing breasts, had jumped right into Cuban life. On those streets, Daniel had become both Catholic and Cuban; an achievement that would accompany him until his premature departure from the island, his forced and painful exit from that noisy city where he'd experienced his greatest sadness and his most explosive joy. Along those same streets, Rufino el Conde had walked in search of the city's most centrally located and well-known cockfighting rings, several times in the company of his grandson, who would become that now-wandering repository of nostalgia and loss, the aging Mario Conde.

He was standing before the large house on Calle Perseverancia, at the address noted on the piece of paper that Manolo had given him. Conde could still see the traces of the run-down residence's former glory days. By the modernist arabesques that survived on the frontispiece and the balcony balusters that still remained, he guessed that it had been built in the early decades of the preceding century. It was obvious that the original owners had enjoyed significant economic prosperity, which they'd been determined to show off with this bourgeois mansion. The stairs, visible from the main door, still retained their marble steps, perhaps Italian or Belgian; the walls were covered with the last remains of some tiles (most of them eroded or removed), perhaps Portuguese or from Seville; there was also the remains of a balustrade of carved wood in the French style, circling up the soft curve of the upper floors. An enormous streetlight of wrought iron, which had miraculously survived periods of both excess and want, was still hanging, its glass panes now missing, from a robust chain extending from the entryway's ceiling. The rest was a jungle: at some point, the house had been broken up into separate rooms to be rented out, and, with the passing of time, those initial divisions had been newly fractured into a kind of beehive in which dozens of families took refuge. Electrical cables hung alongside clotheslines; metal water tanks, sunken floors, and peeling walls accented this old manor; inside, wooden stays meant to hold up the roof, the balconies, the arcades were piled up in a cramped space where, like a tribal battle hymn, lascivious reggaeton poured forth at top volume.

The scaly, toothless Black man whom Conde found on the other side of the entryway, seated on a wooden bench, smoking a cheap cigar, confirmed that Yuniesky Bonilla, alias "the Bat," lived there and specified where: second floor, the room in the back, follow the stink.

"He must be sleeping," the old man said. "He always sleeps during the day. Like a bat, I think he hangs by his legs and everything . . . But tell me, what are you interested in buying?"

"Nothing, right now . . ."

"Whatever the Bat has, I have. And if I don't have it, I know where to get it. More of it and better. Guaranteed."

"Thanks."

"There are whores, too. If that's what you're into."

"No, I'm not into that."

"Young, cheap whores," the old man insisted. "They'll jerk you off for three bucks, suck you for five, and for ten, full service. If you want to give it to them up the ass, that's a separate charge."

"Those are the prices now?"

"For Cubans, in low season . . . If you're an American, it's different. I get the first go!" the old man exclaimed, revealing his toothless, milky gums.

"So where are those women?"

"Not women, girls . . . sixteen, seventeen years old . . . They're at home, watching soap operas, or working. You know, doing *that*, of course. Are you turned on yet?"

"No, still not turned on."

"You're missing out . . . They're first-class. Ah, and I have a guy who sells Viagra. American and Cuban. Certified . . . And another pill for cocks that's called I-don't-really-know-what, but they say it gets you hard as a cannon . . . And at your age . . ."

Conde, a little more anguished now than before, went back to looking around. Yuniesky Bonilla was his only lead to the faux Raydel, since the guy's other known colleague, one Ramiro Gómez, had left little trace of his possible whereabouts. He was nowhere to be found at the various "settlements" on the outskirts of the city where many migrants from the eastern part of the country had flocked. According to Bobby, Yuniesky was called the Bat because he had a congenital defect that caused him to squint his eyelids in the presence of any kind of light. However, the details he'd received from Manolo also confirmed that this vampire wannabe had already spent two years in jail for numerous thefts. Despite the defects affecting his vision, he seemed to have the ability to see through walls, to pass through them, even, in order to appropriate whatever tempted him.

"So, if you didn't come to buy anything, why are you looking for the Bat?" the psoriasis-afflicted old man asked, pointing his cigar at him.

"Not that I'm interested . . . but . . . maybe . . . Since I know everyone around here. How about a ride on the Sputnik?" And he rubbed his index fingers against his nostrils and snorted forcefully.

"I was told to ask him about what I'm looking for," Conde stated, not moving from where he was standing. He understood then that the old man must be working as some kind of "facilitator" for the various businesses carried out there, since only weighty matters, like something involving tons of money, could allow one to stand being in a place like this, where the scent of petrified piss and recently ejected shit came in waves and could knock a person out for days.

"You would know . . ." the old Black man went on, "but if he's sleeping or doesn't have any . . . come see me."

"Of course," Conde said and waved at him before heading up the stairs to the second floor.

The hallway leading to the back rooms was propped up by wooden beams, and in and of itself served as the support for the corridor of the floor above thanks to columns which bestowed upon the place the air of Tatlin's impossible structures. A miraculous architectural balance. This building was a true challenge to the laws of physics, collective proof of the human desire (practiced since Cro-Magnon times) to live under a roof . . . even when said roof could turn into a tomb at any moment, as happened from time to time in this and other parts of the city.

Conde navigated around the beams (from which swung stinking bags of trash, hanging on a nail) and pushed forward in search of the large house's deepest hell. He avoided looking into the rooms—many of them with open doors—skirted suspicious liquids dripping from various walls, and passed two skinny dogs, their fur matted and full of ticks. The animals didn't deign to bark or even look at him: the effort, and their hunger, seemed too great for them.

The door to the room that was allegedly the Bat's was closed and Conde knocked softly a few times. Faced with no response, he knocked more forcefully three or four times, until a voice emerged from the cave.

"Dammit, I'm sleeping . . ."

Conde knocked again and yelled, above the unending stream of reggaeton music:

"Man, I'm looking for something . . . and if you can help me, you'll get your share."

There was no response. A couple of minutes later, after he pounded on the door a few more times, the voice spoke out again.

"What in the hell are you looking for, buddy?"

"You want me to yell it from out here?" Conde replied, and again waited. Despite the noisy atmosphere, he heard some movement coming from inside the room, until the door opened and the inhabitant's mug peeked out: his hair was cut in such a way that it spiraled, sinuous as a snake or maze; and on a sleepy face were small eyes, nearly closed, with which the young *mulato* tried to bring his ill-timed visitor into focus.

"Come on, talk," the Bat demanded from where he stood.

"Jewelry, gold," Conde whispered, as he stepped sideways to avoid the young man's rancid breath, and since he knew he would have only one chance, he played all his cards at once. "Someone told me that your buddy from the east has something . . ."

"What buddy? From what east?" the *mulato* asked him, and Conde had to think quickly.

"Don't play dumb, pal . . . If you help me and I do business with him, for every hundred bucks I buy, you'll get a big cut." And with that, he waved his ten fingers in front of the guy's lids. "I know he's got quite a haul, but he's MIA and I need to find him ASAP, before he sells his own mother . . ."

The Bat opened his eyes a little more widely. Conde noticed that they were the color of coffee that was too weak.

"Hang on, I'm buck naked," the young man said and closed the door.

Conde lit a cigarette and again focused on the deterioration around him. He thought that this physical manifestation of poverty, honed by the years, could only beget more poverty, particularly the worst of them all: that of the human spirit. The faces of the people who stared at him with suspicion were mirrors of their souls, and their souls were the fruit of their environment: pure precariousness, multiplied over the last twenty years by a crisis that cut short the dreams of so many—dreams to improve their lives. The worst part was that the city had hundreds of phalansteries like this one, where thousands of people who had given up faith in society lived, and, as such, they didn't add anything to society: they made a living however they could, like the ticks looking to steal the last breath of starving dogs. Meanwhile, they weakened themselves, if nothing else, with cheap alcohol and massive doses of reggaeton. How many layers of misery, cultural or ethnic destruction, social abandonment, and frustration separated these people from the perfumed and well-fed worlds of Yoyi, Bobby, Elizardo Soler, and others who floated so high above the rest that they were practically invisible? Did they all coexist in the same time and space? And where, between the two extremes, did guys like Conde and his friends fall? What prevented them from climbing the ladder and what saved them from sinking? Conde felt overwhelmed by these recurring questions, with their difficult and painful responses, and for the time being, he was resigned to one thing that was clear: Bosch's painting was reality. Everything else was a virtual world, held aloft by some miracle. Like this building. In the midst of his digression, he remembered an outstanding issue, something he believed was important. Only he wasn't able to remember what. Was that also a fact of old age?

Yuniesky Bonilla opened the door at last. He was wearing only very colorful shorts and had covered his eyes with green-tinted Ray-Bans with metallic frames. Real or fake? When Conde entered, his nose was assaulted by the same odor that reigned in the building's entryway mingled with a concentrated smell of sweat. He saw a large bed with grimy sheets and a pillow without a case; on a side table was a small hot plate coated in petrified grease; there was a gray sink (it might have been white at one point) at the bottom of which lay plates and glasses, and a rope from which some hangers and a few outfits hung. Where did this guy piss and take a shit? Did he even have a fan to chase the heat away? Conde guessed that if the Bat had gotten anything out of the hit on Bobby's house, his earnings would've been minimal and been squandered in the worst way: spent on drugs and alcohol. Maybe on some knockoff shades, *Made in China*, bought wholesale in Ecuador. A backpack and some clothes were piled up on the only available chair. The guy threw the stuff on the floor and gestured for Conde to sit.

"What's this all about?" the Bat demanded, as he lit a cigarette and sat on the edge of the bed.

"Your buddy Raydel or whatever his name is . . . They tell me he made a big score. And I'm into jewelry . . ."

"Who told you? The police?"

Conde smiled. He took out another card and put it on the table.

"That boyfriend of his hasn't gone to the police . . . He's not looking to stir shit up, either. That's why I want to see Raydel: as far as anyone's concerned, that jewelry isn't stolen. Let's just say he borrowed the stuff without the owner's permission . . ."

The Bat watched Conde more closely. This was all probably too complicated for his poor brain to compute. Raydel stole the jewelry, but the jewelry wasn't stolen?

"That dude's missing . . ." the young man said at last.

"I already know that . . . If I didn't, I wouldn't be here offering you money to find him and do business with him. Or do you think I like to just give my money away?"

Yuniesky nodded. The fundamental pull of Conde's offer had won him over.

"Last I heard he'd already sold a whole lot of stuff."

"I can imagine. But jewelry isn't that easy to sell. That's big money."

Yuniesky nodded again. Conde took the plunge.

"Dude, I know you helped move the stuff out of that fairy's house . . . and that you got almost nothing out of it. Look at this." Conde indicated the bed, the table, the sink. "If everything works out, Raydel's going to end up making bank while you stay in this pigsty. But if it goes south, he'll surely rat you out and you'll both go into the hole for a long time. You got a record? Do you know how they treat repeat offenders? Of course you do. Did you know that Raydel's name isn't really Raydel? And that the police would love to talk to him?"

Yuniesky stamped out his cigarette on the floor. He adjusted his green glasses and sighed.

"That's not my problem . . ."

"Of course it is . . . And judging by your reaction, I'm guessing you already knew that Raydel is not his real name." Conde wished he could have taken a good look at the guy's face, but he went on. "A guy who changes his name must have some very big debts, and whoever's collecting, whether they be the police or thieves, is going to take everything when they find him, and if you're in the way . . . Should I go on or are you ready to tell me something?"

"I didn't know anything about that business with his fake name . . . What I do know is that the son of a bitch kept everything for himself and disappeared. *Fuá* . . ." He made a "poof" gesture to mimic the disappearance. "He was all talk about how he was going back to Santiago or some other town out there, but no one believes that. I think he's going to sell everything so he can get a speedboat and head for the U.S."

"That's what he'd do if he had his head on straight. His boyfriend didn't go to the police, but he's not just going to stay still. That guy may be a peacock, but he's a real tiger when it comes to business. He's got some friends who are . . . bad people. And if I made it all the way here, those bad people can, too, you know? Bad guys do bad things . . . 'Raydel's' not going anywhere now."

Yuniesky Bonilla stood up.

"Shit, I haven't even had coffee yet."

He took a moka pot down from a shelf. He prepped it with a brownish coffee powder and placed it on the hot plate.

"So how do I know you're going to give me that dough if you do business with Raydel?"

"You don't. Don't you get it, big guy? I'm your best option. Your other ones are the police, who are looking for Raydel, or the boyfriend's bad friends. So, find your buddy and I'll do the deal in front of you. For every hundred, I'll give you ten. A thousand is a hundred, two thousand is two hundred bucks, et cetera . . . Free and clear. And, from what I know, it could be a couple thousand, so you do the math. I have a guy who has the cash. And besides, you'll charge Raydel what he owes you for having helped with the move, right? You couldn't get a better deal from a Rockefeller . . ."

The Bat nodded again and looked thoughtful. Then, glancing at the stove, he agreed.

"'Kay," he said. "I'll see if I can find him. The Albino might know. They were like two peas in a pod. I didn't know there was so much money involved . . . But I'm warning you about one thing, for sure: after you do your business and give me my taste, Raydel (or whatever the hell that bastard is called) is my business . . ."

"No problem, buddy. That's between you two. I'm only a businessman. I buy, I pay, and *fuá* . . ."

"So how do I find you?" the Bat asked as the moka pot began to steam. It smelled like cheap grounds, overly roasted. Conde hadn't had coffee since he left his house and was dying for a cup, but he'd never drink that awful stuff, not in the dump where he was.

"We'll meet tomorrow at eight p.m. in Parque Central. The part across from the Payret cinema."

"But what if I haven't tracked him down yet?"

"You keep looking for him and I'll keep meeting you there every day until he shows up . . . But the longer it takes you and the more he sells elsewhere, the less money there'll be for you and for me."

The Bat took the moka pot off the stove and took a spoonful of sugar from a bowl up on the shelf. He vigorously stirred it into the coffee and then looked for something in which to serve it. On the shelf was a mug without a handle. He poured the steaming coffee into it and held it out to Conde.

"No thanks, man, coffee really aggravates my ulcer. If you could make me some chamomile tea . . ."

"Chamomile!" the Bat practically shouted. "Do I look like someone who drinks chamomile, dude?"

"No, you look like a bat," Conde retorted. He pulled out a ten-convertible-peso bill from his pocket and waved it in the air. "Tomorrow at eight. The cash machine's ready for us. But if I find him on my own, there'll be none for you. And if the police or whoever else finds him . . . well then, you better hide."

Conde gave the money to the *mulato*, stood up, and held out his hand. The Bat shook it, smiling. Business was looking good. They had themselves a deal.

Practically unconscious from caffeine withdrawal, Conde bravely ordered his medicine at a street stand, one of hundreds that had begun cropping up again in the city. He tried the beverage with trepidation, testing it with several small sips, before concluding that the black broth tasted of linden leaves. At the very least, it would help calm his nerves, and he took consolation in the thought.

When Havana's Parque Central came into sight, swarming with private taxis headed in the direction of El Vedado, Conde lit a cigarette and looked all around him. Some of the city's most beautiful buildings were in this square, and he took delight in their pretentiously eclectic architecture, showing off with their countless arabesques, columns, and vaults. The money and prosperity that had once existed in this singular and unparalleled city! The old Galician Center, now a theater and cultural space, stood across the park from what was once the Asturian Center, now a fine arts museum. The extravagance of these two competing buildings was like a tangible testimony to the unsurpassable economic success of the men who commissioned them. Nearby, the old Inglaterra and Plaza hotels, newly renovated, reveled in their glorious past along with the renovated Telégrafo and Parque Central. The Manzana de Gómez, one of the world's first shopping centers, was being transformed into a luxury hotel and high-end shopping arcade, too expensive for the majority of the island's inhabitants. A return to the past?

It was alarming how this powerful city center had always coexisted, side by side, with the run-down neighborhoods inhabited by the Bat and his cohorts: Blacks, Chinese, prostitutes, criminals, laborers, and practitioners of Santería and Ñáñigo. The magnificent architecture of the buildings surrounding the Parque Central seemed out of tune with the human faces and mechanical monstrosities swarming the ground in the torrid present. Old North American cars still ruled these streets, repaired again and again so that they continued to run for fifty, sixty, even seventy years. Their very existence defied the laws of the market, of universal mechanics, and of the environment. Their prolonged lives meant more noise and lung-polluting black fumes, which ultimately worked their way up into what remained of the ozone layer. Hundreds of thousands of people were walking around under that silent killer of a September sun, and though they should've been working toward a better future, they seemed worn and musty, even more so than those old Fords or Chevys or Pontiacs. They moved like ants whose hills had been shaken: quickly or slowly, but always headed somewhere. Sweaty, with ill-humored expressions, poorly dressed and defeated, many of them carrying an empty cloth or plastic bag in their hands that they hoped to fill with some necessary item or other by day's end. *How were there so many people with so much time on their hands? Who works in this country? Why are there more and more people with such a ragged look these days? Where are they going, and where are they coming from?* He asked himself these questions as he watched the masses parading by, crossing the streets without a cautious glance, as if with a death wish, or else focused on studying the pavement, as though expecting something to emerge from the deepest recesses of the earth.

Conde knew that a Madonna—a black one, at that—was somewhere out there, appearing in his life as if by divine intervention. He knew he had an enviable sum of money in his pockets (thirty, no, now twenty dollars), but he also knew that most of the time he lived on the verge of indigence, no different than the rest of his countrymen, untethered and wandering in circles. He wondered if others saw him—when he hit the streets in search of books to purchase—the way he saw them: as a lost soul. And, above all, he wondered if anyone cared about the regrettable fate that so very many of them had shared for so very many years . . .

The existential reflections of a tropical philosopher are of no use in such a depressed country, as Conde would soon come to learn. Apathy, the path of least resistance, keeping your head down and not playing with fire, these were unassailable life strategies that, for better or for worse, helped people survive day-to-day and maintain their sanities. To hell with philosophy, psychoanalysis, and concerns about climate change! His understanding about the ways of the world was confirmed when Conde got into a private taxi headed toward El Vedado—a 1950s Buick, its body refurbished so it could carry ten passengers instead of seven—and just as he was about to step on the gas, the entrepreneurial driver turned on the radio. At a deafening volume, the beats of a reggaeton song (The same one that was playing in the tenement? Or were all reggaeton songs the same and was that why he couldn't tell the difference between them?) filled the car. The car's eight other passengers and the driver responded by moving their

hips and shoulders in sync and mouthing the lyrics, which all of them
(with the embarrassing exception of Conde) knew, grunt for grunt.

When the car turned onto Calle Neptuno—an area at least as crowded
as the Parque Central—and started to weave around pedestrians, oxcarts,
and pedicabs like a toreador, the driver, now a kind of chorus director, indicated to his passengers that they should all sing along:

Chupa la chambelona
No seas tan llorona
Y mientras tú la chupas
Yo vivo en la luna . . .

As they sang, the male passengers acted out the request for a blowjob
as dictated by the song lyrics, and the female passengers obligingly mimed
fellatio. They pretended to savor the faux ejaculations that had their travel
companions shaking with pleasure. Ladies and gentlemen, young and old,
the indigent and the well-dressed; all passengers of this shared taxi seemed
at that moment to be far removed from the world's tribulations, and especially from those of their own lives, unaffected by the heat and the stench
of gasoline, focused as they were on carrying out a choreography so in
sync that it seemed rehearsed. They were determined to enjoy the reggaeton rhythms on this voyage on the edge of both suicide and homicide in
a roaring 1950s Buick turned *Made in Cuba* diesel limousine.

An alien in his own land, Conde couldn't help philosophizing once
again. *Happy poverty*, he thought to himself. It was the national savior.

His senses were assaulted by the mere approach of a single cell of his body
to the wretched building. A similar assault was suffered upon beholding
its many architectural defects: the naked, dripping metal drainpipes running along the roofs and walls, through which black waters audibly flowed,
and the stairs made of crude concrete, with visibly irregular steps that were
a challenge to either climb or descend. Conde remembered what an old
friend had said of these buildings, which were constructed in the 1980s
to house all the distinguished workers in need of shelter: they were made

of contempt instead of cement. To add insult to injury, in the courtyard where a garden should have bloomed, there were only cigarette and cigar butts, empty bottles, and dog shit—perhaps even some of the human variety—in differing states of calcification.

As he headed up the stairs, the former policeman had the unsettling sense of having entered a prison block with cells on either side. Doors of cheap, rotting wood were crowded together and had metal grilles of assorted qualities and finishes, as if they were merely guarding the invaluable treasures of their inhabitants, the handful of miserable things they'd managed to gather through so much effort. The scarcely lit hallway was damp and suffocating with its cave-like stink of sweat and dirty clothing, of dried-up pungent spices, and of cooking oil. Posted alongside one door was an announcement for the sale of ice; on another, the repair of cell phones; and on yet another, decorated with a heart, was one offering to rent the room by the hour to lovers pressed for time. At the end of the hall, some true believer had offered up their dwelling with an unbelievable sign: "This is Your home, Lord." Conde thought that there was little difference between the Bat's Havana-in-ruins and this cheapened Havana of hastily assembled buildings—only time. And it was quite improbable that the Lord would want to live in either place.

On the third floor, at the end of the hallway, Conde put his hand through a grille to knock on the door of the apartment where René Águila allegedly lived, the most ruthless and unscrupulous art dealer in the city, according to Bobby. This description of Águila's reputation made him suspect that something was off about this place, something more unsavory than just its run-down state, which felt incongruous with Águila's earning potential.

The door opened and the out-of-breath Conde received a welcome breeze of air-conditioning. Soon after he saw the clean-shaven, smooth, well-proportioned face of a *mulato*, about thirty-five years old. The man, undoubtedly handsome and smelling like cologne from Cologne, was wearing a Lacoste polo shirt in a vibrant tomato red, spotless white jeans with a little metallic Calvin Klein insignia, and some dark leather sandals that were unmistakably Birkenstocks.

"René Águila?" Conde asked, trying to dry the sweat from his brow with his already soaked handkerchief and eager for the caress of the cold air coming out of the apartment.

"Who's asking?"

Conde looked up and down the hall, and then behind him, as if waiting for someone else to appear.

"I think I am."

"So?"

"You're René Águila?"

"Maybe . . ."

Conde shook his head. Either the guy was an idiot or he knew too much. Or he was an idiot who thought he knew too much. Maybe he was a real joker who was messing with him.

"I'm a friend of Bobby Roque's."

The handsome *mulato* smiled. He had shining, perfect teeth.

"Well then, that's me," he said and put his key in the lock on the gate. With a wave of his hand, he invited his visitor into the freezing room.

The apartment's interior wasn't any nicer. The living/dining-room area had just a few pieces of utilitarian-looking furniture, including a table with four chairs. His cop's instinct told Conde, nearly to the point of certainty now, that there was definitely something incongruous about this whole setup: the building, the apartment, the decor wasn't what you would expect from someone who presumably did business that afforded him the privilege of dressing only in name brands, and wearing that dry, delicate, overwhelming imported cologne. René Águila announced that he'd make coffee and disappeared into the kitchen while Conde took one of the wooden chairs. At that moment, he resolved to be open-minded: he didn't care what Bobby thought about his host's business ethics, so long as the man could help him find the Raydel impostor.

The *mulato* returned with coffee in porcelain cups served on art nouveau gold-rimmed saucers and handed one to Conde, who immediately noticed a dizzying lowering of his defenses: the liquid had the color and smell of real coffee. With a mere taste of the brew, he felt his senses move organically back into place. It tasted like coffee, like good coffee.

"Did I make it right?" René asked, watching his visitor's reaction.

"It's special. I really needed it," admitted the former policeman, who didn't play around when it came to coffee.

"Coffee is my vice. And I pay a pretty penny for it. What you're drinking right now is a blend of beans I have sent to me from Miami and others that I get from Italy. Did you know that the best coffee in the world is Italian coffee, and that the best Cuban coffee is actually made in Miami?"

"So what, this is an F1 hybrid descendant of those illustrious parents?" Conde retorted. It really pissed him off to have someone try to impart a lesson like that. Everyone knew that thing about Italy and its coffee, even Conde, who'd never stepped foot on that peninsula. That Cuba had the worst Cuban coffee (with the exception of a few, well-supplied places that were inaccessible to mere mortals), and that the best existed in Miami, was the second universal truth of coffeedom. Luckily for Conde, his sister-in-law Aymara supplied Tamara with Kimbo from Naples, and his friend Dulcita, who lived in Florida, tended to gift her former classmates packages of a coffee that drove them wild. Dulcita, who once told them that the Miami airport smelled like Cuban coffee and that whenever she returned from some trip, it was that aroma that made her feel like she'd come home.

The *mulato* laughed, apparently pleased, and took a sip of his brew before driving the point home.

"The point is that I always make it really fucking good."

"No argument here," Conde agreed.

"But the mystery, the key, the quid of everything is in the cups . . . Unless they're porcelain, the taste gets diluted."

"Ah, that I didn't know," Conde admitted, willing to make nice now, as he held up his pack of cigarettes questioningly. The *mulato* nodded: yes, he could smoke. Then he left the room and returned from the kitchen with a clay ashtray. Porcelain cups and clay ashtrays?

"I was also a smoker. It was terrible to quit, but I managed it. What you need is the willpower."

"Where do they sell that? Does it have to be imported as well?" Conde lit his cigarette and they both smiled.

"I love the smell of tobacco . . . So anyway, what's going on with Bobby now?"

"You already know. He was cleaned out. What was stolen was already sold, or is being sold, or is about to be sold," Conde explained. "And since you're in the business . . ."

René Águila showed off his luminous teeth again. Conde imagined he had endless luck with women: he exuded virility and physical charm, even if he was a rat in business, as Bobby had warned him. But those details didn't seem to concern women. Or anyone else for that matter.

"Well, it was just some junk, no?"

"There were a few things of worth . . . Some jewelry, for example," Conde noted.

"Junk, triflings," René insisted. "Nothing that would interest anyone doing big deals, like the ones Bobby does. So, are you helping him find the thief or are you trying to recover what was stolen?"

"Whatever shows up first."

"Why?"

Conde thought for a moment. For money, was what first came to mind, but his second thought seemed more elegant, and it was still true at the end of the day.

"Because I'm a friend of Bobby's from way back. And he trusts me."

"Well your longtime and trusting friend Bobby has proven to be a certifiable idiot. Everyone knew his infatuation with that Raydel was going to end badly. A twenty-year-old pretty boy and a moneyed old man of sixty, my God!"

Conde counted this cruel comment as a check against his host.

"That's life, isn't it? What do you know about Raydel?"

"Nothing . . . Well, just that the kid is a tiger. He made a living however he could, doing a little bit of this and a little bit of that, and Bobby made things easy for him: all he had to do was put his cock to work."

"So, after he ripped off Bobby, you haven't heard any other information about him?"

"No . . . and that's weird to me."

"Why is it weird?"

"You're not a cop, are you?"

Conde decided to come clean: for the moment, René was not his objective, Raydel was. And the fact that he'd had a past as a policeman could help gain his trust. Once a cop, always a cop as Elizardo Soler had noted, and as Conde himself knew, and as René Águila most likely believed as well.

"I was . . . in another lifetime. Now I'm just one more guy trying to make a living however he can, in the most decent way possible. Bobby hasn't gone to the police. Despite everything Raydel did to him, Bobby doesn't want to hurt him."

René Águila thought for a few moments, sighed, and leaned back in his rocking chair.

"Raydel isn't even a skillful thief. If anything, he's an opportunistic crook. He's not the brightest. Bobby laid it all out on a platter for him, and he took what he could get his hands on. But to unload what he stole from Bobby, if there's really something valuable there and he knows that it's valuable, the kid is going to need someone to help him. Stealing beef from a slaughterhouse or quartering a pig isn't the same thing as selling jewelry or high-end furniture, or anything else that's actually valuable. And I'll say it again, that's *if* there's something valuable there. It's a pretty tight circle of people buying and selling that kind of stuff, and we all know each other from doing business. So say someone comes to me looking for, I don't know, a Wifredo Lam and I don't have it, I tell the buyer to wait and I'll go see someone who does, or can get one, and we do a triangular or quadrangular deal. Since I'm the one who found the customer, I get my cut, with a percentage that's negotiated according to the risks."

"Bobby already told me about this. But don't you guys ever play each other?"

"Of course we do, and we compete. We're all snakes in this business. But we don't steal from each other much, because then you lose trust and that's how everything gets fucked up, when we all fuck each other over. The last thing any of us want is for the police to remember we exist."

"Smart," Conde said.

"We all know that Raydel is a crook who stole from one of our colleagues, and Raydel knows that we know. Of course, it's possible that someone from the guild dares to buy things from the Raydels of the world, but then that person would have a heck of a time finding a buyer and would always be known as the one who moved stolen goods. Everyone knows everything around here."

"So?"

"So, Bobby's situation is complicated. We've been talking among ourselves . . ."

"The guild, you mean."

"The guild, yes. I like calling it 'the guild.' It has a nice ring to it, right? It's a word with ancestral history and . . . Anyway, we're all talking to each other. And no one, that I know of, has any idea where Raydel is. The furniture, the clothes, the knickknacks, we don't have anything to do with that stuff. But the jewelry, the expensive decor, and the engravings, the valuable stuff . . . well, that's a different kettle of fish. Bobby says they're not valuable . . . but I should warn you that you should take anything your friend Bobby says with a grain of salt . . . The fact is, we haven't heard anything, and if we haven't heard anything, it's because Raydel sold his wares outside the usual circuit. And if it was outside the usual circuit, then what he earned was a pittance."

"With whom in the guild have you discussed Raydel?"

"I think just one person. We were discussing something else, a deal, and the subject of Bobby came up."

"But who? Elizardo Soler?"

"I don't do business with that pretentious asshole. He thinks of himself as an aristocrat and I don't know what else. A shithead, is what he is. And if you ask me, he's a snitch, too, an informant for the real police and that's why they let him do what he does. Either that or he's a pathological liar."

"I see that you and Elizardo have a lot of affection for each other."

René Águila laughed, shaking his head.

"He really gets me out of sorts . . . No, the person I spoke to was Karla Choy, a chick who truly has a hand in everything, and nothing at all. That woman is a cataclysm."

"What does that mean, 'in everything and nothing'? And how is she a 'cataclysm'?"

"She does a thousand things, and, as far as I know, without ever screwing anyone. As for cataclysm, you'll know what I mean when you see her . . ." he said, eyes twinkling.

Conde mentally noted two details that could be useful in the future: René's animosity toward Elizardo and the recurring mention of Karla Choy. Her name, her abilities, and her . . . attributes.

"Let's assume that Raydel didn't sell the most interesting stuff. Couldn't he be waiting to take them out of Cuba?"

René mulled this over for a few seconds.

"It's possible. And maybe he sold the furniture and the rest to finance that trip. It costs eight, maybe ten thousand bucks to get out of here. Maybe Raydel thinks he stole enough to pay his way out and then live in Miami like a millionaire. And maybe he thinks we wouldn't find out if he sold the stuff over there. But the guild is international, do you understand?"

Conde nodded. It seemed this merchant's network, with its code of ethics and channels of information, was somewhat more complicated and powerful than he'd imagined. It even smelled a bit of the mafia. He decided to change tack.

"Did you know that Raydel's name isn't really Raydel? That he forged his identity?"

The *mulato* squinted, taking this in.

"What's your point?" he asked, masking what nonetheless appeared to be sincere surprise.

"You all think 'Raydel' is an idiot. But he can't be that much of a fool if he posed as someone else for years. And if he's posing as someone else, there must be a reason."

"So, you don't know who he is or why he poses as Raydel?"

"No, I don't. And it's probably important to know what his backstory is . . ."

His interviewee remained pensive. Conde thought he looked worried. He wondered why. Lacking an answer, he decided to take advantage of the momentary hesitation of a man who otherwise exuded certainty.

"René, how did you find out about the theft?"

René Águila smiled once more. Without a doubt, he had the shiniest and most spotless set of teeth that Conde had ever seen.

"Bobby told me himself. I know he thinks I'm a guy without scruples, and that he and Elizardo are Tibetan monks, but don't believe it! Anyway, four or five days ago he came by here with his friend Eli to tell me what happened. He asked me to see if I could find anything out from my networks. Honestly, I think that Bobby and his friend Elizardo wanted to threaten me."

"So, Bobby came here with Elizardo . . . René, I already know you don't like Elizardo very much. Is it just because he's pretentious?"

"He's a proud asshole but that doesn't mean he's worthless," said the *mulato*, more levelheadedly now. "Or that he's making things up. If he's a snitch, then that's something else. That's more twisted, isn't it? But whatever else he is, Elizardo is the king of this business in Havana. He has the best contacts. Important people in this country whom he has in his pocket, through money and little favors."

"Little favors? Material or sexual?"

"Both. According to mean-spirited rumors," René said, amused. "They say Eli is a free-for-all. Homosexual, heterosexual, bi, tri, whatever you want. And he knows when and whom to caress with other things . . . Grease, as they call it these days. Hell, it's obvious that son of a bitch is a rat who's working with the police."

Conde made a note of these rumors, some of which could be well-founded, though he was quite familiar with the way envy could affect one's judgment. But that Bobby was so insistent on hiding the truth was starting to bother him. He felt suddenly out of his depth. What exactly was he getting himself into? What were the members of this "guild" willing to do for one another? He decided to egg on René the Rat a little further.

"So, I should forget about the guild and look elsewhere?"

René Águila took his time answering.

"I would look in Raydel's circle. That's not gonna be easy, though. It could be dangerous for someone who's no longer a cop. When money is involved, these characters can get vicious, you understand? And if this Raydel is not who he says he is, worse still. What I mean is that they're not like the people in the guild. They don't look at things carefully, they don't think of the consequences. They're common criminals."

"And you're not?"

"Touché!" René said and gave the former policeman another of his spectacular smiles. "But no, we're not common at all."

Conde had to admit that his host was much more than a rat. Maybe more like a cat, watchful and with sharp claws. A man who could even play both ends against the middle. To buy some time to think, he prolonged the extraction of another cigarette and before lighting it, asked, "Do you have any coffee left?"

"Yes, but it's not hot anymore because of the air-conditioning."

Conde held out his cup.

"It doesn't matter. The porcelain helps."

As he drank his coffee, still warm, he lit another cigarette and calculated one last move. He started with a sigh, as if he were very tired or overwhelmed or confused. Maybe even a little dumb. All of which he actually felt.

"Excuse my indiscretion, but I'm very curious . . ."

"Naturally, since you were a cop."

"Why do you live somewhere so ugly?"

René laughed heartily.

"Because I am not as idiotic as Bobby. To pull a fast one on me you've got to work for it. It's a jungle out there . . ." Then he raised his voice toward a closed door near the kitchen.

"Yusniel!"

The door opened and Conde could see the face of a young Black man of medium build with a shaved head, his muscles defined under the sleeves of his shirt. The man looked at Conde as though he wanted to cause him pain. At the very least.

René dismissed Yusniel with a gesture of the hand and sent him back into his cave. Conde nodded. He had to admit that René Águila seemed to be very clear on things. Even with the protection of a bodyguard, this New Man must keep his treasures, his money, and his commodities somewhere safer and more discreet. The crude room they were in was just a commercial office. No doubt, this *mulato* was high up in the "guild."

"If you hear anything regarding Raydel, you'll give me a call?"

"Of course," René agreed and watched as Conde wrote down both his and Carlos's numbers on a piece of paper. "We have to protect each other in the guild, and if that Raydel impostor is a dangerous guy, even more so."

"I appreciate it," Conde said after handing him the note. He shook his host's hand. His skin was warm and soft, almost feminine enough to provoke Conde, who quickly withdrew his hand. What the hell was going on here? What was it about this man who seemed so reasonable and attractive, and simultaneously had a reputation for being ruthless in business? He told himself that he didn't care about René Águila's remarkable life, so long as Águila had nothing to do with Bobby and Raydel. He was no longer a policeman and he had enough problems with the missing Adonis and the Black One-Handed Virgin. Nevertheless, that man was giving him a vague presentiment. Impossible to pin down, but a presentiment nonetheless. Like something for which he needed a sixth sense to decode.

He settled his ass down on the wall and felt the heat of the long, torrid day rising up through his skin from the concrete. The glare of the descending sun forced him to remain behind the protection of sunglasses. Though he knew he would begin to sweat profusely, he was resolved to stay seated on that wall—his legs, which had logged almost sixty years of service, had been disproportionately employed all day. Besides, that's where he was supposed to be, on the raised wall next to the steps leading to the Adventist church, when Candito the Red made his appearance.

Earlier, Conde had stopped by the tenement in Santos Suárez where his friend Candito the Red lived, and found that no one was home. A woman with a faded dye job, who recognized that he was a friend of Red's, told him that her neighbors worshipped at a meeting room in the Sevillano neighborhood every week on that night, and gave him the exact address. She knew it because every once in a while, Candito persuaded her and she went along, especially when she felt very pissed. "I said pissed, not at peace," the woman clarified. Pissed about the shitty life she was living—without money to buy anything—and feeling an even greater urge than usual to kill someone or hang herself from the mango tree. And here, she noted, "You have bad days and then you have days that are worse."

Now, focused on awaiting the arrival of his old high school classmate–cum–Adventist preacher, Conde watched the first wave of the faithful streaming into the church's meeting room, which was located on the upper terrace of a nicely painted house with a very well-kept garden in that pleasant neighborhood, and he again thought of the strange ways in which people's lives could be shaped. No one who had known Candito in his high school days, and, especially, twenty or thirty years ago, would have been able to imagine that a guy like him, fed up with being an outcast, would veer toward the path of the intangible in search of a spiritual peace that his surroundings did not offer. Candito, who'd been bred with the rage of poverty and overcrowding, and who, in his days of being a street urchin, had tended to rely on violence as a first recourse in his relations with the world, had never seemed like the most obvious person to become a preacher of prayer and to become at peace—yes, he repeated to himself, at peace—as he awaited the salvation of his soul in the great beyond. He'd always known that Candito's personality had many layers, and that displaying violence had been just one, the one he used as a shield. Ever since they'd been classmates, he also knew that inside the demon-red-headed, nappy-haired *mulato* there was a man with a strict ethical code for whom the values of loyalty, justice, and impartiality carried important weight. That is why they became friends, that is why they continued to be so when Conde became a policeman and Candito a criminal, and that is why they still maintained a friendship in this new era of Candito's militant faith and Conde's overwhelming agnosticism . . . In the midst of his wandering memories, Conde slapped his forehead with the palm of his hand, finally remembering the outstanding matter that had been hounding him: his friend Rabbit's request to speak with him, as announced by Carlos two days prior, to which Conde, busy rushing around with his own concerns, had not followed up. What kind of friend was he? He didn't want to hear his own regrettable response.

The sun had already set when the former policeman saw his old friend appear in the company of Cuqui, his wife for the last twenty-five years, a *mulata* who had just recently entered her forties, voluptuous and compact, with the cinnamon-colored eyes of a tame tiger, still as—if not more—beautiful as when Candito first won her over.

Red spotted him, smiled, and whispered something in Cuqui's ear before holding out his hand to Conde.

"Are you going to convert?"

Conde shook the man's hand and kissed his wife hello.

"It's enough for me to know that Jehovah is large and that the Devil exists. How are you, Cuqui?"

"I'm fine, Conde, fine. And you?"

"No complaints," he said and handed her a plastic bag.

Cuqui looked inside and saw the package of coffee, the packet of detergent, and the bottle of olive oil that it contained. Candito, from where he was, gave a sideways glance at the gifts.

"But, Conde . . ." she said.

"Can't I give you a gift? Does this guy get jealous?"

Candito smiled broadly at both of them before finally stepping in.

"Take it, mama. Conde earned some cash and it's burning a hole in his pocket. He has to spend it quickly."

"I brought you the best kind coffee I could find in Havana and real oil for your salads and look what you say! I didn't bring you rum because you've become boring, practically a saint . . . but the least I could do was coffee."

"Thanks, Conde," Cuqui said and kissed his other cheek.

The former policeman then pointed at the stairs leading to the roofed terrace where there were some fifty chairs set up.

"Red. Is this an official church or a makeshift one?"

"A house of prayer. I'm in charge of it now," Candito said.

Conde looked at the terrace, then at his friend.

"And to whom does this beautiful house belong?"

"Oof, that's a whole novel . . . The owner was a big fish. He was a fixture in the Young Communists, assistant manager and then manager of a business, vice-minister of *el ramo*, as they say, and, because he was efficient and trustworthy, he came to be minister . . . and then, he went down like Humpty Dumpty. He got what he had coming to him, because I don't know if you've noticed, but no matter how bad their bark, and even their bite, everyone gets what's coming to them at some point, right? So first his wife and then he was baptized, and now they're good Christians . . ."

"What a nice story. Pure redemption," Conde said. "So, they weren't good Christians before?"

Candito didn't stop to think about it.

"Outside the church and far from the Lord . . . no. Although they could have been good people."

"I understand, but I don't buy into that redemption stuff. I'm agnostic, you see. Listen, do you have some time to talk about something? I don't need much."

Candito looked at his watch.

"Yes, it's early still. Cuqui, you go on up and start getting things ready."

The woman nodded and gave Conde a third kiss.

"Thanks again. Come by the house soon so I can make you some of this coffee."

"Save it for me and I'll come," and he added in a whisper, "One day when your husband's not around."

The woman walked off, flattered by his flirtation, and Candito took him by the elbow and made him walk to the nearest corner, where they found another wall to rest against.

"What's wrong, brother?" Candito asked him.

"Red, do you think I'm a good friend?"

Candito looked at him with a furrowed brow. He was perfectly familiar with Conde's fits of guilt. Guilt about everything.

"Let's see, buddy. What did or didn't you do now?"

"Forgot for two whole days that a friend wanted to tell me something."

Candito smiled.

"Yes, you're a very, very bad friend. You even come on to my wife . . . But I absolve you," Candito said. "Were you waiting here to give me what you brought and to ask me that?"

Conde shook his head no. He ended up smiling.

"It's just that sometimes I think that I . . . nothing, forget it. Red . . . hey, do you remember Bobby? Bobby Roque Rosell?"

Candito lifted his brows, and Conde lit a cigarette before telling his friend the details of the reappearance of their former classmate, now reinvented.

"So Bobby is gay, a Santero, and a rich businessman!" Candito marveled, like anyone else who'd known Bobby in the past.

"And although you are the chosen lamb of Jehovah, I need you to help me . . . down here on earth."

"I don't know how I can. What do I have to do with Bobby's world, buddy?"

"I'm not sure, but you're going to help me." Conde threw the cigarette butt on the ground and opened the envelope where he had photos of Bobby and his Madonna of Regla. "Let's see. Take a look at this and tell me something."

He held out the two photos to Candito, who moved into the better light of the streetlamp on the corner and put on the glasses he'd removed from his shirt pocket. *We're all a bunch of geezers*, Conde thought, as he looked at Candito with his glasses and his hair, almost all white, just a few remaining traces of the saffron color that had earned him the nickname of Red.

"This is Bobby?" he asked, incredulous, and Conde confirmed. "Oh my, if I ran into him now, I wouldn't recognize him. He's really quite a sight . . . and quite gay."

"'Fag' is what we used to say . . ."

The *mulato*, who didn't say crude things like that anymore, couldn't help but smile.

"But take a look at the Virgin, Candito."

"What about Her? Well, She's Black . . . Is it that She's missing a hand?"

"It's a Madonna of Regla."

"A Madonna of Regla?" Candito looked at Her again.

"That's what Bobby says."

"But She's not the same. I remember . . ."

"Me, too. The Cuban Madonna of Regla always appears standing and this one is seated. Notice the shape of Her crown, too. And the face, Her features . . ."

Candito was listening and studying the close-up photo of the Virgin. He nodded several times, then shook his head.

"No, Conde, this isn't the Madonna of Regla."

"So, what would She need to have to be the Madonna of Regla? If She's Black and a Virgin, She could be the one from Regla."

"Yes and no. There are rules, but I don't really know them."

"I thought that you . . ." Conde seemed disappointed.

"Conde, I was an atheist, then a Santero, then Catholic, and now I'm Protestant. I've had to study to do what I do in the churches, but this is different." He gave the photos back to his friend. "You have to go see someone who knows more about Catholic saints. What I can tell you is that the Madonna of Regla is a copy of one that's in Andalucía. In Cádiz, I think. And they're all the same, as far as I know . . ." Candito stopped.

"What, Red?"

Candito squeezed his eyes shut. He was searching his memory.

"My neighbor Antonia has a Madonna of Regla that I see every day . . . and the face of that Virgin is black . . . But, man, the baby Jesus She holds is white!"

Conde looked again at Bobby's photos: Virgin Mother and divine child, both Black.

"But, of course," he admitted. Bobby's insistence had overtaken his memory, but now he remembered that his mother's Madonna of Regla had also been like Antonia's. Did the fact that this Virgin's child was Black change something essential? He didn't know. And what if it had just been darkened by varnish and time?

Conde put the photos away again and anxiously lit another ciga-rette.

"Candito, if this isn't the Madonna of Regla, then who the hell is it, man?"

"I really can't help you, buddy. Well, I do know of a Virgin who is Black and is seated. She's the Catalan one."

"Of course, of course, la Moreneta. The Virgin of Montserrat. And I think the child is also Black."

"Yes, I think so. But I'm not sure."

Conde nodded and sighed.

"Tell me something, Red. Why is it that when Bobby talks about Yemayá, he touches the ground and then kisses the tips of his fingers?"

"You know that the slaves who came from the kingdom of Ifá identified their orisha Yemayá with the Madonna of Regla, right?" Conde nodded and Candito continued. "The Madonna of Regla is a version of Mary, the Virgin Mother, and here in Cuba, She is the patron of sailors and travelers, the goddess of the sea. But I don't know about in Spain. So anyway, Yemayá also owns the waters, She represents the sea. Both are the mothers of gods. Yemayá is the mother of all the orishas. That's why Africans associate them with each other. So, Bobby makes that gesture because those who have received Yemayá cannot pronounce Her name without touching the ground and kissing their fingers. It's a sign of respect and of understanding: we come from the earth and return to it, right? The earth is the mother of everything. We come from the earth and shall return to the earth, the rivers run through the earth and the waves of the sea kiss the earth."

"You see how you always help me? Let me tell you, you're going to have to give me even more help. With something less religious. There's another reason I came to see you."

"Let's see, let's see," Candito sighed. He was always wary of Conde's requests for help.

"A friend of Bobby's boyfriend seems to live in a neighborhood created by Easterners around San Miguel del Padrón, in the area they call Alturas del Mirador. A terrible neighborhood. If his other associate, called the Bat, can't get me a lead, I'm going to have to go there to find that guy."

"So, what's that got to do with me?" Candito seemed newly intrigued.

"Two things: the first is that I don't dare go into that pit alone. From what I know, not even the police go there."

"Conde, I don't get in fights anymore and don't . . ."

"But you have a tough-guy face. And three people is more than two."

"Three?"

"If I have to go, I'm also going to take Rabbit. But with that dumbass face of his . . ."

"They'll kill you, grind you up, and sell you like ground beef."

"More or less. But there's something you can find out for me, and if so, it would help me a lot. I'm sure there's some Adventists in that neighborhood, maybe even a preacher. You know how to find them and talk to them. If there's a preacher there, surely they'll know the territory fairly well, right?"

Candito had started to scratch his head, not too convinced of being able to carry out what Conde was proposing.

"Look, find out if one of your colleagues knows anyone from your church in that neighborhood and if they can give us a contact. You know how that works, Red. It's not that anything is going to happen to me, but if I go there asking about a guy whose real name I don't even know, nobody is going to give me the time of day."

Candito looked at his watch again and nodded his head. His extensive experience in the world, which had started in the tenements and continued while he was an outsider on the streets of Havana, told him that his friend was right.

"Why in the devil do you get yourself into these messes, Conde?" the *mulato* asked him.

"I've been asking myself the same thing. Well, first of all because Bobby is paying me and I really need the money. You know I'm always just scraping by. And then, I don't know, for the same reason you're going to get involved, Red. Because a friend is asking you."

"So, Bobby was your friend?"

"I don't know. It feels like it. I think so. Not like you . . . But perhaps."

"You never change, Condemned," Candito said, smiling.

"And you think I should change?"

Candito contemplated the house where they would be praying, at peace, and finally looked back at his friend.

"No, don't change. You're a disaster, but a good disaster. And you and I both know it's best not to rock the boat when something is good. You never know what can happen. Don't get down, *viejo*, you've always been a good friend." He held his hand out to Conde, who pulled him into a hug.

"Calm down, no need to get emotional. I'll find out if someone can help us and I'll call you."

"Thanks, Red. And since we're getting emotional and finding things out, tell me something: Does the Devil really exist?"

The most alarming sign that senectitude was quickly approaching for Conde had to do with his relationship to alcohol. For a while now, Conde had been experiencing new and unexpected reactions to drink whenever he took refuge at Carlos's house and partook in their usual game of inebriated chess. The most disturbing of these incidents occurred one night when he came face-to-face with the Devil. They'd been so close, he could smell him.

It had happened a few months prior, during a particularly bloody and vivid battle, sustained by three liters of that devastating rum sold at the Bar of the Hopeless at affordable prices. Since the night was torrid and sticky, Carlos, Conde, and Rabbit had gone outside to drink in back of Carlos's house, and Conde had even removed his shirt. There wasn't a cloud in the sky, just the full moon going from yellow to red as it hung over them the entire time like a lupine omen. By the time they'd finished off the third bottle, no one was bothering anymore to put on a record, and Conde's stomach rebelled, destroyed by the volcanic effects of the rum on his poor, empty insides after having subjected himself to a long fast. Then, the three friends had commenced in a contentious philosophical debate. They'd argued about the meaning of their lives, on the brink of such different precipices. But they'd agreed on this: the fact that at that point, all they had left was to throw themselves into the void or else allow themselves to glide toward the same dark bottom, also a void. It still caused them heartache to acknowledge that they'd lost a majority of their dreams, dreams that had in the past allowed them to forge ahead, that had once forced them to be exemplary, always with their eyes on a future that promised to be fabulous, even luminous. Dreams that were taken from them one by one, or was it by the handful? Whenever the subject came up, Conde wallowed in self-defeat and assigned blame left and right. It was an old and persistent habit, one he could not change because for them, their surroundings never changed for the better. Nor did their lives.

For Carlos, fate had been cunningly merciless. At the age of thirty, he'd been sentenced to live out the rest of his days in a wheelchair, his spinal cord severed by a bullet received in a faraway war. Since then, he had seen his body become a deformed mass, with wells where his sweat dammed up.

Rabbit's plans and fantasies had slipped between his fingers, in part because of the declining surroundings and in part due to his own lack of drive, or else the weight of historic exhaustion. But he seemed to accept his failure without too much drama and found relief in reading history books that served as the best antidepressant and antianxiety medicine for combating his attacks of insomnia and disquiet. History showed him, he would say, that things had always been this bad, that fundamentalism, arrogance, the hunger for power, and the endless strategies used by some to trick, exploit, govern, and, essentially, fuck over everyone else had been around since the cavemen. Even so, he sometimes dreamed of vague possibilities that never materialized, and yet, they sustained him. In recent years, he'd silently suffered the absence of his daughter, Esmé—the girl owed her Salinger-inspired name to a bet won by Conde nearly thirty years before. She'd always been the apple of Rabbit's eye. Almost as soon as she had graduated from college, she'd left the country to make a life according to her own desires. Her departure prompted an outbreak of a sadness most deep that had accompanied Rabbit ever since. That was why he barely ever mentioned her absence during their friendly meetings, despite the fact that it never ceased to needle him, as his friends well knew, like a failure or a sin. Whose failure? And what sin?

Conde, meanwhile, had for many years viewed his own existence as a huge mistake he'd not been able to correct, or even begun to know how, since the mere effort to survive, which had become more pressing since the devastating Crisis, had stolen the better part of his will, and of his seldom-proven talent for carrying out what he most desired: writing squalid and moving stories.

In many ways, the three saw themselves as representative of their generation. They who, instead of opting for exodus like many others, had instead decided to hold tight to their origins. They had believed and fought, only to receive little recompense later for the sacrifice that they had been sys* *matically called upon to make. They were the ones who did not have the strength, option, or desire to leave, not while so much was falling around them. Now, they got by however they could, complaining or not, depending on how their day went, but always on the brink of absolute poverty and envisioning a future that grew narrower and more uncertain. Or perhaps, more certain in the impossibility for them to start over. Presumably, they would languish among opportunists, entrepreneurs, the depraved, and the triumphalism of the new era, some of them still benefiting from having played by the rules of the old one. A universe populated by those gifted with the fangs and stomachs necessary to devour anything digestible in their stunted society, in which only rhetoric, that same old rhetoric, seemed to be in good health, with only slight modifications. Alongside those guardians of corruption and opportunism flourished the weeds of aggression, negligence, and the hopelessness and incivility of so many. What a delightful scene!

On the night when the Devil appeared to him, Conde had been going through another of his cyclical and increasingly more frequent periods of financial drought. The business of buying old books was bottoming out in a country where, for the last twenty-five years, new books had barely entered the market, and the death knell was striking for whatever books had accumulated before that. Given his dire situation, Conde had begun to weigh other alternatives, but the truth was, there weren't many for someone like him, with no technical skills, no capital to invest in a business; not the stomach, lack of conscience, or courage to foray into illegal and therefore more profitable territory. Some of his more versatile colleagues supported themselves by using their book-buying as an in to acquire any other products for sale. For laughable sums, they made off with clothing, pots and pans, decorations, and furniture offered by owners with visa-stamped passports, or else those poorer and more desperate than them, then flipped the items for a small profit, like itinerant peddlers.

One of Conde's business confreres, known in that circle as Barbarito Esmeril, had pivoted his business abilities to set up a sort of flea market in the living room of his house, where he sold a bit of everything, though he specialized in textiles. After his wife washed and ironed whatever used clothes Barbarito had acquired on his search for books, he would place them on hangers or in boxes, offering them to desperate buyers who could not afford to shop in state-run stores. This makeshift market was already known in his neighborhood as Esmeril's Ragshop, and its commercial success was considered a kind of reference point for the entrepreneurial spirit that beat in every Cuban person's heart.

Although Conde admired Barbarito and some of his other more daring colleagues, what little was left of his pride prevented him from sinking to those levels. So, aside from the occasional jackpot of books, he was barely surviving, lately only thanks to Yoyi and his assignments, which were more profitable than the book flipping. With that extra money, he could make do in a country where all goods and services had radically increased in price while salaries had not. He had even come to consider the crazy possibility of working as a custodian, or else teaching classes, or something of the sort, faced with the rate at which the cost of living rose even for a lifestyle as humble as his.

His defeatist—in reality, already defeated—attitude became increasingly aggressive and had accompanied him throughout the entire hot and moon-soaked evening. Among his three friends, he was the one sure to lift his glass the most times, fully aware that he sought the beneficial state of unconsciousness. And whenever the recurring subject of frustrations, losses, and abandonments came up, he was the one who understood it as a matter of principles. Or of how he would come to his end.

"This year, I'm going to turn the big six-oh," he'd said and, with a shaking finger, he had pointed first to Carlos and then to Rabbit. "Just like you, no longer skinny. And you, looking less and less like a rabbit. Now you've got the skinny face of a ferret, dammit. And the shitty handful of years we have left is precisely that—shit and more shit. But you know what? We're not at the bottom of the well. There are people even lower than us." He pointed at the ground, as if he wanted to poke a hole in it with the tip of his finger. He took a drink and his body responded with a tremble. "Ah . . . listen to this, and listen well. It's terrible . . ."

"Don't abuse us, Conde," Carlos begged.

"Let me talk, dammit . . . Look, the other day, I was coming back from walking for I-don't-know-how-many hours looking for books. Even my soul hurt, I had been sweating like a horse and when I was about to enter my house, I saw a man coming up to me and I noticed something strange about his feet. Something strange. When he was closer, I saw that he didn't have any shoes, he had wrapped some plastic bags around his feet. They were filthy; he had surely taken them from some trash bin. Then I looked at his face and realized I'd thought he was an old man, but it turned out that he must be, I don't know, just a few years older than us, or maybe the same age as us. But with that mug . . . A contemporary of ours, gentlemen! And I asked myself, you know how I ask myself things, I think too much, I go over and over shit—"

"Don't tell us something we already know," Rabbit interrupted. "What did you ask yourself?"

"Well, I asked myself, how in the hell had that man come to not even have a pair of shoes, walking around with two bags tied around his hooves? Maybe he drank it all away. More than we do. But maybe what he earned in retirement wasn't enough to eat, let alone buy himself a pair of shoes . . . Are you aware of what a pair of boots costs these days, the kind that look like they're made of dinosaur skin? They cost practically a whole month's salary, dammit! Seeing that old man my age, I suddenly felt pressure squeezing on my heart. I really felt like I was going to cry. Crying for an old man my age without shoes, and for myself, because I saw myself mirrored in that man. I could sink as low as that. If not for Tamara and Josefina, if all of you didn't exist, if Yoyi didn't exist, I could end up walking the streets with plastic bags on my feet . . . Holy fuck! I know that there are people who live like that all around the world, but this guy was the one I had in front of me, he's the one I got, the one who was my mirror image . . . Then I told the man to wait right there and I went into the house. I started looking for some old shoes, some brown ones with laces that I haven't used in years. Do you remember? The ones that were tight in the toes and that I hadn't thrown out, just in case, because you can't throw out anything in this country. But, you know what? I couldn't find them. They weren't in the closet, or under the bed, or in that one drawer where you put your old shit . . . Had I thrown them out? No, I couldn't have thrown them out. Then I remembered that I had seen them in a box with some books I hadn't been able to sell. I looked for them, I took them out, I saw that they were a bit damp because of the humidity and hard as a rock, but they were still good. Anything is better than plastic bags tied to your ankles, right? If he couldn't wear them, he could sell them, exchange them for something, I don't know . . . I shook out the damned shoes and went out to the street. The man with the bags was gone. But I had told him to wait for me! The guy got bored, or thought I had tricked him, I don't know, I don't know . . . Well, even though I was tired as a dog, I went out to comb the neighborhood for him. I couldn't find him, and I started to ask people about the guy with the bags on his feet. It turned out no one had seen him, the drunks at the Bar of the Hopeless didn't know him. A guy with plastic bags on his feet can't just go unseen. What in the hell was happening? Had I imagined him?"

"Are you seeing visions already, Beast?" Carlos seemed worried. To calm that feeling, he finished all the rum he had left in his glass.

"No, no. That day, I hadn't had a drink, I swear to you. So, I wasn't delirious, I'd really met him . . ." As he told his story about the poor indigent, Conde had started to sweat through all his pores and had finished off the half glass of rum in his hand. He tried to dry his face with an already soaked handkerchief, served himself the rest of the last bottle, and took a long and devastating swig to conclude his tale.

"The fact is that I walked for about an hour. I kept asking for him, I cursed and beat myself up for having taken so long to find those goddamned, fucking shoes. I even gave up and went back to my house, sure as ever that I knew what I'd seen and that it couldn't have just been my imagination. I'm not that imaginative. No, of course not. The guy existed . . . exists! And I haven't been able to get him out of my head since that day. I see him dragging his feet so that the plastic bags don't come off, and I keep thinking how in the hell somebody in this country could live like that, without it occurring to anyone to give him a pair of shoes . . . Without anyone giving a shit! Worse still, without anyone seeing him! As if he were a ghost! So, I started to blame myself for not having done what I should have done: I should have given him the shoes I was wearing when I found him on the street. For having tried to give him my castoffs and not what I had on me, which is what I should have done if I weren't such a petty bastard."

Skinny Carlos and Rabbit merely exchanged a look, incapable of uttering any of the sarcasm they usually employed, and, after taking his last swig, Conde looked at his glass, as if he could not explain its emptiness. His friends' silence, the heat, the consumed alcohol, the malignant influence of the dirty, reddish moon on his wounded conscience over the plastic-bagged wanderer must have converged and imploded at that moment, because suddenly Conde felt like all of his engines had shut off, with one final shudder. It was then that an orange stain appeared before his retinas, something between igneous and sanguine, from which festering tentacles emerged with green protuberances that seemed like claws, while a stink of sulfur assaulted him with the effect of an anesthetic. He saw the stain enveloping him, surrounding him with its tentacles and its viscous, indefinite volume, while his body started to heat up, inside out from his bones; his blood beginning to boil with the increase in temperature; his sweaty skin peeling off and becoming part of the plasma of the sulfurous and magnetic image covering him until he felt he was going to explode. Like a balloon, like a bomb, like an eruption of vomit . . .

According to Skinny and Rabbit, Conde had dropped the glass, which shattered against the ground. He was lost for a few moments, as if asleep, though he was visibly shaking. When he came to, he felt a kind of decompression in his body, as if he were returning from a voyage, despite not having a very clear idea of what that meant, since he'd never journeyed anywhere that you could not reach by bus. Finally, he saw the blurry images of his friends and withstood a pressing sensation in his temples, meanwhile feeling great relief. He'd been initiated into the great beyond. But he'd gone and returned, he'd been chosen and sent back. To digest this realization, he drank the drops of rum still nestled at the bottom of the bottle within his reach. Barely having ingested the liquid, he began to twist in his chair like a sawed-down tree, moved by the only remaining force in the universe: gravity. As he was descending into his slow but inexorable collapse, Conde managed to hear Carlos's voice.

"Rabbit, run! Get him, he's passing out!"

"I love that Updike novel," Conde managed to murmur, or at least he thought he had. *Rabbit, run . . .*

Then he fell into a thick cloud from which he would emerge several hours later, lying on a sofa in Carlos's house, bathed by sunlight, in his underwear and clamoring for some dipyrone to come to the aid of his macerated brain mass.

When old Josefina handed him the pills and a glass of water, Conde lifted his gaze and tried to smile at his friend's mother, who was, in a way, also his mother, the mother of the world.

"Jose, I think I'm going to stop drinking."

Josefina shook her head.

"Why did you get so drunk last night?"

"Well . . . well, because I saw the Devil, *vieja!*" he said and sniffed his own armpits. "Don't get too close, I smell like him . . ."

Josefina smiled. Carlos and Rabbit had also smiled when Conde told them the story of his satanic revelation. Rabbit reminded them all that when he got good and drunk he usually saw green mice. It's called *delir-ium tremens*, they said. But Mario Conde knew that it had not been de-lirium, no, but rather a true journey to the bottom of the abyss, through which a man walks aimlessly and without rest and with plastic bags tied to his ankles. And without anyone seeing him . . .

Nevertheless, Conde soon forgot his promise of abstention. After Can-dito the Red confirmed the Devil's existence, he thought it was as good a night as any to tempt the evil one. With two bottles of rum, he made his triumphant entrance to the house belonging to Carlos, who was no lon-ger skinny and who didn't believe in green mice, or in any other infernal apparitions aside from the ones already inherent in his daily existence.

5.

ANTONI BARRAL, 1936

They returned to their home in la Vall de Sant Jaume like black heralds. The country was at war, they announced. At war with whom? This was the question being asked in Molló, in Beget, in Rocabruna, and in other hamlets across the valley, where no one yet knew the bad news. In the larger town of Camprodon, it was said that they were at war with themselves: Spaniards against Spaniards. So why were they fighting? Was it because some were not communists, not anarchists, not trade unionists, not Trotskyites, or fascists, and some were? Because some believed in God, in morality, and in decency, and some didn't? Or believed in them less, and were Masons besides? Because some didn't want a republic and some did; some wanted a monarchy and others didn't; while still others wanted neither? In Camprodon, it seemed that everyone knew something, and nobody knew much. The few radios in town communicated contradictory news. Only one thing was certain: the inevitable war, which many sensed could begin at any moment, had broken out at last.

In Camprodon, Carles Barral and the young Antoni had had to quickly sell off their load of charcoal, at a loss of several pesetas. While Carles rushed to sell their goods and to purchase some necessary supplies to take back to their village, his son Antoni, always curious and inclined to ask questions, had gone to Camprodon's town hall, to the church, to the market, to an anarchist union house, in order to see what he could learn.

Determined to find some cast-aside newspaper, or to be near a radio, or to peel from the walls the flyers still fresh with ink printed from the town's only press, Antoni had felt immersed in a tense and confused atmosphere, among people whose faces changed from fear to hate, or perhaps a mix of the two, and bore ill will. Sympathies were divided in Camprodon, and people thought and talked only of war; many were even willing to participate in it and clamored to obtain weapons so as to go and finish off their enemies—either communist or fascist—as soon as possible. Antoni learned that the Army of Africa had rebelled against the Spanish Republic and that many military outfits had joined in the uprising, although others remained loyal to the government, and still others had no defined loyalties. There has been talk of urgently arming the people of Camprodon, if necessary to defend the Republic; in Catalonia, a majority had already declared themselves loyal to the legitimate government. Word was that in Barcelona, people were on the streets asking for weapons, eager to fight. Though the first gunshot had not yet been fired in la Vall de Sant Jaume, remote and nestled between mountains, it seemed that Camprodon had entered the war as soon as the news arrived. He didn't know it yet, didn't understand too well what was happening, but the war had also entered the life of the young Antoni Barral, twisting it to the point of disfiguration.

They made it home and left their exhausted mules in the shed that adjoined the unchanged stone house with its slate roof where several generations of Barrals had lived. Carles ordered his son to go to the chapel, find Padre Joan, and bring him up to speed on what he'd heard in Camprodon. At fifteen, Antoni was the most educated young person in la Vall de Sant Jaume, one of the few who was capable of reading and writing ballads, and could even add sums without counting on his fingers. He could also decipher maps and identify stars, all thanks to Padre Joan, who'd discovered in the kid a natural intelligence, which he cultivated in whatever small amounts of free time that Antoni, the young charcoal merchant and mountain goatherd, could take away from his work.

Padre Joan was the first priest to have lived in the village for many centuries—at least, no one recalled ever having had one in that poor and remote location—and, to make better use of his abundant free time, he taught reading and writing to the local kids and offered necessary lessons about the catechism and the lives of saints. When he had the energy, he also helped some of the families among his parishioners with their work. Rumor had it that the priest, due to some unorthodox attitudes, had been exiled by his superiors to their village with its illiterate peasants, made to officiate in a small mountain chapel where there was barely space for a few benches, a stone altar, and a crude oak cross, though it had been blessed with an old and beautiful statue of Our Lady, who was pitch-black and had an extensive reputation for performing miracles. Many years prior, a gentleman in the region, after finding that statue of the Black Virgin hidden in the fissures of the trunk of a dried oak, and having been the beneficiary of one of its many miracles, had ordered the construction of the chapel on the very site where the oak had stood and gifted him with a supernatural wonder about whose quality and proportions there existed countless versions.

Antoni had to search half the town to find Padre Joan. He finally found him at the edge of the creek, a book in hand and his drab cassock rolled up to his knees so that his feet, full of blisters and deeply rooted corns, could find relief in the current that came from the arid mountains and ran to the forest-covered valley until it reached the Ter river. Ever since the priest, a city man as well as a man of God, had been confined to this rocky village where all paths went up or downhill, his feet, unaccustomed to such rigor and poorly shod besides, had paid a painful tribute, as a simple glance at them confirmed. The priest, in search of some remedy to better undertake his wanderings, had concocted some ridiculous shoes for himself with raw goat hide, sewn together with hemp fibers. This primitive footwear had caused laughter among some villagers for whom the priest had become, perhaps because of his rather affable nature and advanced age, a kind of ubiquitous authority. He often served as an intermediary in business negotiations and family disputes, and even prescribed remedies for the sick in a village so insignificant that the only government emissaries who ever visited were the obstinate tax collectors, caustic as emery stones, inevitable as the winter flu.

Padre Joan listened to the news, considered the reigning mood in Camprodon as summarized by Antoni, and then read the periodicals and newspapers the kid had collected. The priest, despite being close to eighty years old, could read without glasses and, as he did so, moved his fingers in the creek's transparent waters to shoo away the small fish that approached him, attracted to his sores. That afternoon, while looking at the abused and deformed feet of a man with a hazy past and a boring present, Antoni Barral had a strange feeling. Something lucid passed through his mind with such intensity that for the rest of his life, he would look back on this moment and think of it as a sign, or a premonition. And soon after the moment passed, he was to discover the meaning of that intrusion by his subconscious.

"Poor Spain," the priest said at last and folded the papers to place them within the warm covers of the volume he was reading that afternoon. *The Book of Good Love* by the Archpriest of Hita. "Poor Spain," he then said again.

La Vall de Sant Jaume was a poor and peaceful village that had always lived on the margins of history, or in complete ignorance of it. Ever since the first mountain dwellers had chosen that remote valley in the Catalan Pyrenees as their home—difficult to access but featuring a pleasant climate—the life of all its inhabitants had developed within a limited scope, throughout which the same cosmic and biological cycles occurred again and again, like a gift or a curse. Between the birth and death of each of the villagers, who were determined to stay in the valley, only the change of seasons, the rainy months or tempestuous snowfalls, plagues or epidemics, weddings and baptisms marked the passing of time.

Since neither wars nor scientific advances nor political changes (even those of recent years) had impacted the village's cycles, and since its history had not been documented by the outside world in any known records, nobody could recall precisely its milestones, unless it had to do with some natural catastrophe. And so, it was the case that no one even knew with any certainty whether the old chapel had been built in the village, or if the village had sprung up around the place of worship. According to Padre Joan, the chapel, built with the region's white stones, must have been erected four or five centuries prior, but neither the date nor Padre's estimates mattered too much to any of the shepherds or coal merchants living in the town, for whom time was only vaguely defined by outside forces while being an ironclad physical presence, like the centuries-old lush oak with sweet berries that stood in the chapel's yard.

What distinguished la Vall de Sant Jaume was its chapel and its Black Virgin, which had anchored the existence of the town ever since She was found and the humble site that housed Her was built. Every one of the villagers had been baptized there, all who had wed had received that sacrament amid those stones from some parson who'd traveled from Oix, Beget, Molló, even Camprodon or any other of the larger towns in the area that had their own parish church and the privilege of having a priest on-site. Every one of the area's women had asked Our Lady of la Vall to bestow the gift of fertility on her, along with an easy labor. Such was the faith of the villagers in their Virgin, that even sick goats and sheep were taken before Her in the hopes that She would cure them. Many times, they confirmed, the Virgin had heard their petitions. Her power had revealed itself in cures, pregnancies, and, of course, the oft-remembered miracle of bringing a six-fingered boy back from the great beyond, a boy who had died just a few days after his birth and who, in his second life, as gifted by divine portent, had gone on to live 110 years on this earth. That story, along with Her miraculous appearance inside the tree, were usually the first things villagers remembered learning about the dark statue's powers. And it had been thus going back to time immemorial.

The certainty that the rest of Spain was willing to wage a war, and news that there was already fighting happening in Girona, Barcelona, and a good part of the greater peninsula, barely affected the village's routines in reality, at least at the outset of the hostilities. The first bit of news to actually shake the villagers was that of Jaume Pallard. Jaume, whom everyone in the region knew as the owner of copious land and the patriarch of the curmudgeonly Pallard family, had been summarily judged by the Anarchist Committee as a despot enemy of the people and immediately executed against a wall in Olot. But, for weeks, the greatest concern of families like the Barrals had consisted of whether, with the advance of the war, they would continue to have buyers for the hard cheese produced by their goats and the charcoal that in autumn and winter they concocted on the mountainside, and, of course, if their merchandise could garner even better prices.

Only Padre Joan and his disciple Antoni Barral spoke of the particular events of the war, read the newspapers that the priest had procured from villagers who'd gone down to Beget, Molló, or Campodron, or discussed the news that the priest of Sant Aniol, who owned a radio, sent to his colleague with the odd mule driver or bandit passing through. As a result, they now knew that in Barcelona there had been a great popular uprising led by the anarchists, and that tensions had reached an all-time high, since revenge and violence reigned in the country. It was said that the entire hierarchy of the Catholic Church was supporting the rebel soldiers, while the most radical Republican factions were capturing and punishing priests, nuns, and bishops. The burning of churches and convents, even prisons, and the martyrdom of religious figures did not appear to be just an act of propaganda, but rather, a tangible reality, as was the blessing and legitimization offered by many bishops to the crusade of violent and fanatical soldiers, as most were. Such a state did not cease to worry the old priest.

Antoni Barral tried to understand how they had reached these extremes of violence, vengeance, and hate, and, as such, he always offered to undergo the difficult task of going down to one of the region's larger towns in search of more news. With the deftness of a mountaineer, he wound through the sierra's paths and traveled through areas where he could collect information without calling attention to himself, since on one occasion, during a journey to Camprodon, he'd been captured and taken to enlist in a Republican army or militia, or column, only God knew which—and had had to escape by climbing the walls. While he was vaguely sympathetic toward a republic that promised to improve the lives of Spaniards, the proletariat, and the peasants, he could not bring himself to feel that this was his war.

"But it *is* your war," Padre Joan had insisted when the young man recounted his escape. "First of all, because this war will change the history of the entire country, yes, even this valley where nothing much ever happens. Second, because this time around, neutrality appears impossible. And third, because if you don't go to war, sooner or later, the war will come to you. Revolution or no revolution, no one will escape. Whether you want to or not, you'll have to choose, kid."

Whenever Padre Joan went up to the hillside where Antoni took his goats and sheep to graze, or on the nights when the peasant boy visited the priest in the hut he inhabited on the outskirts of the village, the two would talk about what was happening beyond the valley. And Antoni began to understand more and more: that when hate takes root, it ends up exploding; and when the powers that be manage to manipulate political, religious, and nationalist fanaticism, at some point, sparks fly and you have to expect a reaction. Despite his ten years of exile in la Vall de Sant Jaume, Padre Joan, who'd been born in Barcelona, studied and practiced there, still had his opinions about what was happening. The young Antoni tried to process them: Spain was a country that had lost its sense of justice, and those in power, including the Catholic Church itself, were responsible for this state of mass inequity. Padre Joan's exile and his very appointment as the pastor of a lost chapel in the Alta Garrotxa, the inhospitable "broken lands" of the Catalan Pyrenees, had much to do with his ideologies, which aligned much more closely with the Republicans', sometimes even the anarchists', than with those of the ecclesiastical leaders. His notions and critiques inspired the young Antoni Barral's sympathies and gave the kid a deeper understanding, allowing him to develop a certainty that would accompany him for the rest of his life. Namely, that believing you lived on the margins of history, or acting like you did, was absurd. To believe that History has forgotten you is akin to ignoring that you are part of an ungovernable reality that envelops you. It's impossible to escape it: it doesn't matter if you are in what seems like a forgotten bend in the current, because when the flood comes, everything will be drowned, carried away with it. Every course will be disrupted.

It had been during the catechism classes he organized upon arriving in la Vall de Sant Jaume that Padre Joan noticed how Antoni, a slight boy with large dark eyes endowed with a depth that seemed timeless, had an intellectual ability far beyond that of the other kids in the village. As such, with Carles Barral's permission, he'd begun to teach him not only how to read, but also lessons in history, literature, geography, and science. He soon confirmed that Antoni was a rare specimen in that valley of rustic peasants: he learned, memorized, and processed as if the priest's words were just dusting off knowledge that had been dormant in his memory all along. To make the lessons more exciting, the priest spoke of kings, emperors, generals, and popes as if he were telling stories; he embellished his teachings, whether about animal husbandry or geography, with picturesque anecdotes. Thanks to this, Antoni Barral had his first romantic glimpse of how, beyond the mountains he knew, there was a wide and varied world, and in times past (also known as History), many men had existed who, for better or worse, had either tried or managed to change the world through their acts and ideas. The desire to meet this lively universe beyond the mountains began to take root in the young man's consciousness.

Nevertheless, the priest's proposal that Antoni register at a school in Camprodon was denied by the boy's father: Carles's older son, l'Andreu, was foolish, lazy, and incapable of even properly tending a coal oven, or shearing a sheep without harming it, or assisting in the delivery of a goat. Carles, who'd been widowed ten years prior, needed Antoni to forge his way in their difficult life of limitless suffering and scarcity, to stay in the village, in the valley, in the country. Padre Joan accepted this decision without argument, but received in exchange the authorization to accompany Antoni on any of his tasks, or whenever the boy went hunting for hares, red partridges, and doves. Thus, he continued his pedagogical work and gave Antoni some of the books he'd brought from Barcelona in a cardboard trunk from which, as if by magic, he always seemed to be extracting a new volume that the boy had never seen before.

The desire to know the world on both sides of the mountains and beyond the oceans, to see people who were different from the ones in Oix, Molló, Beget, Camprodon, and even Olot, kept growing in the young man's mind. Nevertheless, Antoni was well aware that he would be hardpressed to have those experiences during his lifetime. After all, he carried out his menial tasks not just with dedication, but also with pleasure. To take care that the coal oven would not explode, to shear the sheep, to wander the mountain paths with the mule cart, to know and care for each of his animals—these were his life's missions. In truth, the lessons and books that Padre Joan gifted him served only to make his tasks more satisfactory and allowed him, in some cases, to associate the business of his life in this village with that of other lives in different places. But on occasion, they also helped Antoni dream.

In one of their meetings, shortly before the soldiers' uprising and the beginning of the war, Padre Joan had asked the kid what he would most like to be when he grew up. Antoni looked at him and smiled: he understood the question, but not its significance. In la Vall de Sant Jaume, no one had ever before asked themselves such a thing. There, one's fate was written before birth and sealed through the moment of death. At fifteen years of age, Antoni Barral was convinced that his existence would replicate that of his ancestors. He didn't complain, and he didn't question it. Overhearing at one time or other a day laborer on his way through the village, speaking of the need to create an equal society, or listening to the parish priest speak to him of times past and fabulous places, or else reading some story also provided to him by the priest, he sometimes dreamed that things—perhaps everything—could be different. But despite this, he knew that this idea was only a diversion, an illusion. Being caught in the middle of history itself was what dramatically forced him to wake from his dreams, since it changed everything.

Anarchists from various organizations, like the National Confederation of Labor (CNT) and the more politically and ideologically extremist Iberian Anarchist Federation (FAI), entered the neighboring town of Beget from Sant Joan les Fonts and caused an uproar among the four dozen villagers of la Vall de Sant Jaume. Especially because it was said they had between twenty and thirty armed men, with the mission of seizing territories and establishing the terms of their very radical and particular revolution, as well as arresting any "enemies of the people" and imposing forced recruitment. Their first objective was to neutralize the city of undesirables, a category that encompassed landholders, the bourgeoisie, and priests. Their second purpose was to begin the creation of a new society in which the people would rule, a society without the vestiges of private property for social status. In other words, they were waging war against exploitation and against the state: the complete revolution of libertarian communism. That didn't sound like a bad idea, although word preceding the revolutionaries confirmed that in other mountain villages and in towns on the coast, forces like this one had undertaken the process of socializing private property, not only small factories and workshops, but even the boats of fishermen and the goats and sheep of shepherds, which ceased to be theirs in order to become a common good of the people. Could it be true? And were they the ones who'd executed Mr. Pallard? Everyone said it was so. Were they the ones who had burned down the church in Sadernes with the parish priest still inside? With all the rumors flying around, no one could pinpoint which policy of governance of the Republic those men ascribed to. The villagers were convinced that the proximity of the anarchists meant the arrival of the war and its effects to la Vall de Sant Jaume, just as Padre Joan had warned.

Carles Barral's first instinct upon the imminent arrival of the anarchists was to flee into the mountains with his goats and his sons. Who if not them, the Barrals, would know how to lead their flocks through the steepest crags and cliffs, guaranteeing pasture and water in the treeless heights; who else would protect them from the coming winter? But it was Antoni who made him abandon the idea: this time, it was not just the matter of a passing storm but a flood, he argued, invoking the priest's metaphor. For how long and in what conditions could they live in those inhospitable mountains? Life was hard enough already in the village, but to try to sustain it in the mountains for a potentially prolonged period of time, at the end of which they could be punished for running away? It was better, he believed, to accept the challenge, as Padre Joan thought. The priest, despite the terrible news of the fate that had befallen some of his colleagues—executed, persecuted, or jailed (as had just happened to Padre Josep María in Beget, it was said, and many priests and nuns in Barcelona)—trusted that the world had not gone completely insane. For the rest of his life, Antoni would ask himself: Had Padre Joan really believed that? Was there a limit to sanity or was it completely lacking? Why had the worst of that war been so merciless to his brother, l'Andreu—a peaceful fool, an angel of God—and to his poor father, Carles? Had that heterodox parish priest with a hearty appetite had the soul of a martyr?

The last conversation that old Padre Joan and the young Antoni

Barral would have took place on the banks of the creek, while they both soaked their feet in the current. The kid was worked up over what was coming, fearful of what the impending arrival of the anarchists, the libertarian revolution, the war, could mean for Padre Joan, but the priest had insisted on calming him down.

"Don't worry about me," he'd said to the kid. "Look at my feet: they are too old by now to take me anywhere else. Besides, I don't think it would be interesting for the anarchists to devote any time to a priest like me . . . If anything happens to me, don't worry. It will have been my fate. Don't feel bad for the goats and the sheep, either. If anything, release them into the mountains, they know how to get by up there better than you do, although you are almost as good as them. I'm going to ask only one thing of you, my son: take care of the Virgin. Some madman could get carried away and do something outrageous, like destroy Her, or set Her on fire . . . She's too valuable to let something regrettable like that happen."

Antoni had been nodding along to each of the priest's recommendations, until he heard the last one. After thinking about it for a few moments, he proposed what he considered to be a good idea: they could remove the statue of Our Lady from the chapel and hide Her, as everyone said She'd once been hidden, in the hollowed out trunk of a tree, or else drop Her into a well, or take Her to one of the region's many caves . . .

"We could do that," the priest hedged, "but it would be worse for us. Everyone in the area knows that the only important thing in this village is Our Lady of la Vall, and if the anarchists don't find Her when they arrive, they will be furious. We cannot give them any more incentive for violence than they already have. Can you imagine if they set fire to the chapel with the Virgin inside, as they did in Sadernes? Could it be true that they wanted to burn down the cathedral in Barcelona as well—that they burned down the one in Lleida?"

Antoni looked at the chapel, the dilapidated doors of which closed only at night to prevent any tramps from taking shelter inside. He remembered the story of the wolf who, during a vicious winter, had entered its perimeter and, when discovered by a villager, had approached and licked the man's hand as if he were a sheepdog. Another of the Virgin's miracles. Just for that, for being miraculous, must She be saved?

"Do you believe in miracles?" the priest asked him.

Antoni nodded. "I do believe, like everyone in the village. And the Virgin is responsible for many." Didn't Padre Joan believe in them?

"I believe in faith," the parish priest answered. "And you already know that faith creates miracles. I believe in the faith that you and the other villagers have in our Lady of la Vall, but I also believe in the importance of symbols. And the Black Virgin is a symbol of many ancient things. No one knows where She came from, or how She got here. Only a sketchy story about a local man who found Her in the trunk of a dried-out oak that looked like a cross, and how the Virgin had repaid him with a miracle. But what I do know is that that statue carved from black wood is the work of human hands and it became a symbol of faith. That statue was created by someone, for some purpose. A devoted artist carved Her specifically from black wood because he wanted to say something with that exact color; he seated Her on a throne because he wanted to represent Her great power to man; he gave Her colors, and made Her lifelike to bring Her closer to us, and more important, to make Her beautiful. Whoever made Her or commissioned Her creation wanted to represent in Her the origins of everything, the earth where seeds fall and life blooms, the mother of the Redeemer who sought to make the world a better place. And I think that someone brought Her all the way here for a reason, because She has some purpose, because they were saving Her or hiding Her from something. I don't know what from, I cannot know, but at the same time, I do know. She knows it, too. And perhaps you will be the one in charge of saving Her once again from human excess, which is infinite and recurring. Save Her, not because of the potential of Her miracles, which we can believe or not, but rather because of the miracle of Her having existed and accompanied men in their disquiet for so many centuries. She is a witness to time. That is sufficient motive to guard and protect Her."

From the lookout to which he led his flock, Antoni Barral saw the militia approaching on the path leading from Camprodon and not, as they had expected, on the one leading from Beget. There weren't as many as they'd said, just over a dozen men, only two on horseback. When they spotted the village, the men stopped and, by the looks of it, had a conversation. Even the two riders dismounted and when they were back at the reins, one of them was brandishing a pole from which they'd hung a piece of cloth, what was perhaps the red-and-black anarchist flag. Meanwhile, in the town, several inhabitants had gathered around the chapel. Among them, Antoni could make out Padre Joan, with his dark cassock and his white hair, and his brother, l'Andreu, who in recent weeks had taken to carrying a pole over his shoulders as if it were a rifle and he were ready to leave for war.

Antoni Barral looked at the September sky, still cloudless, and felt an uncontrollable impulse. He didn't think twice. He herded his goats and sheep toward the mountainside in search of a path up toward another hill, where there was a small valley that was impossible to see from the village, set beyond any trails. What was driving him? Why was he doing this? He knew all too well: he had watched each of his goats and sheep be born, he had named them all, knew the personality of each one, their preferences and stubbornness. They were his.

It was starting to get dark when Antoni finally came down from the mountain after hiding his flock. He had three hares in hand that had fallen into his traps, which could serve as a pretext for his absence. Alarmed by the silence, occasionally broken by some screaming boys, he kept alert, and chose to move between the stone houses down to the creek. Following the current, he managed to place himself as close as possible to the chapel, protected by the old bridge that connected the two banks.

There he overheard a man speaking and cursing everyone: the bourgeoisie, the soldiers, the landholders, the priests, the lawyers . . . They, the revolutionaries, would sweep away every one of those parasites and create a new society in which everyone would be equal. And anyone in opposition would also be mercilessly eradicated, along with the bourgeoisie, the soldiers, the landowners, the priests, the lawyers . . . and the landlords, he added this time: the exploiters. Parasites, all of them, he insisted. The villagers, the poor of the earth—the vociferous speaker clamored—should hand over all the money they had, anything of value, as well as their hunting rifles, since that would be their contribution to the liberating revolution, he assured them, the liberating revolution that would create a society so just that there would be no need for money, the root of all evil.

With goatlike skill, Antoni scaled the stones from which the bridge rose and managed to gain a partial but alarming view of what was happening above him: almost all of the villagers, including his father, Carles, and his brother, l'Andreu, had been placed against the chapel's wall. One step ahead of them was Padre Joan, with a book, or the remains of a book, at his feet. The revolutionary who was yelling—a tall, sallow guy wearing a kind of beret and dressed in something resembling a military jacket— had a rifle in his hands which he pointed at the villagers and the priest throughout his diatribe, until, at a given moment while he was yelling, he suddenly turned the weapon and pushed its butt so roughly into the priest's stomach that he doubled over and fell to his knees, and the revolutionary's companions jeered and asked for more. More what?

With his heart beating wildly, Antoni slid into the riverbed and sought shelter under the bridge. What would happen? What could he do? Is this what all wars were like, or was it just this one? Would the revolution really be established through the violent methods that the beret-wearing man was once again clamoring for? It was then, as fear shook through him, that he had the feeling that whatever was happening now in the village was far worse than what he'd expected, and then he made the first of many fateful decisions that, along with the war, would end up radically altering his life. He removed his hemp-soled espadrilles and waded through the current toward the small ford behind the chapel, just next to the centuries-old oak that had been planted, it was said, in the same place where the Black Virgin had first appeared. He climbed up the slope until he reached the sidewall of the chapel, where one of the village's only two treasures could be found. Lying on the ground and leveraging himself with his arms, Antoni rested his feet against one of the building's stone blocks and, before pressing down, looked at his dirty toenails against the chapel's yellow surface, his prominent metatarsals, the thick veins crossing his feet, which seemed so far away at that moment, almost separate from him. Were those really his feet? Whether or not they were, he pressed down on them now. He closed his eyes and focused all his might: the stone block began to slowly push inside of the building. He wound up and pushed again, yielding another inch. He waited. Nothing. He pushed, waited, but there was no reaction to his increased movement against the block. It was at that moment that he heard some confusion and yelling. A shot rang out. Then, more yelling, and what he thought might be crying. Then another shot. And finally, silence. Antoni was frozen, his feet against the stone, listening to the echo of the explosion ringing through the mountains and the forest of beeches and black poplars until it faded and yielded to a deafening and fatal silence. Why had they fired? Whom had they shot? Why twice? Were both for Padre Joan? Antoni decided not to dwell on it, and instead made a final effort until he felt the stone sliding forward more easily. He waited again and, when he'd recovered more strength, continued to push until he'd managed to make a space in the wall large enough for himself. He climbed through into the chapel, which was mostly dark, since its doors were shut. He crept like a fox toward the small stone altar on which the Black Virgin rested and, for the first time in his life, held Her in his arms. When he lifted Her, he felt that She was heavy and polished, difficult to hold on to, but oddly familiar. As he grabbed Her, the tips of his fingers found a depression in the wood formed by the pleats of the cape covering Her back. Mostly, though, he had the distinct feeling that this was *not* the first time he had held Her, that the black statue of Our Lady was his in an overwhelming and bodily way, a feeling he did not nor would ever understand, one that would never leave him. Antoni managed to grab Her under the arms She held out in front of Her, one with the Child Jesus near Her breast and the other pointing forward in a kindly gesture. To get Her out of the chapel, he had to move the stone he'd displaced a bit farther in order to slide Her through without harming Her.

When he was back outside, next to the old oak, Antoni felt the full weight of his fear and uncertainty. He was shaking. Had he removed the Virgin because of what Padre Joan had said, or because of some irrational and indomitable instinct? Was it bravery, fear, or madness? He placed the statue on the ground and let himself fall against the oak's trunk to calm down and think about his options. Hiding the Virgin in the mountains and returning to the village would be the most rational, but it would reveal the theft. He himself had discouraged his father from fleeing to live in the mountains with his flock, so that was not an option. Taking the Virgin down to the creek and trying to find out the consequences of those shots fired would resolve nothing and risk everything, since it would be very difficult to escape again were he to get caught. Why was it he, he of all people, whom life placed at a crossroads with no clear choice? Had it been madness to remove the effigy? Had it been worth risking everything, losing everything he was, had, and wanted, just to save the statue of a Virgin? But who or what was he anyway? What did he have, and what did he want?

Antoni already knew that any step backward could be suicide, that there was only one way forward. Before putting on his espadrilles again, he looked at his feet and knew that everything would depend on them. He and the Virgin depended on them. He put his shoes on, picked up the heavy statue again, and, seeking to remain hidden by the trees and walls, went toward his house. Luckily, he confirmed, only the outside of the chapel was lit by lanterns and torches, while the rest of the village remained in darkness, as if it were dead. From the shadows there then emerged another black silhouette. Antoni froze briefly again until he saw that the shadowy figure was old Carmeta. When she recognized him, the old woman took his face in her two rough hands, and with her breath that always smelled of garlic and oil, she whispered to him, "Leave. Don't look back. Leave forever. Save yourself, Antoni." Then she blessed him, making a cross on his forehead and kissing the Virgin's outstretched hand. A second later, the old woman had disappeared into the shadows as if she'd never existed.

When he reached his house, his heart beating with fear and Carmeta's words hammering his brain, Antoni pushed open the door, which was already ajar. It was by the light of an oil lamp that he hadn't noticed from outside that he then saw him.

Antoni froze, with the Virgin in his arms. The intruder seemed to be a young man with a double-barrel hunting rifle slung over his shoulder. He was focused on searching the house, poking around and throwing things. Antoni finally understood why the man was there when he saw him shake an old cracker tin and heard the tinkle of coins that, along with the flock, constituted his family's entire savings. Antoni recalled what he'd just heard the beret-wearing man say: everything was done in the name of the liberating revolution. Liberating revolution? Didn't he mean *libertarian* revolution? And why had the anarchists come from Beget, to the east, and not from Camprodon and the Ter Valley, to the west? Suddenly, Antoni understood that they were the victims of the worst scourge of the war: these men weren't anarchists, but a band of criminals taking advantage of the chaos and stealing others' slogans in order to carry out their misdeeds.

Antoni Barral would have many years to ponder what happened in those next moments. Even on his deathbed, looking at his inert feet and the Virgin, he would be thinking about it, trying to undo what had been done, though he knew how fatal and stubbornly irreversible time was. In the moment, however, he had not hesitated: his indignation had won and hatred took over. When the young bandit heard the boy's furious imprecation, he let the tin fall and tried to grab his hunting rifle. Antoni, in turn, released the statue of the Virgin and searched his belt for his mountain knife. The bandit pointed the weapon at Antoni, who, screaming, possessed by fury, jumped toward him. There was the sound of metal against metal, but it was not followed by the expected shot, and before the thief could reposition his extraneous weapon to defend himself, Antoni thrust and felt the knife sink into the intruder's neck, as easily as that of a goat or cow. The blood sprang out in a stream and he shut his eyes against the agonized look on the young bandit's face as he removed the knife from his neck.

Feeling the beating of his temples and with stifled breath, Antoni Barral washed the knife and cleaned off his hand and arm. For a moment, he felt nauseated. When there was no more blood left on the blade and on his skin, he felt a tangible relief. Trying to avoid the dead man's face, he looked under the table for the cracker tin. He opened it and counted 140 pesetas. A miserable sum: it represented *his* misery. He put the money in his pocket and went to the other room, packing the blanket spread out over his straw mattress and an old wool scarf as well as a hat with ear flaps, both knit by his mother before she died. He stuffed it all into a new coal sack. He gathered the small amount of food in the pantry—bread, cheese, a chunk of salted meat—and also put it in the bag. Lastly, he lifted the statue of the Virgin that he had dropped next to the door and, while placing Her in the sack, saw that She had lost her right hand in the fall. In the dark, he couldn't see the hand on the ground. He decided to forget it: there was no time to look for a little piece of black wood. Antoni nestled the Virgin inside the sack and, before leaving, dared to look at the young bandit's corpse: eyes open, with an expression that showed the fear and surprise with which he'd left this world. Antoni understood that the man was barely older than himself: he was only a boy.

Antoni Barral carried the sack over his shoulder and went out into the deep night of the mountains from which cascaded the increasingly cold breeze of a newly inaugurated autumn. He had no idea what to do, where he would go, if he would ever return, and less still of what was happening and would happen next to the village. He didn't know that at that very moment, in front of the chapel, Padre Joan was on his knees, tears in his eyes, praying for the souls of Antoni's brother and father, their corpses going cold in the night, wrongful victims of a war that took them by surprise. All he knew was that he couldn't take the Camí de la Menera, toward nearby France, since it was usually surveilled by groups of soldiers. So, the moment had come to take advantage of la Vall de Sant Jaume's second treasure: a mountain passage on the side of the Pic de les Bruixes through which a cave was hidden by two seemingly compact rocks. The Coll dels Llops, the villagers called it, and its location helped him avoid having to climb several slopes and precipices in order to cross the peak of the mountains. On the other side of that passage was the old mountain path that would lead him to the rest of the vast world that began in a country called France. It would give him a new life.

6.

"So maybe I should put together a brunch."

"A what?"

"A brunch, Conde, I said brunch. My God, how backward you are!" Bobby said on the other end of the phone and laughed.

Then Bobby had to explain to the peddler of old books that the intervening act of nourishment between breakfast and lunch was called "brunch" and had its own characteristics, which Conde would joyfully discover when he arrived midmorning at his former classmate's house and was taken to the terrace where the aforementioned brunch was laid out.

In the center of the table was a tall, etched-glass vase, full of white and spotted lilies, which struck Conde as particularly gay. On the table was a pitcher of orange juice, a plate with a large Spanish tortilla, a tray of toast and exotic fruit spreads like blueberry and strawberry, a stick of butter, a steaming coffeepot, a pitcher of warm milk, a plate of fried bacon, some yogurts, and a platter with both white and yellow cheese accompanied by their respective slicing knives. Dazed by such abundance, Conde's stomach issued a cry: his breakfasts usually consisted of a couple of cups of coffee and a piece of bread that was more or less chewable, wrapped around whatever edible thing he could find (if there was anything at all), and the lunches he ate on the streets were often just greasy pizzas sprinkled with vile cheeses. The morning banquet before him now exceeded all expectations, and the imagination of someone like him, or 90 percent of his compatriots. Not even Tamara could put together a table like that on her days off, since her diet had made a virtue of scarcity. The woman had reduced her nutrition to some low-sugar fruit juice and, to Conde's horror, a tea that was equally bereft of any sweetener. The blessed fear of aging!

As they ate, the conversation revolved around the former policeman's initial investigations and his meager, if foundational, progress.

But when the plates, bowls, pitchers, jars, and platters had been emptied of their contents—Conde had eaten everything, everything he could, with his omnivore's philosophy of life—they gravely got down to the matter at hand.

"Tell me something, Bobby. Something important. Did you know that Raydel was not his real name?"

Bobby sighed and shook his head.

"Sometimes, it did seem like his story was a little weird, that he could be a bit of a liar. But that's normal, isn't it? And it didn't matter too much to me, he gave me what I needed and . . . I never imagined that he was posing as a dead man. Why would he do that?"

"To hide something, or to hide himself from someone . . . Why take over an identity? What pushed him to do that? What had he done that he had to hide under another name?"

"What do you think?"

"That he did something serious, something very fucked-up. The kid you fell in love with was an impostor and God knows what he was hiding. For starters, I don't think he was as simple as you thought. He had some depth. He was looking for something."

"To steal from me?"

"That, too . . . But there must have been a reason. Like we've been saying, he robbed you for money so he could leave the country, for example. But perhaps he needed the money because he wanted to escape from something he feared."

"¡Ay, Dios mío! Why in the hell must I always live so dangerously, man?" Bobby asked, hand on his chest. He had received Conde dressed in white pants, a white long-sleeved shirt, and some upscale espadrilles, also white.

Beneath the shirt, hanging from Bobby's neck, Conde could see a multi-colored bead necklace. Was this the appropriate outfit for brunch? Conde smiled and decided that it was time to put it all out on the table.

"Bobby, do you remember Candito?"

"How could I not, Conde? That light-skinned guy with the nappy red hair who looked like a devil?"

"That's the one," Conde said, smiling.

"I remember perfectly well because I was scared shitless of him. That guy was really, really bad."

"Appearances are deceiving, Bobby . . . Well, sometimes. Candito was always a good guy. And now he's practically a Protestant minister."

"I wouldn't believe it! So, what happened to him?"

"Nothing. Candito, and also Rabbit, think that your Virgin is very strange. She doesn't look like Our Lady of Regla on prayer cards and on Cuban altars, or like the one in Andalucía. Candito thought She reminded him more of the Virgin of Montserrat, being a Black Madonna with a Black baby Jesus and—"

"The thing is, Conde," Bobby interrupted, "She's very, very old. It doesn't matter whether She looks like the Virgin in the church in Regla or on the prayer cards, but rather what Her believers saw and continue to see in Her. How many statues of Christ have you seen? And of the Virgin Mary? Thousands, right? And some of them are Black, aren't they? There are Japanese Virgin Marys, too! Look, I'm sure that the image of Christ you're most familiar with is the one that everyone here has, the Sacred Heart of Jesus."

Bobby imitated the pose of the painting that devoted Cubans usually hung in their living rooms: a Jesus with a kind but condescending face, with His left hand over a chest exposing a wounded heart. Conde recalled that a very peculiar image of Christ, painted by Rembrandt, had led him to discover the extraordinary lives of several Jews in relation to that portrait of a Jesus different from the ones recreated by other painters of Rembrandt's time and, of course, from the Christ of the Cuban popular prayer cards.

"When my grandmother inherited it from her father, she knew it as the Virgin of Regla," Bobby continued. "I don't know if She came from

Spain or if She was carved here in Cuba. What I do know is that She's *my* Virgin of Regla. And that son of a bitch stole Her from me."

"You're right," Conde admitted, serving himself more coffee and lighting another cigarette. "Since She's so rare, perhaps that will make it easier to find Her. Incidentally, Yoyi told me She'd been brought over from Andalucía."

"That's also possible, yes. I think I said that to you before. But I'm not sure, to be honest. She's so old . . ."

Conde didn't want keep pushing the subject, since there was another that had been nagging at him since his arrival.

"Explain something to me, Bobby. If you've always been Catholic, like you said, then why did you undergo initiation with the Yoruba saints?" He pointed to the necklaces his friend was wearing. "And why are you wearing all white today and all of those beads?"

Bobby placed the back of his hand over his eyes: it was the gayest gesture Conde had ever seen in his life.

"My God. Don't tell me you forgot that today is the feast day of the Virgin of Regla?"

The former policeman opened his eyes. How could he possibly have forgotten, involved as he was in this particular investigation?

"In a little bit, I'm going to my *Padrino*'s house. Today, we're going to celebrate Yemayá. And my little Virgin is going to miss it, man."

"I guess I get an F in the saint's day calendar," Conde admitted. "I *had* forgotten. But, tell me, why did you become a Santero if you believe in God and the Virgin?"

Bobby shook his head, leaned back in his chair, glibly stole a cigarette from Conde like it was nothing, and held it between his fingers.

"It used to be practically a crime, but nowadays it's in vogue to practice Santería, you know. When people are desperate they'll believe anything, and desperate people abound around here. The bad thing is that it's all a business now, a pyramid scheme. If you go see a Santera, she'll immediately tell you that your problem is serious and that you need to make saint. And then she sends you to see a Babalawo—who of course is her *Padrino*, her friend, and often her business partner—and they do the ceremony for you and charge you an arm and a leg for all of the paraphernalia relating to the initiation. And you pay it happily, because you become part of the clan and receive divine protection . . . that is, if you even believe in divine protection. And then you yourself get into the business of putting together the ceremony for someone else, especially if they live abroad and come to Cuba with American dollars . . . But I underwent the ceremony with serious people, or so I like to believe. I did it because I really felt that I was going crazy and I needed some relief."

"Was this when they kicked you out of the university?"

"No, later. Like fifteen years later."

"Why, what happened then?"

"When I separated from Estelita and started living with Israel, it was a very big change in my life. It was what I wanted most, what I was truly hoping for, but it had suddenly shaken me from head to toe. My life, my wife, my kids . . . my whole story. It was sometimes a very difficult process. I felt happy about having rebelled, but at the same time I felt dislocated, like I was lost . . . That was when Israel took me to see his *Madrina* and . . . you know . . . they had to do an *asentamiento*, a ceremony by that name. And you know how it goes, one thing led to another . . . Before I knew it, I'd made saint."

Bobby pointed to the blue-and-white beaded bracelet he wore on his wrist and then stroked the necklaces hanging from his neck. Conde thought for a moment.

"Yes, I imagine it wasn't easy . . . So, what happened with Estelita and your children?"

Bobby almost smiled.

"The same thing that happens to everyone else . . . They live in Las Vegas now. They don't want to come to Cuba so I spent several days with them when I was up North. They don't care what the hell is happening here, they don't even want to know. It's fucked-up, isn't it?"

"Yeah" was all Conde said, as he didn't want to get too deep into such tempestuous waters. At least not right now. "So, making saint?"

Bobby reached out and took the lighter. He served himself some more coffee, took a sip, and then lit the cigarette he'd been holding between his fingers—all very slowly, in a manner practically bereft of desire. He inhaled the smoke, and the pleasure was reflected in his face.

"It really wasn't easy," he said finally. "But I think you can understand me . . . I still think, sometimes, that my life could have been something else, if they hadn't thwarted it, Conde."

His words expressed a sad rage.

"Didn't you just tell me that you found yourself in the end?" Conde asked. "That you've been happy?"

Bobby nodded several times.

"Yes . . . In the end. But what I had to go through first was a living hell. And I'm not being melodramatic. Look, my friend, I don't like talking about this, but sometimes I need to."

Bobby put out the cigarette and sighed, as if he were leaking air. He looked toward the yard, and since the effeminate lilies were in his line of sight, he reached out and moved one that seemed out of place.

"Don't tell me if you don't want to," Conde said, gesturing to emphasize, but his interlocutor went on as if he had not heard him.

"When I started going out with Katiuska, in college . . . Well, I did it because I wanted to be a man. I didn't want to be a fairy, I wanted to be normal, do you hear me? Normal. And to be accepted and not have my life fucked up. Do you remember the pressure? So, I did everything I could to fix myself on the inside. But my relationship with Katiuska was weird. When we were alone, we kissed, we got hot and heavy, and sometimes she jerked me off. She'd ask me to lick her down there, but we didn't screw; she wouldn't let me stick it in her. She always stopped me for some reason, which I found out later."

Conde gulped. The love story was getting dark.

"One day, a group of us went to a beach house. There were about eight of us, including Katiuska and her cousin, but Katiuska went back to Havana on the first night because she had a very important meeting the next day, very early at the university with the Young Communists. It was extremely hot that night and we had a bunch of beer and rum, so those of us who were left went to the beach. It must have been after midnight, and someone, a girl, proposed that we swim naked, since it was dark and there was no one around. It was more decadent to enter the sea that way. All of us, half-drunk as we were, took off our clothes. But as soon as I saw Katiuska's cousin and I saw his prick and I saw his eyes . . . Well, I can't describe it. I saw his prick and that gaze—I felt like I was melting inside. The rest was easy. That night I made my sexual debut. I was still a virgin, you know, both at giving and receiving. A virgin in Cuba at the age of twenty-three! Well, that night was an epiphany . . . Can one call it an epiphany? Whatever, it sounds good. That night, he gave it to me and I gave it to him until we had nothing left, and suddenly, I felt like I had found myself, Conde . . . That I was being myself, you know? The next morning, the two of us acted like nothing had happened. That was what we had to do, right? And when Katiuska came back at noon, everything was the same. Or, I acted like everything was the same, although the truth was that everything had changed: I felt it inside, in my heart, I felt it outside, on my skin . . . That night, Katiuska and I kissed, masturbated each other, just like usual, but I realized that sex with a woman now made less sense to me; it was a farce . . . And I had a breakdown. I didn't want anyone to know what I had done on the beach. I repressed myself even more, I forced myself to seem more macho . . . Until one day, I couldn't take it anymore and I fell into a darker pit: an unbearable feeling of guilt, feeling like an impostor, a sinner. So I decided to open up. I told Katiuska what had happened with her cousin and the truth of my life. I asked her to help me save myself. To make me a man, to remove the perversions of my mind. I remember how she listened to me, asked me things, details about how it had been with her cousin, and finally she said yes, she was going to help me, she needed a few days to see how, what she could do. She was very surprised by all of that, she told me."

"You screwed up, Bobby," Conde managed to say, foreseeing the end of this story.

"I don't know, maybe I wanted it to happen? Three days later, there was a meeting of the Student Federation, because of the preparations for that year's Youth Festival, remember? And Katiuska, who was the organizer of the Youth Grass Roots Committee, asked to speak at the end of the meeting and said she had to communicate to the group—I'll never forget her words—'A serious problem that *compañero* Roberto Roque Rosell was facing' . . . And then she told them everything I'd told her, but worse still, she said that her cousin was willing to testify to how I'd taken advantage of his state of inebriation. I ran out of there, Conde. I left that school like a madman, crying, my heart beating so quickly that I thought I was dying . . . Two days later, a professor and the Young Communist League secretary came to my house to tell me that Katiuska's cousin had decided not to accuse me in a hearing, but that I was being expelled from the university for serious moral and ideological deviation, incompatible with the behavior of a young, revolutionary university student . . ."

"What a bitch, that Katiuska!"

Bobby smiled. It was a sad grimace, laced with nostalgia.

"Anyone who has lived through that can understand me. That was the beginning of my time in hell . . . The rest of my story is more or less what I already told you," Bobby said. "Now, you haven't even heard the best part yet . . ."

"There's a best part?"

"Yes, I think so. Well, juiciest, at least."

"What's that?"

"A few years later, I ran into Katiuska and . . . you know why she wouldn't have sex with me?"

Conde smacked his forehead. The image of Katiuska's face, in the bar near the university, returned to his mind like a boomerang. And then the answer to that whole imbroglio suddenly came to him.

"Because she was gay!"

"A complete lesbian, my friend. The dykes call her Joaquín! And now she's the leader of I-don't-know-what lesbian group, a gay pride activist, and a defender of the transformers and the transformed! A leader, a standard-bearer, man! Damn, you can't tell me this story's happy ending isn't the best part, huh, brother?"

Enthralled, he studied the intensely green foliage of the avocado tree that majestically ruled over the yard at Carlos's house. Among its branches still hung several of those prodigious fruits, with their generous green and yellow flesh that Cubans never eat like fruit, only seasoned as a salad. He tried to calculate how many of those avocados he could have shared throughout the forty-plus years of friendship with Carlos, Andrés, and Rabbit. How much hunger had they sated eating wedges of avocado sprinkled with salt and stuffed into a loaf of bread? How many inadequate meals had th y augmented with salads made from those avocados, sometimes even garnished with a bit of olive oil, some drops of lemon juice that brought out their sweet flavor, along with slices of onion that stimulated the taste buds? Moved, absorbed in the observation of that tree, he thought of how they'd shared some intense, full years throughout which they had come to know all that was good and bad in life. Years, decades already, in which they'd enjoyed one another's company until they felt, each of them, fully complemented. They were all individuals and also part of a clan. They possessed an intricate mixture of experiences, accumulated gains and losses, which they greedily protected from outside erosion and converted, he'd always thought, into the bricks of the wall behind which they each took refuge from invasions of all kinds, as survivors of a catastrophe, perhaps many.

The strange mood caused by Bobby's confession had led him to arrange an overdue encounter with his friend Rabbit that very day at noon, and they had made plans to meet at Carlos's house, under the condition that there would be no alcohol. Who had imposed this Dry Law? Carlos, Rabbit, Conde himself? Was it because of a premonition? A fear of the Devil? Conde couldn't remember, but what he did know was that time and life can do away with everything, even noble, old trees like the pleasant avocado he now contemplated from the terrace.

They knew one another so well that Conde could tell whatever Rabbit had to say was serious, just from the way that Rabbit had looked at Carlos and how the latter silently gestured for him to go on, without any of his usual shrill disclaimers. For his part, Conde had looked at the two of them and decided to keep level for once, to patiently wait for the conversation to develop. Perhaps his guilt over having first forgotten and then delayed Rabbit's request for a meeting was making him feel at a disadvantage. This feeling was strange and bothersome to him, and it was aggravated by the growing uncertainty of his true ability to offer friendship. How could he have delayed, even forgotten his friend's request? Just because of the money Bobby was paying him? Still silent and feeling miserable, he accepted the cup of coffee that Josefina brought to him on the terrace and lit one of his cigarettes. The way the older woman was moving, taking extra care to be unobtrusive, Conde assumed that she was already up to speed on the meeting's agenda. His concern overflowed. Unable to contain himself any longer, he looked at Rabbit and offered up the palms of his hands: Come on, give me what you need to give me.

"I'm going to travel, Conde," his friend began. "I'm gonna try to, at least."

Conde sighed, relieved. Was that all? Nobody was dying, everyone's prostates and livers continued on?

"Well, you're going to travel! That's great, I'm happy for you and . . . Nowadays, everyone travels . . ."

"I don't know if I'm going to come back."

Conde felt like he'd been hit. His friend was leaving? Another one? But Rabbit was one of them, the persistent ones, determined, a fellow survivor—and now he was thinking of leaving them, too? Who would turn out the light at el Morro when there was no one left?

"What are you talking about, brother?"

Rabbit looked at him unblinkingly.

"My daughter did the paperwork for me. Andrés is going to cover the costs. If they give me a visa, I'm going to Miami for a while. And there, I'll decide whether or not I'm going to stay. Esmé and Andrés say they'll help me. But I'm scared. Scared of going and not coming back. Scared of coming back and . . ."

Conde felt on the verge of crumbling.

"How long? You, Andrés, Skinny, Esmé, Josefina—everyone and their mothers! How long have you all been planning this?"

"I don't know. Two, maybe three months."

"So why didn't you say anything to me, Rabbit?"

"Because I'm scared," his friend admitted.

"Look, Conde," Carlos interjected, but Conde stopped him with a wave of his hand.

"Scared of what, Rabbit?"

"Of everything. Of traveling, of staying there, of preferring to return," Rabbit said. "Of you being pissed at me."

"Why did you think I'd be pissed?"

Rabbit looked at Skinny Carlos again, and it was Skinny who responded.

"Because we know what you're like, Beast . . . Because we love you. Because you're already pissed, aren't you?"

What Carlos had said was regrettable, but true: this felt to Conde like a question of love, and at that moment he felt like a groom about to be jilted at the altar. Nevertheless, he tried to overcome his ego, his instinct to preserve his tribe, the awakened sense of loss announcing itself on the horizon.

"What the hell are you going to do in Miami? You're sixty years old. Here, it's a miracle that we get by, but we do get by . . ."

"People also get by over there. Things here are getting uglier every day and seem to be headed for worse. Anyway, I really don't know if I'm going to stay there, Conde. I don't even know if I'm going to get to make the trip, if my wife and I will be able to get visas . . . But what I want is to try. At least that. And, if they let me leave this island, I want the opportunity to choose for myself whether I stay in Miami or come back. Once I get there, I'll do the math and figure out if I was wrong to come . . . It's not really that I want to live in Miami. It's that for people like us, we've never been able to choose, and to choose wrong. We had that right taken away from us."

Conde nodded. He knew that any argument he could make wouldn't work against the sound logic of his friend's lived experience. His desires for the privilege to be able to choose, and be proven wrong . . . perhaps even proven right. But Conde's discomfort had nothing to do with logic, but with his feelings. If they kept losing friends like this, what kind of solitude would await them at the end? In what swamp would they drown? In what state would their naked souls reach their final destination? Feeling uneasy, he lifted his gaze and once again contemplated the avocado tree that had nourished them so many times, their bellies and their spirits. The tree, at least, remained. The tree was still there.

"You're right, Rabbit," he said at last. "Yes, you should try, and be wrong as many times as you want. That's how we know we're still alive, right? Ah, and if I find that Blessed Virgin and Bobby pays me, you can count on that money for whatever you need. With what's left over, Skinny and I will go get drunk forty times over and tell the same stories again and again until we burst like fireworks . . . Or until you come back and tell us whether or not you were wrong about what you decided for yourself, about whatever the hell you did because you fucking felt like it. But you know what? I'm not gonna save any avocados for you. I'm gonna eat them all, till I have avocados coming out of my ears."

Shortly before 8:00 p.m., Conde was posted on the side of Parque Central next to the run-down Cine Payret. With the noise of Rabbit's decision still buzzing in his head, he studied his surroundings, which seemed not to change, until the setting of the sun. And not for the better. He saw that many of the policemen patrolling the area had German shepherds and were armed as if they were in *Star Wars*. It was soon obvious to Conde that with the arrival of twilight, the stunned masses that frequented this place in the light of day had been replaced by shifty, shadowy characters, looking for their fix: money, sex, amusement, or all of the above, by any sordid means necessary. It was cockroach time. For not the first time, he was happy that he wasn't a cop anymore, that he had the option of watching this scene from the sidelines as a simple shocked onlooker before the spectacle of a bubbling, growing world—one that hadn't existed back during his days as a cop.

The Bat appeared half an hour later. It seemed that he'd bathed, because he didn't stink like he had the day before. He was wearing a shirt with silver sequins and his eyes looked almost normal, perhaps a little smaller than they should be. Was that because of his defect, or just the effects of marijuana?

"What's up?" Conde asked as the kid sat down on a bench.

"You've had me working like a madman, compadre."

"Don't make stuff up, Yuniesky. Did you buy yourself that shirt with the money I gave you?"

"Yeah," the young man smiled. "It's hot, right?"

"Really nice," Conde confirmed. "Now spill it. What'd you find out about your buddy Raydel?"

The Bat hesitated, then decided to go on.

"The Albino spotted him recently in San Miguel del Padrón, in that 'settlement' where all those Easterners stay. He has a cousin there named Ramiro."

"Ah, I've heard of him. Ramiro what?"

"Ramiro the Cloak. I don't know his last name. But they call him the Cloak, so he must be one hell of a guy, right?"

"How'd you find that out? This cousin, did he do the hit on that gay guy's place with you and Raydel?"

"Listen, you're asking a lot for someone paying so little!" It was clear from his reaction that Conde had hit the nail on the head. "I already told you what you wanted. I don't know Ramiro. Be happy with what I've given you and pay up."

Conde looked at him like he didn't know him.

"Your cut comes later, if I get to do business with Raydel."

The Bat nodded. He seemed relieved. "Shall I tell you something that's worth five big ones?" asked the Bat. Conde waited patiently. "Did you know that Raydel was not his real name?"

"Buddy, I'm the one who told you that yesterday."

The Bat scratched his head, which was a fitting gesture for his namesake.

"Damn, that's right. It *was* you. This stuff I'm smoking is really something. The other day I took a couple hits and that little guy over there"—he pointed behind him, at the statue of José Martí—"he told me about a monster that eats your insides . . ."

"So, do you know what Raydel's real name is?"

"No, I don't. Manduco doesn't know, either—he's the other partner he had in that underground beef business. The Albino was the one who told me where Raydel is. Apparently he's owed him money for a while now. What a *singao*! That's why he changed his name and everyone's after him."

Conde nodded. "I'm going to go out there and look for Raydel tomorrow. Do you want to come with me?"

The Bat opened his eyes, until they were almost a normal size. "You're crazy!" Then, lowering his voice, "Nobody can find out I gave you the green light, not Raydel or the Cloak or anybody else. If they do, they'll fuck me up."

Conde nodded again. "So, when did the Albino find out that Raydel was with his cousin?"

"About a week ago. Raydel told him that as soon as he sold a few things, he would come see him and settle up his debt."

"A week . . . So maybe he's already flown the coop."

"Where was he gonna go? Back to Oriente? Nah . . ." The Bat was thinking. "I swear, if Raydel is anywhere, it's there, in that neighborhood. That's like the pirate cave, where he keeps his booty."

"But he can't be keeping the stuff there. He'd be crazy to do that."

The Bat scratched his head again. Maybe it itched from thinking too hard. "That's true. But he couldn't keep it in Santiago, either, right?"

Conde stood up. "Tomorrow, I'm going to San Miguel."

"What about me? How do I get my cut?"

"I'll stop by your house. You have my word."

"Your *word*?" the *mulato* asked, crestfallen. "Whose fucking word is worth anything in this world, big man?"

"Mine," Conde said. "You're going to believe it, because you'll have no other choice once you see it with those bat eyes of yours. Yeah, your top *is* really nice . . ."

7.

The unhealthy stench of poverty and overcrowding rose up to meet them, stunning them with its aggressive impact. It smelled of lost hope and the currents of dark waters flowing through uncovered gullies, of oil fried over and over again, of the putrid bins surrounded by millions of buzzing flies, of makeshift pens where pigs rolled around in mud and shit. It was a painful mixture.

The night before, as he was drinking with Skinny Carlos, Conde had planned this trip to the city's catacombs as if he were storming Berlin. This hazardous embassy seemed to be the only place he was likely to find the Raydel impostor and Bobby's strange Virgin of Regla. He had no choice but to follow this lead.

Candito the Red had succeeded in finding the name of an Adventist located in the "settlements" of San Miguel del Padrón, and had been willing to accompany him. Rabbit had also wanted in on the adventure. They'd finalized their plans and agreed to meet at nine in the morning in front of Red's tenement building, where Conde picked them up. Despite Yoyi's offer, Conde had opted not to include him and his shiny Bel Air in their risky voyage to an unknown world.

When they'd all climbed into the beaten-up but still functional Studebaker that Conde's neighbor secretly and occasionally hired out, driver and all, the voyagers headed southeast down the Calzada de San Miguel del

Padrón. Shortly before reaching San Francisco de Paula—the village where Hemingway had purchased his Finca Vigía and lived for twenty years, from which Conde had once stolen some panties that had known Ava Gardner's most intimate intimacies—they veered left to a neighborhood on the side of a hill, which had been given the none-too-imaginative name of Lookout Heights. From there, one had a panoramic view of Northeast Havana, including part of the bay and the neighborhood that was home to the Virgin of Regla. From a distance, suspended above all its turbulence, they saw a city that seemed peaceful, perhaps even inviting.

Following directions they received from locals, they had driven through a maze of streets full of potholes, water pipes, people, and wandering dogs, until they reached the last navigable part and what had to be the limits of Western civilization. There, Conde, Candito, and Rabbit got out and took a dirt road toward the edges of the "settlements," as its inhabitants insisted on calling it. The driver remained behind as guardian of his old Studebaker, which had provided him his livelihood and whose integrity he would stay to protect.

Barely three hundred feet from the once-paved street, the outsiders realized that they were entering another universe, as if they'd gone through a black hole and emerged in a dimension outside of time and space. They were approaching a territory that Conde called "the world of the invisible." The alleyways, made of compacted dirt, grew narrower, windier, and more irregular in their shape, physically manifesting a state of instability and deprivation. On either side of the path, which featured ridges that made it impossible for any vehicle shy of a war tank to make its way through, rose dwellings that grew progressively derelict as Conde and his friends encountered what appeared to be the main drag of the "settlement." Upon entering this shantytown, they saw some brick houses with concrete foundations, but soon enough the signs of privation and the sight of makeshift dwellings overtook all aspects of their surroundings. Improvised shelters erected using a few blocks and bricks, others made with rotting wood, still others with metal sheets in varying states of deterioration, and even some out of cardboard. They were covered in a wide range of materials, anything that could be tasked with protecting their inhabitants from the rain and sun: the tin and wooden roofs were shielded with waterproof paper, and the most precarious ones made use of tarpaulins or plastic bags, fixed in place with a rock or iron girder. The laws of urban planning, architecture, even gravity appeared to be unknown in that cluster of miserable dwellings, which resulted in a chaotic and suffocating sprawl.

Conde, who daily kicked his way around Havana in search of used books, had thought he knew the most degraded parts of the city: the old proletarian and poverty-stricken neighborhoods similar to the one where he'd been born and raised. Now and again he'd had reason to visit a "settlement" of Eastern migrants close to where he lived, where an unofficial cluster of houses had arisen in an empty lot between two neighborhoods. There he had seen homes crowding one another, wall against wall, erected without any design or agreement, with unplastered walls . . . Still, one could call them houses. By his standards, *that* was poverty. But now, walking through San Miguel del Padrón, he was confirming the existence of a greater misery. The substrata of Havana: catacombs of the catacombs.

"What the hell is this, Conde?" Rabbit asked, as if he couldn't believe what his eyes saw.

"A parallel life," replied Conde. "It's a different life, but just as real."

"Can you really call this life?" Rabbit said, doubtfully.

"Yes, Rabbit, even if they are invisible," said Conde. "I've told you: there's always someone worse off. Even worse off than me . . ."

"But how is it that there are people doing this badly? Here, in this country? Now?" Rabbit was asking, alarmed. "It looks like Haiti or Africa . . . Or Hell. And I thought I was born in a shitty place. But, man, next to this, my house looks like the Taj Mahal."

"You don't know what poverty is, Rabbit," Candido said, emerging finally from his watchful silence.

Later, these outsiders learned that the "settlements" had begun in the nineties, when a group of people from the east side of Cuba, looking for any solution to their misery, had migrated to the capital. These refugees had ended up in that unpopulated territory, a sort of no-man's-land where they worked to establish themselves with the rocky determination that their reality necessitated: it was a question of life or death. With cardboard, wood, and tin, the pariahs had erected the first of these dwellings and ditches in which to dump their bodily refuse. Then, they began a silent battle for survival, ignored by the majority of the country's inhabitants, since news outlets never covered this refugee crisis, as if these Easterners didn't even warrant that kind of attention. Because it was an illegal occupation of state-owned land, various authorities, including the police, had begun to accost the occupants. But each time they were evicted, the displaced returned, accompanied by new, desperate families from all over the country. Overnight, they would revive their primitive houses in the very spot where the previous ones had been torn down. Some erected other, new dwellings in neighboring parcels and settled there like the conquistadors they were. Facing a cycle of eviction attempts, the dwellers of this nameless shantytown formed human barricades against the offense of legal authorities—links of children and women, even pregnant women, determined to impede the advance of police cars and the heartless bulldozers belonging to construction-cum-destruction deputations. This battle lasted several years, in the absence of other options for a people who were determined to survive, even without running water, sewers, electricity, or the ration books that guaranteed Cuban citizens minimum subsistence at subsidized prices. It was a battle in which there was no turning back and which required all of their efforts and energy. Through perseverance and desperation, the refugees achieved their Pyrrhic victory: incapable of offering them even a minimally dignified alternative, the powers that be decided to look the other way and let the refugees live out their precarious existence there, on the condition that they remain invisible. This truce began the era of "come and contribute," as they came to call it. Under this strange arrangement, families were encouraged to take over a plot of land with enough space to build a dwelling, and a few additional feet to raise a pig or plant some plantains to contribute to their subsistence. With slight variations, this had been the origin story of several such "settlements," which had multiplied like acne around the city's periphery. It was only many years after the "settlements" were first established, when they were already too visible to ignore, that the public was conscious of them at all.

Instinctively Candito took the lead. He hadn't forgotten the lexicon he'd acquired during his time as a street fighter; he had it ready as he approached some of the "settlement's" many inhabitants wandering around the paths. After looking them over several times, one local finally deigned to indicate the way to the house of Oriol the Saintly, as the Adventist was known in these parts. They filed through a steep, narrow passageway alongside which ran an intermittent little stream of fetid water with children playing at its edge. By the looks of it, the entertainment of the season was a game of marbles, which in a few weeks would give way to tops, only to be substituted by the ability to fly kites, then finally abandoned for hopscotch fever, as happened every year. Such was the need to live, grow, and exist—even amid complete shit.

After having stopped for directions a few more times, they finally found the house. Like many of the others, this home was made of wood and cardboard. A man greeted them at the door and, after Candito identified himself, invited them into the house's only room: fifty square feet of dirt floor, with two beds, a small table, a stove, and three chairs. Conde mentally noted that there was no bathroom in sight, but he did see a television set, a video player, and an enormous stereo flanked by two gigantic speakers.

Oriol the Saintly was a sallow-skinned white man, about thirty years old, with closely shorn hair and the eyes of a domesticated animal. He spoke with a strong Eastern accent, swallowing his esses and at a very slow pace, very likely an influence of his religious militancy. As he brewed the coffee that he'd insisted on offering his visitors, he gave them snippets of life, miraculous in the "settlement." He'd only been living there a few months, but had learned from the other locals that for many years now, the houses had had electricity, all because one of the neighbors, an efficient and generous electrician, had risked his life connecting cables from the electrical lines of Lookout Heights. From that moment on, everything had been powered with stolen energy. After all, even if they wanted to, they couldn't pay for it. Since they had no legal housing contracts, said Oriol, or other official documents validating their stay in the country's capital, they couldn't access the usual services from the electric company. They'd had better luck with the water: someone from the Management of Hydraulic Resources had taken pity on them and lowered a supply line from the closest water main, from which the squatters could make water lines to their own dwellings. Every other day, they had running water for four or five hours. The squatters enrolled their children, depending on space, in the schools of nearby neighborhoods, and the area's health clinics guaranteed them medical attention, including the vaccination of minors.

The main struggle that the "settlers" faced was the purchase of food, especially obtaining milk for their children. Without official documents from the Housing Authority, they also couldn't receive ration books. Theirs was a separate country within but entirely apart from Cuba.

Seated in their chairs, the visitors listened to the various miseries and successes of these migrants in their own land. After Oriol served them coffee in glass cups, the man arranged himself on the corner of one of the rickety beds. Conde noticed that both beds were covered with immaculate bedspreads with colorful embroidery. It represented the invincible nature of the human soul.

Candito got straight to the point: they were looking for Ramiro Gómez, also known as the Cloak, and more important, a friend of his who went by Raydel, though God only knew what his real name was.

Oriol smiled.

"I don't know Raydel . . . but Ramiro the Cloak, he's the worst of the worst."

"What does this character do?" asked Conde.

"Whatever there is to do. Surely, some drug dealing. He's also one of the people who runs the casino."

"The casino?"

Oriol the Saintly ran his hands through his spiky hair. He knew that life on the "settlement" was a total mystery to these outsiders.

"Look, you'll have already noticed that things work differently around here, almost as if by our own laws. Many people who live in the 'settlement' don't work for the state because the salaries are too miserable to get by or else because they're not allowed. Since many aren't legal residents of Havana, they're not given jobs. Official jobs, I mean. But we have a bit of everything here: miscreants and businessmen of all kinds, to decent people who are earning a living as bricklayers, landscapers, mechanics, collectors of cans and cardboard. And, to give you an idea of the madness here, our population even includes policemen, wardens, inspectors, a lawyer . . . But if they want to live here, they have to accept the rules of the game and not mix up their professional lives with their lives in the neighborhood. This is apache territory, as the people say. Here, you can buy anything you can imagine—beef, porn, construction materials. There are full-time and part-time prostitutes—and drugs, of course, though people are very careful with that because they know that you people out there"—he pointed toward the city, which may as well have been another planet—"get bent out of shape over things like that . . . Ah, and almost everyone here gambles. *A la bolita*, cards, dominoes, they even bet on the size of the litter a dog will have. So some people running those games had the idea to buy a piece of land with a big room like this one and set up a casino there. The logic is sound: if there's ever a police raid all they have to do is run in any direction. You've seen that this neighborhood is like a maze. Since the house belongs to everyone and no one, the cops can't really take it away, and if anything gets confiscated, it's just the packs of cards, the sets of dominoes, that nonsense. Then the entrepreneurs come back a week later and open up shop again . . . Ramiro the Cloak is one of the organizers. He has a monopoly over the beer and the rum they sell there. As I said, I think he's also involved with drugs . . . A magnate!" Oriol took a long pause, then added, "Ramiro can never find out I told you this stuff, or anybody else . . ."

Conde, Candito, and Rabbit listened, looking shocked. This place was the closest thing to the old Wild West that they'd seen in their lives, and certainly in their city. A lawless land. Or rather, one with its own laws.

"But people already know that we were looking for you," Conde warned.

"I told you where Ramiro lives because you're just looking to do some business with him, right?" the Saint proposed. They nodded; it seemed like a reasonable solution to everyone.

"So, where do we find this scourge?" Conde asked.

"Go down to the main street. Walk up the hill, and on the last path to the left, it's the last house . . . Ramiro lives there because you can see almost the entire 'settlement' from that house, and on the other side, there's a farm that not even God himself would enter, full of rocks and sickle bushes with big thorns. It's easy to get lost."

After thanking Oriol for the coffee and the information, Conde and his friends doubled back to the shantytown's nameless main drag.

"Gentlemen," Rabbit said, "have you noticed that nearly every house is selling something?"

He pointed with one finger at the stands set up in front of the makeshift homes, where people were hawking food, clothing, and other goods.

"Imagine what it's like here when it rains," Candito said, scratching his arms.

"What about a hurricane?" responded Conde, whose apocalyptic nature had made him long-obsessed with cyclones.

"May Jehovah protect them," Candito muttered, though he feared that these people were invisible even to their Creator.

The path on which they were walking grew steeper as they left behind the "settlement's" more central, commercial area, with its cafés, crowded stalls, and ceaseless flow of people. It occurred to Conde that he was just as likely to see a young person wearing jeans and a flashy T-shirt—including the ones with Real Madrid and Barcelona logos that were trending and all over the city now—as he was someone wearing worn-out rags.

To his chagrin, his inner policeman, ever present, wondered where the money for all those businesses and fancy outfits came from. He asked himself once more: Who in the hell works in this country? As always, he had no answer.

Panting, they reached the top of the hill and found a path on the edge of an empty field, covered in hostile vegetation. The dwellings in that area were perhaps the poorest in the neighborhood, made of cardboard and plastic bags held down by wooden posts.

The last house was the only one in that part of the neighborhood that was built with blocks and had a corrugated cement roof. Although it was lacking in plaster, its sturdiness was obvious. Outside, they saw a green-eyed *mulato* sitting on a chair against a mango tree, who looked like an improved version of the Bat. Conde was sure this was Ramiro, aka the Cloak. Not wanting to give the target any time to think, the former policeman quickly approached him.

"Ramiro, I wanted to see you."

When Ramiro opened his lips they were presented with teeth as gold as the thick chain hanging from his neck and spilling over his naked chest. Ramiro exuded self-confidence, a sense of invincibility.

"And who are you?"

"Someone who wants to do business."

"I don't do business."

Conde channeled his street smarts before speaking again, spitting out of the side of his mouth.

"I'm going to make you some money."

"I'm not interested."

"Money that's already yours."

"Mine? What business?" At last, Ramiro stood and walked toward them.

"High-yield. Jewels, for example."

Ramiro studied him, calculating. This guy seemed less simple, more cunning, and tougher than the Bat. The green eyes in his copper face added to that impression.

"That's not my thing."

"Maybe not, but that's what your partner Raydel's got. You know, the jewels he lifted from his sugar daddy. They're worth a fortune."

Ramiro stayed silent. Seeing as these men had come all the way to him, it must've been because they knew something about his relationship with Raydel.

"Let's speak clearly and stop screwing around," Candito interrupted, rubbing his hands like he was starting a fire, then clapping once. "We're not cops. If we were, you'd know it. Clear as day. We wouldn't be coming here, three shitty old men, with some story, especially not like this"—Candito lifted his shirt to show he was unarmed—"but we know that Raydel, or whatever that cretin's name is, was here with you after fleecing that sheep he was living with. And before you start selling the jewels he stole, we want to square some things away with him . . . and with you. Do some business. For starters: Where is Ray hiding?"

Ramiro the Cloak took a cigarette out of the pack he had in the pocket of his very baggy pants, which were hanging around his hips, so that the curly hairs trailing down beneath the waistband of his Dolce & Gabbana briefs were visible. He lit it and exhaled the smoke upward, thinking.

"I don't know what you're talking about. I don't know any Raydel," he said at last.

Conde smiled, shook his head, and gestured to Candito for his permission to interrupt.

"Come on, Ramiro, let's cut the bullshit. We know that Raydel was here with you and we know that he wants to sell the loot and take a speedboat off to Miami. We also know that he can't sell the really valuable stuff to just anyone, much less to his boyfriend's contacts, since they would rat him out. Those guys look out for each other, they have their own mafia, and to them, you're like cockroaches that are better off squashed."

"No need to go that far, honestly," Ramiro muttered. "No need to go that far."

"Don't get all sensitive on me, buddy. We're not screwing around. We're here to catch that housefly, and if Raydel does business with us, you can take the lead and claim your cut. And the Bat's cut, too, if you want to give him anything. That's between you two. We know that you were with Raydel on the day he robbed his boyfriend . . . You see how much we know?"

"What did that blind shithead say? He told you I was in on it?" Ramiro had taken the bait, as Conde had foreseen.

"He didn't have to. A neighbor saw you and told Raydel's boyfriend," said Conde, improvising. "And he described the two of you he didn't recognize."

"So, how do you guys know all this?" Ramiro asked, squinting. He was undoubtedly quick. Perhaps he had his intelligence to thank for the commercial success he apparently enjoyed in the "come and contribute" economy.

"Because I know Raydel's boyfriend," Conde said. "He told me he'd been robbed and . . . Buddy, how many times do I gotta say this? I'm interested in doing business, and for that, I need to find Raydel. Everything else is not my problem. So where the hell is Raydel now?"

Ramiro looked at the three visitors and caressed the thick gold chain against his hairless chest. He was taking his time.

"If you really want to do business, we can talk . . . But if you're thinking of screwing me over, you should know, I'll fuck you up worse than AIDS."

"We know that, too," Conde said.

Ramiro crushed the cigarette under his heel and looked out at the sea of makeshift roofs spread out before him.

"Raydel *was* here, but he's been missing for a week. He's like that: he appears and disappears like a goddamn ghost. He told me he had a buyer for a bunch of things . . . Some jewels, too . . . And then, that crazy bastard disappeared on me. I don't even want to think that he fed me some story and left for Miami, like he always wanted, because if he screwed me—"

"Just one thing," Conde interrupted him. "Raydel's boyfriend told me that your partner's name is not really Raydel."

Ramiro smiled. "Oh, he knew? Well, that shithead Raydel is actually called Yúnior, and he's a son of a bitch, even if he *is* my aunt's son. She's literally a whore, by the way. Anyway, he was on the run and came here to Havana, so I brought him to live with me and got him into the business of selling contraband beef."

"Who was he on the run from?"

"Some guy he conned out in Santiago. I don't really know what went down, but there were shots fired and everything."

"Yúnior had a weapon?"

Ramiro laughed.

"No, the guy he screwed over. Yúnior was so scared he even changed his name and came running out here. The problem with my cousin is that his tongue's too loose. And he thinks he can screw over anyone. But if he thought he could pull one over on me . . . he's gonna have to get plastic surgery, including that one operation where they chop off your dick and make you a pussy instead . . ."

"So, what happened when he got here?"

"While he was running around selling contraband beef, he met that old fairy who fell in love with him. He hit the jackpot with that one; that guy had him living like a prince. But when the old man took a little trip to Miami, Yúnior told me and the Bat that he wanted to do a job and he needed us to help him. Screwing people over is what he likes most. But the day we finally put it all together, with the truck and everything, I didn't see Yúnior take any jewelry. We took furniture, decorations, some paintings, plates, anything that looked like it was worth something . . . And there was a shitload of stuff. Even an enormous Virgin of Regla."

"You stole a Virgin of Regla? There are some things you don't mess with . . ." Conde tried to look shocked.

"Yúnior said he wanted Her for himself. He was really keen on that Virgin."

"So Yúnior sold all that stuff?"

"Almost all of it . . . Except for some small expensive-looking objects, the paintings, and that Virgin. He had this thing for Her, says that She's powerful, or whatever. I don't know, some bullshit story he heard from that fag who was giving it to him up the ass . . . I mean, I guess Yúnior is a believer now, too . . . Or so he says. But me, I don't believe in shit. I don't even believe in my own mother, much less in a dried-up piece of wood with the face of a Virgin."

"So, did he give you your share?"

"Yeah, but we didn't get much, 'cause we had to sell everything so quickly. Where the hell are you supposed to hide a whole dining-room set or a bed with the accompanying mattress? We agreed that when we liquidated the good stuff, we'd divvy up the profits again, but Yúnior never mentioned any fine jewelry. Only a watch and a little gold bracelet that he showed me. Nothing big. Not chains or expensive rings or anything like this . . ." He lifted the chain he had around his neck.

"Well, the guy you robbed says some of the stuff is worth a shitload," Rabbit insisted.

"Like what?" Ramiro asked.

"Chains, rings, some pearl necklaces that were Bobby's grandmother's, antique watches, a gold cross . . ." Rabbit stopped to perform tallying the inventory, before adding, "Two diamond bracelets."

"That son of a bitch! He didn't tell us shit!"

Conde kicked the dirt around with his foot, then looked right into Ramiro the Cloak's green eyes.

"There's a lot of money in this for you, Ramiro. If there's anything you didn't see, it's because your cousin took it without saying anything. But if Yúnior gets picked up by the police, it all goes back to the boyfriend and the three of you are going to the slammer. He may be a fairy and all, but he's got some big connections . . . So, are you interested in doing business with us or not? Are you going to help us find that bastard?"

Ready?"

Conde turned at the sound of the voice. He was seated on a pew in front of the altar. "Not yet," he responded.

He'd been a churchgoer until the age of seven, when, with his First Communion behind him, he'd finally terminated his relationship with religion of any kind. He'd made an incongruously mature deal with his mother, given how young he was at the time: he would make his mother happy by attending catechism classes until the moment he received Communion. After that, Sunday mornings went back to being for worldly activities that, in reality, came down to one: playing ball in the neighborhood's empty fields with the group of ragtag hooligans—friends who lived, as he did, with an indomitable passion for the game. They took it very seriously. As if it were their religion. Or rather, *because* it was their religion.

Still, Conde had gained a few things from his brief experience with spirituality that had stayed with him all these years. For one, he still found peace and harmony inside of any Catholic church. Sitting before an altar, no matter how modest, always brought him a feeling of physical and mental well-being, which he insisted had nothing to do with a connection to the divine. He had declared himself agnostic many years before: he didn't believe in God, just as he didn't believe in the existence of black holes. No one had seen either with their own eyes, and any epiphanies regarding the former or mathematical equations focused on confirming the existence of the latter were nothing more than quackery. Though he generally preferred to keep his distance from churches, just to be safe—especially the humble one in his neighborhood—once inside, he still experienced something tangible, sensorial, constant, perhaps even mystical, capable of bringing him a feeling of spiritual peace by its simple contrast to the unceasing, aggressive pace of everyday life. Just on the other side of those walls, sordidness and the rat race increasingly reigned: the struggle for earthly survival.

The other thing he'd gained was the relationship, based more on friendship than on any shared affinity for mysticism, he'd managed to maintain since childhood with the unflappable Father Mendoza. The priest had married his parents, baptized him, catechized him, taken his confessions, given him Communion in this very parish, only to have the kid say goodbye and launch himself into the atheistic freedom of the streets.

At ninety years of age, the old priest was still active and always in a sour mood. Recently, a younger priest was brought in to help him, but Mendoza insisted that this church was still *his* church and the parishioners in the neighborhood his inalienable property, even though his interactions with them were ever problematic. This was due to his disposition, more fitting of a herder of wild cattle than of a shepherd of souls, despite possessing a kindness that made him seem aloof sometimes, when really he was always willing. But with little Conde, the kid's irony and self-confidence had allowed for a different kind of relationship than the one he had with his flock, more like that of equals, one with which they both felt comfortable.

Whenever Conde got tangled up in spiritual matters, consulting Father Mendoza was an important step of his detective's pilgrimage.

"But are you getting closer?" asked the priest.

"Perhaps . . . Could it be because I'm getting old?"

"The smell of the grave helps many find their way . . . but you still have a while left before you depart," Father Mendoza said while walking toward him, with a book under his arm as he dragged his feet a bit.

"Don't kid yourself, I'm nothing like you. I'm a mess. What I don't get is why everyone is trying to convert me."

"To save you, my child."

"Don't bother. There's no salvation for me."

Dialogue between the priest and the former catechumen was always sharp and cryptic, and pivoted on a bet they had going: before he died,

Mendoza had wagered that he would see Conde return to the flock. Perhaps that was why he was delaying his ascension to the heavens, or else that fall to the circles of Hell reserved for the cantankerous.

Conde looked at the priest's increasingly flaccid face, covered in wrinkles and craters. He focused on Mendoza's eyes: the whites were red and the pupils weepy, the irises were an ever-fading black. He didn't feel envious that this man had amassed so many years on this earth. Such an advanced age did not seem venerable to him, but instead sad, the provenance of all the erosions of which he himself was now the target.

"How are you, Father?"

"Really bad. Now my prostate is acting up."

"What does the doctor say?"

"That I've had it pretty good until now . . . That I should drink as much water as I can so that I piss a lot, because there's no use wasting medicine on me."

"He's right," Conde concluded, because the priest expected him to agree. "So, what are you reading now?"

"Rereading . . . Archpriest of Hita's *The Book of Good Love*."

"Hardly anyone reads that anymore."

"The writer was a colleague of mine, wasn't he?"

"I'm going to have to reread it, too."

Father Mendoza had sat down on the pew and Conde turned a little to better face him.

"The thing is, I saw the Devil the other day . . . and today I was in Hell."

The priest smiled.

"And he let you come back?"

Conde nodded several times.

"The Devil wanted to scare me, but you know that's not easy to do . . . Since I didn't have an inkwell like Martin Luther, I threw a pen at his head . . . What really messed me up, though, was my visit to a 'come and contribute,' one of those improvised neighborhoods that refugees from the east have put together . . ."

"Which one?"

"The one near San Miguel del Padrón, after you pass San Francisco de Paula . . . Father, it's the closest thing to Hell I've seen in Cuba."

"I've heard a thing or two about those neighborhoods. In that one, there's a young priest who's trying to get in, but he says it's not easy."

"No, it's not easy . . . it's terrible. The Protestants haven't managed to get in there, either."

"Those poor people . . . after all those speeches and promises."

Conde shared some details of what he had seen that morning, still agitated by the impression that the "settlement" had made on him and the waves of adrenaline from his conversation with Ramiro the Cloak still rushing through him.

"So, what were you looking for there?"

"A Virgin." Conde waited for Mendoza to take the bait, but Mendoza was much too smooth to fall into his trap.

"I hope you found Her. As far as I know, there's only one Virgin. All other women are born virgins until they're not anymore . . . Younger and younger these days, by the way. The world is lost . . ."

Despite himself, Conde smiled.

"Father, I need your help."

Conde pulled out the photograph of Bobby's Madonna from its envelope. He gave it to the priest, who immediately began studying it.

"Don't you need glasses?"

"Ever since I got the operation, I can see well up close. But from a distance, I can't even see my own salvation." The priest finally looked up and asked, "Where did you get this from?"

"It's a friend's family heirloom. A Virgin of Regla. It was stolen from him."

"Who says this is a Virgin of Regla?"

"*He* does . . . She's Black, so what else would She be?"

Conde was testing him. The priest shook his head and continued studying the photo.

"The Virgin of Regla isn't the only Black representation of the Virgin, there's . . ."

"Yes, I know that in France and Spain, there are others . . . the one in

Montserrat, for example. And there are African versions of Mary that are also dark-skinned."

"Yes, there are many Black Virgins," Father Mendoza confirmed. "In Poland and Germany, too . . . But this one looks more like the Virgin of Montserrat than the one of Regla . . . The one here and the one in Andalucía."

"But what if a Cuban craftsman made Her in the nineteenth century? The majority of craftsmen back then were Black freemen and maybe he fashioned Her after another Black Madonna."

Mendoza nodded again, then immediately shook his head.

"And if not? She looks older than the nineteenth century. I don't know . . . and She doesn't look Cuban at all . . ."

Conde searched his pockets for his reading glasses and took the photo from the pastor's hands.

"What are you trying to tell me, Father? That She could have come from Spain? From Andalucía?"

Mendoza took his time in responding.

"A photo doesn't tell you much. You'd have to get a close look at Her in person. For starters, you'd have to find out if the statue was originally black or if She got darker with time, from the varnish and wood getting weathered. In Spain, there are Virgins that are painted black and others that have simply darkened, as is the case with the Virgin of Montserrat."

"So, la Moreneta isn't Black?"

"No, She didn't start out that way. But if She's a Virgin of Regla like you say, She's exceptional and I'd say rather old, and a rather liberal imitation. The Virgin of Regla traditionally is in a standing position and carrying a baby Jesus with a white face. And if She's not a Virgin of Regla, as I suspect, then She's even more exceptional . . ." He paused, reflected, and concluded, "But no, I don't think She is. There aren't many authentic Black Virgins and the ones in existence aren't just lying around like that . . . The genuine ones are medieval, Romanesque sculptures. They're almost ten centuries old . . ."

"So . . ."

"Yes, it's possible that the craftsman, whether there in Spain or here in

Cuba, was inspired by the Virgin of Montserrat, thinking that they were all alike because they were Black . . . Or because the sculptor was Catalan and gave it to the client as if She were a Virgin of Regla, but was actually a replica of his Virgin, from over in his land, where there are other Black Virgins. In any event, it's a strange statue . . . How in the hell did you say your friend got it?"

"He told me he inherited it from his grandmother, who inherited it from I-don't-know-who . . . He's just as likely to say She's Cuban as he is to say She's from Andalucía."

Mendoza looked at the image again.

"In the Sanctuary of Regla, there's a young priest . . . young! Hell, he's around your age," Mendoza corrected himself. "He knows quite a bit about the subject since he's been there for over twenty years and has decided to study dark-skinned Virgins. He knows more than I do about this . . . If you need to see him, tell him I sent you. Gonzalo, Father Gonzalo Rinaldi . . ." He returned the prints to Conde. "For all that's holy, Conde, yesterday was the seventh of September, the feast of the Virgin of Regla! And today is the feast day of Our Lady of Charity! Oh, sweet Mother, my memory! I'm going senile!"

Conde smiled. "Isn't there a mass for Our Lady of Charity?"

Mendoza also smiled. "Of course, of course there's a mass . . . Do I have Alzheimer's or am I turning into an imbecile? My assistant is going to officiate the mass today, at five . . . Oof, what a relief . . . And, well, since you're already here, and I have time, and since it's criminally hot out there, and today is the feast day of the Virgin of Charity, and your parents were so devoted to her . . . why don't we make the most of it and hear your confession? You can just give me a summary, come on . . ."

Such a proposal was bound to come up in every encounter with Mendoza. Conde suspected that the priest felt more of a mundane curiosity about his accumulated sins than any shepherd's duty toward him.

"There's not enough time, Father, not even for a summary. I'm going on a trip next week. I'm finally going to Alaska."

Mendoza flashed his white, straight, unabashedly false teeth. "Weren't you the one who said Alaska can kiss your ass?"

"And it still can, Father . . . Will you give me your blessing?"

"Of course, my son . . . Go to Alaska with God. And with the Virgin . . . if you can find Her, I mean."

Sticky and scorching hot, the night announced the presence of the summer's heat waves that tended to last through October or whenever the tropical climate felt like it. Conde and Rabbit, sitting with Skinny Carlos on his porch, benefited from the efforts of an old Chinese fan that had survived many battles. They were drinking tall glasses of juice made from guavas that Conde had purchased and Josefina had blended with lots of ice. Carlos was swallowing it deliberately, as if it were a healing elixir, while Rabbit drank it in great slurps, barely breathing, disinclined to come out of his stupor. It had been Conde's mandate that they only drink juice that night. He felt so exhausted, physically and emotionally, that he'd decided to undertake an alcohol fast and, if possible, improve his health and ward off the old age that would soon debut, as Skinny Carlos now reminded him.

"Beast," Skinny said. "Your birthday's in a month and a day . . . We've got to plan your party and . . ."

"Party, what party? What the hell do you think I'll be celebrating? The fact that this one wants to get the hell out of here?" He pointed at Rabbit. "Or that the Easterners live the way they do in that foul neighborhood?"

The visit to the "settlement" had left a persistent bad taste in his mouth and had wounded his sensibilities. Conde had grown up in a country that had reduced its misery through concerted will and effort. When he was a boy, he recalled that in his house—itself never abundant—they'd talked about families that were very poor, like Rabbit's. At the time, Rabbit and his family had lived in a small room with bare brick walls and a fiber cement roof that, with much sacrifice, they'd improved little by little during a time when his father's salary had made it difficult, but still possible. Later, the qualifier "poor people" had fallen into disuse on the island since, one way or another, many Cubans had managed to improve their existence, overcoming the limitations of their origins and at least gaining in dignity what they didn't gain in comfort.

In reality, everyone on the island was poor, more or less. Conde remembered the years in which he'd had only one pair of Russian boots, harder than the ice in Siberia, and some plastic slip-ons that made fungus grow like polka dots between his toes. Nevertheless they'd all had opportunities to rise. Like many others, even a guy like Rabbit, the son of practically illiterate parents, had ended up with a degree in history and dreams for his future, while others like Candito barely managed to overcome their humble origins, which stuck to them like mollusks . . . However, in recent years Conde and his compatriots had witnessed a social distention that raised some up while pulling others down. If those who rose did so through their efforts, will, and creativity, then to Conde, it seemed like a deserved recompense. But those who drowned, swallowed up by circumstance, seemed like innocent victims trapped by fatalism, politics, and history. And the men, women, and children who had taken refuge in a "come and contribute," as they were lamely euphemized, had tested the limits of his understanding.

Conde's sadness infected the others, and so the night was spent relaying the day's experiences, so that Carlos would have some notion of the abyss through which his friends had passed. Their chat was made only somewhat lively by Conde's news that Father Mendoza had confirmed that Rabbit and Candito's suspicions regarding the Black Virgin's identity were well-founded.

"I knew there was something off about that Virgin . . ." Rabbit quipped. "Give me a couple of days to see what I can find out."

"About what?"

"About that style, the era, I don't know, something that will shed some light on this story for us. I'm going to send a message to a friend of mine in Spain . . ."

"A letter?"

"Don't be a shithead, Conde. An email."

"You have email?"

Rabbit smiled. "Since a month ago. I just entered the twenty-first century."

"I'm stunned . . . Brother, you sure you want to get the hell out of here and abandon us?"

"Stop screwing around, Conde," Carlos scolded him. He'd been so absorbed in the conversation that he had finished his juice almost without noticing. "These days, people go and come back. Miami is closer to us than Santa Clara. So stop messing around and save this useless chatter for when we have some rum . . . Incidentally, Rabbit, when *you* go and come back, which you certainly will, what will you bring me as a gift?"

"Today, I remembered how I used to say that I wanted to go to Alaska," Conde announced.

"Well, I went to Angola," Carlos offered and pointed at his useless legs.

"Fucking hell," Conde said. "The only one of us who's traveled anywhere and . . ."

"Come on, let's leave it alone," Carlos hurried to interject, trying to keep their chat from falling into ever darker pits. "Let's see, clear something up for me: Did Bobby's little Eastern lad know that there was something special about that Virgin?"

"To hear it from his cousin Ramiro, he said She had powers," Conde began. "Maybe Yúnior believed Bobby's bewitching story."

"Or it could be that Bobby really believes in those powers, Conde. That explains his obsession with recovering the Virgin," Rabbit added.

"That, too," Conde admitted. "But there's something strange about all this interest in that darned Virgin. I think what She represents doesn't matter nearly as much as what She is: a strange, perhaps antique Virgin . . . And, incidentally, yesterday was the feast day of the Virgin of Regla . . ."

"Yes, I remembered," Rabbit remarked. "What a coincidence, right? My grandmother was . . ."

But at that moment, Carlos stretched his arms forward, as if trying to stop an approaching avalanche, until his friends went silent and gave him their full attention.

"What if Bobby is hiding something?"

Conde stopped in the middle of lighting a cigarette. "I don't know. He's certainly capable of it . . . Hiding what? All the miracles his Virgin has performed?"

"Don't be a shithead, Beast." Skinny seemed annoyed. "What really matters is the Virgin . . . *That* Virgin, as you yourself say. Whether She be from Regla or Burundi . . ."

Conde looked at Carlos and then at Rabbit, who was nodding his head. "Bobby is an SOB . . . Yoyi thinks he's capable of selling counterfeit paintings, even, but . . . What exactly are you trying to say, Carlos?"

"Easy, my friend . . . Everything you know about that Virgin is what Bobby told you, right? Well Bobby could've told you only what he wanted you to know. It's Rabbit, Candito, and Father Mendoza who have put the Devil inside of you . . . What? It's just an expression. Did you really see the Devil, Beast, or are you messing with us?"

"Forget about the Devil and keep going, come on . . ." Conde encouraged him and finally finished lighting up his cigarette.

"Well, what if the Virgin is loaded inside, like dice? With objects that are valuable, very much so, and that's why Bobby told Raydel about Her powers, so that he'd be afraid . . . But instead it had the opposite effect."

Conde was listening, thinking. "You mean that the Virgin might actually have real jewels inside?"

"Diamonds, for example," Carlos added. "Like the ones in the bracelets Rabbit made up when you were talking to Ray's cousin . . ."

Conde and his friend looked each other in the eye, the wheels in their heads whirring efficiently, since in place of alcohol they were using red guava juice as fuel, which, according to scientists, was rich in vitamin C and antioxidants. Then he heard Rabbit's voice (he was always the most logical and accurate of them all), weighing his words carefully.

"So . . . I mean . . . What if what is truly valuable is the Virgin Herself? That Black Virgin."

8.

To wake up without any expectations can be a painful or satisfactory experience, depending on how you choose to look at it. And that morning, Conde opted for the latter. The night before, he'd made love, and maybe that's why today, he didn't feel any older, although in reality he'd had to take half of a sildenafil, without telling Tamara, of course. As soon as he opened his eyes, he decided that he would not hit the streets in search of private libraries for purchase, and he enjoyed the certainty that whatever he did or did not do, he would earn one hundred dollars that day, double what Tamara, a dental specialist, would earn in an entire month. For doing nothing. He wouldn't even think about Rabbit's travel plans, the pain of which lingered like a dagger in his side. And he would think even less of the Black Virgin and everything surrounding Her, he told himself, as if it were possible to fool himself and to block out his obsessive-compulsive thoughts. For the time being, he felt almost happy with his decision, since he was also convinced that he was well on his way to finding the young man who, thanks to Manolo, they knew was actually called Yúnior Colás Gómez, and who seemed like little more than a full-time con artist. Neither did he feel any rush to read the state newspaper (the news was always the same, and never very good), nor did he have even the slightest desire to sit in front of his old typewriter and contend with what increasingly revealed itself to be beyond his reach. How could he aim to write a squalid and moving story, like Salinger, after having seen life in the "settlements," where there were thousands of people for whom squalor was not at all a Salingerian feeling of Buddhist spiritual lightness, but rather, something both physical and moral in nature that was oppressive and inescapable? No, he would do nothing. A whole lot of dolce far niente. In short, the freedom of choosing an awakening satisfied.

Tamara had gotten up early to go to the clinic, since she had to be in surgery that day. And on the wide and beautiful bed, in the well-ventilated room, surrounded by a welcoming and sustained silence that he never got to enjoy in his own neighborhood, Conde basked in its compact softness, and in the fresh scent of lavender, woman, and sex emanating from the sheets, and he had no problem delaying the moment he'd have to leave the bed in order to brew the day's first cup of coffee. If not for the pressure in his bladder (or could it be that his prostate was already screwing with him?), he wouldn't have moved from there for hours, years, centuries . . . Once he was in the kitchen, he looked out the window at the patio. Thanks to the money her sister Aymara sent from Italy, Tamara had managed to maintain the same level of care for the house that it had received from their father, ever the ambassador, both before and after 1959. The efficacy of such help became more pronounced when one compared the Valdemira house with another of a similar style and vintage just a few blocks away, on Calle Mayía Rodríguez: while the one belonging to the twins maintained its appearance, the latter, abandoned by owners who now lived in Dallas, Texas, had had the bad luck of being used by a low-level state agency and now appeared rotten with termites . . . Lost in his thoughts, Conde drank his coffee, lit a cigarette, and pondered moving himself full-time into this clean, well-lighted home, even as he knew he would never do so definitively: neither he nor his dog, Garbage II, would be able to adjust to the refined discipline that ruled here. Besides, he'd have to inherit the responsibility of clearing out the dry leaves from the house's garden, something he chose to do voluntarily this morning, since in addition to feeling satisfied, Conde also felt responsible for saving the environment. Or rather, like a sucker.

When the telephone rang, he didn't even consider answering. If someone was calling Tamara, it was best that they left a message on the answering machine, since he usually forgot to relay her messages. If it was for him, he would respond whenever his state of satisfaction ran out. It rang eight times before the answering machine clicked on: "You've reached . . ." Then came a human, vociferous voice, one very well-known to him: "Listen, Conde, dammit, I know you're there, and . . ."

He leaped up and lifted the receiver from next to the refrigerator. "What the hell is wrong with you now, Manolo?"

"Were you still sleeping?"

"No . . . I forced myself not to think, I swept the yard, I listened to the birds singing, I decided I'm going to write again, and I was just drinking a freshly made coffee that was . . ."

Sighs and tongue clicking came from the other end of the line. "How lucky you are, you son of a bitch . . . I've barely slept and coffee here tastes like shit."

"Here where?" Conde asked.

"From headquarters, *viejo* . . ."

"So why are you calling me from headquarters at this hour, my friend?"

"Because I believe that *here, at headquarters*, I have something that *you* would be interested in," he said, emphasizing his intentions.

Conde noticed the reawakening of his latent, but vivid police instincts. "Something like what, Manolo? Come on, talk, buddy, you love being mysterious . . ."

Conde could hear the smile in Manolo's voice: in reality, he liked that game of parceling out information, but since he'd reached the end of the line he came out with it.

"There's a corpse at the morgue . . . And the fingerprints belong to one Yúnior Colás Gómez . . . who looks quite a bit like your friend Raydel. So much so that, well, I'd say it's the same person."

Even back when he was a policeman, he'd avoided visiting the morgue whenever he could, so despite the invitation from Major Manuel Palacios, he decided that he wasn't going to start going now, and much less to see a body that had already begun to decompose. According to forensic estimates, when they found the body, he'd been dead for anywhere between 120 and 140 hours: five or six very hot days. A malodorous corpse with a bashed-in skull, as if he'd been beaten with a meat tenderizer, according to Manolo's description. And, to make things more interesting, he had traces of many other blows to the rest of his body, all too similar to the lacerations sustained from being tortured or subjected to a fit of sadism.

The body had been found the previous night by a volunteer border guard, near Boca de Jaruco. The vigilante, a former low-ranking soldier, as part of his battle against imperialism and the defense of the homeland, went out almost every night to cover some part of the rocky coast, to the east of Havana, fulfilling the self-assigned mission of surveilling possible supplies of drugs dragged in by the Gulf current or of preventing clandestine exits by those compatriots who desired to land on any of the Florida Keys. It was not yet midnight when he'd arrived at an outcrop of the coast where the strong smell of putrefaction came to him from a small cluster of sea-grape plants growing between the sharp rocks, known by fishermen, with good reason, as "dog's teeth." As soon as he saw the corpse, the guard sounded the alarm and local police, upon seeing the state of the body, immediately called in the criminal division: for there was not the least bit of doubt that it was a homicide, and a rather bloody one at first glance.

Ever since he'd left the police force twenty-five years prior, Conde had not reentered the office that oversaw criminal investigations. There, he'd fielded hundreds of meetings of all kinds—from the most pleasant to the most acrimonious—along with his former boss, Major Antonio Rangel, and there, he had handed in his resignation to Colonel Alberto Molina, when he managed to leave the corps, two weeks after old Rangel's defenestration. And now, the person in charge of that place (for several years now) was his former subordinate turned Chief of Investigators of Greater Common Crimes.

"It appears that they beat him with a rock," Manolo said as Conde examined the office, even taking in the scene that was visible through the window that ran along one of the walls. Manolo was sitting in his high-backed chair behind his desk, and Conde settled into one of the two wrought iron and vinyl armchairs opposite him. "But quite a few times . . . More than necessary. With gusto."

"So have they found the rock?"

"Not yet . . . And I don't think they will. If it was thrown in the sea . . ."

"Any other clues?"

"The other injuries could have come from a fight, but it doesn't seem like it. There are many . . . some could be from kicks. The specialists are examining everything they picked up at the crime scene now: a couple of soft-drink cans, some papers, a cigar butt . . ."

Conde was dealing with a wave of nostalgia. It was a half-smoked cigar that had helped them resolve one of the last cases that he and Manolo had worked on together, such a long time ago, perhaps in another life.

"So that's why this kid wasn't showing up anywhere," Conde muttered.

"That's why I called you. I need you to tell me everything you found out about him."

"Ah, I thought it was to help me with my lost Virgin case . . ."

"Man, never mind the damn Virgin, or anything else! Now a guy is dead!" Manolo protested. "I called you so you could help me with my case. But I have to warn you, Mario Conde, it's a case you can't get involved with, not even to dip your toes in! Now, that whole business with the Virgin is just one more detail. Perhaps an important one, perhaps not, but it's part of a serious homicide case. And, as you can imagine based on what you told me the other day, the first suspect I have is your friend from high school . . . What was his name?"

Conde shook his head. "Bobby? No, Manolo . . . Not Bobby . . ."

"Yes, Conde . . . Yúnior Colás left him, robbed him, humiliated him . . . He himself told you he was crazy in love with the kid . . . What more do you need to suspect him? Look at how he was killed, with what passion . . ."

"No one who's in that deep makes waves, Manolo . . . Let's see, what do you guys think happened on the beach?"

Manolo leaned back in his chair.

"That whole area between Havana and Matanzas is where clandestine escapes frequently happen. Maybe the kid and the murderer went there to leave the island . . . Or else, someone took Yúnior there under the pretext of getting him out, but with the objective of snuffing him out or getting information from him about what he'd stolen and hadn't yet sold, right? If that robbery hadn't happened at your friend's house, we might be looking at other leads. But with that story right in front of us . . ."

"I really don't believe that Bobby . . . Roberto Roque Rosell . . . No, I don't believe that he's capable of that. Not the Bobby I know. You know he's my friend."

"I don't care about that: we have to fully investigate this and have a serious talk with him . . . Give me his address . . ."

Conde scratched his arms: it was a physical reaction to the situation in which he now found himself. Barely comforted by the conviction that he wasn't revealing anything too sensitive, he dictated Bobby's address to Manolo. The Major lifted one of the three phones at his disposal in one corner of the desk and dialed some numbers. When he got through, he repeated Bobby's name and address, hung up, and renewed his focus on Conde.

"Now tell me what you've found out."

Conde understood that he didn't have a choice. Besides, the rest of the information in his possession in some way exculpated his former classmate. What sense did it make for Bobby, if he really was Yúnior's murderer, to come and ask him for help on the very next day following the kid's murder (according to the established chronology)? What good would it do to shake things up like that? But what if Bobby had sought him out with the intention of creating a smoke screen after having committed a crime? Conde tried to cast this possibility aside: it was too contrived and dangerous, not to mention dramatic, since it implied staging a whole series of interactions that required Bobby having very cold blood and a very twisted mind.

"Okay . . . but I have a condition . . ."

"There are no conditions, Conde!" Manolo stood up and his chair rolled backward. "We're investigating a homicide, and you know very well that—"

"Let me talk, dammit! Don't be such a cop, *viejo*! I want only two things: first, that you keep in mind that Bobby is my friend . . . And second, if you find any evidence related to the Virgin of Regla or any of the other things that Yúnior stole, you let me know . . ."

Manolo puzzled at Conde's misplaced intensity. "Fine . . . But, why are you so hung up on that damn Virgin?"

"Because in this story, everything that appears to be one thing ends up being something else. And this version of Her does not appear to be what people say or think She is . . ."

Manolo crossed his eyes and attacked. "Okay. I don't know what in the hell you just said about what appears and doesn't appear, but talk."

Manolo sat down again and, with his feet, pulled his chair closer to the desk. In a notebook, he began to jot down the details of Conde's investigation. That the robbery of Bobby's house had been planned by Yúnior and carried out with the help of Yuniesky the Bat and Ramiro the Cloak; that part of the loot had been sold almost immediately to someone whom Conde had not yet been able to identify but could find, if necessary; that, following the robbery, Yúnior had retreated to the "settlement," seeking the protection of his cousin Ramiro, who in turn confirmed that he'd not heard from his accomplice in several days, despite having asked relatives who still lived on the eastern part of the island if they had seen him around there; that Yúnior had changed his name because he was on the run from someone he'd conned back in Santiago who'd threatened him, a fact that could not be ignored since it could have something to do with the way the kid had met his end. Finally, he noted the possibility that, along with the Virgin of Regla and some engravings and decorations that by the looks of it—only by the looks of it—were not too valuable, Yúnior had also kept some jewelry, the value of which Conde did not know (an engagement ring with semiprecious stones appeared to be worth the most) but that the kid might've thought was valuable. Perhaps Yúnior, believing that the jewels were his meal ticket, had been seeking a potential customer, most likely someone outside the circle of buyers and sellers that Bobby himself ran in, where René Águila had stood out, due to his unscrupulous reputation. But Conde kept to himself the speculations that he, along with his friends and Father Mendoza, entertained regarding the Virgin and Her potential value, due either to Her supernatural powers or to Her being a historical or cultural artifact, if that were the case. As a matter of fact, what worried him was that Bobby had been positioning himself as an old friend, and had the ability to soften Conde's heart by invoking that relationship, but was in reality a stranger to him, capable of shape-shifting time and time again, both successfully and unsuccessfully, to hide who he really was. Bobby, who had reappeared out of the distant past and who, despite the passionate, anguished pleas for Conde's help at their first meeting, had intended on conning him, offering him less money than what he had previously agreed upon with Yoyi the Pigeon. Could Conde really trust someone like that? he asked himself, alarmed, afraid that Bobby, who had claimed friendship, was actually manipulating Conde on the basis of Bobby's own past and current ethical-ideological prejudices against the police as a homosexual man in Cuba.

As he told Manolo what he thought was pertinent while simultaneously organizing the information he had gathered through the perspective of a criminal investigator, Conde felt he was entering a precarious terrain that he took no pleasure in traversing. Often, during his career as a policeman, he'd resorted to inflicting various kinds of duress in order to obtain useful information to aid in his investigations. Only now, it was he who was offering the details that could implicate other people, or even betray their guilt, among them Yuniesky and Ramiro's in connection with the robbery, men whom he had approached as Bobby's representative, and not as an agent of the law. And, even though his conscience was telling him that, ultimately, he wasn't hurting anyone who had not already hurt someone else, and even though he knew that violent crime turns all logic and responsibility upside down, something inside of him rebelled against this sort of collaboration, or to put it simply, ratting them out. However, while he was doing everything he could to distance Bobby from the events, by portraying him as a victim and as a person incapable of committing the bloody act of smashing another human being's skull to bits, Conde was nevertheless subjecting his friend to Manolo's scrutiny as he pursued the guilty party, or at minimum, uncovered some clue capable of identifying the guilty party. And in that process, Bobby's personal and professional life would inevitably come under deep investigation from which all kinds of shit could come to the surface.

"Is that all?" Manolo asked him when he had finished relaying the information he'd accumulated.

"Yes," Conde said.

"Are you sure?"

"What the hell is wrong with you, Manolo?"

"What's wrong is that I know you very well. If that Bobby is a friend of yours . . . I know you, Conde," he insisted.

Conde smiled.

"You're also my friend, Manolo . . . And, like you, I want you to find out who crushed that kid like a bug . . . like a cockroach."

"The violence was extreme," the policeman agreed. "Whoever killed him is capable of even more dangerous acts. This was not just a fight, but a very cruel act, potentially with torture involved."

"Did you guys already know that Yúnior had conned some guy out there in Santiago? That could be why—"

"Yes, we already have Yúnior Colás's file . . . But the guy he was on the run from, one Braudilio Castillo, couldn't have killed him: he's dying of cancer in a hospital in Manzanillo."

"But couldn't he have sent someone?" Conde tried to lend power to the possibility.

"Anything is possible, but I don't think so . . . Why would he do that now, just as he is dying and Yúnior was trying even harder to hide because he'd screwed over someone else?"

"Yeah, it's messed up, it's messed up . . . Tell me something, are you going to be in charge of the case yourself?"

"No, no," Manolo sighed, tired. "I have a thousand things going on . . . I gave it to a kid who's the new rising star here. He's very smart and knows how to get the most out of computers and all that electronic shit we have now . . . And he's a real bulldog. When he latches on to something, he won't let go."

"So, who's this prodigious beast?" Conde asked, somewhat stricken with envy. Long ago, he had been the hero. The star of the department. And what the hell was he now?

"His name is Miguel Duque and . . . damn, they call him el Duque!" Manolo exclaimed, only just at that moment realizing the semantic operation of relating the last names, via nobility, of his former mentor and his current disciple.

"I hope he really is good . . ." Conde admitted ill-humoredly and added, "because there have only been two Duques in Cuba: the old one, who died, and the young one, who went on to a better life . . ."

"No kidding, Duque Hernández, the baseball player, died?"

"I said he went on to a better life . . . He left for the States, won four World Series, and now he's loaded . . . He plays golf and everything."

"You're always talking shit and thinking about shit, Conde!"

"What about you, what are you thinking about, Manolo? Seriously."

The major looked his former colleague in the eye. His pupils started to look as though they were seeking refuge behind his septum.

"Stop getting all cross-eyed and just tell me. I already told you what's on my mind . . ."

Manolo refocused and his eyes regained their balance.

"I think that there are many loose ends to this story. For starters, I have a compulsive con man who could have screwed over many people, and I can't help but consider a settling of accounts for something about which we have no idea . . . On the other hand, I have your friend Bobby with a broken heart, who, on top of that, was upset about being robbed, and no matter what you say, a person like that is capable of many things . . . But then, I've also got a trio of criminals who do a job and then one keeps most of the haul and screws over the others . . . And he's the one who shows up dead . . . There's also the fact that the whereabouts of the stolen goods are unknown, the value of which is hypothetical, because we don't know if Yúnior tried to do business with anyone, nor do we know with any certainty how much money we could be talking about if the jewelry the deceased stole was truly valuable . . . I also have what was potentially an attempted clandestine exit from the country, with objects in tow that could be valuable or could not be, which someone decided to take without sharing the profit . . . But, above all, I have a violent criminal and a story that, no matter how you look at it, is rotten, not unlike Yúnior Colás Gómez's body . . . In other words, Conde, I have too many bad things and nothing pleasant. But it's cases like this that you used to like, remember?"

Conde nodded, feeling like a stranger to himself. "Yeah, I remember . . .

Well, the truth is that I'm happy I'm not the one who has to solve it now. Luckily, you have the brilliant Duque!"

Certain that he was about to ruin every good memory he had of the place, Conde crossed the threshold of the rusty gates, more evocative of a prison than anything else, that guarded the shadowy, dilapidated ferry building on which the sun still beat down. The only relief the shed offered was the promise of freedom that one always gets from the sea. At the door, a sign enumerated the instruments of war that were not allowed inside, which seemed to say all but the Dantesque warning: ABANDON ALL HOPE YE WHO ENTER HERE. Cannons, rifles, machetes, saws, and hammers— all were forbidden. The most dangerous of the prohibited weapons: a bottle of rum. Standing under such warnings (ending in an ET CETERA that amplified what was inadmissible into infinity), the gatekeepers ensured that these demands were met. The guardians, an ill-shaven man and a woman equally in dire need of a shave, were dressed in olive-green uniforms, custom-made for people other than themselves. They scrutinized him with critical, well-trained eyes, and both seemed to conclude that he was just a harmless old man, letting him pass without subjecting him to the customary pat down. Other people who arrived before and after him were made to show the contents of their bags, and one or another was subject to a body search, as if they were about to board a space shuttle to a galactic destination, instead of the slow, sputtering ferry that went in circles every day, from sunup to sundown, year after year, between the corner of Havana's main port, known since colonial times as the Emboque de Luz, and the other side of the bay, where there was the small town of Regla, named after the seafaring Andalucían Virgin that had been deposited there when the village was first founded four centuries ago. Because the route never varied, the two or three ferries that completed the trajectory had become a national institution, and had acquired a single, proper name: the Little Boat to Regla. And because the island's inhabitants felt periodically or permanently anxious to escape, the little boats had been considered a strategic means of transportation for the last two decades.

Conde recalled having boarded one of these ferries for the first time in the company of his grandfather Rufino, some fifty-five years earlier, during one of his tours of Havana's cockfighting pens, before their revolutionary abolition was decreed. Back then, the Little Boat to Regla had always been operated by an engine plagued by whooping cough, and usually had its wooden sides painted a vivid orange with benches lining the port side and starboard. Its principal mission was that of taking and bringing inhabitants of the "overseas" town, as people in Havana insisted on calling Regla, from one side to the other of the inlet's coast, as well as transporting believers and pilgrims who'd left the city in search of Regla's venerable chapel, and distracted passengers who'd boarded the vessels merely for fun and relaxation.

On that first occasion, enjoying the thrill of the venture, the breeze as it caressed him, and the sea that, at that point in time, still smelled like the sea, young Conde had observed, free as the wind and with all of his childish wonder, how the ferry cast off, the process of leaving behind one shore in order to approach another, the game of perspective and how distances can alter sizes and proportions: as Havana became more remote, fitting neatly in sight, more magisterial and permanent in its profusion of towers, belfries, cupolas, eaves, and masts, Regla became larger, proudly displaying its perpetually proletarian modesty. The growing vista of the small town offered, first and foremost, the yellowish plaster walls of the small chapel in which the Black Virgin was worshipped. This was the Virgin of Regla, the direct descendant of a statue from Chipiona, which, according to legend, was itself fruit of a mystical revelation and stroke of artistic inspiration received by Saint Augustine the African, Bishop of Hippo, who must have carved Her with his own hands.

Following that initial voyage, Conde had used the Little Boat's services on many occasions. The last time he'd made this journey, so typical of life in Havana, he had done so to seek the wisdom of an old practitioner of the Bantu rite of Palo Monte with the hope that the ancient Black man would help him understand why someone might steal the bones of a Chinese or Jewish person from a cemetery. He'd learned then that in the Palo religion, an evildoer could have no more effective possession than the bones of a Chinese or Jewish person, placed in a powerful receptacle known as the *nganga*. A belief from the heart of Africa, seasoned by Cubans with the human remains of Jews and Asians! What monstrosities arose from the nation's lack of limits, which were so beneficial and dangerous at once! That time, the emblematic orange of the ferries had appeared to him as nothing more than a stain, and the smell of the sea had been replaced by the sickly, fetid odor of acid and fuels that clouded over the ocean's surface. The yellow walls of the chapel, meanwhile, were peeling, dissolved by sun, salt, and national apathy.

It was shortly after that last trip of Conde's that the ferry's circular route was forcibly altered by hijackers who turned its dormant compasses toward a new and unforeseen destination: north. Or rather, the North, as Cubans tended to call their neighboring country in their fanatic way of nicknaming all things. The messy and brutal North. It was at that time that the Crisis devastating the island had grown and swelled to the point of homegrown pirates beginning to hijack the shuttles in order to take them beyond their usual, predictable horizons. The hijacking attempts followed one after another, insistent on improving and prolonging the journey. However, it turned out that the fuel in the Little Boat's deposits was barely enough to make it a few miles inland, so a solution was proposed to increase the capacity of its tank and, therefore, the distance it could cover. The ferry that went the farthest was also, as it turned out, the most festive. On Havana's docks, it was boarded by some *cumbancheros*, weighed down with whistles, maracas, and guitars, allegedly en route to celebrate the wedding of a Santería high priest from Guanabacoa and a Santería priestess from Regla. They boarded with their crates of beer, their bottles of rum, and even some very large cakes . . . The celebration was to be carried out much farther away, as the bottles of beer and rum turned out to be carrying not jovial alcohol, but fuel, and beneath the flowery meringue of the pastries were even more canisters of gas . . . At knifepoint and with guns extracted from their guitar cases, they took control of the steering wheel to embark on the journey of their choice . . . After that hijacking incident, the Little Boat of Regla became a militarized shuttle, with police on board and guards on the dock in order to avoid new and creative attacks by pirates and modern-day, homegrown corsairs.

Now as he settled in on the ferry, Conde was still unclear as to his purpose in carrying out another pilgrimage to the overseas town. Yúnior-Raydel's death had shaken him from his satisfactory stupor and charged his investigation with macabre resonance. The drama had gone off the rails, it was out of Conde's hands, and the proof that greater and worse interests were at play was now tangible.

As he crossed the bay, to whose origin the city owed its existence, glory, and prosperity, the former policeman felt the extent of his disorientation and was certain that if he wanted to know where Bobby's Black Virgin had ended up, as well as the possible motive for the murder of his ungrateful lover, he had to review all the details again from the beginning, with due and necessary diligence, and fill in all the gaping holes.

After they docked, he walked to the nearby chapel, a work of brick and tile masonry, with a bell tower and a very modest cupola. Already more than two hundred years old and pleasantly humble, the church had been erected on the very site where the original precarious chapel was erected in 1696, one after another to house the Virgin, most likely brought to Cuba from Cádiz, who was the patron saint of sailors, travelers, and migrants. The first chapel, with wooden walls and a guano roof, had been leveled just three years later by a hurricane with the name of an archangel, Saint Raphael, as if to bind the Virgin's fate to that of an island always at the mercy of the sea—*the cursed condition of being surrounded by water on all sides*—and of hurricanes—*Lord of the winds! I feel thee nigh*—to which the poets sang.

It was just a few steps from the dock to the church, and Conde traversed them as if pulled by a magnet, or else by his policeman's instinct, which had never completely evaporated. Without stopping, he crossed the threshold into the sanctuary and saw, at the back, the modest main altar and the small, black-skinned Madonna that presided over it, with Her white child in Her arms. Dozens of generations of Cubans, sailors and otherwise, Catholics and Santeros, Blacks and whites, rich and poor, had requested the favor of Her divine intervention, and a few swore that She had produced true miracles. On each side of the altar rose various effigies that kept watch over the Holy Mother, and thanks to his catechism classes, Conde managed to identify: Saint Teresa and Saint John Bosco; Jesus of Nazareth and His putative father Saint Joseph; Saint Anthony of

Padua and his namesake Saint Anthony the Abbot (accompanied by a long-snouted pig); Saint Francis of Assisi (with his doves); Saint Lazarus (with his dogs); the two mothers known respectively as the Virgin of Mercy (also known as the powerful Obatalá, according to Afro-Cuban tradition) and the Virgin of Charity, the spiritual mother of all those born on the island, syncretized as Ochún—the most beautiful, the most fertile.

At the foot of the altar today was an enormous pile of flower bouquets, already going musty and emanating a rather invasive scent, which hovered between perfume and rot. In the church's pews, he saw several people, perhaps a dozen, the majority of them senior citizens, although a couple of young people, dressed in the obligatory pure white clothing signifying their recent initiation into Santería, caught his attention.

Conde sat in a front-row pew in the center section, which was closest to the Virgin. From there, he observed the small wooden statue; She was covered save for Her face and hands, both very black, indicating Her African provenance. The rest was foil that had been layered and colored—from blue to yellow, passing for silver and gold—and giving Her the pyramid shape with which She was associated. This figure was the basis of thousands of plaster replicas, destined for domestic worship, an image that any of the island's native sons would recognize. The face, Conde said to himself, was inscrutable, nearly expressionless, more stoic than other incarnations of the Virgin that tended to be magisterial or maternal. Meanwhile, the juxtaposition of the white child held in Her black hands was accentuated by the sense that She was projecting Him forward, as if She were offering Him to someone in front of Her, or else, to the entire world. It was as if She were presenting the Redeemer.

From his shirt pocket, he extracted the photo Bobby had provided and compared the two statues: apart from their color and solemnity, there were no other notable similarities. In truth, it was as he'd already known. It was not the case that Bobby's Virgin was a liberal copy of the statue Conde saw before him. No, without a doubt, Bobby's Virgin was something entirely different. It could be that some whim on the part of the sculptor accounted for the difference in Bobby's Virgin, but the carving on it suggested great skill with the gouge, and a trained artistic sense.

So, why was the Virgin in the photo sitting majestically, while the one in the chapel stood? What about the bonnet? And why had the sculptor changed the position of the Son of God, so that His arms were in His lap, close to the breast of the Virgin, when the Virgin of Regla's baby had His arms extended out? Why was one baby white, while the other Black, like His mother? Did the difference in the color of Their skin connote specific meaning?

Conde's hazy premonitions, his questions, suspicions, and gathered evidence, grew into a caustic mass of anxiety that increasingly alarmed him: so, the Virgin that had been stolen from Bobby had never been a copy of the patron saint of Regla, nor of the original Virgin who came from Chipiona. And if anyone knew this, it would have to be Bobby. Conde had now confirmed that he was dealing with a completely different variation of the Blessed Mary, and he had the increasing certainty that this difference held the real reason for Bobby's obsession, as well as the motive for the statue's theft. Not to mention, an explanation of its value.

With this conviction, Conde approached a woman—who was as Black as the Virgin—as she came out of the sanctuary and walked toward the altar with baskets in her hands into which she began to deposit the bouquets of wilting flowers.

"Good morning, ma'am, please . . ." He addressed her from the railing that protected the altar.

"How can I help you, sir?" The woman's voice was as sweet as the expression on her face.

"Why are there so many flowers?"

The woman smiled. "Don't you know that the day before yesterday was September seventh, the Virgin's feast day?"

"True, true," he murmured. "And was there a pilgrimage?"

"Procession," the woman corrected him. "Yes, we now have permission to hold one outside the church. For years, we had to do it right here inside, or else in the atrium."

"I didn't know that . . . Thank you."

"You're welcome," the woman said, smiling again and returning to her task of gathering the dead flowers. Only then did Conde remember why he had approached her.

"Ma'am, would it be possible to see Father Gonzalo Rinaldi?"

The woman abandoned her task again and approached him, her smile never wavering.

"I'm sorry . . . Father is giving classes at the seminary . . . But, let's see, maybe I can help you with something? Would you like to be baptized, confess, or get married?"

"No, no thank you, I've already been through all that . . . Don't worry, I'll come back another day," he said, and, before turning around, he looked again at the Virgin of Regla, this time from even closer. And he had the impression that the statue met his gaze.

Ay, Conde! Ay, Conde! For God's sake, and for the sake of the Virgin . . ."

Bobby's face, which on previous occasions had alternated between cheekiness and dramatic sorrow, now held an expression of fear. And his pleading only accentuated the picture.

Urged by his conviction, Conde had traveled straight from Regla to the house of his former classmate. He hadn't even taken the precaution of eating something along the way, and the hours of awaiting Bobby's return from the precinct had become such torture to his gastric system that he was about to abort his mission, which was to get to the man while he was still hot from being raked over the coals by Conde's former colleagues.

When he saw Bobby and heard his pleading, Conde knew he'd been right. This was his chance and he jumped at the opportunity.

"Did they put the pressure on much?" he asked when Bobby, still invoking divinities, had collapsed into one of the wrought iron chairs on the porch.

"Much? They practically had me on the rack and sicced the dog on me . . . Those guys are savages . . . Were you like that when you were a cop?"

Conde smiled. "It depended . . ."

"On what?"

"On whether I knew if the person I was interrogating was telling me the truth, or was a lying piece-of-shit-son-of-a-bitch-motherfucking manipulator . . . Like you, you cocksucker!"

Bobby jumped from his seat when he heard Conde howling the string of invectives in his face. Conde confirmed that his reaction had achieved the desired effect, then he reloaded.

"You're in shit up to your neck. They let you go, but they didn't really let you go. Don't believe that. They have their eye on you, since there's a ninety-nine-percent chance you're somehow involved in the murder of Raydel, or whatever the hell that kid's name was . . . *Or* maybe you did it yourself! They were only getting started with you today. When the games begin for real, you're gonna shit your pants."

Bobby brought his hands to his chest and began to cry. Conde let him unburden himself, just enough so that he could speak again.

"So?"

"I didn't kill him, Conde."

"I know, that's why I'm here."

"So, help me, *viejo*. Help me, for the years we've known each other, for our friendship . . ."

"Are you afraid, Bobby?"

Bobby looked at his former classmate and more tears fell from his eyes, but of a different kind.

"Afraid? No, man, I'm terrified. There's a difference. I've been afraid my whole life. I've always lived with fear. In this shitty country, fear is a permanent condition and guys like me are its poster child . . . But this is something else, something else."

Conde nodded. But now was not the time for him to get soft and allow himself to be led astray by emotion. He pulled out the photos of the stolen Virgin and threw them at Bobby.

"What's with this fairy tale about your grandmother's little Virgin of Regla?"

Bobby started as if Conde had just thrown acid on him. His tears disappeared.

"What are you talking about?"

"Bobby, cut the shit. I'm serious. If you don't tell me the truth, I can't help you."

Bobby sobbed again as he looked out at his pristine garden. A rosebush of black princes held the place of honor, boasting its bloodred flowers in all their splendor. Conde suddenly recalled, like an arrow flashing across his memory, the black princes that had once adorned the small garden of his childhood home, as they were his mother's favorites. How many years had it been since Conde himself had pruned that old rosebush? He'd maintained an intense love-hate relationship with it, due to the flowers' beauty and the ugly aggressiveness of their thorny stems, which had attacked him so many times, drawing blood the same color as the petals. Bobby's sigh as he recomposed himself brought Conde back to the torrid present.

"It's a Virgin, Conde, and my grandmother considered Her to be the Virgin of Regla. But it's true that She came from Spain, with the Catalan man whom my grandmother married, who was practically my grandfather. Josep Bonet, he was called, but everyone here called him José. But actually, neither of those was his real name. For some reason I never learned, he'd changed his name when he arrived in Cuba, or maybe before he got here, and I never knew his real one. Anyway, José brought the Virgin here from Spain."

"Bobby, are you telling me another tall tale?"

"No, *viejo*, I swear I'm not . . . José came to Cuba during the Spanish Civil War, and he never wanted to show anyone the Virgin or talk much about where he'd gotten Her . . . He would just as easily say She was from Andalucía as from Catalonia . . . Maybe the Virgin had some dark history. Maybe not. I don't know . . . What I am sure of is that José *did* have a dark past. But anyway, no one cared about any of that when they saw the Virgin, you know? She was a Madonna, She was Spanish, and She was Black. What else could a Black Virgin be in Cuba but the Virgin of Regla? What, do you need the Vatican's permission to worship a Black Virgin as if She were Our Lady of Regla?"

"But you very well know that She's not a Virgin of Regla. Maybe other people don't, and maybe Raydel didn't . . . but you have to know, Bobby. Maybe none of that usually matters, but with this Virgin, it does. And what matters most is that you didn't tell me the truth from the beginning."

Bobby stroked his chest with his open hand several times, as if that gesture were helping him lower the tension that had built up there and expel it.

"Yes, of course, I asked around. She is modeled after a Catalan or Basque or Southern French one . . . In that general area, there are several Virgins that look like mine, and are of the same style. Some are very old, medieval. And the one that José, my grandmother's husband, brought over here was inspired by that Romanesque model. But She's just a regular replica. She's smaller than most of the original statues."

"How do you know She's a replica and not an authentic medieval Virgin?"

"Because José always said that he'd bought Her in some street fair in a town called Camprodon. He kept Her in his house . . . His own *moreneta*, as he would say."

Conde sighed. "Bobby, how the hell do I know you're not pulling one over on me?"

"Dammit, *viejo*, it's the truth. The truth as I know it. I swear on my grandmother. On the Virgin, even!"

Conde looked at the rosebush again and thought about how deceptive its beauty was. Could he believe Bobby even when he was swearing by the Virgin? He had no choice, he told himself. But he would not let his guard down anymore.

"So why do you think he brought Her to Cuba?"

"Well, there was a war, so he came here . . . And he brought his Virgin with him. Isn't that normal?"

"I don't know . . . There's nothing inside Her? Something more valuable than the statue itself?"

"Inside Her? What do you mean?" Bobby's surprise seemed real.

"A cavity in the wood, maybe . . ."

Bobby paused for a minute before responding.

"No, not that I know of . . . She's a wooden statue, Conde, bought at a street market! She's valuable because of what She means to me personally, what She meant to my grandmother, what She meant to her husband . . . And do you know why? Well, because that Virgin has powers! José said so, my grandmother also! And I know it's true, Conde. That's why I want Her back. Who said She could have something inside Her?"

"It's just an idea, Bobby, just an idea . . . An idea that could have occurred to Raydel or anyone else noticing your fixation on the Virgin.
Maybe the person who bumped off Raydel, for example, in order to keep
the Virgin."

"And the jewelry . . ."

"Besides the engagement ring, what else did they steal from you that
had real value?"

"Trinkets, family things . . . The engravings weren't very valuable, either. But Raydel thought it was all treasure . . . The truth is that the ring
isn't worth much, either. It's a memento . . . like the Virgin!"

Conde tried to think. He needed to think. He still didn't know why,
but he was convinced that there was a trap somewhere in this web, a void,
a trick, and it needled him that he didn't know what it is. Did it have to
do with the Virgin's "powers" of which Bobby spoke? Conde didn't believe in those powers, but he knew that other people did—some had even
felt their benefits. Were these mystical powers a greater factor in the disappearance of the Virgin than any material value the Virgin might have,
and which Bobby denied anyway? Was She really not worth anything more
than those powers, a connection with the divine embodied in a statue,
as Bobby insisted? Conde knew that he was getting tangled up in a farce
that probably had a simple explanation, and not one of the more complicated ones he was wont to cook up. But nothing about this case was
what it seemed, and what seemed important ended up being nothing . . .
Had someone killed Yúnior in order to make off with a powerful Virgin,
or was it just a valuable object they were after? Was the motive faith or
reason? And what if the crime had nothing to do with the Virgin, and
Bobby's insistence had merely clouded Conde's judgment? Maybe these
were good questions, the former policeman told himself, then decided
that he needed to be in the most propitious physical and mental conditions to come up with the answers.

"Treat me to brunch," he said to Bobby. "I'm so hungry I can hardly
see straight, and I can't even think anymore."

"It's not brunch time, Conde."

"So, crunch, then! Anything for me to chew on, buddy . . . And then tell me more about the people who deal in art and antiques. Let's see if we can find out anything through them . . . And then I'm going to tell you how you need to behave with the police. I know all their methods for getting a confession."

"Really, Conde?" His friend seemed moved, more than hopeful.

"Yes, but come on, let's eat. I'm starving to death, dammit."

Bobby had a refrigerator that was better stocked than any of Havana's supermarkets, and Conde's pernicious hunger was resoundingly defeated. His stomach full and his nerves relaxed, the former policeman outlined Bobby's strategy for talking to the cops—saying only what was necessary to help determine the Black Virgin's whereabouts, never accepting blame—and then the two friends forged a plan for Conde's next move, in light of recent events. After a second pot of coffee, which they drank down to the grounds, the former policeman decided that he still had time to make a little headway in his investigation, and he started to take leave of his old friend.

"There's something I haven't told you," Bobby whispered when they were already walking across the living room.

"What else, buddy?" Conde said harshly, immediately unnerved. He couldn't take it anymore. When would the surprises end? Dealing with Bobby was like peeling an onion.

Bobby was serious. Dead serious. With a gesture, he pointed Conde toward one of the living room's armchairs and turned on the ceiling fan to cool off the place. The host took his place on the sofa, barely sitting on the edge, as if he were ready to bolt. He rubbed his hands, looked at his friend and then at a blank wall where there once was a painting. Conde was certain that an important revelation was imminent, and decided not to push it.

"Look, I don't really like to talk about this and I've barely mentioned it to anyone, but since I know you and those awful cops don't believe me . . . Conde, that stuff about the Virgin's powers is no fairy tale . . . Not my own and not my adopted grandfather's. He told me that She has healing powers. He said the Virgin had resuscitated a boy from his village who had six fingers on each hand . . . He saw it with his own eyes, he said! I'm telling you, it's true that She performs miracles. I can confirm it myself."

Conde stifled a smile. He considered making a joke about the boy with the six fingers but refrained. Bobby seemed too serious, and Conde couldn't bring himself to ruin his story.

"Well, when I made saint and received Yemayá," Bobby continued, "and I carried out the appropriate rituals, it wasn't just because I was confused about my life, like I originally told you . . . although that was also true."

"Dammit, Bobby! What now?"

"Man, I did it because I was dying. I was diagnosed with breast cancer. Don't look at me like that, this doesn't have anything to do with being gay . . ." Bobby unbuttoned his shirt, exposing his chest. Conde noticed that his nipples were perhaps thicker than those of other men, and below the small hill of his pectoral muscle were two curved scars, almost imperceptible, in the macabre shape of a smile. "You see it? Men, even manly men, can suffer from breast cancer, and it got me. It seemed to be super aggressive. Of course, I went to see a specialist, I underwent medical treatment, but since I've always been religious, I decided to take other actions . . . Israel's *Padrino* was a Santería high priest, and he consulted Ifá for me and determined that I should receive the attributes of Yemayá, the Virgin of Regla. Do you think that's a cosmic coincidence? Do you know how many different orishas there are? What are the odds that I should receive Yemayá and not any of the others? It was a sign, and I decided to follow it. I got ready to make saint, but like my grandmother recommended, I put my trust first and foremost in my own Black Virgin. I prayed to Her, I asked for Her help and strength, and I went through the whole initiation process in Her company. That was when I made a promise to the Virgin that in exchange for my health, I would crown Her with a golden tiara, and I swore to never leave Her and to worship Her like a mother."

Conde needed a cigarette. Bobby's story was moving, but also pitiful.

"So did the Virgin perform the miracle?"

"Yes, She did, though you might not believe it. During the ceremony where I was to receive Yemayá, I was in a room where you're supposed to be alone for several days while meditating and purifying yourself, but I had my Virgin with me . . . And on the second morning, when I woke up, I saw that my Virgin was dripping wet, as if She'd just been taken out of the water . . . I looked up at the ceiling in case there was a leak, and I asked my *Madrina* if someone had wet Her, but no . . . The water kept dripping off of Her, almost as if it were coming from inside of Her, as if She were sweating from a fever. She also had a strange smell. I dared to run my finger along the Virgin and taste the water and . . . it tasted like salt, but it smelled like grease, like lard . . . It was seawater, greasy seawater! You don't have to believe me, Conde, and don't look at me like that, because now comes the really incredible part . . . A few days after receiving Yemayá, I went to the hospital . . . And to the surprise of my doctors, the cancer had receded at a medically impossible rate, given the stage of treatment I was in. It was something so extraordinary that even these oncologists said they had witnessed a miracle . . . of nature. I, of course, knew otherwise but didn't say anything to them. The tumors had become so localized that they were able to operate. For two more years, the doctors observed me, in case it came back, but I didn't have any cancer left in me, it was as if it had never been there at all. If you want, I can show you my file from the clinic; I have it saved here. An oncologist even wrote that the cause of the tumor's remission was 'inexplicable.' How the hell do you explain something like that? Something that's inexplicable even to a scientist, a specialist? Now do you understand why I believe in the powers of that Virgin, and then some? And why I feel like I failed Her by allowing Raydel to take Her? Why I'm scared shitless without Her by my side, so much so that I'm even telling you this story that you're not going to believe? But I do believe it, because I've lived it. It's because of a miracle that I'm alive, my friend. Or rather, it's because of the Virgin."

9.

ANTONI BARRAL, 1472

At this pace, a full day, sir," Antoni had lied, after pretending to make some calculations, and the gentleman Jaume Pallard had admitted, "I won't make it, Antoni, I won't make it." And Antoni knew that if not for a miracle, the gentleman would never make it. With their mediocre and overtaxed animals, moving forward over rocky terrain through which the gentleman had obstinately decided to take a shortcut, it would take them at least two days. But with a fever that wouldn't lessen and bloody vomiting that smelled of sulfur, Lord Pallard's hours on earth seemed to be very few. "Is this your valley, Antoni?" the gentleman asked, and Antoni responded yes. At one point, it had been. "And what's that peak over there?" "The Pic de les Bruixes, sir." "Let's make a stop. After all, any place is a good place to die. Right, Antoni?" And the squire responded yes again, but said that the gentleman was not going to die. What else could he say? Any place. Although, for Antoni Barral, exposed as he was to the aggressive whiff of black fever that had infected and was killing his master, that valley that returned him to his origins might actually be the best place. His place.

After ten years of absence, years of war, violence, hate, and death, Antoni had barely managed to recognize the place. And not because the valley had radically changed: it was just that he was a different man now, like anyone who has ever lived through war and had made blood run. Antoni was able to identify it by the eternal outline of the mountains, the dark and treeless mound of the Pic de les Bruixes, the creek's stubborn path plagued with coarse turns, and the intense green that made it distinct in the entire region. Nevertheless, what had once been an orchard, with its olive trees and vineyards, its fields of wheat and barley, the most beautiful flocks of sheep and goats in the region, had become mere brambles in which some rocks and blackened wood piled up, marking the site where there had been a dwelling, a stable, or a silo for grains and grasses. All of it obliterated by the war, all of it conquered by neglect. Not even the bleating of sheep broke the silence. No cocks sang out. The desolation was complete and, for Antoni Barral, was overwhelmingly an omen.

It had been exactly ten years since the Catalans of the Kingdom of Aragon had battled among themselves: enough time and effort to devastate everything. They had fought in Barcelona, Girona, Lleida, on the coast and in the valleys, in any corner of the country. They had gone to war for King Joan, against King Joan, for Prince Carles even after the prince had already died. They battled for the right to the land, to mobility, to keep or eliminate tributes. Some even said that they had fought for the kingdom's independence from outside powers both visible or as ethereal as ghosts: the king of France, who was trying to take over the lands of the rich county of Roussillon, extending beyond the Pyrenees and promised by the Aragon king in return for the French sovereign's military aid; the ambitious monarch of Portugal, inclined to increase his territories; the powerful René of Anjou, Lord of Provence. Although many claimed they knew why they were fighting and which side they were on, Antoni had the impression that many had also forgotten their reasons and their loyalties many times over, that these had changed throughout the years during which they'd devoted themselves to killing one another, as if there wasn't already enough accumulated death, as if hating one another were the main design of their existences. As if being against one another constituted part of their ancestral spirit.

With the exhaustion of the battle, few remembered that the war had begun as a conflict of radical factions, who had widely extended the defense of their great interests, dragging the kingdom with them, involving both gentlemen and peasant farmers, generating great chaos. Sometimes, the disputes escalated without giving anyone time to consider what side they should or wanted to favor, and men ended up linked as troops, forced by more or less fortuitous circumstances, as had happened with Antoni Barral, a rural farmer and servant, squire to the powerful family of the Pallards. Antoni did not know or want to know anything about wars in which people like him always ended up the losers, but even so, he'd had to spend ten years of his life in a fratricidal fight that he never completely understood, in which there was no defined winner in the end, but rather a commitment to finally laying down arms out of sheer exhaustion. Because as time went by and pacts were made, it came to be that fighting for or against the monarch boiled down to a simple question of geography or loyalty to a master or the real desire to do away with something that did not work or that someone had decided did not work. And suddenly, regions, cities, towns, hamlets, even families found themselves divided, considered one another enemies to feed a devastating civil war that, a decade later, had not left any victors or conquerors, nor had it changed the country for the better: everything would be the same. Actually, worse. All of Catalonia was a wasteland populated by corpses, and the king was still the king, and the mediocrity into which the kingdom had fallen was a burden as heavy as the Pyrenees that the squire was now beholding. Thank God, after ten vain and devastating years, Antoni Barral had held on to something that, in reality, barely belonged to him: his life.

The squire took the reins of Lord Pallard's mount and decided to descend a little farther, in search of the small forest of oak and beech trees in what appeared to be a bend of the mountain creek. Water, shade, and grass were what they needed at the moment and were all that the fertile valley could offer them during this return journey that would perhaps conclude here. A bad or a good place, it was all the same, Antoni thought. At least it was pretty.

Lord Pallard's fevers had begun two days before and perhaps the best option would have been to return to Girona, in search of a doctor or a healer or even a witch doctor who, at the very least, would have bled him, placed a poultice on him, and offered him a less terrible way to die. But Jaume Pallard, stubborn and willful, had insisted on continuing on toward Camprodon and from there to the family dominion, convinced at first that his physical strength would allow him to arrive at his destination, from which he'd been absent for several years. The previous day, however, he had awoken with swollen lymph nodes all over his body and had been seized by his first fits of vomiting. Even so, they took up the trek again and Antoni Barral had the premonition that they were both embarking on the path to Hell: with that illness of which almost no one was cured and few who lived near it resisted its invasive capacities for infection. It was well-known in these lands, beyond decimated by the plague before being bled again by the spears and swords of the fratricidal war.

When they crossed the low, crystal-clear stream, they saw a strange oak, of exaggerated proportions, that seemed to reign over the small forest set off by the horseshoe of water. Separated from the rest of its species, without a doubt dead for many years, the tree had kept only two large branches, open like arms, which formed a nearly perfect cross. Meanwhile, its trunk, eaten away by insects and green with moss, seemed cracked in the middle with a deep, dark wound that had never closed up, cauterized by the fire from when a lightning bolt had struck the oak, God only knew how many decades before. Antoni, who had kicked around those valleys for years, found it strange that he had never before noticed such a peculiar tree—though, of course, what most surprised him was seeing, at the foot of the scorched oak, in a strange bowing position, the remains of dry skin, cloth, some strands of white hair, and the bones, eroded by the sun and rain, of what must have been, doubtlessly several years before, a human being. To what real and sentient man had that skeleton now lying under the dried tree belonged? How was it possible that the body had not been completely destroyed by wolves or scavengers? Was it true that predators didn't eat meat infected by the plague? Hadn't anyone seen him and decided to give him a proper burial? Even though he knew so much about death, the image of the corpse lying there gave Antoni Barral such a fright that he had decided to get far away from that place, until Lord Pallard gave what was perhaps his last order in this world from his mount: "Let's get down here, Antoni. Next to the dead oak and the skeleton. That way, I will have eternal company."

Antoni Barral had been born quite close to that very green valley, in a small, nameless hamlet nestled in that mountainous region whose magnificent range separated the Catalan Garrotxa from the county of Roussillon. His family—peasants, shepherds, coal merchants—had lived in that place forgotten by God and by History since time immemorial, always dependent on the Pallards: each member of the family occupied the social position with which fate had marked them before their conception. It was Antoni's skills as a rider and hunter that had brought him to the attention of Jaume Pallard, the young lord who was only a few years older than he was. And those skills would come to change his life—for the better, Antoni thought—because he went from the work of tilling the land and tending sheep that had marked his fate, to that of being a squire to the young gentleman, who was so given to undertaking adventures that often transgressed the limits of what was permissible, even for someone of his lineage. Thanks to this close relationship, Antoni was the first of his clan to learn to read and write—and was perhaps the only one who would achieve this for centuries—and he had enjoyed the privilege of sailing to Naples and drinking that kingdom's strong spirits, of galloping across half the country several times, of wearing leather boots with buckles, and of sleeping at inns in Aragon, Castile, León, and Navarre (more often in stables, this had to be said), places where they drank, ate, and fornicated until they were spent and where they had sung of the deeds, real or imagined, of the wandering knights and the Mediterranean sailors of which Antoni became such a fan. For some reason, one of those stories had always attracted him in particular: that which told of the journeys, glory, and death of the Great Captain Roger de Flor, a character who straddled myth and reality, and who, the story went, had commanded the *Falcon of the Temple*, the pride of the Templar maestros, which in his time was the largest and most powerful vessel that had ever existed. Later, devoted to piracy by then, Captain Roger de Flor had destroyed the coasts of the Mare Nostrum by commanding a band of corsairs known as the Catalan Company. What a character, that Roger de Flor . . .

What at first had been an unexpected benefit, capable of changing Antoni's fortunes, thanks only to his physical skill and natural intelligence, would later seal his fate. History took him by surprise and he found himself where he could not escape: for ten terrible years, Antoni Barral would have to fight next to his master in a war he was keenly aware that he was fighting for the interests of others, the same powers that be as always, the ones who force History.

How many men had he killed during the long years of battle? That he was skilled with a sword—more so, even, than Lord Pallard himself—had kept him alive after much combat, although his own survival depended on the death of others. When the war first started, persuaded by Lord Pallard's riveting speeches, Antoni had believed that he was entering a struggle that could improve the lives of men of his station. With a certain insistence, there was talk of fighting to break the bonds of peasants' dependency on the land and on their masters, to end mistreatment and excessive tributes, and to revive the dead *masos*, those farms that had been abandoned after the most difficult decades of the plague. But, as the battle continued, the young squire lost his way because, suddenly, his masters were fighting for opposing causes, or else new or different ones. What Antoni Barral did learn was that, like so many others, he was in fact no more than a peon moved by the interests of those high enough to surpass all of his understanding. Because he had neither land nor textile workshops nor businesses in Barcelona nor warehouses in Alexandria and Sicily, he was not an oligarch belonging to the *bigaires* nor a rich merchant belonging to the *buscaires*. He was not even a devotee of the king or a follower of the prince. He was merely what he was: a skillful sword manipulated by his betters. And thus he would continue to be after the war was won, with his abundant merits and his place in Hell for having killed so many men, the majority of them poor and of his station, just as miserable he was, as dragged along by the avalanche of History as he, in a war that was neither just nor holy. The only consolation for his guilt was having once heard that the war was waged for freedom, that, those in the know said, was one of the main pursuits of upright men, since servitude was comparable to death. Could that freedom also be his?

An intense decade on the battlefield had served to further hone Antoni Barral's physical abilities and survival skills. Thanks to these, after nestling Lord Pallard next to the dead oak with branches in the shape of a cross, he had managed to trap two hares and even a red partridge that he was now browning over the fire. Relieved by the knowledge that there would be food, he watched the sun set behind the valley while submerging his bare feet in the creek's soothingly cold and rushing current. A few hours before, Antoni had begun to feel an ache in his joints on top of the accumulated exhaustion after his chase of the hunt. Seated on a rock, he looked at his aching feet, whitened by the water, and they suddenly seemed like strange animals to him, definitely unfamiliar. Lost in contemplation, Antoni Barral was surprised to shake from a sudden chill coming from deep within his body, and he had the illuminating revelation of having been in that same place, in an identical position, perceiving very similar sensations and asking himself the silliest questions: What would you have liked to be in life? What would you have liked to do with your life? Who could think of asking himself something like that? The lives of men like him, those at the bottom of the social ladder, had always been and would continue to be determined by decisions and wills beyond their own, placed in the hands of fortunate men who boasted of wanting to change the world and, at times, truly desired to do so, but who, as Antoni had learned during a long civil war, mostly ended up making it worse. The strange experience of replicating a forgotten personal act, in all certainty only a dream, was so vivid for him that it seemed to have occurred outside of chronology, since he perceived it as if it were fixed just beyond the limit of his memories. Most disturbing of all was that he could also sense, in another sudden flash of insight, that he would repeat this moment in a distant, instant future, one he would not reach in the years that he would spend on this earth. All of these sensations were so outrageous, and yet crystal clear, that they were accompanied by tangible physical feelings but with certain inexplicable details that he could not pinpoint (the scent of lard and the ocean, of poorly tanned hides, of burning incense, of lavender candles), that were vague (could he smell them or not?), their contours altered by a prism, as was occurring now with his submerged feet. He then thought that he was seeing time through a transparent drop of rain, hanging from a branch. Or traversing the years with his gaze fixed on the untarnished lucidity of the tear that an overwhelming and altered mood had brought forth from his eyes.

"Could you give me more water?" the sick man requested, and Antoni

Barral emerged from the marvelous and incomprehensible enchantment into which he had fallen. The real smell of the food over the fire must have revived Lord Pallard, who was leaning against the trunk of the dried-out tree on the side opposite the unburied skeleton, so that he had opened his eyes and was almost smiling. Before obeying his master, Antoni again looked at his feet submerged in the creek and saw only that: his feet, solid and now clean, still aching. When he stood up, the squire finally answered his master: "It might make you vomit . . . At this point—" "Give me water, I'm burning up inside!" his master demanded, and Antoni Barral refilled the cup in the creek and brought it to the gentleman's lips. Jaume Pallard took the container, raised it himself, and managed to take a few sips. In the brief moment in which Antoni's hands brushed against the other man's, he thought that he had never before touched a human being whose skin could peel off from such a fiery temperature. In reality, he was burning, inside and out. Was this the prelude to his entry into the igneous eternal condemnation?

Antoni turned the pieces of meat. "If I die here, don't bury me," he heard his master's voice again. "After all, they're expecting me in Hell, you know that . . . Leave me here, near my neighbor. Many years from now there will be two mysteries here, instead of just one. And in the meantime, we'll keep each other company. Let's see if my friend will tell me who he was and how he got here." Antoni Barral nodded. His master was given to these types of thoughts. "Your Grace is going to get better," Antoni lied, and the man smiled again. "So, if you don't catch the plague, what will you do with your life, Antoni?" the sick man then asked, and his servant was startled. No one had ever asked him something like that, and the question was coming just after the strange experience he'd had, when he was asking himself the same thing. What was happening in that valley? Were they the playthings of the invisible rulers of the forests and mountains?

"I don't know, sir," the servant said at last and explained: "It all depends on you. If you die, I don't think that your gentlemen brothers will pay me the salary they owe me or give me the lands you have promised." "Is that why you're making the effort to lead me home?" "You know very well that's not the case, sir. I've been in your service for twenty years." "Do we have something on which to write?" "I'm afraid not, sir." Jaume Pallard smiled. "Then feed me. Your only salvation is that I survive." "You'll vomit." "But first, I'm going to eat. Hares' thighs are the juiciest meat."

They ate as night was falling over the valley. Antoni fed the flames to provide them with light and heat in the ever-cold autumn nights in the mountains, and settled Jaume Pallard such that his back was to the skeleton leaning against the dead tree. At some point, he heard the knight speak, as if delirious, of the shameful end of a shameful war that had ruined the country; of how some gentlemen and dignitaries had manipulated the kingdom's inhabitants into a sense of belonging by saying they were threatened by outside forces, only to hide their true interest in power and riches; of the barely altered fate of the downtrodden peasants after so many years of battle. The civil war, Jaume Pallard said vigorously and with a strange lucidity, had been just one more in the chronicle of wars past and to come: a game of power, the explosion of ambitions, the expression of the worst of the human condition. Listening to his master repeat these arguments, Antoni wondered whether his words were the result of a feverish madness or of mature reasoning, particularly since that rich, powerful man, who himself had often been despotic and whose actions ranged from gallant gestures to regrettable banditry, was expressing ideas that were alarming to Antoni and unforeseen, while simultaneously seeming intimately familiar since he had heard them at other moments of the recently concluded struggle. Or, perhaps he'd gained new understanding thanks to the revealing illumination that typically came with the approach of death. What was happening to him, to this place, in this translucent moment of time?

Night had fallen and, after throwing up, in violent fits, everything he'd consumed, the gentleman Jaume Pallard had fallen into a kind of spasmodic shaking that Antoni calculated would be the prelude to the end. When he lifted him to place him against the trunk of the damaged tree, the squire again felt the heat rising off his master's skin and onto his hands, and he crossed himself. It was incredible that that boiling-hot man was still alive, he thought. Antoni watched the periodic convulsions that shook the sick man's body; he was taking care so that his head would not beat against the tree too much, when, almost without warning, he himself was overtaken by a fetid, dark vomiting that tore him apart. He had no doubt: it was not that the hares didn't agree with him or that he'd swallowed something putrid with the water. His fate as a servant was so tied to Lord Pallard's that he had also been infected by the black plague.

Stirred by the first round of shivers, Antoni approached the hearth as closely as he could and covered himself with a blanket. There was nothing to be done. He thought, nevertheless, that before losing consciousness, he should untie the horses so that they wouldn't die once they'd exhausted the grass surrounding them, but he knew that he was already losing the strength to stand up. And lacking other alternatives, he began to pray. He was praying, submerged in a litany that left his mind blank, asking for forgiveness for his own faults and excesses he didn't deserve to bear, clamoring for a new chance in life or in the other promised existence, when he heard a noise that was perhaps fueled by his feverish state, the echo of which bounced off the mountains surrounding the valley: first with a prolonged crack, then a dull thud, one of the branches of the dried oak that gave the tree its cross-like shape had come loose from the dead trunk and fell on the head of Jaume Pallard, who remained lying under the enormous piece of dark wood.

Crawling, Antoni approached his master's body. He saw a dark stream of blood coming from his forehead, but he was still breathing. How could that burning, dehydrated body, wasted away by plague, have survived the branch's crushing blow? Antoni tried to move the branch and only managed to displace it. He thought quickly and knew that he could only lift the wood with the help of one, maybe two of the horses. Carrying out an enormous effort, he began the operation of tying the branch with a rope. He assayed and felt how his body was beginning to burn, his joints screaming out their agony, his vision blurred by the pain searing through his temples. Twice he vomited waste with more blood while he was making the beasts pull the limb. When he at last saw that the body of Jaume Pallard was free of the weight of the branch, he cut the rope and, incidentally, let loose the nags. Leaning against the dried trunk, he waited until he'd recovered his breath. Nearly dragging himself, he approached the creek to drink and to dunk his head in the cold current. With what remained of his energy, Antoni Barral—servant, peasant, mountain shepherd, and squire, son of Carles Barral, also servant, peasant, shepherd, and a soldier who'd died in another war that wasn't his own, grandson of Pau Barral, of the same occupations in peacetime and the same fate in war—allowed himself to fall next to the body of his lord Jaume Pallard, the man thanks to whom he'd come to know the wider world existing beyond his valleys and mountains. He had even had the dream of being able to be a freeman, owner of a piece of land where he had planned to plant robust grapevines brought from the Levant and the Duero lands, of raising goats with long beards and flowing coats typical of those rural places. An impossible dream for a man of his origins and his miserable fate, shaped by decisions that had always surpassed him, manipulated him, even debased him.

When the sun came out the next day, Jaume Pallard opened his eyes and saw with regained clarity the light shining over the valley bed. His head hurt and he touched the wound and the bulge he had on his forehead, over which the blood had dried. How had he been wounded? He couldn't remember. Next to him, he saw the inert and cold body of his squire, Antoni Barral, with his neck deformed by the buboes that had contributed to his death. But wasn't he the sick one and Antoni healthy? Was he alive and delirious or dead and on the way to disappearing into the void? Behind Antoni, he saw the large branch, green with moss and lichen, to which he saw tied a rope. At that moment, his thinking became clearer. He looked up and saw that the cross made by the dead oak's dried branches was missing an arm, without a doubt, the limb that was on the ground in front of him. Then, making great effort, Jaume Pallard dragged himself to the creek's current and took some sips of water, which felt pleasant despite the ulcers covering his mouth. Exhausted, but with his breathing more settled and fever lowered, he allowed himself to fall backward into the creek so he could feel the miasmas and putrid blood that had come forth from his body run downstream. From that reclined position, he observed the dead oak, split in two by the fall of one of its branches, and then he saw it. Or at least thought he did. No, he saw it, he *was* seeing it, because he wasn't delirious or dead. There She rested, seated in what remained of the trunk damaged by lightning and rotted by time. It was a black statue, majestic, without a doubt a very beautiful representation of Our Mother and Lady who with Her left arm held the Child Jesus against Her lap and held out Her right hand in the very direction in which he found himself, on his knees, pointing at him, choosing him. Jaume Pallard knew at that moment that he had witnessed a miracle, and would say so over and over for the remaining thirty years of his life. He was the beneficiary of a miracle. At that moment, he realized why the dried-out corpse was in a prayer position next to the blackened tree. Still prostrate in the creek's current, his vision fixed on the Black Virgin, he promised to live in chastity for the rest of whatever existence the heavens would grant him, to not unsheathe a sword ever again, and, as soon as was possible, to build on that same site a monument to house and honor that miraculous Virgin who had returned life to him. There he would also bury, beneath the altar, the remains of an unknown man who had died in a posture of adoration of the statue born within the magic tree, and those of Antoni Barral, the faithful servant who had led him to the site where the miracle would bring him back from the world of the dead.

10.

To kill a man, she didn't need firearms or projectiles or biological weapons or atomic arsenals: she herself was bullet, knife, arrow, anthrax, and neutrons. To bring a man to his knees required much less effort: perhaps merely a look or a smile. Her face caused the usual response in Conde; even with advance warning, no man could help but feel his hormones surge upon viewing that living work of art. Imagine the effect on someone specifically seeking her out for her attributes. She was a cataclysm, yes, a cataclysm! Because Karla Choy was a bombshell and you could see that her fuse was lit from a mile away.

Moved by Bobby's confession and convinced of the real affection that his former classmate and his Catalan grandfather could have for a miraculous statue, Conde reexamined all of the possible connections that could be made between the lost Virgin's fate and that of the murdered kid. Karla's name came up again like a card in a marked deck: just the previous night, Bobby and his friend Elizardo Soler had eaten dinner with the young art dealer. Over dessert, Karla had revealed a detail that seemed too significant to Bobby now: yes, as they had suspected, someone had prompted Raydel to commit the robbery. Could it have been a believer, Catholic or Afro-Cuban, a Babalawo, a Santería high priest, for example, convinced that the Virgin really was powerful? How much could the power of the Virgin be worth to someone who truly believes in it, and who would risk whatever necessary to possess it? All of the money in the world, concluded the woman, who knew a lot about both. And that could explain many things, Bobby thought, from the disappearance of the statue to the death of Raydel. A fanatic is capable of anything and everyone knows it from some firsthand experience, he said.

Called by the persistence of the idea and by the art dealer's reputation (and by what was said about her beauty, he had to admit), Conde was determined to see her and asked Bobby to make him an appointment with her as soon as possible. Once the call had been made, Bobby told him that Karla Choy was in her private gallery right then, mounting an exhibition, and that she'd agreed to see him.

The gallery had been opened in one of those mansions on the main avenue of the Kohly development, very close to the bridge over the Almendares River. It was a building from the 1940s, with a high stanchion, many lead-glass windows, and a quiet elegance; one of those structures that was capable of withstanding the passing of time and trends with dignity. Conde conquered the short set of stairs that raised the mansion about six feet above the world and entered through the entryway's columned hall. He crossed a space with shining granite and peeked into the open door, about to knock or announce his presence, when he saw coming toward him, from the back of the house, the nymph's unmistakable figure. When she was just a few feet from him, the mere vision of the woman made him feel the heat rising up from the bottom of his feet, similar to the one he'd suffered the night on which he had seen the Devil. But this was a much nicer fire.

Her very black, straight hair moved to the rhythm imposed by her swaying body, on display under the spaghetti-strapped shirt hugging her body, and the spandex shorts clinging to her hips and thighs. You couldn't ask any more of that body: her tanned skin was taut over two small and perky breasts, crowned by nipples that shot out through the shirt; over a flat, tight, hard abdomen and across generous hips between which nestled that magical trangle, the real philosopher's stone—capable of transforming matter—that which disoriented alchemists never had a clue where to find; to finish things off, the color and magnetic quality of her skin continued down to her thighs, which were toned without being too muscular, and down her legs to the shapely ankles and well-proportioned feet, which proudly supported this magnificent specimen of nature and genetics. But the finishing touch was in the eyes. Everything is in the eyes, Conde had once heard or read somewhere—and the eyes of Karla Choy, a Chinese Cuban, demonstrated this in an irrefutable way: they were black, deep, almond-shaped, brilliant, intelligent, perhaps even cunning. Without a doubt, murderous. Bolero eyes.

"Are you Rey, Bobby's friend?" Karla asked the statue of salt at her threshold. Her voice was not out of tune with the rest of her body; it contained the necessary warmth to announce that its owner, ultimately, was real, human, and not a replica handmade by the creator of dreams.

The man gulped and regained his breath. He made the effort and managed to speak.

"I don't get called that very often . . . I'm Conde."

She laughed, forcefully. "Oh, that's right . . . Forgive me. But, come in, come in . . ."

In the living room, against the columns charged with dividing the ample space into equal portions, there were several works by one of the Cuban painters whom Conde hated most. His art itself spoke to his lack of talent, but his fame and presence were oppressive. God only knew what political or economic favors he'd done to get on top. The work was all more or less the same. A chubby, smiling girl, with the features of an angel, took first position in the pile of canvases, and at the mere sight of the image, Conde felt himself returning to reality from the unreachable orbit into which the figure of Karla Choy had launched him.

"Is this the painter you're promoting now?" he asked when he saw three young people, two men and a woman, measuring paintings and spaces, preparing the exhibit.

"Yes. Why?" Karla asked and stopped before the canvas of a happy child dropped among angels.

"Well . . ." He didn't dare. That was not his business and he feared crossing a line.

"Tell me the truth, don't be shy," she encouraged him.

"It seems like utter shit to me," Conde whispered, so that the curators wouldn't hear him. Karla laughed again. She was even more attractive when she laughed. Absolutely and efficiently lethal.

"No, it *is* shit . . . But this world is full of people who buy shit. Even people who prefer shit . . . And I . . . If you want it and you pay me, I'll sell it to you," she said and added, "Come on, let's go to the dining room."

Conde enjoyed the show, watching her walk ahead of him. It's what he'd been missing, that rear view of this woman, and what was true was that it did not disappoint his expectations in any way. *What must it be like to live with a woman like that?* he asked himself as they walked, and answered immediately: a round trip from glory to the Inferno. If Tamara's subdued and relatable beauty had been the source of jealousy and discomfort evident in the faces of other men, then to walk around with Karla in Havana, where far less attractive women were undressed by the male gaze, would have required the use of armor and flamethrowers.

The mansion's dining room was also in keeping with the rest of what he had already seen: in fact, it elevated his estimation of the house's luxury. It was closed off by stained-glass windows (which cast the light in geometric patterns) and benefited from the hum of the generous air-conditioning unit. The room was welcoming and familiar, thanks to the cupboards covered in what was perhaps Venetian glass and, most of all, to a mural boasted by one of the walls. The author of the mural was one of the contemporary Cuban painters whom Conde admired most. His scenes were naïf, dreamlike sequences, at times depicting identifiable characters and at other times populated by distended dolls, as was the case in the piece he now contemplated. The masterfully controlled pastel colors created an ethereal, gauzy atmosphere, but somehow, it also felt familiar. The artist, highly admired, very well-known, had been recently experiencing a period of public ostracism and social and cultural invisibility due to his public opinions and attitudes, of a bitterness that went beyond what was admissible by the powerful and castrating orthodoxy. Nevertheless, to Conde's satisfaction and—he imagined—that of many people, the painter had not given up and was still working on his oeuvre, creating invincible beauty against which neither cultural marginalization nor other human fatalities had any power.

"Now *this* is a painter," Conde said.

"Of course . . . But not everyone will buy him! That work alone is worth ten times as much as the twenty-five pieces we are exhibiting up there. It's easy to do the math. I'm a broker, not the Minister of Culture."

Conde sat down on the chair Karla presented to him.

"What can I get you?"

"What are you offering?"

"Whatever you want."

Conde accepted the challenge. "Irish whiskey?"

"Coming up!" Karla exclaimed and walked over to a tall cabinet, opened one of the doors, and returned with two glasses and a bottle of twelve-year-old Irish whiskey. "I'm going to have one with you. I need to relax . . ."

She served the liquor in the glasses, placed a few ice cubes in them, and, without waiting for them to cool, took a sip from hers.

"Thank you," Conde said before drinking. As the distilled drink slipped down his palate, he confirmed that there was still such a thing as glory. Only, it must be very expensive and was, as such, elusive.

"So . . ." Karla probed. "I have to get back to work . . ."

Conde took another drink, took out his cigarettes, and gestured to ask permission, which she granted with a nod, while pushing the heavy glass ashtray in the middle of the table closer to him. It turned out that this cataclysmic beauty was one of the few people in this country who did actually work.

The former policeman began to explain the reason for his visit: the theft Bobby had experienced, the complicated situation he now found himself in upon the discovery the night before of the murder of the presumed thief, who was Bobby's former lover and protégé. He also shared the speculations about the crime having a connection to the robbery. He felt loquacious, encouraged by the young woman's disarming look and the aura of powerlessness that her presence created. He revealed the information without having a clear idea of what was prudent. He was that vulnerable.

"When Bobby called me and told me they'd killed the kid . . . Terrible," Karla commented. "But I really don't know how I can help you. Poor Bobby . . ."

"The problem is that until today, I thought that the key to finding that damn Virgin was Raydel, or Yúnior, which was the thief's real name. But now, I think there's someone else behind it all. Someone smarter than

Raydel who set him in motion . . . And since I've been told that you are of the same opinion, and that you simply know everything about everything that happens in this business . . ."

Karla smiled, seemingly flattered. "And you're sure the Black Virgin is valuable? As art, I mean."

"Valuable, yes, but I don't know how much," Conde admitted. "That depends on many things. How rare and old She is, especially. These are details I don't have, because according to Bobby, She is neither antique nor rare . . . Although She could be valuable solely from a spiritual perspective. At least to those who believe in such things."

Karla nodded. "Yes, that's what I told Bobby . . . But, did the police have any leads? Do they suspect anyone who could have killed Raydel?"

"No, they're lost. I think more lost than I am, since they don't know what I know about the Virgin . . . They're going to come down hard on Bobby and on Raydel's buddies, until they get something out of them, or get tired and start looking at other possibilities."

"What could they get out of them?" she continued.

"I don't know . . . anything at all."

Karla nodded. Then, she smiled again. "Rey, what kind of cop are you?"

"Just Conde," he corrected her.

"Can't I call you Rey? I like it better than Conde."

The man was on the verge of melting, and with a final flash of lucidity, he wondered whether the woman was trying to manipulate him to get information out of him. And whether she was, in fact, doing so with her looks, smiles, Irish whiskeys.

"Okay, call me Rey. It's an honor to be seen as a king . . . I've never been so high. Nearly in the clouds." He raised his drink, without turning away from the young woman's gaze.

"Tell me, what kind of cop are you?"

"More or less like you in your business: a cop who works for himself. I'm not the kind who puts people in jail . . . Instead, I look for them when they're lost. I have to make a living somehow . . ."

"I like that: you're the first Cuban private detective since 1959 . . . You're a king, I knew it! I have a sixth sense . . . Hey, listen, do you need a P.I. license?"

"Not that I know of . . . I'm clandestine . . ."

"Clandestine, I like that . . . Well, Rey . . . The problem is that I don't know how to help you . . . How to help Bobby get out of this mess he's in or to recover his Virgin. If this is a matter of Santeros and believers, then I give up. That's not my world. I don't believe in anything."

"But you don't have to be wedded to the idea that there's a fanatic behind this. It could be a business deal that got complicated. And as you know . . ."

"I don't get involved in those swamps, Rey. You see me here, half-mad," she said. "Fast and furious, as they say. But not in business. I can't lose what I have just to earn a few more pesos. I've gotten all of this by working, skillfully but persistently. And it has cost me a lot. Fights, enemies. There are also some up there"—she pointed beyond the rooftop—"who don't like me too much. To have this gallery was my dream . . . And I achieved it. I studied architecture; I like to build things . . . But if you can't build bridges or houses or anything in this country . . . then I make magic. This is magic, Rey."

Conde admired entrepreneurial spirits, possessors of the impetus that he was lacking. And if the effort was clean, then he applauded it. And if the person behind it was someone so beautiful, he drooled.

"I'm not going to tell you my life story, but since I can't help you with your problem, while we have this marvelous drink, I am going to tell you *something*," Karla announced and took another sip. "My grandfather was a starving Chinese man who came from Canton to make money, and he broke his back working. My father and mother were two starving Cubans who also worked like animals. Today, they're two sixty-year-olds, exhausted, disillusioned with everything, and they're not starving on their fifteen-dollars-a-month pension because I support them . . . As for me, the truth is that I had other options, but it seemed like in the end I was going to get more of the same: a desk in some dark office. To be frustrated and, if possible, be corrupt in order to escape . . . Geographic, historic, even racial fatalism? You know that Chinese genes are very strong, right? They keep recurring for generations. And I have those genes: the good ones, the bad ones, the visible and the invisible . . . I can break my back working, like my family. But, being half-Chinese after all, I can also make business out of anything . . . as you already know. Have you seen those Chinese refrigerators they sell to people here? Junk, absolute junk . . . But they sell them! Well, I entered college right in the middle of the Crisis. There were no buses, I don't even know what I did to get to the School of Architecture every day; there wasn't food, either, and I don't know what else, or how I studied because there was almost never electricity. I never had a peso . . . But I was screwed, so I hit the pedals hard, of both life and of the shitty Chinese bicycle I got around on. And I graduated. Then, I told myself that I wasn't going to be like my grandfather or my parents or like my Chinese bicycle. To live a little bit better, I wasn't going to do what so many girls of my generation did, either, who found themselves an old foreigner to get them out of Cuba and support them, but drool all over them. No, I don't have the stomach for that. I don't have the soul of a prostitute, not even a married prostitute. I don't want a man to support me, because if they support you, they control you. And the controller is made . . . I wasn't going to do what some of my classmates did, either, whose only exercise of their architecture degree is taking money from people who need their approval for government workers to fix a house, to buy one or sell one. Don't think I'm criticizing them. None of them, no matter how much of a bitch or or a son of a bitch they are, because ultimately, they are victims. Each one takes what he can, especially when the flood comes after so much rain. These people putting their asses on the line, those people stealing from the bastards who have the money to buy themselves big houses and also from those poor slobs whose roofs are falling in over their heads. Because you have to make a living. And anything goes in that business . . . In sum, I don't want to bore you: what I did was put my pants on, I made my way into this business without really knowing how, but with the will to do it. Because I told myself that this business was going to make it possible for me to live better than I was meant to according to my origins and my present conditions. So, I started from the bottom, without anything, but with effort, with will, working fifteen hours a day, and . . . Now, you see, I can offer you that drink you just had or whatever you could have thought to ask for. Brandy, port, Finnish vodka, mescal . . ."

Conde was listening to her pragmatic lecture and was slowly recovering his ability to process information. Although she had not meant to, Karla Choy was revealing to him the basis for a life philosophy that more and more people were practicing in the country: that of making do on your own so as not to fall into the pit.

"Is there a line you won't risk crossing?" he dared to ask.

"Of course, I take risks . . . To be able to keep what I have, I take a lot of care. I do thousands of deals, but I don't get dirty. Everyone around Havana knows that . . . That's why no one is going to come and try to sell me a fake painting by some Cuban master and, of course, less still, some shitty, stolen Virgin who isn't even worth a hundred pesos, and only an imbecile like your friend Bobby or that potato with eyes Raydel or a crazy mystic could believe that it's worth something, in money or in esoteric powers or whatever you call it. And if it's really worth something, then I don't really care, either, it's dirty and now, on top of that, covered in blood . . . That's the thing, Rey. I don't get sullied. And well, since I like you, some other day, I'll invite you to have another drink. Today, my consultation is over. I have to work. Work."

Karla Choy smiled and held out her hand to Conde. The salt statue was now a stone. Who in the hell was this woman? Where did they make them like that?

When Tamara asked how hungry he was, Conde puckered up his lips, pretended to be thinking, and finally said, "Just a little." He would be happy with any trifle, he assured her seriously, that way he gave his stomach a break, while still keeping her company in her healthy, frugal meal. Tamara looked at him with an expression that said, "I know you, Mario, you can't pull one over on me," but did not speak her opinion. Of course, he would not confess even under torture that at five in the evening, Bobby had prepared a banquet for him with only the delicacies at hand in his fridge and powerful pantry: pickled mackerel, crackers with foie gras, egg and potato salads, Serrano ham, sliced Manchego cheese, anchovy-stuffed olives, a bottle of Malbec, a slice of coconut pie with two scoops of mamey ice cream, and . . . real coffee, in nonrationed quantities. And Tamara, playing the role of a woman who is happy to see an improvement in her lover's nutritional reeducation, punished him by making him share with her just one bowl of asparagus soup with a side of green salad.

What Conde did tell her was the turn his current investigation had taken. A death changes everything, he said to her. Now his head was going a thousand miles a minute, since he intuited that some important piece of the puzzle didn't fit, was missing, or was left over. Because of that, without mentioning the mystical story of Bobby's miraculous cure much less the cerebral commotion caused by contemplating the cataclysmic Cuban-Chinese woman, he asked Tamara to let him shut himself up for a couple of hours in Dr. Valdemira's office, the same one that the deceased Rafael Morín had usurped for a few years. Conde needed to make a few telephone calls and give himself time to think.

"Before you start thinking about Bobby and the Virgin, let me tell you something," Tamara interrupted him, and Conde, feigning greater interest, lit a cigarette and settled into his chair.

"So, what happened?"

"What happened is that you're an egotistical piece of shit and you don't deserve the friends you have."

The unexpected blow stirred something within him. The words, unusual coming from Tamara's mouth, especially in the tone with which she said them, carried along an accusation that was too heavy.

"What are you talking about?"

"You see?" she said. "You don't even know what I'm talking about. You're impossible. All this silly talk about friendship, freedom, loyalty, and—"

Conde finally reacted. "Did you see that gossip, Skinny?" he ventured.

"I stopped by to see him because he wants to put together a good birthday celebration for you. Like the good friend he is . . . And he told me that you scolded Rabbit because he wants to travel, because he might stay in Miami to live with his daughter, because of what he might want or could do with his life . . . What right do you have, Mario Conde?"

He looked at the woman's eyes. They had their ever-present wet-almond shine, but they shouted out a deep cry of pain and reproach.

"I told him I'd help him out however I could . . . Rabbit is helping me look for the Virgin . . ."

"Ah, because on top of everything, you take him to that godforsaken neighborhood knowing that Rabbit can't even take candy from a baby!"

"Don't mix things up, baby . . . I told Rabbit that if Bobby pays me, I'll . . . But what in the hell did I do?"

"It's what you didn't do," she said. "You didn't tell him that his right to choose is the most important thing. Or don't you believe in that anymore? Mario, no one has to live their lives according to yours, to what you want or need. Not even me, so you know . . . Aren't you the one who spends his days talking about freedom, huh?"

He crushed the cigarette butt in the ashtray and took a sip from his mug of herbal tea—sweetened with the honey of bees who only fed on Turkish jasmine—and finally nodded.

"You and Carlos are right . . . I'm an unbearable narcissist . . . But I can't help it, Tamara. Understand me, dammit. It's that I can't stand one more loss. Dulcita and Andrés left; Candito is a saint now; Josefina is an old woman who could die at any moment, you know that . . . And I have to be happy because Rabbit also wants to get the hell out of here? No, I can't . . ."

"Well, you have to be able to, Mario. If you end up alone, if we end up alone, that's our lot. Do you think it makes me happy to have my son and my sister living in Italy? Do you think that the anti-cellulite creams they send me make up for their absence? Of course not, but I don't judge them," she said, and her damp eyes turned into tears rolling down her cheeks. "Just like they can't judge me for having stayed here, bearing all possible disasters . . . including you. That's my right. My choice."

Conde stood up, walked around the table, and placed himself behind Tamara. He leaned over and kissed the trace of her tears. And he whispered in her ear. "You'll never leave me?"

"I don't know," she said. "One never knows."

"This is very serious, Tamara. If you leave me, I'll die," he stated and kissed her lips, which tasted salty, like her tears, like the flavor of life. "Am I really a disaster?"

"You're asking me?" she said and reached out a hand to caress her lover's face. Tamara was not surprised to feel the wetness of other tears on her fingertips.

With his gaze fixed on the office's decorative fireplace, Conde sat down at the beautiful wooden desk and had no choice but to remember the ever-more-distant times, of gains and future perspectives, days and nights in which he, Tamara, Aymara, Dulcita, Carlos, Andrés, Rabbit, and other friends would get together there to study, drink soft drinks, and listen to early records by the Beatles, Creedence, and Chicago that Dr. Valdemira, a silent accomplice, had brought for his daughters from abroad. Youth and dreams made the period that was very arduous for so many people seem perfect to them. Old age and frustrations, spiritual and physical losses— Andrés, Aymara, Dulcita, and, perhaps soon, Rabbit's distance—had not made these other times—the promised future—something that could be called pleasant. And on the horizon, he was barely able to make out that final solitude of which Tamara spoke and a grim collective fate. This was their due because of historic evolution. This was the great and worst disaster: dispersion, solitude, accumulated and amassable losses, hushed dreams, pain over the present, and fear of the future.

Resolved to remove the burden of dramatic thoughts from his head, he dialed Manolo, who picked up ill-humoredly. He was exhausted, dead with exhaustion, he said. Nevertheless, he opened the conversation with a new warning to Conde to keep himself far from the case of the murder and continued with a brief discussion of what he could and could not reveal. Later, Major Palacios gave him a precise outline of the case, summarized in three words: they had nothing. Interrogations of Bobby, Ramiro the Cloak, and the Bat had not yielded any revealing information. By the looks of it, no one had heard from Yúnior Colás in more than a week, and that could be true, since they firmly resisted the pressure of those conversations, as Manolo euphemistically called their interrogations. They had learned, through the Bat, the destination of the furniture stolen and sold by Yúnior, but the buyer—despite the threat of being accused as an accomplice—couldn't add any valuable information about the later path of the young man who was killed. And neither the jewelry, nor the engravings, nor the Virgin had shown up anywhere. At the end of the day, they had released the dead man's boyfriend and friends, convinced that they'd have to call them in again and officially accuse Ramiro and Yuniesky of aiding and abetting.

Conde hung up, none too frustrated, since he was almost expecting a response like that. He closed his eyes for a few minutes and tried to free his mind of previous judgments in order to try to gain some clarity. To engage in zhi, as the Buddhists said. Many years before, he had learned the usefulness of that mental cleansing and also that the best disinfectant liquid for cerebral burdens was alcohol, the more aged and distilled, the better. He owed the lesson to a Chinese man, a Chinese man from China, like Karla Choy's grandfather, who had also arrived in Cuba full of dreams that never came to fruition. But for a long time already, Conde had strictly disciplined himself not to drink rum or anything similar at Tamara's house unless it was a party or celebration, or unless invited to do so by her. For the sake of their mutually agreed upon system of cohabitation, because of the disaster that he was, it was already rather complicated for him to show up there with alcohol diluted in his bloodstream, worse still to transport it in bottles on top of that. That was why, with very few exceptions, on the most alcoholic nights he enjoyed with Carlos and his friends, he usually ended up at his own house or, when he went too far and even met the Devil, on the sofa at Josefina's house, with a spring piercing his lung and his ass sinking into a depression. As such, he would have to limit himself to soap and water for spiritual cleansing. Or with the herbal tea sweetened by the honey of Turkish bees.

Despite his convictions as a militant agnostic, Bobby's story about the Black Virgin's powers had alarmed him more than he could have foreseen. If his philosophy made such a quality in a piece of carved wood absurd, Conde knew well how these links to mystery worked in true believers. They simply worked: and they became corporeal, real, even verifiable. According to Bobby, besides concrete miracles, the effigy's power revealed itself through prolonged and concentrated contemplation of the little wooden statue, which caused a patent sense of spiritual peace, like a chemical sedative entering your soul by way of faith, meditation, and prayer. The Catalan man who would end up being his adopted grand-father had been the one who revealed that mystical gift of the Virgin, a capacity that had been obvious to him since the first time he'd seen Her, while he was still very young, amid the other religious figures at a market in the small town in the Catalan Pyrenees where he usually went with his father to sell the charcoal that they made. Bobby had told him that, according to Josep Bonet, the discovery had occurred during the first occasion upon which he arrived in town without his father, who had died two weeks before when he fell into a ravine. Then, as if She had been waiting for him, he said, he'd discovered the Virgin in the little antiques market. He was so moved by his encounter with the image that Josep Bonet, before he was called Josep Bonet, invested all of the pesetas he'd earned by selling his coal in the acquisition of the Black Virgin. From that moment, the statue would accompany him and light his way. Bobby's grandmother, strong-willed and practical, had for years insisted that this whole yarn had seemed like a Catalan tall tale. Instead, she maintained that the impression the Virgin made on young Josep was the logical reaction of a boy who had suffered personal trauma, whose world had just lost its center with the death of his father and the arrival of war. Josep, she would say, needed a lodestar, if not a physical one, then at least a spiritual one. The thing about the boy with six fingers who was resurrected, about the sterile women who ended up pregnant, and about the cured goats, it all fell into the bag from which Josep pulled out the fanciful stories of an unredeemed believer.

Stories or no, Bobby had assured Conde, what was true was that his near-grandfather maintained a relationship with the figure that went be-yond a mere matter of physical representations of the divine or a lucky tal-isman, to the point that, sensing the moment that he was about to die, he had asked for the Virgin to be placed between his feet. Not in his hands or on his chest: between his feet, to guide him in the final step as She had guided him before . . . And he exhaled his last breath. For his part, Bobby, perhaps due to the difficult experiences of his life, full of things hidden and masked, had come back to the statue many times, just like the Cata-lan Josep, in search of consolation that, he could swear it to Conde with a hand on the Bible, the Black Virgin had granted him. Peace, serenity, spiritual rest. Later, when he got sick and was cured of his cancer, even his unbelieving grandmother let down her guard in the face of the Virgin's tangible power.

Peace, comfort, spiritual rest: eternal and universal values or aspirations. Supernatural power capable of manifesting itself in what is earthly: more complicated territory. In that roundabout way, Conde's visual memory recalled the high-contrast image of the house where Ramiro the Cloak lived and worked, with the appearance of the "settlement" of migrants from the eastern part of the island. That place, so foreign to peace or comfort, had now (Conde was beginning to feel it with the power of an impertinent and overwhelming premonition) something that didn't fit, insistent on disturbing him, a peculiar quality upon which he had not focused and that, he didn't know by what association, had arisen in his mind just as he was meditating on peace and comfort. But he concentrated: it was not that Ramiro's house was a little less miserable than the neighboring homes, that whole chaotic accumulation of desperate solutions to navigate the poverty of a people determined to better their lives, or at least the lives of their children. Because all of them, including Ramiro and Yúnior, pursued an opportunity to advance that they could not visualize happening in their places of origin, cities and towns on the eastern part of the island where survival had become so arduous that they preferred to throw themselves into an exodus of nearly biblical proportions and limited horizons. The wave was so populous that, in recent years, it had become a common cliché to say that those from Havana went to Miami or Madrid, and for each vacancy in the capital, someone from the east came to fill it. Or three people from the east. Except that, even though it was in some way a real process, the substitution was not even: the house of a Havana native or the job where one could be close to some redeeming source of income rarely ended up occupied by one of these pariahs. That was why so many of them had to work in jobs that were looked down upon by those in the capital (including the street police), and many had established themselves in very poor "settlements" that had begun and grown on the city's outskirts. There, at least, they lived, and life always (or almost always) implies hope, no matter how remote or baseless it may be. Peace, comfort, spiritual rest? Perhaps that was asking too much for those poor people . . .

But if in the tangible world, Ramiro the Cloak moved in commercial circles that were more profitable than the work as agricultural peons, bricklayers, dumpster divers that his brethren practiced . . . why was he still there, amid all that shit? Perhaps for the simple reason that within his own tribe, he could find customers to sell his deathly drugs or clandestine pieces of beef. But anyone knew that such merchandise tended to move better in more elevated spheres, with people in a condition to allow themselves such tastes and luxuries. So, if Ramiro didn't do his most profitable business there . . . perhaps all he had in them were commercial offices and warehouses: his own refuge. His cement-block house, built on the small promontory from which he oversaw the whole neighborhood, was like a feudal castle. The elevation implied—or could—power, protection, physical and even social superiority . . . Besides, behind the Cloak's dwelling began the unconquerable world of a wild farm, barren land that was too rocky or overtaken by aggressive marabú bushes with thorns like spears, a space that didn't seem to be worth much as land for cultivating crops or raising animals. The preservation of uncultivated land jibed with the fact that it had a legal and private owner. That was why, as Oriol the Saintly had told them, it was set off by spiked-wire fences that served as a warning that it was forbidden to those who sought a place to erect four walls and a roof. Nonetheless, that same rustic terrain, with its rocks, damaging bushes, and possible caves, could be no better place for the hiding of certain explosive materials, he thought. Although if, and only if, the Cloak had some kind of protection, including police protection. Because if all the paths that Conde was pursuing ended up being more or less right, couldn't other people have considered them, for example, an astute cop who knew the region and its characters? Could that be the source of the mystery?

Pushed by his premonition, Conde dialed Yoyi the Pigeon's cell phone number. He asked him if they could talk for a few minutes, and with the affirmative response, he inquired whether the Pigeon had a landline nearby on which to call him and make their communication less onerous. Between a call made on a landline that's paid for in Cuban pesos and communication via cell phones that is paid for in foreign currency, the price for the use of a mobile device was twenty-four times higher and—Yoyi told him to stop fucking around and just talk, he wasn't going to look for a landline in the restaurant where he was eating and paying the equivalent of the average Cuban worker's monthly salary for a shrimp dish and a chilled bottle of Galician Albariño.

"Suit yourself," Conde acceded. He told him a very abbreviated summary of his recent findings and asked Yoyi if he would dare accompany him the next day to Ramiro the Cloak's lair. Because, of course, Conde had a premonition. And his were usually painful and, especially, productive.

Overwhelmed by the weight of his worries and premonitions, by Tamara's reproaches, by the excitement caused by the expedition planned for the following morning, and worried, besides, about the abandonment to which he was subjecting Garbage II, Conde decided to return to his own house for the night. Tamara, who could tell from afar when her lover was telling her the truth, accepted his need to leave in good humor: she consoled him, saying that she wasn't going to abandon him in the shadows of the night, although at that moment she was glad for him to leave her alone because that way she could watch that movie about the mother who gives her all to save her sick child . . . unsuccessfully. The woman well knew that Conde rejected the consumption of that type of story, and more so if it was preceded by the note that it was inspired by a true story: in his daily and surrounding existence, he was already struggling with too many hyperrealist tragedies to then consume more voluntarily through an aesthetic medium.

Since he had enough money, he made a stop at the new cafeteria that had arisen from the remains of what had once been the kiosk where, as a boy, he'd bought guava cake bars, coconut pastries, and watermelon juice during breaks from the interminable ball games in which he invested every possible hour of his youth. He ordered four hamburgers, clarifying that they were to go, and calculated that the expense amounted to something like four or five days' salary of one of his proletarian compatriots. Why did everyone on the island spend their time, whether they had money or not, making that macabre calculation? A national obsession.

Alerted by the smell of the food, Garbage II welcomed him at the door with barks of justified reproach as well as a visible measure of happiness.

"So, you thought I had forgotten you, huh?" Conde said to the animal as he opened the door. Garbage II, wagging his tail, followed him, and he spoke to him again. "Well, now you and I are going to eat, because what Bobby gave me has left my stomach already . . . And that asparagus soup . . . Can you imagine what it's like to eat asparagus soup and a plate full of grass, huh, Garbage?"

Conde served himself a glass of the remains of the last bottle of rum he found in the kitchen. Four fingers full. He knew that all he had left was that minimal dose, sufficient for what he was thinking of doing.

"Come on, let's go," he told the dog and opened the back door. With the hamburgers in the bag and the glass in the other hand, he went up to the roof via the metal stairs and looked for the cement block where he liked to sit, on the outside edge of the house, with the street at his feet. When he was settled in, he extracted a hamburger and, bun and everything, let Garbage II take it in his jaws. Conde loved seeing that, even when he was very hungry, his dog had manners when it came to accepting food: he did so with a delicacy capable of revealing his gratitude. But there ended the formality of eating: in three bites, Garbage II made the bread and the meat patty disappear. Only when he finished his portion, always under the watch of the animal who didn't blink or move his tail, did he reach into the bag again and give Garbage II another hamburger, taking the remaining one for himself. The animal slammed back with the same speed and put on his best expression of doggy humility. Conde ate three-quarters of his second hamburger and, as a prize for good behavior, gave the rest to the dog, who somehow knew the banquet was over, since, as soon as he finished his bite, he disengaged from the man, shook his tail, and went in search of the best place to take a piss.

His mouth invaded by the taste of cheap mustard and meat of dubious origins, Conde began to cleanse his palate and his brain with his minimal drink of rum. He contemplated the clean and starry September sky. As the night advanced toward the wee hours, the heat receded and a cool breeze flowed. It was pleasant to be in that place, close to his dog and so many memories, with his full stomach at work digesting, a drink of rum in one hand and a cigarette in the other. So he refused to think about old age lying in wait, about the lost Virgin, about Rabbit's departure, about unfulfilled dreams, about the miserable lives of the inhabitants of the "settlement" and the beatings that from any and all sides would change their existence, always at the mercy of greater designs beyond History and power. No, he wouldn't get into that, nor would he engage with the increasingly stabbing desire to write. He even forbade himself from thinking of Karla Choy, with or without spandex.

Contemplating the dark stain of the fence and house rising up now on the other side of the street, his memory returned to the image of the place when it was occupied by a wooden house with French terra-cotta eaves, always painted green, the house behind which, in a kind of stable that was also made out of wood, the cages piled up in which his grandfather Rufino and two or three of his old neighborhood friends raised fighting cocks. The peculiar and unmistakable smell of the cock pen, a golden place in his memory and the most nostalgic, returned to his olfactory senses with incombustible clarity: the dust of cedarwood chips, chicken shit, wet feathers, decomposing tamarind leaves, and ripe mangos. Following the smell, as usually happened, he saw the solid image of his grandfather's face, under his straw hat, his inseparable knife at the waist, an impish smile on his lips, and a red-feathered cock in his hands. From the boy's height at five or six, grandfather Rufino always seemed like a giant to him. How old could his grandfather have been at the time? Surely more than sixty. Conde could not specify the number, although he clearly remembered his grandfather's calloused hands with their protruding joints. Through the prism of the years, the man whom he now was, on the verge of turning sixty, seemed solid, happy, because he was the owner of a cock with feathers the color of blood and old gold, and he offered his grandson advice that was so oft repeated in the years they shared on earth:

"Never play if you are not convinced that you'll win."

Why, just at that moment, did he again remember those words? A mystery of the subconscious, he told himself, to stop spinning his wheels, but it kept poking at him, because he finished his drink and felt how the alcohol wound its way down, heavy with nostalgia. He never had managed to find the kind of certainty his grandfather had possessed and, besides, he had lost every game in which, willingly or no, he had participated in his life.

His vision blurred by the dampness brought about by these ruminations, accumulated pains and guilt, when he saw him come out of the darkness and cross the piece of sidewalk in front of his house. He knew it was him, it could not be anyone but him, and knew that he had to be completely and definitively real when he saw the dirty white shine of the bags covering his feet and heard the plastic murmuring caused by their grazing of the cement. There was the invisible man!

He didn't stop to think about it. He dropped his glass and raced to try to intercept the vagabond. He went down, crossed through his house, opened the door, and, without bothering to close it behind him, went out onto the street in the direction the man had taken. Once on the sidewalk, he searched for him with his gaze, unsuccessfully. No, it could not be that he had disappeared again. Desperate, he ran to the corner, the very street where he used to play ball, and, halfway up the block, in the shadows, he made him out, thanks to the unmistakable white bags. He quickened his pace, but he had to go even faster since the man was traveling at an accelerated rhythm, as if he were in a hurry. When he managed to be just a few feet behind him, he called out to him.

"Hey, sir, sir!" he said, still fearing that his words were capable of breaking the spell and causing the disappearance of the evanescent figure.

The man turned around for a moment, without stopping. Surely, he thought that the title of "sir" didn't apply to him. When Conde was a boy and running around those same streets, he had participated, like all of his friends, in the cruel entertainment of calling the crazy and the destitute by the names that bothered them the most and thus provoking generally aggressive reactions in them. They would have nicknamed that destitute man, Conde thought, "Baggies." For that reason, he repeated his respectful call, but only when he was very close to the man.

At last, the Lord of the Bags stopped and turned around. Conde was violently shaken at that moment: light-colored eyes looked at him with an expression that did not seem like that of someone who had lost his mind. On the contrary, a certain reflection of intelligence came from the gaze beneath the dirty skin, unwashed hair, and unkempt beard. The belief that he was not dealing with a madman—at least not an everyday madman—disconcerted Conde. Who was this eccentric being? Was he sick or not? How had he arrived at that state? Where had he come from? The stench coming from the vagabond's body and clothes was not accompanied by the smell of alcohol, so Conde discarded the possibility of extreme alcoholism. Why did he look at him like that? Where was he going in such a rush? Where was he coming from?

The silence of the man with the bags didn't help, either. Conde didn't know how to approach him, since it gave him pause that he was convinced he had no right to interrogate him, no matter how much he wanted to know anything about him. Even with so much grime on him and those ridiculous bags tied to his ankles, the man, perhaps just a little older than he was, exhibited a neat, tangible dignity. It was impressive.

He finally dared to speak, and what he did was excuse himself.

"A few weeks ago, I told you to wait in front of my house, back around the corner, do you remember?"

The man looked at him more intensely and, after a few seconds, nodded his head and added:

"Perfectly."

Conde smiled, as if apologizing, and began to ask him to accompany him to his house so he could give him a pair of shoes, but then he recalled his ideas regarding the miserable donation of leftovers. And at that moment, he made his decision. He leaned back against a wall and began to remove his shoes. When he had them both in his hands, he held them out to the man with the bags and dared to say:

"I hope they fit you."

The destitute man, barely surprised, accepted the offering, and nodded his head. And, before turning around, Conde looked him in the eye again, with the latent fear of having wounded the dignity of a wretched man who usually wandered all over the neighborhood without anyone noticing his presence. He headed home, feeling the sting on the soles of his feet of every rock on the battered sidewalk. Only when he'd traveled a few feet and was searching in his pockets for the cigarette he craved like few times before in his life, did he hear the man's voice behind him.

"I think they fit me . . ."

Conde halted his retreat and turned around. The man was beginning to untie the bags from his ankles, with his back leaning against the wall to keep his balance. Conde took two steps toward him and saw his dirty, deformed, calloused feet, with their knobby toes. He again recalled his grandfather Rufino's hands.

"Try them on to see . . ."

"I've walked a lot with these feet," the man assured him in the middle of loosening the laces to facilitate putting them on. "More than anyone can imagine. I've been in many places with them, some that could seem incredible, others that I don't even remember . . . My feet are all for me. That is why I take care of them not as much as I should . . . But I do what I can. What would I do without my feet? I wouldn't be able to go back, I wouldn't be able to go back," the man repeated and finished putting on the shoes.

"Go back where?" Conde dared.

In the man's eyes, there was an unfathomable depth, as if it came from some remote region of time and reason. But it was not a demented gaze, but rather of a powerful lucidity.

"I've forgotten," the gentleman admitted, and Conde could tell he was ashamed of his inability to remember. "It's that I couldn't live remembering where I've come from. I only know that I have to return . . . That is my fate."

Conde nodded a couple of times, as if he understood something.

"Yes, my shoes fit you," he said. "I'm glad . . ." And he began to distance himself again, cursing the rocks that punctured him.

"Thank you, good sir . . . May the Virgin repay you."

Without turning around, Conde made a gesture of understanding and of goodbye, he kept walking. Had he called him "good sir"? When he reached the corner, before turning toward his house, he leaned against the telephone pole to remove the stones that were stuck on the bottom of his socks so he could walk better. From there, he looked in the direction where the man with the bags had just been. He saw only the dark of night, a disquieting emptiness that, by some strange association, made him think he was contemplating the world through the transparent patina of time.

11.

While Yoyi drove his sparkling Chevy Bel Air down the Calzada de Güines, as that part of the Central Highway was called, Conde was deep in reflection. He knew he was forcing open the door to a dangerous precipice, into which he could tumble without anything to break his fall: he was about to play another mind game without the slightest certainty of how it would end. But he didn't have the option of turning back. Something in his instincts assured him that, behind that foreboding door, there could be a path. And he was going to take the risk and try to follow it—even while wearing the boots of cardboard-like leather that he'd chosen from his limited options. Ultimately, he thought, this is what they paid him for. Was this what they paid him for? Yes, and no, he answered himself. And he avoided offering any clarification for his Solomonic response: he was entering this labyrinth out of curiosity and, especially, because he was an imbecile, the psychological component that best expressed his anachronistic sense of responsibility and what was just.

Excited by the adventure, Yoyi had stopped by to pick him up earlier than the agreed-upon time; although, with foresight, in order to maintain the physical integrity of his beloved car, he had brought along his trusted mechanic, a character that everyone in Havana knew as Paco Chevrolet. The man, who had a bullet-shaped bald head and the face of a prisoner, was considered the best specialist on the island for Yoyi's make of automobile, and Yoyi treated him like the eminence he appeared to be.

When they crossed in front of the intersection leading to Finca Vigía,

Conde took a look at the dive bar where the toilet that had once had an intimate view of Ava Gardner (escaping from the nervous exhaustion of Hemingway besieged by a literary dry spell) must still be. The association happened in his brain immediately.

"I'm feeling weird, you know? For days, I've had the urge to write," he said, as if he were commenting on the weather.

Yoyi took his eyes off the road for a moment. "Like a real urge?"

"I don't know, an urge . . . At some times more than others. Last night, something strange happened to me. Like an illumination," he said, without being able to bear to speak of his experience with the apparition to whom he gave away his shoes.

"So, get to it, man . . . Before that light goes out. Remember all the blackouts we get here . . ."

Conde nodded. If it were only that easy. He lit a cigarette and chose to change the subject. "Incidentally, yesterday I met Karla Choy," he said to Yoyi.

"And what'd you think of that specimen?"

"A cataclysm," he dropped his assessment. "Does she have a husband?"

Yoyi smiled. "I don't know if he's a husband . . . They say he's an Italian who's swimming in cash."

"An old guy?"

"What do you mean old, man? That woman has options, Conde."

"So, what do you know about her?"

Yoyi thought for a few seconds. "Very little, almost nothing . . . I don't know why but I've never done business with her. Although we know each other, of course . . . But she's a strange woman. She doesn't open up; she's mysterious; she knows she is disarming to men and she uses that to her advantage . . . Women like that are a hazard . . . In business, of course."

"Well, yesterday, she told me her life story," Conde said, with a measure of pride.

"Be careful with those Chinese fairy tales, man."

"She seems like an intelligent woman who knows what she wants," Conde opined.

"And she is, she is . . . That's what makes her more dangerous. With that face and that body, young, intelligent, manipulating . . . Too much," the Pigeon declared. "That's why I say it's best not to do business with her . . ."

"Well done," Paco Chevrolet pronounced from the back seat before returning to his usual silence.

"Do you think she could be involved in this mess with Bobby's Virgin?"

Yoyi thought for a moment. "I don't know . . . Now, there's a dead guy in the story . . . A dead guy that I don't think she killed, right?"

"Sometimes things get out of control and . . ."

"That's also true . . . Tell me, where do I need to turn?"

Conde pointed out the turnoff, and when they had left the avenue to run along the devastated streets of Lookout Heights, he began to reveal his strategy to his friend and partner.

"If Ramiro the Cloak is there, I want to speak with him alone."

"But, man, didn't you bring me along to take care of you and to see what I think of the guy and try to negotiate with him?"

"Yes," Conde admitted, "but leave the opening to me. You wait nearby, and when I call for you, you'll come and help me. I'm going to introduce you as a buyer with lots of money, who is interested in everything . . ."

"Is this the face of a trafficker?"

"A little bit, yes. Not as much as Paco, but you'll do," Conde said, as he gave the mechanic a look and Yoyi smiled, a little proud, even, so the former cop kept going. "Yoyi, can I ask you something personal that . . . ?"

The young man, without taking his eyes off the road, responded, "Shoot . . . Paco is silent as the grave. Note I trust him so much that I gave him this car with my eyes closed. And see how he keeps it . . ."

Conde chose his words. "Well . . . It's that, I wanted to know . . . Have you ever sold drugs?"

Yoyi stopped smiling. He turned toward the last navigable stretch of street, on the border of the "settlement," and focused on his partner.

"Are you seriously asking me?"

"It's just a question, my man."

"Then no, I don't get involved in that, and you know it. I am involved in a thousand other things, but that, no, not in that."

"Well done," Paco Chevrolet added.

"Out of fear or ethics?" Conde continued.

"I don't find anything appealing about drugs . . . And besides, I don't get involved with them because I'm smart . . . Let's see, Conde, you know that in this country people do five thousand kinds of business and that four thousand nine hundred ninety-nine of them are illegal, because in Cuba, whatever is not forbidden is illegal . . . And I do all of those businesses. I make a living from those businesses, but there are two . . . branches of business that are best to stay away from: politics and drugs . . . Your former colleagues and their superiors are usually bothered by those subjects, because they imply power. Real power. And when those gentlemen get angry, they are relentless. So, it's best to go down another path, since everything is lacking here and everything is needed, then someone has to facilitate obtaining things . . . And here I am, right, man? Besides, I can't stand those guys who sell drugs: they're rats . . ."

Conde held his hand out to his friend. Yoyi the Pigeon was a wise man and his economic and general good fortune were the best evidence of that wisdom.

"Let's go," Conde said and left the car.

Yoyi gave the car keys to Paco Chevrolet, who had also gotten out.

"I leave it in your hands, Paco. Remember that this is a patchy territory. Make sure that not even a fly lands on it . . ." And he caressed the automobile's hood.

Paco smiled for the first time that morning. His missing teeth hurt just to look at. "Damn, Pigeon . . . Not even the fruit flies will get close to it," the man assured him. "Go on, waltz away. Not even the butterflies!"

Owner and mechanic bumped fists. Pigeon could calmly be on his way.

They entered the "settlement" through one of the paths that led to the main artery. For the occasion, Yoyi was wearing double-soled boots, jeans, and a wide shirt, underneath which he could hide anything, including his protuberant sternum. And, of course, he had left his thick gold chain with the gold medallion at home, when he usually wore it daily. As Conde observed the reigning poverty with immutable surprise, Yoyi contemplated the scene with a critical and distant eye, as if no part of that surrounding urban and human disaster were capable of surprising him. The twenty-year difference between them had created different perceptions of the same reality. While to Conde the place's misery proved it was social, political, economic aberration, to his partner, it constituted the mere result of the country's social, political, and economic situation. *It's exactly what I expected, man,* he would have said.

When they reached the point where the path veered toward the hill where Ramiro the Cloak lived, Conde asked his friend to wait for him at that spot until he called.

"Are you sure you know what you're doing, Conde?" Yoyi insisted. "The other day, no one knew Raydel had been killed and Candito and Rabbit were with you."

"And today Ramiro knows the police are marinating him and that I'm here with you. This guy knows everything . . . Let me do it my way. Remember, I'm old but I'm not yet an old fart."

"Okay. But take this with you in case something comes up . . ." Yoyi held out a compact cell phone to him.

"I don't know what to do with that, buddy," Conde protested.

"Don't fuck around, man. How can a Cuban in 2014 not know how to operate a cell phone, not have access to the internet, and, once in a while with his salary, not buy himself a trip to London and stay in a good hotel so he can understand up close how decadent British reality works?"

"What in the hell are you talking about?" Conde was looking at him as if he'd gone mad. A cell phone was a luxury (ever since the government had finally authorized their possession) of which he and millions like him could not allow themselves the purchase or the use given the Cuban prices and rates; the internet only seemed to work on national television (which Conde never watched, since he didn't even have a TV in his house and he abused himself enough already with alcohol to then withstand such an attack on his neurons); and, to all of them, London was the foggy place where Jack the Ripper and Sherlock Holmes ran around and where there was a street with a zebra crossing which the Beatles had walked.

"I'm talking about how far we've come, and you haven't even found out, man. I read it in a magazine the other day . . . You don't make any progress, Conde, no progress! You're stuck! Look, take it. If you need it, you lift the lid, press this key, and then these two, and I'll respond on mine." And Yoyi showed him his touch-tone device of the latest make and generation.

Grudgingly, Conde put the gadget in his shirt pocket, adjusted his shades, and began his ascent toward the place where he had met the Cloak two days before. When he arrived at the ramshackle gate that led to the property, he turned around, confirmed that his colleague was still in sight, and entered. He stepped across the few feet of flattened, dry earth separating the gate from the little house. Once he was at the door, he called out to Ramiro the Cloak and identified himself. A few seconds later, a voice called out, "Hang on . . ."

Conde took out a cigarette and lit it. Down the hill, Yoyi had moved so as not to let him out of sight, and, a couple of times, he showed him his raised thumb and, laughing, motioned like the police in the movies before they began a sting operation. A few minutes later, Ramiro opened the rotting wood door and gestured to Conde to come inside, closing it again behind him.

"What's up with you now? They already found Yúnior, so stop looking for him," the Cloak said. "That business is fucked. I've got the police on top of me . . . And not just any police . . . Even State Security is involved in this!"

"State Security?" Conde was puzzled.

"What other Security do you know, *pipo*?"

"No, this doesn't have anything to do with State Security . . ."

"Suit yourself . . . Why don't you just disappear already?"

Conde asked himself what Manolo could have done to make the Cloak think things were even more serious than they already were, and he feigned not understanding the invitation to evaporate. As if he had time to spare, he looked around: inside the large room, with its sanded cement floor, Conde saw a refrigerator, two working fans, a muted television set, a bed, and a square table with four chairs. No bathroom or kitchen. He supposed that if the Cloak ate there, it was because someone brought him prepared food, and that he took care of his personal business elsewhere, perhaps in some neighboring house or on the rocky terrain outside, visible from the room's back window and through which a powerful, almost blinding reflection of sunlight was entering. On the table, he saw several mugs and a thermos that, he assumed, would contain coffee. In a corner there were several empty rum bottles. And on a small shelf, some type of lidded wooden receptacle, colored a bright blue, inside which he supposed there must be some kind of religious artifact, perhaps even the bones of a Chinese or Jewish person. But Ramiro did not display any ritual necklaces or bracelets, although close to his shoulder, Conde discovered on him the discrete lines of two scars: that of the "*rayados*" in the Palo Monte religion. In the air, like a winnowing presence, floated a peculiar odor, sweetish, like blond-tobacco cigarettes . . . American cigarettes, he thought.

"Bobby told me that they killed your cousin with gusto, Ramiro," Conde said and settled into one of the chairs without having asked permission to do so.

"Yes, and because of that old faggot, they came after me and held me for four hours while they questioned me and fucked up my business life. Now I have to lay lower than whale shit . . . They even forced me to identify the body!"

"Bobby didn't say anything about you," Conde lied. "It could have been your partner the Bat."

"It wasn't the Bat . . . That one knows what he can and can't say," Ramiro assured him. "But now it's all the same . . . Because I didn't have anything to do with what happened to Yúnior . . . Well, come on, tell me, I'm not in the mood for you today. What the hell is going on with you now? I already told you, there's no business to do . . ."

Conde got up and went over to the window to throw his cigarette butt outside. The bare land of the neighboring lot shimmered under the sun.

"What's going on with me is that Yúnior's body showed up, but no trace of the Virgin or the jewelry . . ."

"Because whoever did away with Yúnior took off with it, right?"

"That's a possibility . . . Well, I'm not sure."

"Your problem . . . Look, Yúnior didn't say anything to me about that operation or about any jewelry. What I do know is that he was thinking of getting the hell out of here. But he said that every day, especially since he'd had to race out of Santiago. He was kind of an idiot, you know? Anyway, he had goals and was thinking that in Miami, he would live like a prince because he had a big dick and a pretty face . . . They completely disfigured him!"

Conde took his time.

"Sit down, Ramiro, I have to tell you something that greatly concerns you . . ."

The young man looked at this gate-crasher who was ordering him around in his own house. His initial inclination was to act affronted, but something stopped him and Conde knew at that moment that he had hit the target: Ramiro was scared. The *mulato* drew back a chair, to give himself some space, and sat down, with his forearms on his knees and his body leaning toward the other man.

"I already told you that I was once a cop and no longer am," Conde began. "But I know something about the way stories like the one your cousin Yúnior got involved in go . . . If the person who killed him was the same one who was going to get him out of the country, and if that guy took what Yúnior had, the story ends there and the deal is fucked . . . Now, if they killed Yúnior because of what he stole and didn't get the things they were looking for, things that include something that must be worth a lot, at least to a few people, then the story isn't over . . ." Ramiro, who had initially listened with indifference, became slowly absorbed by his visitor's reasoning. He looked away to find a cigarette, which he placed between his lips without lighting. It was black tobacco, like the ones Conde was smoking. *He's thinking*, Conde concluded, and continued his speech. "And the person or persons who killed your relative are very fucked-up people, truly fucked-up. They tortured him, they beat him with everything and with gusto . . . Well, you saw him . . . They disfigured him . . . Why? I think they did it because Yúnior didn't have what they wanted, and they tried to get out of him where he had hidden everything . . . Don't you think?" Ramiro didn't react, Conde sighed. "So now we don't know if Yúnior said anything or not." Conde paused and launched his best missile: "Nor do we know if he told them where *you* and he hid those things . . ."

Ramiro dropped his cigarette without lighting it and protested at last, exasperated.

"*Oye, oye*, what in the hell are you saying? Why does everyone think that I know . . . ?"

Conde made the cautionary gesture of pointing between the other man's eyebrows with his extended finger. The motion was effective, since the Cloak immediately stopped.

"Ramiro, to do what you do and still be on the streets, you can't be an idiot. You know a lot . . . But the cop or cops who protect you so that you can do your business here in the neighborhood are not going to get involved in this mess. There's a dead body involved . . . And now even State Security . . . So, keep listening to me and think, because it behooves you: I would guess that Yúnior didn't talk and that those guys lost control of things and killed him before they meant to. They are bad guys, but they're not professionals . . . Although you know well that there is something in this whole robbery that is worth so much that it could warrant the risk of killing someone if necessary. And you also know something else or you should learn it right now . . . If it's worth it, the person who kills one guy, can kill two . . ."

Ramiro picked up his cigarette and finally lit it. Conde felt the desire to imitate him but stopped himself.

"What could be worth so much, Ramiro? Whatever it is, I'm interested in it, I could buy it . . . Outside here, I have a guy with big bucks, and he's desperate to do a deal."

The *mulato* smoked and looked out the window, then back at Conde, and lowered his voice.

"You're nuts, *viejo*! Do a deal while the fire is raging? I don't know if there were diamond bracelets or not . . . What I do know is that the Virgin is worth a boatload of dough . . ."

"A wooden Virgin of Regla?" Conde was playing his cards and embracing the other man's style: he also lowered his voice. "Not even my neighborhood priest would believe that . . ."

"It's worth millions . . ."

"What are you talking about, Ramiro?" The former cop finally felt like he was on promising ground.

"A friend of Yúnior's, one who spends his time screwing rich old men and women who he finds on the internet. He says that the Virgin comes from Spain and is worth millions . . ."

"Everyone knows she comes from Spain . . . But that she's worth millions . . ."

Ramiro got agitated and recovered his tone. "That's what Yúnior said, *viejo*! That the Virgin was on the internet!"

Conde thought a moment, looking for the best way to move forward. "Who is this friend of Yúnior's?"

"I don't know him. He's a gigolo, he screws old American ladies . . . and men, too, if they pay him . . . They call him Platero, because he's hung like a donkey."

"So, where does he live?"

"I don't know that, either. I think around el Cerro. But I'm not sure . . . It doesn't matter."

"So Yúnior offered the Virgin up for sale after finding out that she was worth a lot of money?"

"I already told the police that . . . He told me that he was going to see someone who could find him a buyer for the things that were worth the most money. But he didn't tell me who. And then he got lost . . . I didn't see him again . . . I thought he had screwed me over . . . He loved screwing people over . . . And it turns out he wasn't showing up because they had eaten him alive . . ."

Ramiro threw his cigarette butt out the back window. Conde followed the perfect parabola of what remained of the cigarette with his gaze, keeping his focus on the visible scene of rocky terrain, populated by the wild bushes of marabú. So Yúnior had spoken with someone who could buy the Virgin, someone who had to be worth a lot of money. Someone from the guild? Conde noted that detail and decided to go in for the kill, although he felt that in that whole imbroglio of deceptions and deals, there was still an essential detail missing. But he didn't have time to think, he just had to put on the pressure.

"Ramiro, I know that I look like a world-class idiot . . . But you must have noticed that I'm not such an idiot, right? You're telling me some truths, as well as some lies. And sooner or later, I'm going to prove it and figure out what's what . . . So, don't lay it on so thick, buddy . . . This is a matter of earning money . . . I know you know where the Virgin is . . ."

"What the hell?!?" Ramiro protested. "Stop fucking around and disappear already. I already said more than I should have. Come on, come on, get going!"

Conde stopped to look at the young man before moving.

"Fine," he said and stood up. "But let me say something else, the most important thing . . . The ones who killed Yúnior must also know that the Virgin is what's worth a lot . . . And they're hell-bent on finding that statue, and they know that you and Yúnior were like two peas in a pod. They could think as I did . . . That over there, next door"—Conde pointed at the fallow land—"you could have hidden Her . . . And all they have to do is go look for Her because you—"

Conde noticed a fleeting change in the lighting in the room and the spark of stupor on Ramiro's face. A whiff of American cigarettes and, immediately, a violent commotion. Then all the lights went out.

On the third or fourth slap, Conde cried out and opened his eyes, recognized Yoyi, and closed his lids again. His head ached with a beating, explosive intensity and the smell of vomit assaulted his senses. More out of instinct than any ability to think, he put his hand at the base of his skull. Delicately, with fear, he touched the burning, sticky bump he now had there.

"Wake up, man, come on, come on . . . What in the hell happened here? What in the hell happened?" Yoyi was pleading, his voice agitated, and Conde made a gesture, asking for a minute. His friend granted him just a few seconds and again asked, "Can you get up and walk!? Tell me, Conde, dammit!"

With a gesture, he again asked for calm, until he spoke at last, "I don't know, I'm dizzy and it hurts a lot, so much! They broke my head open! I'm bloody, look at this! What happened?"

"That's what I'm asking you! How the hell am I supposed to know what happened, *viejo*? You're the one who was here . . . Look at what they did to this guy, look at what they did to him!"

He forced his eyes to open, to react, to try to understand. "To Ramiro?"

"I don't know, to this guy they fucked up . . . Look at this, I think you can see his guts, man, you can see his guts. What a fuck of a lot of blood . . ." Yoyi said, as alarmed and freaked-out as Conde had ever seen him.

He sat up, leaning on an elbow, and looked around. The images came to him in double, and to his right, beyond the tables, near the windows where the sun streamed in, he managed to see Ramiro and his double, lying on the floor, with his faces—the same face—with a grimace and his eyes clearer and vaguer, no longer with their satanic brilliance, and his abdomens bathed in blood, a lot of dark blood.

Conde let himself fall to the ground again and lowered his eyelids once more.

"Call Manolo, Yoyi," he told his friend, and, as if he were returning from a trip, he touched his shirt pocket. "The cell phone! They took the cell phone you gave me, Yoyi! Don't touch anything. Come on, dammit, call Manolo."

"Are you sure?" Yoyi asked. "This one is done for, and if we leave . . . I want to get out of here, man, there's a dead guy, they ripped his guts out," he insisted, getting more and more agitated. "I don't want to have anything to do with this, man."

"Get a hold of yourself, buddy . . . Call Manolo, dammit, call him already. Tell him they killed the Cloak and that they almost fucked me up . . . And then give me some water . . . Better still, rum. And if you find it, have a drink yourself, too, and see if you calm down . . ."

From his position, Conde could see his young friend turn and vomit any of the remaining liquid he still had inside of him.

He knew all the protocols, so he didn't let Yoyi remove two of the chairs from the Cloak's shack to sit on while they waited outside the crime scene for the police. They got as comfortable as they could beneath a mango tree, up against its dried-out trunk, since he and his partner both needed to rest: Conde, because of the wound that had stopped bleeding but was still beating; and the young man due to nerves that caused him to repeat

several times that it was the first time he'd encountered a dead man . . .
And what a dead man.

Beneath the tree's tired shade, they kept their silence until the first
patrol car arrived, manned by area police. Those in uniform tried to
seem professional, but it was obvious that they were just neighborhood
agents, if anything, good for breaking up fights and the pursuit of mi-
nor criminals. And they seemed very annoyed to have been called to a
place that they normally tried not to enter. Behind them came people from
the "settlement," who viewed the arrival of the police force, with whom
they tended to have a tense and problematic relationship, with a mixture
of curiosity, animosity, and fear. *What happened?* was the question running through the entire neighborhood. Twenty minutes later, two 4x4s
and the forensics van brought specialized units led by Lieutenant Miguel
Duque and the already-aged medical examiner Flor de Muerto, a veteran
specialist from Conde's days with the police.

After observing the scene, and before the technicians got down to
work, Lieutenant Duque approached Conde and Yoyi to listen to their
version of what had happened, while the medical examiner cleaned the
wound on the back of Conde's head.

"That's quite a blow," Flor de Muerto proclaimed.

"Will it require stitches?" He was asking because medical procedures
terrified him. He was the guy who turned his face when they took blood
from him for lab work.

"I can stitch you up a little . . . To be safe, but it won't be pretty . . .
But you have thick skin, Conde . . . Let's see, how many fingers am I showing you?" The medical examiner made a V with his fingers in front of the
wounded man's eyes.

"Eight?" Conde asked.

"You're all set," the doctor proclaimed. "I cleaned up the wound for
you. Sit and take a pain reliever and don't have sexual relations for forty
days . . ."

"And how do we break the news to your wife?"

"I'll do what I can. She's understanding . . ."

"Thanks, friend, you're always so . . . Damn, Flor de Muerto, do you
remember that time that Major Rangel caught you—"

"Can we talk?" Duque interrupted, exasperated and resolved to put an end to the former colleagues' camaraderie and nostalgia.

Miguel Duque was a light-skinned *mulato* with amphibian eyes and a bearing that was excessively military. He had a serious, commanding voice, and, despite having been born in the province of Guantánamo, he pronounced all of his letters and syllables with the precision of a newsman . . . Born in Guantánamo. Conde well knew that kind of policeman who was capable of fully enjoying the state of being a policeman twenty-four hours a day. Some could even be good policemen, and the fame of his efficiency preceded Duque who came from the eastern extreme of the island. A Palestinian, like the deceased Yúnior and Ramiro.

Conde told him what little he knew: he had come to speak with Ramiro about the death of his cousin Yúnior Colás and of the possible fate of the objects they had stolen from the house of Roberto Roque Rosell. Conde was doing it because Roque was his friend. While he was speaking with Ramiro, he had received a blow to the head (he pointed at the site of the wound without touching it) and did not see the attacker. Perhaps that was why he was still alive. He had awoken when his friend Jorge Casamayor Riquelmes, who had remained about three hundred feet from the house, went to see what was happening, since Conde had not come out or answered the cell phone that, incidentally, had been stolen from him when he was unconscious. It was the first time he had a cell phone all to himself and, before using it, it had been stolen from him. That was why he had never wanted a cell phone, look what happens when . . . Duque muttered his protests and Conde finished his story: the rest of what had happened was what could be seen in the large room of the now-deceased Ramiro Gómez, alias the Cloak.

Duque was listening and taking notes, without interrupting the story. He knew that, despite his premeditated inquiries, the former lieutenant would make the kind of summary a policeman could put together, so, for now, Conde would only tell him what he was interested in telling him. The officer turned toward the doctor and the two technicians who were waiting by the front door and ordered them to proceed.

Duque looked at Conde with more intensity. Conde also knew those looks. "So, do I have to believe what you told me?"

Conde shrugged his shoulders. "I don't think you have any choice, Lieutenant. Even the secretary-general of the United Nations, that Chinese guy who doesn't even know where he's standing, knows that I didn't kill that man."

"Korean."

"I get them all confused . . ."

Duque nodded. He took a deep breath. "In any event, we're going to fingerprint both of you. And you should give me your passports," the officer added.

"If you find mine, please take care of it for me. I was thinking of making a trip to Alaska . . ."

The policeman furrowed his brow. Was he putting him on? "Remember that I am an officer and"—Duque pointed a finger at Conde and then said something that the others didn't manage to hear—"What did Ramiro tell you about the stolen objects?"

"He didn't know anything about them. You and your guys already know that Ramiro didn't know that his cousin had been killed until you called him yesterday. I don't think this kid had anything to do with Raydel's death. At least not directly."

"So, did you suspect that Ramiro knew something about those objects?"

"I assumed so, that was all. I was pressuring him a little . . ."

"Did it seem like Ramiro was nervous, that he was afraid, that he was waiting for someone?"

Conde thought before answering. It was a good string of questions. So, he decided that police intervention was necessary and, besides, could be useful to him. A person, or more than one person, capable of killing two guys and of doing so in the way that they had were true dangers to society. And if the police work could even serve to prevent their making off with the stolen objects and disappearing from the country on a speedboat, then it would be better for everyone, even for him and Bobby.

"I thought he was a little nervous because you had interrogated him yesterday . . . Now I think that before I arrived, it's possible that Ramiro had a visitor . . . When I entered here, I got a whiff of blond tobacco and he smoked black tobacco . . . He also took a while to let me in, perhaps . . . On the table, there were two cups of coffee, and I think that when we left, they weren't there . . . What I now think is that Ramiro was hiding what Yúnior stole, at least a part of it. And, I have a hunch that that was or is in the terrain that starts on the other side of the fence."

"A hunch?" Lieutenant Duque wanted to clarify.

"Do you have something against hunches?"

"I don't like them," the officer admitted and added, "I'm a Marxist."

Now it was Conde who imbued his gaze at Duque with more intensity. A real Marxist, alive and healthy?

"Well look at that," Conde said. "I'm a dialectic. Of the Heracleitus school, of course . . . That's why I believe in telepathy."

Duque tried to regain his authority, on the verge of being beaten down following the untimely announcement of his philosophical militancy. "Forget that . . . Why are you so sure that what happened in there had something to do with the theft from Roberto Roque? As far as we know, Yúnior Colás had other outstanding debts, and Ramiro surely had some out there, too."

"You're right, Lieutenant . . . But my hunch tells me that the theft was just the tip of the iceberg . . . So, Marxists don't like hunches; what about subjective conditions?" Conde asked, willing to poke the wound just as the police were shooing away the curious in order to allow in an unmarked car, from which Major Manuel Palacios emerged. Conde thought he saw smoke emerging from his former subordinate's ears and decided to put a lid on his sarcasm.

Duque put away his notepad and went out to meet his superior. He greeted him with a precise military movement. For three or four minutes, the two officers spoke. From where he was, Conde watched them and reminded Yoyi of his part in the script: all he knew was that Conde was taking a long time, so he came to get him. Yoyi listened, without saying a word.

The lieutenant went toward Ramiro's house, gestured at the forensic examiner to follow him, and they both entered the large room, prepared to join the examination of the sites and the body. For his part, Manolo walked very slowly as he approached Conde and Yoyi. He did not shake their hands.

"What a shitty place. What the hell is this? My car almost fell apart trying to get up here . . . How do you feel?" the policeman asked his former colleague.

"This one isn't going to kill me . . . It only hurts when I take a dump . . . Or when I see your face . . ."

Manolo walked around him to look at the wound, returned to his position facing Conde and looked at him seriously. "Well, it must hurt a lot because you really turned this to shit . . . What in the hell did I tell you very clearly about this case? When are you going to fucking understand that you are not a policeman anymore, or anything close to it? Huh, huh? Are you ever going to . . ."

Conde was shuffling his feet during Manolo's barrage of questions and insults. Next to him, Yoyi was looking at his nails, to see if some speck of dirt had soiled them.

Conde sighed at last. "Manolo, don't be foulmouthed . . ."

Major Palacios pointed a finger at his former colleague and his eyes crossed. He was on the verge of exploding when the other man made a gesture to stop him.

"Okay, okay . . . You're right, right as anything. I'm an idiot who sticks his nose where it doesn't belong and can screw up police work and—"

"So why did you do it then, *viejo*?"

"Because I can't help it, Manolo. You know, buddy, that I can't help it," Conde confessed to him. "It's that I had a hunch . . . And now I have two . . ."

"Are you going to go on with that story about your hunches? Look, I'm—"

"Are you also a Marxist?"

"What in the hell—"

"Can I speak?" Yoyi interrupted. He looked more together. His face had recovered its color and his wise gaze.

"What happened, Yoyi?" Manolo asked. "Do you also have a hunch?"

The young man paused, shook his head no, and finally spoke.

"Manolo . . . The guys who killed *that one*"—he pointed toward the deceased Ramiro's room as if it were a considerable distance away—"and who clocked *this one* on the head took a cell phone that I lent *this one* . . . I already told *that one*, the *mulato* officer who went into the house and . . . Can't you track the phone? I mean . . . like on the American TV shows?"

Manolo looked at Yoyi, then at Conde, and turned around to yell: "Lieutenant Duque!"

It was painful and comforting. Devastating and educational. That disaster also—or above all—was life. That was why whenever he had time to spare, he carried out this kind of pilgrimage with which he paid homage to friendship and the past, as he simultaneously completed a personal and nontransferable mission. And he never ceased to carry it out when he had problems. He no longer obtained practical solutions to his conflicts, of any kind, or even advice or scolding. Nor did he expect miracles. On the contrary, he felt a tangible relief running through his body and spirit when he engaged in this sort of confessional sacrament with which he mitigated his debt of gratitude and love for the man who observed him in silence, with barely any visible expression. Even thus, he knew, Mario Conde knew, that the man was listening to him, processing the information he was receiving, and it felt electrifying to have the slim but constant possibility of being the confidant of somebody who loved him, who needed him, and who, perhaps, understood him.

It had been five years already since the former police commissioner Antonio Rangel had suffered a violent stroke that robbed him of nearly all his speech and mobility. Until shortly before the treacherous attack by his own body, Old Rangel, long retired, had seemed ten years younger than the eighty he had actually accumulated. He even still played some sports—his body remained as erect and muscular as it was in the days when he wore his officer's uniform, always ironed, without a speck of dirt. Immediately following the stroke, when Rangel's life was hanging by a thread for several days, Mario Conde insisted to the former major's wife and recently arrived daughters (they resided in Europe) that he be in charge of the sick man's overnight care, and he took over a plastic chair that he placed alongside his friend's bed. He spent each night telling him stories, in the hopes of helping him return to life or at least make the passage to death less sorrowful. The anecdote he repeated the most times, because he knew how much Rangel liked it, was the one about the day he stole a Montecristo No. 5 from him, to try to prove the culpability of a suspect. And the words the major spat at him for this unforgivable provocation: a Montecristo No. 5 cigar, played with as if it were a mere paper garland!

Later, when the man's life was no longer in danger but his body was left devastated, Old Rangel was sent home and, whenever possible, his former subordinate and friend visited him and tried to make him a participant in some life pleasure. Conde, who always smoked cigarettes, took a cigar along with him on each of his pilgrimages and lit it so that Rangel could inhale that smoke he had enjoyed so much when he was a whole man and not the human wreck he was now that, after years of so much exercise and playing sports, his body refused to release his soul and allow him to rest in peace. Because a man like Antonio Rangel didn't deserve that miserable fate.

Now, as with each possible opportunity, Conde pushed the wheelchair in which the old man vegetated and took him out to the porch of his house. From there, one could see the garden that Rangel had taken care of from his premature retirement until his sudden physical decline, the pleasant street of the Bahía neighborhood with a smattering of passersby, and a sky (that on that September afternoon was cloud-free) of an immaculate blue. It was a nearly idyllic world, diametrically opposed (so completely diametrically opposed) to the "settlement" where that very morning Mario Conde and Death had been.

After Rangel swallowed the painkillers that his wife, María Luisa, offered him and drank her recently brewed coffee, Conde lit the cigar he'd bought on the way and bathed his former boss in smoke.

"This cheap cigar is a piece of shit, but it tastes good," he proclaimed. "It's not one of those Montecristos or Cohibas or Rey del Mundos that you liked, but it's not bad, I swear it's not," he commented and took another puff on the thick cigar, then exhaled more perfumed smoke. "Would you like some?"

From his wheelchair, Rangel was watching his former and most unruly disciple, and greedily breathed in the cigar's smoke, moving his eyelids, accepting, enjoying . . . *What a disaster*, Conde thought. *What a shitty life*, he knew Antonio Rangel must be thinking. And, almost certainly, appreciating his former subordinate's incombustible loyalty, while simultaneously lamenting that his friend could not help him with what he really needed most: ending everything.

"The problem is that my hunch feels real, *viejo*," he said after telling Rangel about the mess in which he was involved and showing him the protuberance on the back of his head and describing the murder scene of Ramiro the Cloak and even his stop at police headquarters to have his fingerprints taken and for the inspections of his and Yoyi's fingernails. "The investigators say that someone was walking around that vacant field. The man left footprints, but they don't know if he found anything . . . But if he knew where what he was looking for was, then he nearly certainly took it and flew the coop, so Manolo says it doesn't make much sense to keep looking, and I'm of the same opinion . . . And that somebody who took it is almost probably the murderer, of course, because if he isn't, then who the hell is it going to be? This seems to leave aside the possibility of a settling of accounts and focuses everything on the robbery . . . Now the hope is that the shitty cell phone they stole from me helps them track down the guy . . . Although I don't think he would be stupid enough to start using it. Do you know how you find a cell phone if no calls are made? Because I don't have the foggiest idea, and I imagine that you don't, either. My friend Yoyi says that in the American movies it's so easy . . . And if they find this character, I don't think that the son of a bitch Manolo will call me to tell me. That lazy bastard is raging at me. Those madmen asked for my passport. My passport! Look, Manolo acted just like you used to when I did some outrageous thing, remember?"

For ten years, Antonio Rangel had held the responsibility of being Conde's supervisor in the Criminal Investigation Unit. Before that, he had been the one who'd discovered the potential as an investigator of a young, unorthodox, and irreverent policeman who was allergic to weapons and violence, who read too much, aspired to write, and said he was fueled by his gut feelings, prejudgments, and premonitions: a compendium of what a policeman could not be. And, in essence, Rangel had not been mistaken. Throughout those years, always tense when it came to work, both men had learned that there existed between them deeper affinities, and they became friends. But the friendship born and nurtured did not represent any authoritative weakness on the part of the major, who had been on the verge of putting Conde on leave several times, and even, on one occasion, had cut back his responsibilities and returned him to the records pit from which he had previously extracted him once he'd noticed his powers of deduction. Ten years after their initial encounter, when Rangel was found guilty of ignoring certain acts of corruption by his subordinates, the least drastic solution was to make him take an early retirement and send him home. In the face of what he considered an injustice, Conde's response in solidarity had been to leave the police as well, something he had been planning to do for some time already.

Following that disaster, Rangel had chewed on his frustration, without allowing himself the additional humiliation of lowering himself to protest the arbitrariness to which he'd been subjected. He punished himself so diligently that in the end, he managed the rebellion of a vein within his skull. It had been a difficult time, in which the former major always looked more like a bird who'd fallen from the nest, since his demotion coincided with the unleashing of the Crisis, throughout which, as on more than one occasion the old man's wife had confessed to Conde, they had survived (in truth, they still did) thanks to the financial help provided by their two daughters, who lived outside Cuba: because the official police pension would not have been enough to get through even half the month. Less still when the man's physical decline occurred and he needed special attention to keep him alive.

At one point, sometime after his onerous exit from the police, Rangel had confided his frustrations to Conde:

"Sometimes I think I really should have let myself be bought. Now I might have something to get by on and I wouldn't be dependent on what my daughters send me . . . Living on charity, even when it's from your own family, is humiliating. At least, for me, it's humiliating. And I don't want to ask anyone any favors to get me a job as an assistant manager or head of supplies for the hotel for foreigners or any of that crap soldiers and old policemen do to try to make some extra cash and feel like they can keep ordering others around . . . They fucked up my life; I am an untouchable. The only son of a bitch who comes to this house is you, Mario Conde . . . What a disaster . . . And you know what? I haven't hung myself from one of those trees in the yard because I know that I would also kill María Luisa and make my daughters suffer . . . That's why I'm still alive, but enraged each day, from morning to night . . . That rage and humiliation are going to be the death of me, Conde . . ."

Those words, said by a man who had always seemed to be made of stainless steel, returned to Conde's mind on each visit he made from Rangel's initial decline until his nearly vegetative state. And he knew that the greatest desire of the best head of police he'd ever known was to be able to die as soon as possible. But nature punished him by keeping him in his shitty life.

"What worries me, *viejo*, is that because of the Virgin or whatever it is that is worth so much or that someone believes is worth so much, they've already killed two people. Because that's how things are these days: they'll kill anyone over anything . . . Or nothing. To give you an idea of what it's like out there, listen to the story . . . Manolo told me a few days ago that three guys had killed a kid just to look tough. You heard right. They challenged each other to see who would knife him, and the poor kid who was just walking by, not bothering anyone, they knifed him so repeatedly that they killed him: they perforated his liver and his lungs . . . twenty-two times. Just to play, to show off, because every one of those characters had a knife on him and they were drunk and bored. That's what we've come to, *viejo*. So be happy you are no longer a policeman, as I am happy, because now, it's a jungle out there. And it's getting worse and worse . . . You cannot imagine the state of things. This same neighborhood of Easterners where they gave me this knock to the head, you've never seen anything like it, how those people live, amid shit and violence, subsisting on whatever they come up with. Yes, *viejo*, that's what we've come to . . . And it's happening right in Havana and all over the country; don't think this is geographic determinism. No, no . . . Dammit, my cigar went out!"

He lit the cigar again, which he had forgotten as he was relating his sorrows of a former policeman. When he saw that it was properly lit, he looked out toward the street.

"I wish you could say something to me, *viejo*. At least to tell me if I'm wrong. Like you used to do . . ."

Conde registered movement with his peripheral vision. What had it been? He looked at Rangel, because the fluttering seemed to have come from him, and then he saw that the old man was lightly lifting his pointer finger. Conde looked at his hand, then at the sick man's eyes.

"Did you move your finger because you wanted to move it?"

Conde waited. Rangel moved his finger.

"Well . . ." He hesitated, thinking. "Look, *viejo*, if the answer is that you moved your finger because you wanted to move it, lift it twice, okay?"

He waited again, concentrating on Rangel's pointer finger which finally rose once. And, a second later, he repeated the motion.

"Well, damn, this is great," Conde rejoiced and thought he saw a flash of intelligence cross his former boss's face. "How long have you been able to do that?"

Conde waited for a response that didn't come.

"Well, that doesn't matter . . . Now tell me something, do you think I'm a hopeless imbecile?"

Rangel lifted his finger, and moved again.

"So that's what you think of me . . . Well, you always thought it . . . But, tell me, do you also think that among what they stole from Bobby's house, there's really something worth a lot?"

Conde remained expectant. One, two movements of the finger.

"And what's worth a lot is the jewelry, right?"

More waiting: Rangel's hand remained at rest.

"So then, *viejo*, it's really the Virgin?"

Conde leaned a little closer toward the old man. And he saw him move his finger twice.

"The Virgin! Because She has something inside, diamonds, I don't know what?"

The old man's hand remained static, as if dead.

"Because of the Virgin Herself?"

Twice, the finger confirmed, perhaps with more precise strength.

"Because She has powers, or someone believes that She does?"

Rangel lifted his finger three times.

Conde was about to scratch his head, but stopped himself. Two times was yes. Three times?

"Yes and no?" he hazarded a guess.

Two motions of the finger.

"Aha . . . So then . . . Because She is an antique?"

Rangel confirmed again.

"And because She is an antique and the internet says She's worth a lot of money, as the Cloak told me?"

Another confirmation.

"So, they're killing people for an antique Virgin who is worth a lot of money. And because She has powers?"

Rangel controlled his fingers.

"Because someone believes in those powers, like Bobby?"

The former major moved his finger twice more. Conde knew it, Rangel was still the best boss the Criminal Investigation Unit had ever or would ever have. And at that moment, he discovered that his deathly quality cigar had gone out again. Since he had money on him, how in the hell had it not occurred to him to buy a Montecristo so he could gift its aroma to old Antonio Rangel?

"Is this cigar a national disgrace?"

Two movements of the finger. Said and confirmed: a disgrace.

Since the headache had diminished but not disappeared, Conde decided to take refuge in a safe place. But, before going to Tamara's house, he stopped by his own and devoted some time to making dinner for Garbage II: a sort of risotto loaded with fairly bad chicken picadillo to which he added some strips of Cuban pork shoulder to improve the taste. And a pinch of salt, just like Garbage II, who loathed flavorless food, liked it. Watching his dog eat, Conde thought about the possibility of taking him with him during his stays at Tamara's house; it caused him pain and shame to leave him alone, now that that whirlwind Garbage II had become old and dependent. *Old age and neglect surround me*, he thought. *What if I take him to Carlos's house?*

When Tamara saw him arrive with his new look, she put a hand over her mouth. With the gesture, Conde motioned at her to remain calm and went to the guest bathroom mirror and looked at himself for the first time since he'd received the knock to the head. What little hair he had left looked like a matted glop, and his face like a field after a battle. The shirt, two sizes larger than his own, made him look like a scarecrow.

"María Luisa, Rangel's wife, lent me the shirt . . . Mine was covered in blood," he said as if he had just returned from the dead. "I have to take a shower, come with me and I'll explain."

Tamara followed him to the master bathroom and watched him undress and enter the shower. Only when he'd allowed the water to run over his head and body and drain darkly did Conde begin to narrate his peripatetic day. She asked him some questions and went out to get him the other set of clean clothes that he strategically kept at her house. When she went out, she took the dirty clothing with her, holding it by the tips of her fingers, as if it were infectious material.

Naked, Conde sat on top of the toilet and Tamara delicately dried his head. Then, she examined his wound.

"It's not big . . . But any scalp wound causes a lot of bleeding."

"They almost killed me, Tamara . . . They hit me so hard. And I was bleeding and bleeding," Conde exaggerated. "Dry my back, please, everything hurts."

The woman agreed and with similar care went on drying the man's skin until, standing in front of him again, she saw Conde's physical response.

"Really?"

"You are my Viagra . . ."

"Well forget about doing the tango . . . There's nothing for you today. You have to rest."

"The warrior's rest," Conde admitted, watching himself quickly and inexorably go flaccid as Tamara approached him with a bottle of hydrogen peroxide in her hands. While she treated him, he yelled as if being tortured.

They ate in the kitchen and Tamara offered him a long drink from the bottle of whiskey a patient had given her, that she had been saving for special occasions. When he felt more relaxed, he searched for the cordless phone and dialed Manolo Palacios's number.

"It's me, Manolo."

"I know that already . . . Aren't you dead?"

"I'm more alive than ever . . . Tell me, what happened with the cell phone?"

"Nothing, they removed the card and threw it out. They might have thrown out the device, too. They took it from you so you wouldn't able to call anyone."

"And did they end up finding the Bat?"

"Yes . . . And he couldn't have been the one who killed Ramiro . . . He was at the League Against Blindness from eight in the morning until two in the afternoon . . . He started shaking when he found out about Ramiro."

"So, what do you have, then?"

"Several footprints in the vacant field, but nothing that looks like anything was buried. We took the search dogs to cover the sites where Ramiro could have been and it looks like that son of a bitch went there to piss and shit. Too many tracks . . . The dogs were worthless. We also have traces that someone entered through Ramiro's window, but this could have been anyone, even Ramiro himself when he went to the field . . ."

"So, almost nothing," Conde concluded.

"Besides the two dead people . . ."

Conde nodded. "So did the coffee cups show up?"

"No. And the thermos didn't have any prints. It was wiped clean."

"So why did you tell Ramiro that you were with State Security?"

"What are you talking about, Conde?"

"About Ramiro telling me that someone from State Security was after him because of Yúnior . . ."

"Ramiro was talking shit."

On his end, Conde nodded and closed his eyes. "You know what, Manolo? I was at Major Rangel's house."

There was a brief silence on the other end of the phone.

"How's the *viejo* doing?"

"The same."

A guilty silence.

"I need to go and see him. I'm a fake . . . But this job. I'm still stuck in this shitty office . . ."

"I spoke with him . . . Yes, I spoke with him . . . Not with words, but I spoke with him . . . And the *viejo* also thinks that the key to everything is the Virgin. Everyone thinks so . . ."

Manolo engaged in a much more prolonged silence on the other end of the line. He knew that Rangel's police instincts had extraordinary abilities.

"And what do you think?"

"I think you can set aside any possibility that all of this has something to do with Yúnior's old debts or even Ramiro's . . . That's why, early tomorrow—"

This time, Manolo immediately reacted. "Don't even dare, Conde! Here at headquarters, I have your friend Bobby and the Bat, the guy who bought the stolen things from Yúnior and a certain Manduco the Albino, who was also a buddy of Yúnior and Ramiro's . . . And we're putting the screws to them to the max because one of them has to know something. Do you want me to bring you over here, too, huh? Tell me. This is a police case, Conde, there are two deaths, and, even if they were completely scum, I'm getting a lot of pressure from the higher-ups . . . There's even talk of a serial killer! So don't even get involved. Because I swear to you that I'll also reserve a room for you at this hotel. I swear on my mother that I'll do it, Conde, on my mother."

"Fine, fine. I'll stay still . . . But anything you find out, you'll tell me, right? For old times' sake, Manolo. So I can tell old Rangel later . . ."

Manolo sighed. Conde closed his eyes and raised his shoulders to protect himself from the explosion.

"Mario Conde, you are the most twisted, blackmailing son of a bitch on this island and all of its damned keys!" And he hung up.

Conde opened his eyes and smiled. He showed Tamara the empty glass and grimaced in pain. He needed more medication.

12.

ANTONI BARRAL, 1314–1308

The mountain silhouettes rising until they blurred and broke into the clouds, proud, indifferent to the passing of time, gave him the pleasant feeling that he was beginning to recover the man he had once been, too many years before or perhaps in another life: a boy, a teenager, a young man for whom those snowy peaks, seemingly crude, like telluric explosions, were the beginning and end of the world. Because thus had it been until the glorious or disastrous day—he still wasn't sure; perhaps, he never would be—on which he had crossed the mountain range in order to start another life. A turbulent existence, full of such extraordinary shock that, distraught by the events he had recently experienced, he often persisted in thinking that perhaps it should not have been his. Or had his fate always been written by a greater power in a book of indestructible pages that were impossible to erase or alter?

Despite having been so far away for more than thirty years, Antoni Barral felt the capacity to remember every one of the secrets of that arrogant landscape. The peaks, the valleys, the steep passes, the ports, the forests, the birds, and the pests all spoke to him in an ancestral language, and, guided by his heart, he began the ascent to the mountain range's initial ridge, confident that his old knees could handle it. He felt certain he could find the intricate but favorable pass that would allow him to cross the rocks without having to climb them, and emerge from the mountainside through a strangely propitious path, opened by the capricious hand of the very Creator. From there, he would at last be able to descend to the mountain valley of his millenary line. When he was already entering the low, dense forest, Antoni Barral had the distinct feeling of penetrating a different dimension of time, an oppressive, circular, prisonlike space that hounded and would hound him, a distorting but revealing patina, like the water from the mountain creeks, through which he could see himself undertaking his own paths again and again, with the persistence of the eternal and the unappealable, like a creature wandering within and outside of time.

It had taken him two months to cover the last leg of his pilgrimage to the mountain range. A year before, when the surprising and implacable persecution of the knights of the Order of the Temple of Solomon had been unleashed throughout the territories subject to the French monarchy or one of its kings, princes, or allied nobles or vassals, in his directionless escape, the Templar brother Antoni Barral had found refuge in a small post the brotherhood had in Rousillon. The farm was so modest that no one would guess that any treasure was hidden there, and it would hardly spark any interest in those hunting the members of the outlawed order. Those vultures, motivated by conviction, compensation, or purely envy, destroyed the Latin kingdoms in order to stalk some men who had once been venerated, considered exemplary Christians for decades, and had suddenly become, due to the implacable defamation machinery pushed by the powers that be, something worse than criminals or bandits. Enemies.

A sergeant brother, an old and blind chaplain, more than a dozen serf brothers, simple peasants from that place, made up the population of the unremarkable enclosure guided by the order, whose main function had been to give shelter and food to pilgrims or members of the brotherhood traveling through far-off territories and to extract some barrels of a very delicate olive oil from their carefully tended-to orchard.

Brother Antoni Barral had turned to that corner of the world following a bewildering journey that had begun in Marseille, the port where he had disembarked following the Great Defeat that marked the catastrophic loss of the Holy Land. Like the handful of his brothers and several hundred civilians, he had arrived there aboard the *Falcon of the*

Temple, the magnificent vessel under the command of Roger de Flor, on which, through something he could only qualify as a miracle, he had managed to board and, thus, save his life. Since then, always in wait of a new military or monastic destiny that would never be assigned to him, he had lived for fifteen years in the city overlooking the Mare Nostrum, a place where all the world's paths crossed. In Marseille, like a treacherous knifing, he had been surprised by the royal band organizing the detention and imprisonment of all the members of the Templar order, accused as heretics, blasphemers, sodomites, worshippers of idols, and disrupters of the peace in Christian kingdoms.

Alarmed by the accusations and foreseeable punishments, Antoni Barral had something like a revelation and decided that, this time, he would break the rules and not obey the mandates of his hierarchical superiors. A veteran like him could not understand that his leaders would urge him to submit himself to royal justice and not papal law by which he should under code, while they forced them to recognize the commission of the worst sins that could be imputed to a human being educated in the faith of Christ. Because of that, instead of placing himself at the disposition of King Philip's soldiers and inquisitors, Antoni Barral didn't think twice about taking off with his bags of coins and gold pieces taken from the area that held the treasure, and escaping the order's headquarters and the noisy port city. Without any certainty of what his fate would be or what his immediate future would look like, the seasoned knight could not help but place on his saddle the black statue of Our Lady who, upon his arrival from Africa, he had placed himself on a pedestal in the chapel of the brotherhood's grounds. Whatever his fate, he would share it with the miraculous effigy that he had saved at least twice from destruction at the hands of infidels and to whom, also at least twice, Antoni Barral owed his life.

He would never know if it was his instinct, the magnetism of the path marked by stars in the sky, or a deep calling of his belonging that made him take the dangerous paths of Provence, without yet thinking of the ever-fretful crossing of the mountains to reach the cattle and valleys of his origins. Before leaving Marseille, Antoni had taken the precaution of abandoning his habits and any signs that could associate him with the order, including the beard that distinguished them, and as such, at inns, serf huts, and pilgrims' lodgings where he had stopped, he always introduced himself as a repentant sinner en route toward the sepulchre of the apostle Santiago. Under this cover, the knight had been able to follow, shock after shock, the course of dark events which were oft discussed in the noonday countries. He came to find out that thousands of his brothers in the order were detained and jailed over a few weeks, especially in Paris and the larger cities of the French kingdom. The travelers spoke of enormous quantities of goods seized, incalculable amounts of gold, coins, and relics that the superiors of the fraternity kept in some of their fortresses. They claimed that satanic pacts between the initiated, systematic ridiculing of the cross, and generalized sodomy among the knights had been revealed. Some came to say that it was already known that the great secret of the Templars had been their dominion over God and the conquest of their powers via the exercise of will and mental energy, arts they learned to control in dark, secret meetings in which bewitched Jewish Kabbalists participated . . . And, alongside all of those feverish claims destined to feed people's worst imaginings came the description of confessions, obtained through and without torture, summary sentences for those who recognized or denied the heresies of which the brotherhood was accused, and all of the bonfires on which the bodies of Knights Templar had begun to roast, such as those lit in the forest of Vincennes, in which in one single night, fifty-four warrior monks had perished as if they were Jewish wizards! The humiliating and defamatory processes extended all the way up to the order's Grand Master and his main marshals, locked away in the dungeons of Paris, Lyon, Liège, by the inquisitors under King Philip, called the Fair.

Throughout months of danger, fleeing, hiding, brother Antoni Barral had too much time to think about what was happening to his brothers, and too little capacity to understand it. However he thought about it, it seemed inconceivable that so many of those men, distinguished for their valor and convictions, should kneel down without fighting. Because they were the same knights whom he had seen fight until the death so many times: similar to the ones who immolated themselves in Safed; who withstood in the beautiful Tripoli; who died in the towers, walls, and under the ruins of the fortresses of the magnificent Acre; and who fought again for their faith in Ruad, when they well knew that all was lost. These courageous men now folded and admitted to being the most recalcitrant sinners; they accepted that, by their attitude or earthly ambitions, they had allowed the last loss of the Holy Land and acted, as such, to the benefit of the Saracen Muslims; they effectively admitted to being heretics, sorcerers, sodomites, and blasphemers. What fears, threats, and pains could have broken them, not just one, not just some cowards and opportunists, but rather hundreds of proven and proud warriors, loyal soldiers, thousands of which, for two hundred years, had fought and died for their faith in the Holy Land?

When he reached the small post, located in the territory over which the dominion of King James of Aragon extended, Antoni Barral knew he was safe, at least for the time being. He knew that the Iberian monarch, due to old political disputes and his own ambitions, would not at first join the hunt organized by his French colleague, and a few months later, when he finally accepted to do so, he didn't seem very committed to the work, although he was quite interested in using the situation to take the order's goods. In the post's chapel, just a roofed altar, the fugitive had deposited the statue of Our Lady, alongside the small figure of the Virgin, of a less noble wood and of much rougher and more imperfect features, who had reigned there for one hundred years. And despite enjoying the peace in that place, participating in the harvest and working the olive trees, and even assisting in the improvement of the chapel, brother Antoni Barral never stopped having the feeling that at some point, sooner or later, the ill winds of History would arrive in that pleasant place, since what was happening was not a simple storm, but rather a devastating flood. Such defenselessness in the face of great events willing to revolutionize or involve the world seemed to be his fate and, he already knew, as an individual, he could do very little to protect himself.

The unsettling idea was confirmed for him when, during a visit to a nearby town in order to shoe two of the post's horses, he found a recent powerful proclamation, posted on the small chapel of the place, urging the fugitive members of the order to appear before the diocesan bishops to be interrogated and judged, sentenced or exonerated. The document advised, besides, that any reluctant fugitives would be excommunicated and, at the end of the year, considered heretics and candidates without appeal for burning in the bonfire.

The exhausting idea that he was a creature at the mercy of the erratic will of History became a conviction when, a few weeks later, a couple of roving troubadours, on their way to a fair that occurred every year in Toulouse, were hosted at the post for several days. The night before their departure, they decided to compensate their hosts' hospitality and some neighboring serfs by playing the most popular songs in their repertoire. At first with pleasure and then with pain, Antoni Barral listened to them narrate the indispensable epic of Roland, the exciting tribulations of Robert the Devil, and the story recently turned to verse of what they called "the real and extraordinary adventures of the very magnificent Captain Roger de Flor," which told the peripatetic existence of the mythical Great Captain of the *Falcon of the Temple*, the man who had been a sailor, crusader, Templar, and later the fearful pirate commander aboard *La Olivette*, under the flag of King Frederick of Sicily. To Antoni's distress, in the song's final verses, the troubadours narrated the conditions of his death, dismembered like a pig following a surprise ambush, in the lands of Byzantium. Once the rendition was over, Antoni Barral interrogated the bards about the veracity of Roger de Flor's tragic end. And even though the troubadours couldn't specify a source, they assured him that for a few months already in Marseille, Venice, and Genoa, all were speaking of the death of the captain of the *Falcon of the Temple*, the majestic vessel aboard which, they assured, Roger de Flor had taken from Saint Jean d'Acre and Cyprus many of the treasures of the covetous and now heretical Knights Templar. Among the relics extracted by the captain were, according to what they said, the only surviving fragment of the True Cross, the necessary maps to locate the Ark of the Covenant, and a black statue of Our Lady, carved in the times of the last pharaohs of Egypt, and famous for being a prodigious granter of miracles . . .

The Coll dels Llops it had been called by the serfs of the nearby valleys, although, in reality, few of them knew its exact location. Many mountain dwellers even doubted its actual existence and considered the opening of such a low pass to be an old wives' tale. Worse still: some of those who avowed to its strange presence through the tangle of rocks considered it as nothing short of one of the mouths of Hell open on earth. But Antoni Barral did know of the existence and location of the pass since he had used it on several occasions, although, as he was able to confirm with growing anguish, it was much easier to find it from the meridional slope of the mountain range than from the northern slope, for the simple reason that he'd been born and raised in the valleys to the south and there held all reference points as a habitual wanderer of its paths.

The mule he'd taken from the "settlement" and on whose back he'd carried the statue of the Black Virgin and his provisions was much less skillful in scaling the mountains, which made movement more difficult. Even when Antoni could swear that the gorge that lead to the pass was in the area he was now scouring, his discovery had become complicated to the point that he was thinking of abandoning his search and undertaking the risky ascent. But, with that mule accustomed to flat lands and his sixty-year-old knees, he couldn't imagine another possible way to go across the rocks if not through the lower pass: scaling the slopes, edging around precipices, withstanding gales and very low temperatures in search of a higher port would be impossible for him. And the option of going back along his path to cross the mountain range through the Camí de la Menera or, farther to the east, by the routes on the coast seemed like suicide to him, since everyone knew that the Perpignan and Portbou route was the best one, if not the only way of escaping toward the Hispanic kingdoms for the knights fleeing persecution by the French and Provençal kings.

On the verge of desperation, brother Antoni Barral made a decision with which, he well knew, he risked a lot: leaving the mule in one spot and, with greater mobility, looking for the Coll dels Llops. Before leaving, he took two important precautions: he hid the image of the Virgin in a small grotto and buried at the foot of a dying chestnut tree the coins and objects he still had. He then took his mount to a clearing where he could drink from a small current of water and feed off the abundant pasture. And with his sword, a bit of bread, cheese, and a blanket, he went into the mountains.

Three days later, when he had at last located the nearly invisible Coll dels Llops and returned in search of his mild-mannered mule, he didn't find a trace of it. Again, he had to carry on his shoulders the heavy statue of the miraculous Virgin who, thanks to his prudence, was waiting for him in a Pyrenees grotto.

When Antoni Barral contemplated the valleys, creeks, and ravines of his childhood, he felt his life coming back together, and, simultaneously, he faced the quandary that, in his forced escape, he had barely considered. What would he do there? He wanted to think that perhaps that remote place would find him exempt from persecutions, interrogations, torture, and punishment, which was improvement enough. But while it was true that at some point he had belonged to that lost place on the planet, so many years later, it no longer belonged to him: at his age, he didn't even dare think about a life as a shepherd or farmer in the service of a greedy local noble. Perhaps he could go down to one of the small towns in the southern valleys, on the banks of the Ter river, and find a way to earn a living there; he could also offer his protection to some gentleman in the region; he could even risk tracking down one of his brothers' castles or posts, like the ones in Miravet and Monzón, where, as far as he knew, they had reluctantly taken a post when King James had accepted the papal order and set fire to the Templars of Valencia. As a last possibility, there was that of crossing nearly all of Spain and taking refuge in Córdoba, the mythical city of the old caliphate, where, it was said, many thousands of Muslims, Christians, and Jews lived in harmony . . .

The fugitive was well aware that every one of those options, more imaginary than real, held the danger of being revealed, detained, and judged. And he, Antoni Barral, was not willing to accept the ominous fate to which so many of his brothers, without a fight, had subjected themselves. His only possessions in his now-extended life were a powerful Black Virgin with whom he had covered half the civilized world, and the proud and ferocious history of his life, built on a capricious twist of fate. His fabulous existence had begun when he was still an illiterate peasant boy and received the seemingly simple task of leading to the northern slope of the Pyrenees two Templar knights who had been called by the

Pope to a new Crusade. But the chore would lead him to be the young man who, because of his skills and natural intelligence, had earned the exceptional honor of surpassing his humble origins and of being initiated as a knight and receiving the Cross of the Temple. The same skills and intelligence that, with complicated logic, when he was already a warrior monk, had led him to participate in dozens of battles and, in the name of faith in Christ, to kill so many infidels that he couldn't remember the sum. With his brothers, Antoni had managed to stand before the imposing walls of Jerusalem, had watched the fall of beautiful Tripoli, and had seen magnificent Saint Jean d'Acre go up in flames. Because of all this glory he had lived, he resolved that he would never subject himself to the scorn of a trial and a sure sentence in a process that barely concealed dark political aspirations and spurious economic interests. Nor would he allow vassalage to some monarch who presented himself as the custodial prince of the purity of Christendom, when in reality, installed in his Parisian palace, he had never done anything but conspire, prosper, and take on unpaid loans. No, not Antoni Barral . . . What if at another juncture of his life, he became a bandit and made his living from pillaging? he asked himself, and then responded that that would never be an option for him, since he hadn't even done so when his now-deceased friend Roger de Flor—already expelled from the order for supposed theft of the relics that were now being discussed—proposed that he join his Catalan Company and, as a mercenary and pirate, become rich in just a few years.

From the depths of the valley, he saw the curling column of white smoke, an unmistakable sign that there was a bonfire where wood still full of water and sap was also burning. He estimated that the exact site could be behind the forest of beeches and oaks on the banks of the creek that ran alongside it, and so he decided to follow it downstream.

In the last two weeks, ever since his mule was stolen along with his last provisions, Antoni Barral had fed himself from only berries, edible roots, a few eggs, and a hare he had managed to spear. His hunger tormented him and the nearby bonfire could signify the existence of food.

He walked until the smell of food reached him: yes, someone was roasting a goat. The Templar stopped for a few moments to think, and then, with nearly all his remaining energy, he went down to the horseshoe made by the creek's course. There, climbing on some rocks he piled up, he raised the statue of the Black Virgin and let Her fall in the hole opened up by a ray of lightning in the trunk of the gigantic oak. The dead tree was an unmistakable reference point, since its only branches made a nearly perfect cross. Since he didn't know what he would find around the bonfire, the fugitive didn't want to risk losing to some bandits the statue (whose miraculous nature he knew well) with which he had lived for the last seventeen years. Antoni Barral confirmed with satisfaction that only God in the sky or a gigantic Cyclops on earth could look into the oak's hollow and discover the presence of the Virgin. But, while this certainty was reassuring, he was concerned about what he should do when the time came to rescue Her. Would he have to tear down the oak punished by celestial fury?

When he rounded the curve made by the creek, he saw him: it was a man, perhaps his age, perhaps older, in possession of abundant white hair that fell down his back and a beard, also white, that reached his chest. On his shoulders, he wore a type of cape made of various furs, and underneath, he was dressed in what appeared to be the last vestiges of a monk's habit. On his feet, by way of shoes, the man wore some cloth-and-fur bags, tied at the ankles. His gaze was absorbed by the body of the goat roasting over the fire. Antoni thought that, in reality, he was more dangerous to the man than the man was to him, and he decided to approach him.

When he saw him, the old man with a long beard gave a start. From the ground, he lifted the mountain knife with which he must have sacrificed and dismembered the goat and pointed it in the direction of the recently arrived man. Antoni raised his left hand and with his right pointed at his sheathed sword: Did he want to fight? The other man knew that he stood to lose and lowered his weapon. Then Antoni, returning to the language they spoke in that country, greeted him, gave his name, and offered him a gold coin for half of the meat over the fire. The white-bearded man displayed his nearly empty gums in what must have been a smile, and asked if he knew how to speak langue d'oc, and when Anthony nodded, he told him to put away the coin since it had no value whatsoever there and that he was welcome to share the meal.

Fray Jean de Cruzy was the most talkative hermit anyone could ever imagine. During the long time they lived together, Antoni Barral did not manage to conceive how it could have been possible for that character to have maintained a vow of silence for two years, since he heard him speak so much that he learned everything about the life of that monk of the Cistercian order who had spent four winters already living in a retreat of solitude and meditation in a grotto in a valley of the Catalan Pyrenees.

With the instruments that Fray Jean had made for himself and for Antoni's never-forgotten skills, meat was never lacking over their bonfire while they were supplied with greens and roots that the hermit had cultivated in an orchard. Thus, they spent the rest of their days and nights talking about the human and the divine, even though both preferred the matters of men before those of God.

Brother Antoni Barral, assuming the role of the hermit's visitor, had no issues telling him all the ins and outs of his existence, starting with the years he had lived in the region's valleys as the son of a serf who paid tribute to the very poor lord of the feudal territory of Camprodon, a certain Jaume Pallard. That hollow, so close to the mountain's high ridge, the beneficiary of the mildest climate, the most fertile land, the most crystal-like creeks and plentiful hunt, had been thus named with the very unimaginative name of la Vall. Antoni also confessed to him that, in reality, he was an outlaw without any idea of what his earthly fate could be, although, amid all the possibilities, he was sure it would not be that of a hermit without worldly contact, like Fray Jean de Cruzy. He told him how he had escaped from Saint Jean d'Acre on the last day of that city's Christian existence, which he had watched burn from the bridge of the *Falcon of the Temple*, the powerful vessel at which he had arrived after throwing himself into the sea from the remains of the city walls in flames, when he had been caught by an enormous and unforeseeable wave that deposited him alongside the vessel as it retreated. What he did not confide in the hermit was that the miracle had been the work of a Black Virgin, proven to be miraculous and loaded with legend, the same statue that listened to their conversation while hidden just a few feet away.

The man who was actually a former monk, meanwhile, confessed to him that five years prior, he had abandoned the Abbey of Thoronet, in Provence, which he had entered as an adolescent and where he had lived for more than forty years, time that must have been more than sufficient for the attempt to surpass the worst of his human condition, rage, and, incidentally, what had become his most unsettling conviction: that the glorified Bernard of Clairvaux was a demon and not a saint. But neither education nor prayers nor the cloister nor penance had managed to save him from his own character and convictions. Because of that, after committing a mortal sin he never specified, he had taken his few belongings and gone out in search of the most remote place on earth to live in solitude, without contact with other humans, as a being with his defects and accumulated sins deserved. In the four years he had lived in that valley of broken land that seemed so desolate and welcoming, brother Antoni was the fourth person with whom Fray Jean had spoken. His last visitor had been a converso Jew on the pilgrimage route to Santiago who, almost a year before, had gotten lost and, God only knew how, had ended up in this complicated spot. Among other news, the wandering converso, who said he was called Frederick of Geneva and ended up being more talkative then Fray Jean himself, told him what was happening in France and other kingdoms with the order's *milites Christi*. Although, when he considered it, in light of what the brother had confided in him, perhaps the pilgrim who introduced himself as a convert from Toledo, who was confessing a name that was so Sephardic and speaking the language of Castile with exaggerated enunciation, as if he were singing, was in reality another of Antoni's brothers, an outlaw like he was.

In possession of such news, Fray Jean had not been too surprised by the story of Antoni Barral's escape. Besides, the hermit thought that, for years, the knights of the Order of the Temple had begun to forge their perdition committing the venial and all too human sin of arrogance. They had created the aristocracy of faith and the sword, of esoteric wisdom and commercial abilities, when in reality they were failures. Yes, because the loss of all of the Christian kingdoms in the Holy Land had left them without a reason for being the custodians of devotees who could no longer embark on a pilgrimage toward the Holy Sepulchre and, above all, because no European monarch wanted to cohabitate in his own territory with an army not under his command. Thus, mundane sins, military failures, and the very structure of the order had decreed the perdition that the ambitious and cunning King Philip had taken charge of executing so easily, and of course, with the consent of a pope whom he, Philip, had placed on Peter's throne, as all of Christendom knew.

If at first the former monk's considerations seemed excessively harsh to judge a brotherhood that had done so much for the defense of the Christian faith, the arguments Fray Jean laid out in successive chats and Antoni's own vision of the order's actions and projections ended up convincing the knight that his opinions were astute.

But a mystery persisted that would not cease tormenting him and for which Antoni Barral remained without any satisfactory explanation: How was it possible that so many of his brothers, including those with the greatest responsibilities in the order, had admitted in their confessions the generalized and stubborn commission of sins and the heretical behaviors and thoughts that were said to be common in the brotherhood? Of course, it could be—in fact it was—that some brothers, in the solitude of the camps and posts, had been given to the practice of acts of sodomy, as also happened in many military camps or monasteries—and the hermit nodded when they spoke of the matter. It could also be that some had sworn in vain for the cross solely to gain the privileges and the prestige of belonging to the order, and until one or the other had given to speculating for his own benefit or that of his post. But Antoni Barral, who at the age of twenty had had the honor of becoming initiated as a knight of the Temple despite his plebeian origins, who had covered half the world wearing the unmistakable insignia of the eight-pointed red cross, fighting with its battalions in the most difficult combats to take place in the Holy Land, he could confirm that there were exceptions. The supposed secret initiation ceremonies had nothing of the esoteric, since they were essentially similar to any knightly ordaining of vassalage. There was no blaspheming in them, much less with spitting on the cross or disowning Jesus and the Virgin. The kisses on the cheeks were only a way of making patent the love between brothers that was implicit in the initiation of the neophyte, and the legends of worshipping pagan idols was the most absurd of the lies. Or not: the most outrageous one concerned the pretension of conquering the powers of God . . . That was why Antoni Barral asked himself again and again how it was possible that the condemning confessions piled up by men who held the same convictions as him and whom he had seen fight and die in the cruelest battles.

Fray Jean de Cruzy, who recognized himself as irascible, a sinner, and very little given to believing in miracles and saintly men, proved many times to brother Antoni that he was, above all, a wise individual, and, despite the many years he had lived as a monk, Fray Jean knew everything about the dark corners of human consciousness. Because of that, he was able to give his companion in the eremite grotto a response that was capable of unsettling him: "More powerful than faith, the hope for forgiveness, or material ambitions, the most invincible thing is fear," he had said to him, his eyes fixed on the fire warming them that December night in the year of our Lord of 1308. "Fear and the survival instinct and not other feelings are the essence of the human condition, the power that when it works, dominates everything: even the love for God." Brother Antoni Barral immediately shook his head: "I saw that those men did not have to die. I saw them agonizing, clutching the cross and with their swords plunged into the heart of an infidel. I saw them fight knowing that if they were captured as prisoners, the ritual throat-slashing of the infidels awaited them, or the most feared inferno of slavery in Muslim lands . . ." Fray Jean had taken a few sips of the mint leaf infusion sweetened with honey that he had that night in his bowl. "And speaking of a different fear, worse than the fear of death, brother Antoni," he said. And he got back on track: "I'm well aware that many of those who now confessed to be blasphemers and sodomites would have died like martyrs on the walls of Acre if they had been in Acre. Because you are warriors made for one kind of battle and used to one kind of enemy: the infidel. You were prepared for sacrifice you knew, which you did not fear, which even tempted you.

You knew, as you say, that Muslims wouldn't waste any time in torturing Templar pris ners, and you faced it courageously. Thousands of knights have been immolated for their faith in Christ and have entrusted themselves to Our Lady. But now the tables have turned. Now, you are told by the hierarchs of Christianity that you are the allies of the Saracens and that, because of you, the Holy Land has been lost. Suddenly, some proven defenders of the Catholic faith turn out to be accused of the contrary and classified as heretics. And they are shown or the aim is to show them that the best service they can still render to humanity, to Christianity, to Jesus and Our Lady, to the better world to which our faith inspires, consists precisely of confessing. The king of France, Christianity, and the Pope, their protector, the closest thing to God that there is on earth, asks it of them . . . And if they do not confess all of those sins and thus help Christianity, they threaten them with submitting them to torture or they actually torture them . . . Do you know how torture works?"

"On the basis of pain?" brother Antoni hazarded, opting for the obvious.

"It's much more than that," the hermit proposed. "Torture is a concoction that causes hallucinations. When a man is tortured, all that his life has been comes back to his mind and explodes. Then, the miserable man, who has started to cease being the person he once was, says not only what the inquisitor wants to hear, but also what he imagines would be pleasant to him to hear, since a link is established—certainly a diabolical one—between them . . . Under torture, a man can tell the most absurd lies, since he is no longer the one who speaks, but rather his unleashed fears, all multiplied . . . And do you know who the best torturers are? Not the rough goons who hang and cut heads off. The most efficient ones are my former brothers from the mendicant orders, the Dominicans and the Franciscans, men of great faith and militancy, who know of the weakness of the body and spirit, because torture is a specialty and the one applied today is refined, it's recently created . . . But, I am convinced, it will be eternal. What we have discovered about the manipulation of fear and the essence of torture shall be applied for centuries to come, in future societies to come . . . Even when, fortunately or unfortunately, neither you nor I will be in this world to confirm it. But I can see as if my soul were flying through time that it is a greater truth than these mountains that surround us."

Winter was long and aggressive that season, even in that valley in which, Antoni Barral knew, it rarely snowed. Without the knowledge of the area and the recovered skills of this mountain dweller, perhaps Fray Jean de Cruzy would not have withstood the rigors of the drawn-out season.

When the spring of 1309 arrived, Antoni Barral was already resolved to do something with his life, without being able to gather what. He found out through the first pilgrim who came through the valley when the snows started to melt that dozens of his Templar brothers were still being held in several Catalan fortresses and there was talk that King James had promised to pardon them, only after seizing their goods, to then send them to fight against the Moors in the occupied Iberian territories. Nonetheless, the experiences of the recent years had prompted great disillusionment in him concerning his beliefs: all of the utopias in which he had believed had come undone before his eyes, further still, had been twisted. He now dragged along the terrible conviction that making war had been engineered by higher powers, the same that, when no longer useful, wanted to incinerate him in a pyre; the eternal powers who aspired, with the hope of defeating Islam, to make off with all the riches of the territories of the Levant and the commercial routes toward the very rich Asian lands. Solely for this, he now knew—his friend Roger de Flor had always known it—he had been pushed to participate in History, he had invested his sweat, his blood, and his tears in the name of the belief in a world closer to the heavens, better, more just: a world that was not nor would be.

The days on which thoughts of that nature tormented him the most, the knight went to the oak with its death wound and its branches shaped like a cross where the statue of Our Lady rested in hiding. There, he prayed to the point of exhaustion, with the ever-vivid hope of receiving some sign from the Virgin, like the ones that had favored him in the days on which he had been closest to death. Because he continued to be a believer, he would be his entire life, although he would no longer be one of those puppets moved by a hidden and deciding hand. The mystical practice of praying to a tree, impossible to hide from Fray Jean de Cruzy, had forced him to lie to him, inventing a story about how with a piece of that oak wounded by the sky and its branches shaped like a cross, his father had carved a small Virgin since, for centuries, the dwellers of the valley considered that that specific tree had celestial powers: solely because of it, it had survived standing the tremendous impact of a lightning bolt and had not burned to the roots. Besides, lacking any other attributes, the tree in the shape of a cross, carved by the very hand of God, served his spiritual purposes.

But no matter how much he prayed and thought, he could not find a satisfactory alternative. He was well aware that he did not have the soul of a hermit or the right to break the solitude chosen by the pleasant Fray Jean for much longer or the possibility of going to some place and introducing himself with another name and another life history. Since in the supposed case in which they would not discover his affiliations, what would they do when he showed up with a Virgin so extraordinary that even the kings coveted Her possession? What convincing story could he invent about Her?

As if that weren't enough, Antoni Barral had just turned sixty years old and knew that his life was entering its final phase. He was already an old man for whom it was an effort to scale mountains and to eat with the few teeth that had still not fallen from his mouth. And it was on a summer afternoon, as he urinated and was cooling off his legs in the creek close to the hermit's grotto, when he felt, following a deep shaking, that his feet were demanding his return to the road. Antoni Barral knew that the vigorous revelation was the call of his fate, although he was also ruled by the conviction that, before, he should fulfill an incontrovertible assignment from that same personal destiny, already written or in the middle of being written: to safeguard the miraculous Virgin.

As soon as he had the revelation, he decided what the statue's fate would be: a convent or a monastery. Although before that, he thought, he should make necessary confirmations. Antoni knew that in the feudal seat of the region, the place called Camprodon, they had raised a monastery or abbey, but he was not familiar with the order to which it belonged. And in his decision to hand over to some men of the cloth a powerful Virgin, the conviction had also arisen that some monks did not deserve Her. And since Fray Jean de Cruzy had only vague news of the existence of that abbey, the only possible option turned out to be going down to the village and asking the relevant questions.

Under the pretext of carrying out an excursion to buy the hermit some more appropriate tools for the work in the orchard and ropes aimed at preparing traps for larger hunts, brother Antoni Barral took his leave of his host, the hermit Fray Jean de Cruzy, with the promise of returning in two, three weeks maximum. And he asked the former monk to prostrate himself before the cross-shaped oak every once in a while and pray for his fate. A few extra prayers were never too many.

The winter of 1314 was even harder than that of 1309: the entire valley was covered in a thick layer of snow and some of the fords of the creeks turned to frost. Since the provisions gathered in the warm months were not enough, Fray Jean de Cruzy, hounded by hunger and cold, had to finally leave his grotto in search of something to eat and branches to warm himself. He wandered for hours in the snow, following the tracks of animals that never appeared until, at some point, he felt lost. He then went back over his steps without any certainty that he was returning to his refuge, and when he was starting to lose hope, like a ray of light, in the distance he saw the dark oak shaped like a cross. Because of that, when he was getting close to his grotto at nighttime already, frozen stiff, without a thing to eat, and sensing the outcome that awaited him, the old hermit thought that could be a good place. After he blessed himself, he kneeled before the broken oak and, beneath its cross-shaped branches, he did the only thing he could do: he prayed. Two hours later, there died, prostrate, frozen, Fray Jean de Cruzy, without having ever again heard from the former Templar Antoni Barral, the sole companion he'd had in his years as a hermit in a nameless valley, surrounded by mountains whose peaks seemed to climb and pound into the heavens and eternity.

13.

That corner of the old neighborhood of el Cerro was known as el Canal and had always been famous across the island as a place where human temperaments heated up. It had been the stomping ground of bad boys, switchblade owners, fight-pickers, and hit men ever since colonial times. In its territory and in that of the neighboring el Manglar, the *negros curros* who came from Seville had settled down, these loud Andalucíans with dark skin who distinguished themselves from their poor African relatives by the red handkerchiefs they tied around their necks, their skill at spitting to the side, and the knives of shining Toledo steel that they always wore sheathed at their waists . . . until the time came to take them out.

As Conde followed the hazy directions that would take him to the house of Yúnior Colás's friend, known as Platero for the similarity in his phallic proportions to that of the most famous—and, to Conde, the most idiotic—donkey in Spanish-language literature, he wondered whether this story about the Virgin that he was following wasn't forcing him to see each and every side of a city that, if you really looked at it, seemed affected by leprosy.

By asking around just enough not to turn anyone off, his shirt soaked with sweat and his feet burning inside the killer boots, Conde came to find out the exact address of the young prostitute. In front of the house, whose peeling-paint door opened right onto the sidewalk, Conde saw that on the nearest corner, three of the neighborhood's inhabitants were analyzing him with an interest he would not qualify as anthropological. It was to be expected, he thought, and he dried off as much sweat as he could from his face before finally knocking at the door.

An old woman opened the door. She was about seventy, with a poorly coiffed mane that was a mix of black hair, gray knots, and tresses that had once been dyed and were now faded from chestnut to rat-colored. Conde greeted her and asked if he could see Platero. The woman studied him more slowly than the delinquents on the corner had, perhaps evaluating whether the visitor was a policeman or some perverted client.

"What do you want him for?" the hostess asked.

"I need to talk to him . . . regarding his friend Yúnior, or Raydel, I don't know which one he knew him as. The *mulato* from the east . . ."

The woman immediately cast aside perverse reasons and opted for police-related ones.

"That's the one they killed, right?"

"That one."

"Poor boy. Yes, my grandson knew him, but he had nothing to do with him . . ."

"The thing is, Platero talked to him about something important . . . Incidentally, what's Platero's name? I don't like to call him that . . ."

"My grandson is called Yamichel and I already told you that he doesn't have anything to do with that Raydel . . . My grandson studies at the university."

"I'm glad," Conde said. He was beginning to understand some things and not understand many others. That Yamichel could be someone who was well-informed, maybe even refined, a university student. But at the same time, he was in the profession of dispensing pleasure for pay. Was that also normal? Was it normal now? "Ma'am, I only want Yamichel to tell me something he found out about a Virgin that Raydel had seen."

The woman with the multicolored hair and nearly grimy appearance muttered, "The Virgin of Regla who was not from Regla."

"The very one." Only at that moment, seeing the cavity-filled grin of the grandmother of Yúnior-Raydel's friend, did Conde have the certainty of the rapid loss of his faculties. If Yamichel knew about the Virgin's real value . . . couldn't he be part of the plot that led to Her disappearance and the death of two people? He felt like punching himself, although he was relieved when the woman spoke again.

"Are you a policeman?"

The question was bound to come up. And he decided to test a response that would allow him to advance a few steps.

"More or less."

The woman weighed the information. And she deemed that Conde was more or less a policeman. And she surely thought, since she must be well aware, that when there's nothing else to be done, it's better not to annoy the police: the ones in that fraternity, even with faces like Conde's, were usually ill-tempered.

"Yamichel is at the university. But he'll be back in a moment. He's coming home for lunch . . . Do you want to wait for him?"

"Yes, of course," Conde reacted, surprised by that possibility.

"Well, then come in."

The old woman held out her hand to wave him in toward the small living room that looked more like a grotto. Like most of the houses in the neighborhood, built one wall against the other, it lacked side windows and the light came from the street or from the door that, in the back, should lead to a small outdoor area for washing. On one of the side walls, on an angle broken up by one of the columns holding up the ceiling, Conde saw the image of the small version of Our Lady of Regla that he had always known, the cheap, popular replica of the original that existed in the chapel dedicated to the Holy Mother.

"Take a seat." And she pointed at the old armchair made of dark wood, of the same model as the ones that Conde had had in his childhood home. "My grandson is a good kid. He's young and does things young people do, but he's good . . . Did I tell you that he's studying at the university? Can I offer you a lemonade?"

"Yes, thank you, this heat . . ." he muttered, after refraining from the impulse to ask if she would use boiled water. No, he could not give in to that.

"And that's with it being September already," the woman added as she headed toward the kitchen. "This country is an inferno . . ."

"It would be better to live in Alaska," Conde dared to add.

"On the moon, even!" the old woman let out before immediately adding, "Because of the heat, I mean . . ."

Half an hour later, the lemonade ingested and Yamichel's spotless student and political biography, in his grandmother's version, told, Conde saw the young man arrive and was no longer surprised by his face: he seemed like a normal kid, very different from the shady aspect of the deceased Ramiro the Cloak and the Bat. He only noted the fact that Yamichel was blacker than shoe polish, while his grandmother was, or appeared to be, white. The young man's gestures and face were without a doubt masculine and accentuated the shine of his shaved head and the volume of his weight-lifter arms.

The grandmother hurried to explain to Yamichel who the visitor was. Conde did not have any difficulty decoding the message the woman was transmitting to her grandson: *Careful, he's a policeman; I warned you.* So he decided to provide more information and told him what he was looking for: he needed him to explain why Yamichel thought Raydel's Virgin was valuable, just that.

The young man listened to his grandmother and the presumed policeman silently as he drank his glass of cold lemonade. Conde knew without fearing he would be wrong that he was dealing with an intelligent person, and perhaps because of that, he was as or more dangerous than the common criminals of Raydel's sort with whom he had been dealing.

"So what can you tell me?" he asked, waiting.

"I don't have anything to do with Raydel's mess . . . But I'm going to help you. Just a moment," Yamichel said and grabbed the backpack he had brought in and removed a laptop from it. With the skill of systematic use, he opened the machine, turned it on, waited a few seconds, and operated the built-in mouse in search of something. When he found what he was looking for, he handed Conde the laptop. During the operation, the grandmother with tricolored locks had followed the young man's precise movements with admiration, as if she were trying to figure out a magician's tricks.

Conde took the machine carefully. On the screen, wide and tall, was the image of a Virgin very similar to the one he had seen in Bobby's photos.

"She looks a lot like Her . . ." Conde moved cautiously.

"Too much . . . As if they were sisters . . . That Virgin is in a church in the north of Spain. She is a medieval sculpture, Romanesque, and it's possible that She was brought from the north of Africa in the time of the Crusades, twelfth century . . ."

"That old?"

"Yes, very old . . . And priceless."

"What do you mean priceless?"

Yamichel smiled at last. He had very white teeth that contrasted with the brilliant black color of his skin and even his gums.

"That those Virgins are very rare and are not for sale . . . And if someone sells one, they can ask a fortune for Her. I don't know how much, but a serious amount of money. It all depends on how much the buyer wants Her and of the seller's skill. And on how dirty She is . . . These are relics."

Conde nodded. He was thinking. "So you told Raydel this?"

"I told him because he told me about a Virgin of Regla who had some power and he showed me the photo he had on his cell phone. I knew right away that it was not a Virgin of Regla," he said and pointed at the sculpture to his left. "I grew up in Regla and I know that Virgin by heart . . . The rest I found out on the internet."

"So, what was Raydel going to do when he found out what the Virgin's worth could be?"

Yamichel smiled again. "Steal Her, of course. And then go to Miami and try to sell Her there . . . There is no buyer here for that gem."

"So whom did he speak with to get out of Cuba?"

"That, I don't know . . . I didn't want to know, and I'm glad . . . Because it seems like the Virgin punished him. Or that Raydel spoke with the wrong person, right?"

Conde, Conde, Conde . . . How generous . . . Well, if you're letting me choose: an aged Santiago. You know that rum is the only one that they still make in the old Bacardi factory with the same formula that they used to use to make original Bacardi? Well, what the hell am I going to tell you about rum, right? But that's why it's so damned good. Look, you can have a whole liter and the next day you're good as gold, without the hangover you get from this hooch they make these days with pretty labels, and they put coloring in them and say they've been aged for whatever time they damn well feel like, as if you're an idiot, right?"

Miki Dollface was a couple of years older than Conde, although he already displayed a collection of folds, wrinkles, and stretch marks on his face. He had once been so good-looking as to earn the nickname which compared him to female beauty. The implacable revenge of time, Conde thought every time he saw him. And despite meeting with him as infrequently as possible, the social information accumulated by the supposed writer who did not write forced him to seek him out again and again.

In the private, ice-cold bar, where everything had to be paid for in Cuban convertible currency, Conde observed the line of spirits behind the bar with attractive labels, like powerful magnets: scotches and bourbons, gins and brandies, creams and vodkas, wines and cordials all arrived from the most varied parts of the planet. The possibility of sitting in a bar like that, with the option to torment oneself over not knowing what to pick had been a dream of his throughout his whole life. The strange thing was that it was thanks to the circulation of strong currency and even to the renaissance of burgeoning private enterprise on the island that such a worn possibility had been recovered. So he decided to give himself the pleasure and the luxury as part of a commercial and work transaction. And because in a place like that—clean, ice-cold, discreetly lighted—it was easier to egg on Miki Dollface's loquacity than in the noisy bar belonging to the Writers' Union, where Miki was a usual, or in the aggressive Bar of the Hopeless, where, surrounded by the drunks of his neighborhood and four flea-ridden dogs, Conde tended to buy his daily alcohol. And because he would later send the bill to Bobby.

When he inhaled the aroma of the Santiago añejo served in the low, round-bellied cup, the most propitious one for those golden, warm contents, he felt like the character out of a novel who'd been moved to another book. A mistake.

"My thing, you know, is not people looking to deal works of art, but one hears about everything. Look, to give you an idea: there's a writer, well-known, who has moved heaven and earth to build himself a collection of Cuban paintings that would make you shit yourself. Those works of art must be worth millions. And he gets them through all the ways you can imagine. As favors, through tricks, however . . . He's insatiable. And he's good friends with René Águila. Since that writer likes to be told he's the best in the world, when you tell him that, he feels so deservedly recognized that he begins to talk like a parrot . . . And he'll tell you some things! He was the one who told me that René bought himself a house in the Alturas de Guanabo. A house that looks like a fortress. He completely remodeled it, put some medieval castle walls around it, installed cameras and alarms, and even has a bodyguard, because what he has in there is madness: furniture, sets of china, paintings, jewelry . . . That René buys everything, but always at a deal, without paying what it's worth, because he's a son of a bitch without any scruples or rules and he would trick even Muhammad . . ."

"That guy talked to me about the ethics of the guild . . ." Conde recalled.

"Ethics? My friend, the only ethics I know are the ones Spinoza wrote . . . Do you understand anything Spinoza says? Well, it's that this is no longer what it used to be, brother, don't think that for a second. Look, before, only the big, big fish and the sons of the big fish and the wives and the beloveds of those big fish had things and lived the good life. Now, besides the big, big guys, there's a whole lot of sons of bitches who have made themselves cash getting what they can out of people who are fucked and need some money to get by. And that's what René Águila does. Ethics? That guy is capable of any son-of-a-bitch move. But killing a kid who's a shitty thief who doesn't really know what he has in his hands? I don't know, Conde, I don't know . . . That's another thing entirely."

"What about the other guy, that Elizardo?"

"I can tell you lots of things about Elizardo: The first is that he has a geographic history that is strange as all hell. Imagine, he spent about fifteen years living in France and came back about ten years ago, when taking that backward step was more difficult in this country than buying soap that wouldn't scratch up your skin . . . But he did it. How did he get to France; what was he doing there; how did he come back? All urban legends. They say he married a rich Swiss woman. That he went in search of the inheritance from a Catalan grandfather who was a millionaire. That he was a double-oh-seven super agent sent to fight against imperialism in that battleground . . . There is enough to choose from. The fact is that he has money or at least seems like he has money, and if he has it, it's also because of the things that he has bought and sold here. And the house where he lives! A palace . . . But when I say palace, I mean paaaaaalace . . . One of his businesses, and this seems true, is that since he met several art dealers in France, and Switzerland, and Germany, the guy puts them in touch with some Cuban painters and charges a commission for the sales. And he gets a ton from that. Because in Cuba there are more painters than sparrows: they're rustic, but some end up being really good. And since everyone thinks that at some point, around the twenty-fourth century, things between Cuba and the United States could improve, American collectors have come in search of what there is and . . . Everything is going to be bought and sold already. And whoever wants something will have to pay for it dearly to those who have harvested it now. Elizardo also focuses on Cuban classics: many of the works by good twentieth-century painters that move go through his hands and that's another nice sum. What's interesting is that this character has class. René is a smooth talker who comes off as nouveau riche, as a businessman; Elizardo tries to come across as a cultural promoter or facilitator or whatever in the hell you want to call it, but something more refined, and he has friends in official circles . . . Or at least, that's what he says . . . The truth is that, at heart, he's just the same, because he also buys and sells jewelry, ornaments, furniture, sets of china, but he does this through front men, so that he doesn't seem like a flea market, like René . . . The guy is insatiable, he has delusions of grandeur, that's certain . . . But to kill for a valuable piece? I don't really think so, to be honest . . ."

"I have my doubts . . . Money's a bitch."

Miki took a sip from his glass. "Yes, when I really think about it, brother, things have gotten so fucked-up here that anyone does anything to stay afloat. Look, I still remember when today's bestselling painters were giving away their works to their friends, or would trade them with foreigners for a pair of jeans or a tape recorder. Here, nobody knew what their work was worth, and less still how to sell it. But not even a memory remains from that romantic time, Condemned, not even a memory. In this country, people have to fight tooth and claw to live, because if they don't, they don't live . . . Tell me, how do you live, how do Carlos and Rabbit live? In a permanent state of poverty, purely by a miracle. And look who came to throw you a lifesaver: Bobby the goose . . . Because that one, who was Marxist, Leninist, Stalinist, and all the other-ists you know, what he was doing was hiding his homosexuality so they wouldn't eat him alive, and when they ended up eating him alive anyway and he decided to open his eyes, he said no to communism and yes to consumerism . . . He went into business and they say—they say, don't believe me, but they say"—Miki lowered his voice—"that he had something to do with some fake paintings by Tomás Sánchez that they released in Miami . . ."

Conde made a gesture to stop Miki's speech. "Bobby was in the falsification business?"

"I couldn't swear it, but there are rumors . . . Do you believe that because he was a moron before he can't be a tiger now?"

"I believe in less and less lately, Miki . . ."

"Good for you . . . Anyway, the fact is that there's Bobby, rolling in cash and living like a king with sexual servants and everything. But he's in a sorry state, because he was fucked over by the revolt of the humble and they left him stark naked . . . That's why I'm telling you, Conde, I don't know what the police must know, but a guy like Bobby has to know what that shitty Virgin was worth and he was hurt because his boyfriend fucked him over . . . Do you really think he wouldn't be capable of killing that kid the way they killed him? I don't know about that other criminal, Ramiro, you said? Well, this looks more like a Raymond Chandler book, including the blow to the head you got . . . You tell me if that isn't true . . ."

"Marlowe got knocked on the head every once in a while . . ."

Miki drank again, almost as if he was thirsty, and drained the rest of his drink.

"But Raydel or Yúnior, I don't even know his name, Bobby could've taken it out on him . . . In a fight, when he was angry . . . I'm saying . . . Damn, Conde, my rum ran out. With everything I told you, I earned another one, didn't I?"

Like he had seen it done in movies, Conde lifted a finger to the bartender and carried out the classic gesture of asking him to refill both drinks. He felt fulfilled through this action he had never imagined he could practice and with the success of it in the Havana commercial arena. How long would this miracle of private cordialness and efficiency last? That would cause itching and they would fuck it over: mark his words.

"Earn it for real, Miki . . . What about Karla Choy?"

The barman refilled the glasses and, to pick on, he placed a plate with several olives and some dried fruit. Were they living in reality or in one of the Bogart films that Conde loved? A mystery with a femme fatale included?

"Whoever tells you something about that woman and thinks it's the truth is a moron. Because the only thing known about her that is absolutely sure is that she is fine and has a face that . . . can stop traffic. When you see her . . ."

"I already saw her . . . And I had a drink with her . . ."

"Damn!" Miki couldn't help but exclaim. "Did you see what a thing of beauty she is!"

"*Bocato di cardinale . . .*"

"No, of the Roman bishop . . . In my time . . ."

"Forget that dirty old-man bullshit and talk, Miki."

"Well anyway, no one knows anything about her . . . There are some who say she's the lover of a super minister, one of the historic ones, as they say now, and that the guy is her shield. Others say that she's actually the daughter of one who is even higher up, one of the big, big fish, and that that father is her antimissile shield and that's why she does what she does . . . There is even talk of a husband who is an Italian count, the owner of vineyards in Tuscany. But I think those are all tall tales. The truth, for me, is that the chick is a rainmaker: she has the art of doing business in her blood . . ."

"Her Chinese genes . . ."

"Yes, but the Chinese of today . . . That's why I am telling you that, as far as I know—and it's not that I know much, Condemned—that woman wouldn't get involved in any business like that, and less still if there are dead bodies in the way . . ."

"The dead bodies could have come later," Conde advised, "like unforeseen complications. Collateral damage . . ."

"So you think that . . . ?"

"I only think that for three or four million euros, anyone could take the Bastille and bring it down, Miki."

"Well, that's true . . . as true as this being the best rum in Cuba because it's the one made in . . . Hey, listen, did you hear that Rabbit is outta here?"

Conde felt his heart leap. That Miki knew about his friend's plans was already outrageous, but that he would talk about them in public was suicide.

"Listen, Miki, do you have to yell it out like that? We don't talk about that . . ."

The other man smiled and sipped from his drink. "What world are you living in, Condemned? Damn, you seem like an extraterrestrial . . . That already happened, it left, it's over . . . Before, if you knew someone was leaving and didn't say anything, your light and water got shut off. Just remember what happened to your friend Fernando Terry . . . Now, the ones who leave, whether they're doctors or baseball players or writers, they have a party before taking off and everyone's all *easy*, smooth. Good luck to you, my friend, we'll see each other here in a couple of years or maybe there if I get the visa . . . Of course, there are still some morons who have an issue with that, and talk all low . . . But the fuss is over. Have you seen how many baseball players leave every week? And have you seen how many later come back to Cuba on vacation? And how many people have a Spanish passport now and bring back packages from Panama or from Burkina Faso for two hundred dollars a trip? No one can stop this now . . . Even Rabbit is leaving us, buddy, he's leaving us!"

When he left the ice-cold bar, forty dollars less in his pockets because of the six drinks he bought, Conde was hit by the humid heat of that September afternoon. He immediately felt himself being overcome by an overwhelming lethargy capable of taking his emergent desire to write about the feeling of being outside something and being close to it, of belonging and apartness that he had felt in that bar which had seemed to him—God knew why—squalid, Chandler-esque, and moving. Besides, the base of his skull still hurt from where he had been hit; the information accumulated in his mind was a tangle from which he did not manage to gain any clarity; and the certainty of how the world worked now, according to Miki Dollface's conclusions, was not a landscape that could be seen as encouraging for the country in which he had lived all these years, where slowly and silently the scramble and rush seemed to be taking shape for any solid useful castoffs available. Someone had summarized it for him in two words in his police days: the jungle.

Exhausted, he decided to retire to the safety of his winter quarters, but before that he resolved to improve the health of his feet with some affordable option in a nearby store that sold in dollars. Once he was wearing his new moccasins—another forty dollars down the drain—he took a private taxi to his house (traveling for half an hour to the rhythm of reggaeton and breathing in carbon monoxide in its purest state), where he fed and spoiled Garbage II for a while, took a long shower, cold, disinfecting— Miki was contagious and the aroma of gas from the old taxi had stuck to him like a tick—and he changed his outfit. When it was beginning to get dark and the sun's fury was lessening in intensity, he took the route toward Skinny Carlos's house after making a stop at the Bar of the Hopeless to stock up on a liter of the terrible alcohol they usually drank there. He didn't feel like having another drink. With the mood he was in that afternoon, there was a high possibility of another encounter with the Devil. But he sensed that Carlos would be itching to drink. And indulging him was one of his greatest life missions: a bottled dose of unconsciousness was always well received. Although, he suddenly felt petty. When he thought about how, just to get some Havana gossip, he'd drunk Santiago rum with a bad writer and a fake with a viper's tongue like Miki while he was taking flammable liquid to his best friend. His burden of guilt won him over in round one, and, before he reached his destination, he went into another one of the stores where everything was sold in convertible currency, bought a bottle of rum (at least it had a label), and tallied the day's expenses: he had already spent the hundred dollars he was supposed to have earned. How could one live in this country without a hundred dollars to spend a day? Wearing shoes that killed and drinking rotgut, that was the only possible response.

As soon as he saw him arrive, Skinny immediately noticed his old friend's bad mood. He confirmed it when Conde handed over the two bottles of rum, one good and one bad, and asked him not to serve him a single drink, not that night, and to tell Josefina he wouldn't dine there, since he wanted to arrive early, sober, and hungry at Tamara's house.

"You're not fucked-up, Conde, you're dying," Skinny Carlos proclaimed, in the face of his surprising state. "What in the hell is wrong with you, Beast? You're not going to drink rum and you're not going to eat the arroz con pollo the old lady is cooking up? Did that knock to the head make you stupid?"

"I don't know, I'm . . . I don't know . . . I think that . . . I'm all confused in the head."

"In my opinion, it's menopause. And an asparagus soup isn't going to make you feel better . . ." Skinny decreed and served himself a drink of rum, from the labeled bottle, of course.

Conde tried to explain his lethargy to his friend: without needing to think about it too much, he went over everything he'd been through in those days, from learning of Rabbit's plans and the scolding he received from Tamara, to Bobby's confessions, Miki's revelations, the visit to Rangel, and the journeys to the Inferno of the "settlements," and all the way to an almost intimate knowledge of two bloodied murders and even a shoeless destitute man. It was like a tsunami of emotions that had shaken him badly and connected him in the worst way with the reality of life and of his country.

"That really is a bitch," Carlos admitted. "Please clarify something . . . Is all of this rum for me?"

"All yours," Conde confirmed and watched as his friend raised his shoulders, grabbed one of the bottles, and served himself another drink. Conde made an effort to restrain himself, but didn't manage it. "Did you say something about an arroz con pollo?"

"*A la chorrera* . . . soupy, with some red peppers on top and . . ."

It was already dark out when he left for Tamara's house. He decided to walk, to accelerate the digestion of the arroz con pollo, and tried to piece his spirits back together by absorbing the beneficial air of a neighborhood that was not his own, but that awoke sentimental memories: his high school years, his friendship with Carlos, his relationship with Tamara, the small stadium where he played ball with friends like the now-absent Andrés, the image of the area's pleasant, cozy parks where he kissed his first girlfriends. Even though he knew that between his memories and the present, there stood decades deployed in demolishing everything with intensity and malice, with a nearly calculated perversity, he was still surprised by the tangible state of deterioration and abandonment that also extended over everything there like a plague. Braced houses that had never been painted again; mountainous heaps of garbage on the corners; sidewalks and streets recently imported from the Gaza Strip; new businesses erected on the basis of improvisation, poverty, and poor taste; stray dogs who would have given a leg to trade places with his poor Garbage II. Nothing that could improve his mood.

Tamara greeted him with a kiss capable of removing half of the burden of indifference that accompanied him, admiring how well his new shoes fit and giving him the news that Yoyi had been calling his house, Carlos's house, and her own. He wanted to see him urgently, his business partner had emphasized, regretting again that Conde did not have a cell phone, although he was already aware of his incapacity to operate them and his tendency to lose them.

As he watched Tamara skillfully cutting vegetables to make a soup, Conde called the Pigeon from the landline in the kitchen. When he got through, Yoyi's voice surprised him with its capacity for anticipation.

"Where the hell were you hiding, man?" his friend asked.

Conde made the gesture of looking at the receiver. "Yoyi, you have half of Havana calling you . . . How in the hell did you know it was me?"

"Oh, Conde . . . The cell phone recognizes the numbers calling you . . . And on the screen, because you know they have a screen, right? Well, Tamara's name came up because . . . What kind of an idiot conversation is this, man?"

Conde smiled in the face of his partner's exasperation. "Well, what's going on that's so urgent?"

"Something I found out and other things I'm thinking about. We have to talk . . ."

"Aha, talk to me."

He heard the Pigeon sigh. "Not on the phone, it's very complicated . . . Look, get yourself a car and come over to the *paladar* where I'm going to eat with my girlfriend . . ."

Conde looked over at Tamara, who was putting the vegetables in a pot.

"It's just that today . . . Tamara is cooking . . . And I already . . ."

"This is important, man. And you know I don't play around with important things. Come on, write down the address and come over here . . . Besides, I want to introduce you to my girlfriend and for you to see with your own eyes what a luxury *paladar* is. This one's in vogue . . . Look, look, come with Tamara, I'm treating."

"But . . ."

"Conde, come on already . . . Let's see, get Tamara on the phone," Yoyi ordered.

He turned around and told Tamara that Yoyi wanted to speak to her, while he wagged his finger no. The woman, intrigued, dried her hands on her apron and took the receiver her companion was holding out to her.

"Hello, Yoyi," she said, listened, and repeated "aha" to him three times, capping it with a smile and a nod. "I won't forget the address. I'm getting dressed and we're headed over there. I'll drag him by the ear. Yes, okay, see you soon," she confirmed and hung up.

The little mansion in El Vedado had enjoyed glamorous times as well as long years of decay on the verge of ruin. But when a Cuban entrepreneur managed to purchase it (at a bargain-basement price) with the idea in mind of starting a restaurant, the building was revived and, befittingly, entered its glory. The reparation and remodeling of the property covered everything from the front gate to the last inch of the roof, and now everything gleamed with the shine of lamps, furniture, folding screens, daringly designed decorations, polished metal, lacquered paint; everything arrived from far afield in unknown ways. The first thing Conde asked himself as he entered the place, reserved for foreigners and very privileged Cubans (or others like him, invited by either of those two possible options), was how much they must have paid for the building and its reparation and decoration. Just imagining the raw sum made him feel dizzy and awoke more questions like, for example, where had the money come from to make this investment before there were any profits? Another Cuban mystery. The last question he would ask himself, three and a half hours later when Yoyi paid with cold, hard cash for everything they'd consumed, just like the dozens of diners preceding them and who would follow, was how much money that place generated per day. Instead of dizziness, what Conde felt was suffocation. That place was a gold mine. Thus were made the fortunes that Miki Dollface was talking about that very afternoon, and he could not help but ask the same question: How long would that last?

The Pigeon was a regular customer of the restaurant and the maître d's college friend, since both had received their engineering degrees and now barely used their diplomas as decoration, since they earned a living doing other things and in more productive ways for their personal economies than designing bridges that would never be built, like Karla Choy had said. Knowing that Conde was a chain-smoker when he drank alcohol, Yoyi had asked his friend for a table on the terrace, the most set apart and comfortable one possible, and to keep cool two bottles of a good Spanish red for when his guests arrived.

With a glowing, beautiful, and perfumed Tamara hanging on his arm (so she could better show off her wedding ring), the plebeian Conde (who, luckily, was shod with dignity) crossed the room in search of his business partner, and confirmed that his long-running girlfriend was still capable of attracting attention: coming and going. He felt proud to be the exclusive beneficiary of such attributes. But when he arrived at the table reserved by Yoyi and saw his friend's new girlfriend, he felt his legs shake: the woman was finer than the house in which the restaurant stood, almost, almost as fine as the Chinese-Cuban Karla Choy. Her platinum hair, green eyes like traffic lights saying go, her thick lips, and carefully sculpted body with abundance in all the right places proved that Yoyi was a gourmet in all of life's important ways. The beauty of the day was named María de la Merced, she liked to be called Merche, and with the additional feat of having a classic name and nickname, Conde felt that the whole package was perfection: she was one of the few people of about thirty years of age born in the country who did not have an invented name or an outrageous nickname, of which one or the other began with a *Y*. To cap her virtues, Merche was the general manager of a private interior-decoration agency and was even a good conversationalist, reasonably educated, sufficiently well-informed, as discreet as to remain silent or chat directly with Tamara when the men entered rocky territory. Where in the hell did Yoyi find angels like this one?

Following the introductions, they each had a whiskey, enough to read the menu, put in their orders, and ask for the cooled-off Ribera del Duero wine. As usually happened when he had to choose between many possibilities, Conde opted for the first thing on the menu that promised to satisfy him gastronomically: grilled hogfish with herbs (what kind of herbs?) that he asked for with white rice, black beans, an army of fried plantains, and malanga fritters, plus an avocado salad with plenty of olive oil, since his stomach had already forgotten the arroz con pollo he'd ingested a few hours before. Tamara, meanwhile, decided on a Cuban plate with a French name, of sparse quantity and low in calories, while Yoyi and Merche opted for green salads followed by an octopus carpaccio with slices of Parmesan. Abundance, abundance, dammit!

As he savored the wine and picked at some olives and anchovies, Conde focused on observing the surrounding landscape, without ceasing to think of the unbearable variety on the menu and the wine list, a crossroads of selection whose possible existence his generation had never experienced in the establishments of socialist gastronomy, cultivated on mental agility and the most affectionate treatment: "My beautiful boy, there's this and this and nothing else, and hurry up and order, because you know it will run out: this and also this. And, you already know, heart of my hearts, that it's two beers per person. And they're not very cold, honey." He had to control the policeman he carried inside, and studied the atmosphere with interest while trying to demonstrate class, something that was complicated in a brute like him. He listened with real attention to Merche's explanation about the restaurant's decor, where, she said, neo-Nordic and minimalist styles converged, with straight lines dominating and light-colored wood, and he contained himself when it occurred to him to ask how much that building and everything in it had cost, further still, where it had all come from. As far as he knew, the closest stores selling neo-Nordic or minimalist or even well-made furniture were on the other side of the sea, of the damned circumstance.

When Conde was beginning to suspect that Yoyi's rushed invitation had as its only objective inviting him and Tamara to dinner in a pleasant place with exclusive prices, the Pigeon took advantage of their silence to reveal his other reason: incomplete but rather reliable information had reached his ears regarding the presence in Cuba of a Catalan antiquarian, Jordi Puig-something-or-other, who was very well-connected in the sale of artwork from Europe. According to what they said, the man, although he dealt in everything, specialized in pieces of medieval origins . . . As far as Yoyi knew, during the medieval period, in Cuba, there was no art: just some starving Indians, who were hunting Cuban hutias and eating cassava, without any *mojo*, to boot. And based on what Conde had said, Bobby Roque's lost Virgin could very well be a piece that was nothing less than medieval. Two plus two, Yoyi calculated with his knowledge as an engineer, equaled four, Conde. Or, almost always, he corrected himself. Confirming that he'd awakened his business partner's interests as a detective, the Pigeon promised to find out a little more about the reason that had brought that specific antiquarian, medievalist, Puig-something-or-other, to Cuba, who was, of course, Catalan, like Bobby's grandfather, like the statue of the Virgin, Catalan . . . Puigventós, dammit!

"If the man came for what we are thinking," Conde began after receiving the new information, "it's because someone was already talking to him about selling him something that interests him. And if that something is Bobby's Black Virgin, who appears to be a truly valuable antique, it's because She is or is supposed to be in the hands of someone who knows the Virgin's worth and where and how to find Her . . . And that person is not on the same team on which Raydel and the Cloak were playing. It's a guy in the business . . . or in the guild."

"Which means," Yoyi continued, "that if we're talking about the Black Virgin, who is still in Cuba, and that people from the guild are behind the robbery or connected, as far as I know, there are only four or five lions in Cuba with those connections, man, among them your friends René Águila and Elizardo Soler. And that Chinese earthquake . . ."

"So do you know the others?"

"At least two others . . . A guy who worked for years on restoring old Havana and who they say even stole nails from the cross . . . He's called Enrique Garcés. And he is gay, just like your friend Bobby, but he has more spurs than the finest fighting cock . . . The other one I remember is an Italian guy who comes and goes, a die-hard whoremonger, Guido I-don't-know-his-name-either, because everyone calls him Guido Corleone, pronouncing it as if it were a Spanish name, without the *u* . . ."

"So how are you going to find out more, Yoyi? This story is red-hot. Remember there are already two and a half dead guys . . ."

Merche stopped the fork in midair with which she was taking a portion of the carpaccio to her mouth and opened her green eyes so widely it seemed possible to see them fall on her plate. To speak so calmly about two dead and one half of another was far beyond her universe of designs, fashion, decorations.

"Two and a half dead guys?"

Yoyi smiled and caressed his girlfriend's hair. He winked at Tamara, asking for her help, and the doctor put all of her capacities into the task, acquired in the long years of living with a former policeman.

"You exaggerate so much, Mario! Two guys get killed in an accident racing motorcycles and you stick them in the story . . . I know that you fell in the bathroom and almost killed yourself, but it's because you're old."

Merche looked at Tamara, who smiled at her, then at Conde, who was looking at Tamara with a dour grimace, and last at Yoyi, who was looking at her.

"*Mami*, you know that my business is with people like the owners of this place . . . And they only kill you when they bring you the bill. Or, when you want to leave without paying . . ."

The young woman, who was not completely convinced, took the carpaccio to her lips and caressed the remains of the octopus as she chewed.

"Anyway, Conde," Yoyi added, "if I hear anything, I'll tell you and that's it . . . Okay, man?"

At that moment, the maître d' with an engineering degree approached the table and asked them how things were going. They all responded, "*Marvelously*," and Conde enjoyed watching the man refill their wineglasses with the dry and simultaneously delicate Ribera del Duero.

"Well if you'd like, I can set aside a table for you up at the bar on the terrace. Tonight, there's live music," and he mentioned the name of a famous musician. "Some Mexican tourists hired him to play for them."

"What do you say?" Yoyi asked Tamara and Conde. "This doesn't happen every day."

"It's fine with me," Tamara accepted, and Conde went along without any resistance.

"We'll finish and go up, so don't close my bill," Yoyi communicated to his friend, who withdrew to his other tasks.

Half an hour later, the two couples went up to the terrace's bar, where a loving breeze from the nearby sea glided across them. While the Mexicans had paid for the show (how much had they paid, Conde was asking himself, withdrawing numerical question marks from his bottomless pit of questions), the table that was set aside for Yoyi and his guests was in the first row, in front of the small stage along which ran a bar with all the necessary attributes to make it typical and pleasant, including strings of lights.

Since they had decided not to eat dessert, Yoyi ordered a plate of French cheeses and a bottle of Bordeaux, according to him, the best accompaniment. Conde, in addition, asked for coffee. In the conversation that followed, Yoyi informed them that Merche was choosing to take a specialization fellowship in Canada and that, if she traveled that way, she had plans to remain and explore the territories in the north . . . Conde watched the girl who glowed and felt that her beauty and good taste were attacking him: Another one who was saying goodbye? What in the hell was this?

The ambience of the bar-terrace was lively, youthful, full of conversation and laughter, music that was perhaps by pure miracle projected at a volume that did not interfere with the communication among the clientele. Conde, his professional baggage on his back, looked around and confirmed that the majority of those present, except for the long table occupied by about ten Mexicans, were members of the national fauna and almost all of them were young. The feeling of finding himself in a place where he didn't belong, where he was more of a foreigner than the Mexicans themselves, became very tangible at that moment. But he managed to even feel happy because of Tamara's happiness, although at the same time he was dissatisfied that he could not treat himself to enjoying places like this with his old friends, who would surely be incapable of even imagining their existence, which were becoming more common in the city (per Yoyi), spaces that were so in demand they required previous reservations and where people didn't fight each other for anything because there was enough for everyone. For all who could pay those prices. And, asking himself—what a damned tic of his, he just couldn't avoid it—Conde questioned the source of the money in the hands of those young people who were so young and seemed so at ease, comfortably installed with genetic harmony in the reserves of Havana's revived bon vivant scene with which he himself had been in intimate and well-fed and well-imbibed contact that day.

The musician joined the stage with his band and began his concert. It seemed significant to Conde that the young people present, including Yoyi and Merche, knew the words of the songs he sang by heart, some of them made to listen to, and others to enjoy while dancing, dancing. Yoyi and Merche went out to the dance floor and, under the pretext of observing her abilities, Conde was in ecstasy contemplating every inch of that woman's magnetic body. Was he seeing her for the first and only time? Then Tamara asked him, more out of duty than conviction, if he wanted to try to move a little. But he said no with all of his fundamentalism: in Cuba, there were only two ways to dance. Well and badly. And he danced badly. And people look down upon those who danced badly. It was enough already that people were looking at him because of his face, his age, his surprised expression before the revelation of an exotic world sprouted from God knew what folds of society that shone in all its splendor with new riches, and exultant post-anything glamour. Tamara said yes to everything, said of course, but left her chair and her tormented near-husband, and went to dance.

As he savored the drink of cognac—courtesy of the house—with which he resolved to end the night, Conde remembered for a moment the circles of Havana's Inferno through which he had traveled in recent days. He patted the still-painful wound on the back of his head and told himself that in reality, that Inferno existed as much as this paradise under the stars where he was drinking cognac, also French, whose price would guarantee food for a day for an entire family. Two neighboring worlds between which a wall was rising similar to the one that, in the time to which Bobby's Black Virgin seemed to belong, separated nobles from plebeians: a wall perhaps more subtle although no less distinct than on the island they had tried to demolish but that, persistent like life, continued to rise at the slightest chance. Then, in the midst of his socio-historico-philosophical meditations about the circularity of time and its worst manifestations, through the extreme left angle of his vision, Conde sensed a gold reflection, luminous, powerful, capable of making him turn his face. In that sector, in front of the bar, a long dozen of girls, amid whom was Merche, danced and sang the musician's song, and Conde understood that the vigorous light that had touched him came from those bodies, those dresses, those shoes, those perfumes, the expansive elegance, and the sparkling hair of those women: all were beautiful, elegant, svelte, and blond. The wall existed and imposed its segregation.

14.

He moved through the room as stealthily as a thief. Tamara was sleeping, with the elegance and class that she exhibited even in that state, and with the remains of her satisfaction of the previous night still marked on her Sleeping Beauty face. Once he was in the kitchen, he prepared the coffee, drank two cups, and smoked two cigarettes. Between the first cup of coffee and cigarette and the next ones, he made a generous stop at the toilet, where he deposited the mixture of the exclusive foods from the previous night's exquisite dinner and thought about the regrettable end of those French cheeses.

Fully awake and his mood weighed down by annoyances and unleashed bitterness over the experience of recent days, he went out in search of Bobby and of the truth without which he could not work. Or even live. Even if he lost the highest salary he'd ever earned in his miserable existence.

Without allowing himself the calm of contemplating the sea, he went directly to Bobby's house and banged on the door. The inhabitant welcomed him with piercing fear reflected on his face that was barely alleviated when he realized that the visitor was his friend and not the persistent police. He was wearing a Chinese silk robe and did not appear to have had a good night.

"Conde, those police won't leave me alone . . . Now there's another dead man and they insist that I have something to do with what happened! I'm the victim, the victim!"

Conde followed him to the terrace where, without saying a word, he awaited Bobby's return with the tray on which the porcelain cups tinkled with the coffee. He drank his calmly, enjoying the gift it was on his palate, and then he lit the indispensable cigarette. Meanwhile, Bobby had continued his lamentations, his invocations to the power of the Virgin and to Yemayá, his justifications, until Conde energetically lifted a hand to ask for silence.

"That's enough already with the boo-hooing, Bobby . . . I don't know about the police, but I don't believe a goddamn word of what you're saying. You are a shitty liar and you deserve everything that's happened to you. And more . . . !"

The other man's eyes were bulging out. He rubbed his hands as he listened to his employee's speech.

"I deserve what Conde, I deserve what?"

"Everything, Bobby."

"But you know I didn't kill anyone . . ."

"That's the only thing I think I know . . . And sometimes I have my doubts."

"But how can you, my friend . . . ?"

"Bobby, you disappointed me," Conde stated, looking into his eyes. "You tricked me several times, you used me, asking me one thing when what you wanted was another. You've told me whatever you feel like whenever you feel like it, and, to boot, you spoke of the years and our friendship and I've believed it . . . Guys like you are capable of anything . . ."

Bobby lowered his gaze. He seemed truly affected. "You're right, *viejo* . . . Forgive me."

Conde regretted having to use that method, but he thought he had placed his former classmate where he needed to. So he continued.

"I don't forgive jack shit! Let's see, to begin to fix your disasters and lies, tell me the whole story of the Virgin. The truth, dammit! And don't talk to me about how She has powers! Because if She does, it's to screw over people. Because of the Virgin or because of you, there are already two dead guys and—"

Bobby shook his head, denying something, but began to speak.

"Forgive me, forgive me, please, if I didn't tell you something . . ." Bobby insisted. "But, understand me."

"I don't understand. I want the truth . . . Come on, spill it . . ."

Bobby changed the focus of his gaze again and placed it on an ornamental malanga plant's enormous leaves, of a shining and spotless green.

"Why do these things happen to me, my God?" He paused, looked up at the heavens, blessed himself, sniveled a large quantity of mucus. "None of this had to have happened . . . She's a medieval Black Virgin," he said and stopped again before finally getting on with it, his gaze directed at his interlocutor already. "And She really does have powers, Conde, She really does: She cured me; in Spain, She saved people, She did miracles . . . You have to believe me, *chico*! That Virgin was brought by the Spaniard who was my grandmother's husband, like I told you. José came from a small hamlet in the Catalan Pyrenees that isn't even on maps . . . He brought the Virgin and always had Her with him, and he didn't like to show Her to anyone. But if anyone from the family saw Her and asked him about the Virgin, the first thing he said was that She was a Virgin of Regla . . ."

"Bobby, Bobby, I already know that story . . . How long . . . ?"

The other man sighed before he continued. "José told that story I just told you to everyone . . . But it was made-up. He only told the truth to my grandmother. And that is the truth that I know: that that Virgin had been in the chapel of his hamlet for centuries, ever since She appeared in the trunk of a tree and performed a miracle . . . José said that in that area, She'd always had the reputation of a miracle worker, of someone who cured, that She helped women get pregnant, things like that. But he insisted on telling my grandmother that he had not stolen Her. That he had saved the Virgin, was what he said . . . That to save Her he did very serious things and had to escape from Spain. He never said what he had done, but serious things are serious things . . . All of this was during the Civil War, when the anarchists and others were killing priests, burning churches and saints . . . They even burned down Gothic cathedrals and that's no lie . . . They killed one another for any reason and even no reason . . ."

"You really don't know what serious things José did? Couldn't it have been that, that he stole the Virgin?"

"I don't think so, he seemed like a good man. But the truth is that I don't know what in the hell he did over there during the war, whether José was one of the ones who was going around killing priests to make the great revolution . . . What he did say is that with the Virgin in a sack, he crossed the Pyrenees through a path he knew. He went across half of France with Her. In Le Havre, yes, I think in Le Havre, he made his way onto a ship as a stowaway that was coming to Havana and Buenos Aires. When he was discovered, they were on the verge of throwing him overboard. They punished him by making him clean the ship. Then, when he arrived in Havana, he recovered the Virgin whom he'd hidden, and escaped the ship . . . Ending up in Regla. And in Regla, he saw another Virgin, the one from here . . . From that moment on, he began to tell anyone who asked him that his was a Virgin of Regla. I think that even my grandmother believed that at the beginning . . ."

Conde lowered his gaze. The story sounded believable, although incomplete. "But those two Virgins don't look alike at all . . . Well, they're Black . . ."

"It seemed logical to me: to any person in Cuba, a Black Virgin has to be the Virgin of Regla, right? Later, my grandmother found out that it was not and he told her his story . . . Or, the other way around . . . But before my grandmother told me, I, who am curious, discovered what She really was: a medieval Virgin, authentic Romanesque, originally Black, older still than the Virgin of Regla of Chipiona. From what I later found out, over there, they called that statue Our Lady of la Vall, because she is one of the statues who disappeared in that time, during the Civil War, so in that respect, José was not telling a lie . . . In sum, before she died, my grandmother handed Her over to me and told me José's story, at least what she knew, which could be true or not, although she confirmed what I already knew: that She was a Virgin who had spent centuries in the church of José's hamlet and that José was not called Josep Bonet and everything else . . ."

"But the story doesn't end there."

Bobby shook his head. He gulped. Conde knew he was missing the essence of what he needed to know.

"I started to find out more," Bobby continued. "I knew that one of these Virgins, if sold, could be worth up to three or four million dollars. Perhaps more. Because there are very few of those statues left in the world, in the South of France, in the north of Spain, a few in Germany, some in Poland. Today, they are museum or catalog pieces . . . Imagine, Saint Louis brought some when he returned to France from his Crusades in the Holy Land . . . But I never wanted to sell Her, Conde: I want Her for me, to leave Her to my children later and for them to do whatever they want. Worship Her or sell Her. But after I'm dead. That's why I want to recover Her. Because it's true what I told you, but also what José used to say: that Virgin has powers. I don't know if it's because She's Black, medieval, because She is rare, perhaps because She came from Africa, from the Holy Land, like some historians say, I don't know: but She has the power to give you peace. And strength . . . And health . . . It's a mystery, but it's true Conde, I swear it to you. Because of all of that, I want to recover Her without making a fuss . . . Because I don't know if the Spanish government can claim Her as the country's cultural patrimony, and because if I make noise, everyone will know what She is worth . . . Conde, almost no one knew that I had this Virgin. Now even the police know and those are statues that even appear in books . . . You'll see, you'll see . . ."

Bobby stood up and smoothed his robe before going upstairs, from where he returned with two books, one of them coffee-table size, with a leather cover, that he opened and placed on the little table, in front of Conde.

"Here She is . . . Our Lady of la Vall . . . Romanesque sculpture from the twelfth century. Disappeared from Her chapel in 1936. Unknown whereabouts."

Despite the dubious quality of the printed image, Conde recognized Her immediately and had the feeling that the pieces were finally starting to fit together. The one in the book was the Virgin from the photos that Bobby had given him. She could also be the one that Platero had shown him on his computer, in a retouched and improved image.

"It's obvious that José stole Her . . ."

"Or that he saved Her, as he said. The war was ongoing, they were burning churches . . ."

"The one in this photo has two hands . . ."

"The missing hand is one that José lost when he took Her . . . That's what he said."

"Do I have to believe that whole story about the Catalan and your grandmother, huh, Bobby?"

"I swear on what is most sacred that it's true. Where in the hell else was I going to get a statue like this one, how was I going to obtain it? Where was I going to buy it?"

"So, what's this Jordi Puigventós doing in Cuba?"

"Looking for my Virgin," Bobby responded without hesitation. "That guy is a pirate and somehow he got wind of the Virgin existing and being lost . . . I'm sure it was René Águila . . . What I told you, Conde: people already know She exists and that She is in Cuba . . ."

"And for sale," Conde specified.

"Yes, for sale. But who has Her, Conde, who? Whoever killed Raydel and the other kid?"

Conde nodded; he shook his head; he was thinking. "All of this means that the Virgin is still in Cuba . . . And whoever has Her is Raydel and Ramiro's murderer or knows who killed them, and he recovered the darned Virgin . . . So, the good news is that they cannot sell Her because it would give them away."

"Whoever has Her is someone who knows what the Virgin is worth. I'm thinking that it could even be the person who asked Raydel to steal Her . . . and then things got complicated."

Conde had already considered that possibility, which seemed more and more probable, although it seemed strange that the fake Raydel would steal such a valuable Virgin, with which he hoped to become a millionaire and leave Cuba, and at the same time would carry off even the kettle to boil water. He had also calculated that the murderer could take the risk of selling Her to someone like Jordi Puigventós, capable of buying Her without too much thought, and once She was sold, try to escape with the money. How much money? Where would Puigventós get that money from? Conde piled up reasons and doubts to then spar with Bobby a little more.

"Who could buy that Virgin worth millions and that somebody took out of Spain, let's say, to save Her? Worse still: Who would dare buy Her knowing that behind Her, there are at least two dead and behind the two dead, some Cuban policemen who, I can assure you, are not idiots and already know there's a valuable Virgin stuck in this whole mess? Bobby, if that Virgin was stolen in Spain, over there, they can't do business with Her either. No, I don't understand . . . Do you think that Jordi would go so far as to . . . ?"

"Puigventós knows a lot, Conde. To have the business he has . . . And here in Cuba, there are also people who know a lot and have cash and—"

"People from your guild?"

"Yes . . . But there are others who invest in things with assured value. Houses, jewelry, paintings . . . Now there are a lot of people in those businesses. It's like a plague that's been set loose. And some must have contacts to get things out of Cuba. And someone in Spain or Miami, someone with a lot of money, could want the Virgin: not to exhibit Her or resell Her, no . . . But rather to keep Her, for Her powers."

"Don't fuck around anymore with that thing about Her powers, Bobby."

"Okay, I won't fuck around anymore. But She has powers! She cured me! That's what gives Her the most value! Don't you understand?"

Conde shook his head and gave himself a few moments to think. He had begun to feel like he had before him the true entry to the spiral, but without yet possessing the certainty of where it would lead him . . . Or even whether it would lead him to that darned Virgin who was prompting the story that was getting more and more macabre. He had to do something. And he was going to do it.

"You'd have to be crazy to want to buy that Virgin, although . . . Bobby, get dressed right now. We have to go out."

"Where to, Conde?"

"Where my hunches lead me. Come on, let's go . . ."

What in the hell is wrong with you, Bobby?"

"I'm just nervous. I'm scared . . ."

"It doesn't seem to me like you're very scared . . . Because you don't care if you die, you son of a bitch . . . But I do . . . At least in this way . . . It's going to hurt very much . . ."

"Ay, Conde . . ."

"Ay, nothing, take it easy, dammit . . . Red light!"

Bobby slammed on the brake beneath the traffic light, and Conde was about to slam into the windshield to then fly out of the small German artifact when, without transition, the driver went into reverse.

Conde thought he'd made the worst mistake and was risking his life in the most absurd way he could have conceived of. Bobby Roque turned out to be the most disastrous driver he'd ever seen in his life. Ever since he turned on the ignition of his VW Beetle and drove up Miramar's Séptima Avenida, he had begun to make every possible blunder along the way. From running through stop signs and a red light to being on the verge of running over an old man, a motorcyclist, and even a dog who, in the most classic and disciplined style, was pissing on a fire hydrant.

Twenty minutes later, sweaty, clutching the seat and the door, Conde let out his breath when he was able to step foot on firm ground in front of the mansion of Elizardo Soler. And there, he went from a state of terror to a feeling of perplexity.

That house on El Vedado's Calle 19 had attracted Conde's attention, but, for some inexplicable reason, he had never asked to whom it belonged or had belonged. Something distinguished it from the area's other mansions and large dwellings. Its singularity was not due only to the majestic proportions of a building that was exemplarily eclectic or to its magnificent state of conservation amid the buildings in need of paint and love and care, but rather to its capacity to give off an air of mystery, at least for the somewhat novelesque perceptions of the former policeman. That enigmatic condition, now that he thought about it, was perhaps due to the conjunction of the tower—lookout, crowned by a rooster wind vane, the roof gutters that imitated Gothic gargoyles, the pediment decorated with two cornucopias facing each other from which poured fruits native to the country and paradise, elements visible over the tall gates covered with metal sheets that were always painted black, and the dense vegetation, from which exotic date palms stood out.

"Bobby, I need you to tell me what Elizardo knows, because if he was in the know about what they stole from you and how much it was worth . . . For starters, tell me who in the hell this Elizardo Soler is who lives in this mansion and about whom I've heard some strange stories . . . Come, let's sit down." And he pointed at the benches in the park that was laid out on the next block, one of which was permanently occupied, for several years already, by none other than a bronze version of John Lennon. This would be the first time Conde used the park since the Beatle's face was unveiled, at last rehabilitated as an exalted figure of the counterculture after his music had been stigmatized, for years, on the island as a product of capitalist and bourgeois ideological penetration.

Elizardo Soler, Bobby began to tell him when they sat down and Conde lit his cigarette, was the natural-born grandson, if you could call him that, of the former proprietor of the house, one of the members of the Sarrá clan. Like his entire family, Emilio Sarrá had left Cuba when the revolutionary government began to voice its revolutionary purposes. An illegitimate son of that Sarrá, whom the magnate had not been able to give his last name, but did give his affection, then came to live in the mansion with his mother, the dancer Adela Soler, in the fleeing aristocrat's confidence that he would soon be returning to the island and his properties. If there was something Emilio Sarrá wanted to keep in this world, it was his tropical version of Xanadu, the mansion of dreams and glory of a stock of successful and well-heeled *indianos*, the owners of great fortunes of origins as dark as the Black Africans purchased and sold by many of them. To achieve it, Sarrá trusted in his lover and his offspring. His natural-born son, Octavio Soler, was, as Conde could imagine, Elizardo's father. And at some point, Octavio had to fight to avoid that the house of his progenitor, in which he had lived until then as an occasional guest, be revolutionarily repossessed, as the sugar mill, the rum factory, several stores, and the Camagüey haciendas of his blood father had been repossessed. It was of great help in that effort to preserve the property the fact of having been, like other young bourgeois university students, an active collaborator of the anti-Batista revolutionary fighters in the Havana clandestine movement. Very soon, thanks to some friend with real power, his case was covered up, like the house's garden, and Octavio Soler was considered the legal usufructuary and later owner of the mansion of the man whom, he said, was his biological father.

Meanwhile, Elizardo, Bobby continued, had been a wild bon vivant in his youth, a member of the clan of the children of powerful fathers. To finance the best possible life for himself, he had begun to empty the house as soon as Octavio died. In the mid-1980s, when Elizardo most needed it to move his life along, the government opened the so-called House of Gold and Silver, soon renamed the House of Hernando Cortez, where one could trade gold for trinkets. And Elizardo handed over a fortune in jewels in exchange for a new Russian Lada and some appliances that Cubans had no other way of accessing. Later, when the Crisis came, he sold furniture and decorations to maintain the rhythm of his expenditures and consumption in the midst of general sparsity. Then, like in a fairy tale, a French noblewoman appeared on his horizon who, if not rich, at least had a bit of money. Money enough, Bobby thought. Elizardo married her and went to live in Switzerland . . . Or was the woman Swiss and he went with her to France and, in reality, she was very rich? The fact is that he spent about ten years over there, between Paris and Geneva, while his mother took care of the house in Havana . . .

When Elizardo's mother got sick, he returned. The family mansion was the magnet that dragged the Sarrás, like a call of their blood. For Eli, it was easier to return because he invoked his father's name and his father's friends, and they gave him special treatment . . . When he repatriated himself, with the experience of what he had lived and learned in Europe, he decided to change the focus of his interests, and instead of selling, he recycled himself as the buyer who would later sell and gain. From that time on, thanks to the connections established in his time as a seller who consumed everything and anything, to his knowledge, and to the relationships established in Paris and to the capital he managed to extract from his French or Swiss wife, he had entered the business, or the guild, with exceptional force and ability and, one would almost say, with crazy luck. Because, as if he had some kind of special magnetism, the most valuable and sought-after pieces came his way, the ones that brought him the most cash. But he soon diversified his interests and made himself a kind of representative of several painters, the mediator of some European merchants and gallery owners interested in Cuban art and . . . There was Elizardo Soler, earning money like a madman and living in that house of dreams, which would never see the return of the original owner, that grandfather Emilio Sarrá, from whom, Eli says, and with this Bobby finished his story, he received an inheritance in Spain, but that must be completely made-up.

"Urban legend," concluded Conde, who had been connecting the story Bobby laid out with the information Miki Dollface had offered him earlier to confirm how both fit and complemented each other at the most basic level, even in the parts that were legend.

"Yes, I think Eli is a compulsive liar," Bobby confirmed.

"Someone told me it's possible he was also an agent . . ." Conde probed.

Bobby laughed heartily.

"If he's a State Security agent, he's the best in the world . . . With the dealings he gets involved in, the things he says and does, with how boastful he is . . ."

"But couldn't he have been one? Maybe he no longer is, but if he was, he continues to be so . . . Like what happens to policemen. That might give him a certain impunity, or he might think he has it, I don't know . . ."

"No, Conde, Eli is too much of a bigmouth and takes too many risks. Sometimes he says and does things that make you wonder whether he's mad or pulling your leg. But an agent, a spy, any of those things, I don't believe it . . . If he ever swears it to me, I'm going to think it's another one of his lies, his boasting . . . Well, let's go. Although the truth is that I don't know what you're going to get out of this conversation with Eli . . ."

Following Bobby's steps, Conde at last crossed the threshold of the iron gate, walked across the granite paved path that led to the mansion, and his previous and foreseeable surprise multiplied. The house's garden, cared for with obvious professional attention, was adorned by a true procession of marble sculptures of winged angels and crowned Virgins that seemed familiar to the former policeman. Couldn't they be some of the valuable pieces stolen from the richest pantheons of Havana's cemetery? The porch, which ran across the front and sides of the first floor, was protected by tropical awnings behind which were placed wicker and iron seats and tables with a fruit motif. In enormous cages, some birds of multicolored feathers and long golden beaks were resting in the midday heat.

Conde identified them as toucans. And alongside the gigantic mahogany door that gave way to the mansion, like one more adornment, there was Elizardo Soler, smiling, dressed from head to toe in white, evoking a boy who was ready to receive his First Communion.

"To what do I owe this honor?" the man asked, looking at the recently arrived pair, although addressing Conde.

"How are you, Eli?" Bobby, whose embarrassment was visible, greeted him and, when he reached Elizardo's side, kissed him on the cheek. "It's that Conde needed to speak with you and—"

"Well, come in," Elizardo extended the invitation, and Conde said hello and thank you, although he managed to avoid shaking his hand.

The mansion's foyer had the same dimensions as Conde's house. At the back, a curved staircase led to the upper floor and received the multicolored illumination of an enormous stained-glass window that displayed a sailing scene, perhaps Mediterranean, like the original owner of the house. Marble floors and columns, stylish lamps and furniture, very fine glass ornaments were scattered about on every surface, establishing a harmonious game that relied on an elegance dictated by quality and good taste.

With a hand on Bobby's shoulder, Elizardo led them toward a side room where he had put together what appeared to be his work studio. Built-in bookcases ran along the wooden walls where several encyclopedias that had once been very highly prized (Conde, because of his business, could tell from afar) rested in boredom, now devalued due to the arrival of digital alternatives. On the front wall, behind the desk, shelves gave way to open space on which Conde could contemplate, as he gulped, an enormous canvas by René Portocarrero, which, in the maestro's aesthetic, represented the house in whose interior he now stood. Who was Elizardo Soler in reality; who was his father; who was his mother, the forgotten dancer? How many of his urban legends might not be the most extraordinary real stories of a country where they aimed to create an earthly kingdom of equality and where it was still possible to find places like this one?

Elizardo invited them to sit down on a leather sofa while he took his place on a high-backed office chair, seemingly his preferred throne.

"It's a miracle you caught me here. That Cuban habit of dropping by unannounced."

"It was my fault," Conde interrupted. "I needed to speak with you and—"

"Leave the formalities, my friend . . . What's going on?" Elizardo asked, and Conde thought he sensed some hostility in his tone.

"What else have you been able to find out on your end about the story with Bobby's Virgin?"

Elizardo smiled. He seemed relaxed, confident, as always. Superior. Elizardo made it tangible that he belonged to a native breed of the powerful who had lorded over things and people, the possibility of an easy life: a mark that would be almost impossible to get rid of. And that power seemed to affect Bobby in a special way, who became smaller spiritually and even physically in the presence of that venerated friend.

"I found out about the other kid they killed. And that means that things have gotten complicated."

"Besides the dead guy . . . Why else?" Conde asked.

"You want more complications than two dead in connection with Bobby's Virgin?"

"Oh, God," Bobby muttered.

"Yes, because the deaths are a result of something . . ." Conde probed.

Elizardo thought for a few moments before speaking. Conde knew that, just like René Águila, the man was a bird of prey, difficult to follow, impossible to corner. His gaze reflected an intense wickedness. Or was Conde merely seeing what his prejudgments indicated?

"That the Virgin is still in Cuba, right?"

"Yes, and what else?"

"That there's someone who wants Her . . . And that that someone was behind the theft."

"Possibly . . ." Conde admitted, "and that that someone lost control of what had seemed easy. To steal a Virgin of Regla should not be complicated. Especially if the thief was an ignorant like Raydel . . . But that he was ignorant did not mean he was an idiot. He couldn't be if he was capable of taking over another identity for three or four years without anyone discovering him . . ."

Bobby was following the conversation with his eyes wide open. Elizardo nodded periodically.

"Did Raydel know what the Virgin was worth . . . ?" Elizardo proposed.

"He knew. Price and everything. A friend of his told him. A kid who knew where and how to find out . . . To his buddies, Raydel sold them Bobby's story that She was a Virgin of Regla and had powers, without telling them what She was really worth."

"She does have powers, dammit!" Bobby protested and closed his eyes for a few moments. "Don't be so mistrustful," he added. Because it seemed he was beginning to understand something that until the moment he had not imagined, and he again invoked God, the Virgin, and Yemayá, without forgetting to touch the floor and take his fingers to his lips.

"But before the matter got out of control, everything seemed so organized that there was even a buyer for the Virgin already," Conde added, and Eli reacted.

"Puigventós!" Elizardo exclaimed, who seemed to have realized a revealing connection.

"Yes, that is why Puigventós is in Cuba . . . Do you know him, Elizardo?"

"Why do you insist on treating me so formally?"

"It must be because of this house, I don't know . . . You know Puigventós, right?"

"Everyone in the business knows him. He buys a lot and pays well. I myself have sold him some things. Antiques . . . But all of it legal, like I told you the other time. I wouldn't risk losing what I have just to make a little extra money."

"Sometimes, it's more than just a little extra . . . Like the value of the sculptures in your garden. Whose dead are they?"

"They came from the pantheons of my maternal great-grandmother and my paternal grandfather. I mean, from the Sarrá and Valladares families," the man responded with confidence and a touch of pride. "Before some vulture could take those sculptures that belong to my family, all of them made in Italy with Carrara marble . . ."

"Belonged," Conde rebutted.

"Depends on the point of view. For me, they belong, first person plural present perfect of the indicative of the regular verb *to belong*. The pantheons are still private. That is why I transferred them here . . .”

"Third," Conde noted when the other man allowed him to speak.

"Third what?" his host asked.

"Third person . . . *They*, the sculptures, *belong* . . . Although in the past it's *belonged*."

"It's all the same . . . I could give a shit about grammar. They are mine . . . In first person."

Conde had no other option but to smile, despite not having any desire to. "Because everything will go back to its original owners?"

"Anything could happen . . . This country is changing and is going to change more. It has to change more."

"To go back to being what it once was?"

"I already told you: anything could happen . . . Like you, I know that nothing will be what it once was. It will be something else. And, we have to be ready for that something else. Or you're going to get an offside."

Conde nodded: Elizardo was right. As a matter of fact, many things were happening and he had tangibly confirmed it in recent days. There were already people left out of the game. But the past was the past, and the future . . . only God knew. Because maybe it was all just a simple question of verb tenses and the best conjugations.

"That's why I don't like soccer," Conde said, trying to gain time to go back to the subject he wanted to explore. Elizardo, meanwhile, smiled in satisfaction.

"Of course something is going to happen here. I don't know what, whether we're going to make a somersault backward or forward . . . But something is going to happen. I don't know when, but . . . I have that presentiment. And no, they're not going to catch me off field . . .”

"Yes, that has become fashionable . . . The thing about having presentiments. And now, I myself have one called Jordi Puigventós. Have you seen him already?"

"No, I haven't seen him. He hasn't called me and—"

"But you know where to find him?"

"At the Meliá Cohiba. He always stays there . . . Because he's friends with the manager and he gives him discounts. He's Catalan, after all . . ."

"Yes, this story is full of Catalans . . . Even the Virgin is Catalan . . . Even his grandfather was Catalan . . . Too many . . ."

"That's why I'm a Barça fan!" Elizardo exclaimed and, from the pocket of his very white pants, extracted a blue keychain in the shape of the shield of the Barcelona Fútbol Club.

Conde demanded that Bobby accompany him. He sensed that a conversation with a guy of Jordi Puigventós's background would end up being complicated and that the presence of the owner of the Black Virgin could be useful, even when he wasn't sure for what and despite feeling disappointed by him. At the hotel front desk, Bobby asked to be connected with the guest's accommodations, but following several rings, he was convinced that he was not in his room. Conde then looked around and his police sense picked out a man, black as coal, dressed in an immaculate guayabera and leaning against one of the lobby's bars, facing a cup of coffee. The man was trying in vain to not look like a security guard (or was he simply not trying at all?). Conde approached him. He sat down on the empty stool to the right of the Black man in the guayabera, and, without asking whether he was or wasn't one of the location's guards, without even looking at him, he told him, as if he were making confession with a priest, that he was a former colleague of his, that he was helping the head of the Criminal Investigation Unit on a case, and that he was there because he needed to obtain some information about the guest Jordi Puigventós. The blacker-than-night man in the immaculate guayabera looked at Conde the entire time with great seriousness and as if he were an insect.

"So how do I know that what you're telling me is true?" he asked at last.

"Call the Criminal Investigation Unit and tell them to put Major Palacios on the line for Conde. Conde is me."

The man in the guayabera looked at him with all his attention. His lips moved slightly. "Conde? Lieutenant Mario Conde?"

Up until this point, as far as he knew, he was Mario Conde and had been a lieutenant.

"What's left of him. How do you know . . . ?"

"I'm the nephew of the deceased Arcadio Jorrín, the captain . . . My uncle had a lot of affection for you. Ariel Jorrín," the guard added and held out a hand to Conde, who felt the sharp return to the past: a nephew of Captain Jorrín! Many years before, he and Jorrín had been policemen alongside each other and friends, and Conde had felt the captain's death deeply. He didn't want to remember anymore.

"Well, if you can help me . . ."

"Come with me," Ariel Jorrín said, and Conde followed him. When he walked by him, he made a gesture to Bobby to wait for him. Behind the guard, he entered an office close to the concierge's desk and took the seat his host indicated.

"What I'm doing goes against protocol . . . You know. I know that you are not a policeman anymore. I'm doing this because it's you," Jorrin's nephew advised him.

"Thank you."

"Puigventós is a client of the hotel. We know he focuses on buying art in Cuba. He buys what can be bought and, almost certainly, many times, what can't be . . . But we haven't been able to catch him red-handed. He knows a lot . . . Perhaps some diplomat helps him take out what he shouldn't or somebody whom we don't suspect, but who is very well-connected. The man knows how things are and does not speak of anything important on the hotel telephones or inside the hotel," the guard said and dialed a number on the phone that was in front of him. "Alfredo, it's me, Ariel . . . Tell me, what do you know about Puigventós?" he asked and listened for a long minute, as he nodded, and voiced his thanks before hanging up. "Well, well . . . The Planta Real folks tell me that he hasn't been by the hotel in two days . . . And he has an open reservation . . . His things are in his room, so it doesn't appear that he has left Cuba. Strange, right?"

Conde was nodding as he received the information. And then he considered it only for a moment.

"Ariel, now you really have to call Major Palacios . . . That that man has been lost for two days could be a real issue."

The betraying beat of vertigo trapped him when he pressed his forehead against the cold glass and observed the generous landscape splayed out at his feet: the dark, snaking avenue along the Malecón, the gray line of the concrete wall that was the end or the beginning of so many dreams and the tempting extension of the sea, both multiplied by the height: the extension and the temptation. He closed his eyes for a few moments, waited for the shaking of the void to dissipate and took a deep breath before returning to the contemplation. From that twenty-fifth floor, all perspective was altered. He confirmed that it was possible to distinguish the sea's many color changes. It went from a pleasant green which revealed the layers of rocks beneath it and, going farther out, went up through the cool palette to an intense blue capable of hiding the contents of the depths. Not a single boat was traveling between the coast and the remote horizon. The absence of visible life on the whole liquid plain contributed to increasing the feeling of unfathomability and calm, but also the certainty of what the challenge of crossing it in any floating artifact represented, as so many Cubans had attempted so many times throughout the years. As the young Yúnior Colás Gómez, alias Raydel, had dreamed of crossing it. A dream that had perhaps cost him his life.

Absorbed, he didn't even hear the voice calling for him. Observing the sea from the hotel room, Mario Conde navigated through general meditations and landed on the most regrettable and concrete realities. Involved in an investigation in which he responded to the interests of his former classmate Bobby, he had allowed himself to be dragged by the current of an elevated and deceptive perspective, like the one he was enjoying now, and assumed as guilty Yúnior-Raydel, his cousin Ramiro the Cloak, and even their pal the Bat, when in reality, they had been victims: of society and of much more elaborate ambitions, capable of surpassing them and, even, of devouring them . . . Conde regretted having made that error in judgment that, perhaps, had prevented him from seeing with the necessary clarity a process in which he was participating as a catalyst. The ease with which his own prejudices and conditions led him to distort opinions was pathetically obvious.

When he turned around, he saw that Manolo had occupied an armchair and Bobby, terrified, with his hands between his legs, was sitting on the edge of the bed. In the ambience of the typical hotel room, the image of the two men, practically knee to knee, seemed ridiculous to him: Would they make love?

"Tell me it's not," Conde let out.

"Not what?" Manolo asked.

Conde took a chair and dragged it over to the glass wall. He wanted to remain there, facing the sea. "Nothing, just me being silly . . ."

Major Palacios and Lieutenant Duque had arrived at the hotel just twenty minutes after Ariel Jorrín had called them. While Duque was focused on compiling information with Jorrín and the head of security of the office where the guard command post was located, Manolo had asked for a quiet place to have a conversation with Conde and Bobby and was given the key to a room that served as a sort of ground zero for security work. Conde knew that at the hotel, the walls were transparent and the telephones were speakers, and when he had the mental clarity to do so, he confirmed that everything in the cubicle presented the most pleasant image of hotel normality that happened to hide more cameras and microphones than those placed in a television studio. The scene was of a macabre reality show.

Manolo let out a long sigh and slapped his thighs with both palms: the work was beginning.

"Citizen Roque Rosell . . . you are making too much work for us," he began, and Conde saw how Bobby nodded: yes, he was making too much work for the police, he admitted without protest, pushed by his fear. "Theft, murders, disappearances, false identities. An encyclopedia: and you are at the middle of it all . . . Let's see, tell me a good story . . . One that I don't know."

Without any need to be pushed further and without entrusting himself to any of his divine protections, Bobby began to speak, almost as if he needed to confess himself. The story he told turned out to be very similar to the one Conde knew, including the tale of what he'd confirmed with his own flesh—so aptly said—of the Virgin's curative powers and the fact that he had known for years how valuable the stolen statue was, although he kept the detail to himself of the possible sums. Of the lost Catalan Puigventós, all he confirmed was that he focused on buying art, but that he had never dealt with him directly. Other people from the guild had, but not him.

Manolo nodded. Conde knew that the major was exhausted, and he preferred not to ask the reason. There must be one. For a police officer, obliged to deal with the worst human miseries at all times, there always were reasons.

"What about you, Conde, what do you have to say? Do you also believe that the Virgin cures the sick and that we should post Her in front of the Ministry of Public Health?"

Conde's retelling added the unsettling conviction that the Catalan antiquarian Jordi Puigventós had come to Cuba in response to the possibility of taking that Virgin. A Virgin that was not just any Virgin, he specified, since, mystical powers or not, She had faculties in which many people have believed throughout many centuries and in which so many people still believed. The medieval black wooden statue could fetch a sum of several million euros. Although, he warned, he could not imagine how Puigventós would be able to sell Her with the effigy's criminal history. Old and new, known and yet to be discovered. But, whatever his motives may have been, it did not seem fortuitous at all that, just one day after his arrival on the island, Puigventós had disappeared from his hotel without anyone, even his friend the Spanish manager, having the slightest idea where he was or what could have happened to him.

"He just miraculously evaporated?" Manolo said ironically.

"Mackandal the one-armed flew from the pyre where he was being burned alive and the people saw him rise. And the people yelled: *Mackandal sauvé!*"

Manolo squinted trying to follow Conde and saw that Bobby was nodding, as if endorsing the known origin of the quote: Alejo Carpentier's *The Kingdom of This World*.

Then, Conde speculated about the possible solutions, the least serious and elevated for the foreigner's absence: a clingy Cuban girlfriend, steady or rented by the hour or day; a stay in the provinces devoted to meditation; a willful disappearance for some unknown motive. Or, the most suspected one at the moment: the search for the Black Virgin. Because the initial investigations dutifully completed by Ariel Jorrín and his colleagues that were carried out as well as if they were the Ministry of Control clearly showed that Puigventós was not at any other hotel in the country, or at a private hostel, or at a hospital. At least not under his known identity. Where in the hell could the man be, all the guards asked themselves and repeated their question to Conde, who opened his hands before Manolo to show that he did not have the disappeared Catalan in them.

After thinking about it for a few moments, Major Palacios ended up calling one of his policemen to accompany Bobby to the reception desk. Citizen Roque Rosell could go home, where he should always be reachable. But Mario Conde was to remain in the room, since he needed to have a private chat.

When Manolo closed the door behind a Bobby who didn't tire of thanking the policeman, Conde jumped up.

"Don't scold me, Manolo."

The major returned to his armchair and sighed again. "I'm not going to waste my time . . . There is no hope for you."

"Not even for improvement."

"You're repeating yourself. You've already said that."

"Because it's true."

Manolo stretched his arms, rubbed his eyes. "And don't try to show off making yourself out to be so educated. Who in the hell is that Mandrake?"

"Mackandal. A Haitian Black man who was a shape-shifter and transformed himself. Or so it was believed. People believed it . . . Just like they can believe in the miracles of the Virgin or in the powers of divination of a Babalawo's shells."

Manolo sighed in exhaustion. "Okay, okay . . . What's your best guess here?"

Conde took out a cigarette and asked before lighting it. "Who's watching us?" And he pointed at the room's walls.

"As far as I know, no one," Manolo confirmed. "I asked them to turn it all off . . . So talk and tell me a better story . . ."

"Better? Well, I'm thinking the worst, Manolo. The person who's behind the theft of the Virgin must also be behind the deaths of those two miserable souls, directly or indirectly . . . That person manipulated Yúnior and Ramiro and took them out of the game when things got dangerous somehow. And he must have a connection with the Catalan and with the fact that he's not showing up. I don't know if it's a personal connection or through some intermediary, perhaps one of the sellers in the guild, but there is something."

"The problem is that Puigventós appears to be the hen with the golden eggs, right?"

"Yes . . . King Midas . . . The one who can turn a piece of black wood into a tremendous amount of cash . . . That gives him protection . . . And might even be dangerous."

"What kind of danger, Conde?"

"I don't know . . . I'm just making guesses . . . Throwing stones . . . Puigventós must be more of a pirate than all of his Cuban colleagues together. He knows how to take care of things very well . . . I don't know, I don't know, it's that I have a premonition that isn't quite a premonition. Something I have right in front of me and can't quite make out . . . Because in all of this, there's something I can't manage to understand, something irrational, sick, I don't know . . ."

Manolo clucked his tongue: Conde's premonitions and doubts were the last thing he needed at that moment. "Do you want something more irrational than going around believing in celestial powers?"

"It's something else, Manolo. It's not a question of faith . . . It's something different."

"Why did you say irrational?"

"Because I can't find any reason for it. That makes something irrational, doesn't it?"

Manolo shook his head. A slow, tired gesture. "Did you already forget about when you were a policeman, my friend? Irrational? We only get to deal with the worst, run around with shit, and you know . . ."

"You could end up smelling like shit."

"You didn't forget . . . Well, so how deep in it is your friend Bobby?"

"That's something all of you already know. Did you see how the sight of you makes him shake? They've wrung him out like a mop. They stole his Virgin and he wants to recover Her, and he's not going to go around killing people. He might be a trickster, but not a murderer. I think that everything he told you is true, although it might not be the entire truth. Nobody tells the entire truth . . . And less still to the police."

"I noticed that he didn't mention what the Virgin could be worth . . . Conde, whoever killed Ramiro has the piece. And he killed Ramiro because somehow he knew that he had it . . . And because beforehand, he knew or confirmed in the worst way that Raydel or Yúnior didn't have Her."

"Did you keep looking in that field behind Ramiro's house?"

"Yes. There was a hole in the ground from which they removed some jewelry . . . But none of it was what Bobby says they stole from him."

"I knew there was something there . . . So how would you say the lost Catalan fits into all of this?" Conde asked. In his time as an investigator, he moved the Ferris wheel of information in one direction and another and used to ask Manolo strings of questions to test his theories. A notable number of times, one of Major Palacios's theories matched the reality of what had happened.

"I don't really know . . . We already have enough messes without a man getting lost on top of that . . . Who do you think is behind all of this, Conde? Someone from the art sellers' guild? Or a woman?"

The former policeman thought for a few moments.

"A woman is always a good reason to get lost . . . From the people in the guild, the truth is that I wouldn't dare point fingers at anyone, Manolo . . . Because, despite my prejudgments, or because of them, I'd point out all of them. But no, it's not the same thing to be a rat in business or a petulant asshole as someone willing to knock off two guys . . . Or three."

Manolo sighed. He looked at Conde with an intensity that ended up causing his eyes to cross. "So why don't you include Karla Choy on that list?"

Conde smiled, and when he was about to respond, he closed his eyes. Had he spoken to Manolo about Karla Choy? Had Bobby? No, he didn't remember it.

"Manolo . . . Has one of you been following me? What do you know about Karla Choy?"

"Don't think so highly of yourself, Conde. Who the hell's going to follow you and why? The police are the police, and we know things. Or we're fucked . . . And that's it, we're done . . . Get out of here now, let us work. And for God's sake: don't keep fucking around and sticking your nose in the investigation. This is getting uglier and uglier . . . Just imagine if they kill the Catalan, too . . ."

"Or if they already killed him," Conde said, and Manolo looked at him with his eyes more crossed than ever, with hate.

"Don't even say that, dammit . . . If they killed that guy, they're gonna cut my balls off."

"Ask the Virgin for a miracle, *chico* . . . And there's something I want to ask you, but I just can't remember what it is right now . . ."

"Because you're old . . . Come on, let's go, goodbye." Manolo moved his hand just at the moment there was a knocking at the door. Without getting up, he asked, "Yes?"

The door to the room opened and in came Lieutenant Duque. In his arms, he carried a portable computer with the screen open.

"There's something I want you to see, Major," Duque said.

"Let's see, what is it?"

"But . . ." Duque looked at Conde.

"It doesn't matter, let this one see whatever it is . . . We'll see if it serves him for something besides going around making messes and having premonitions . . ."

Duque walked over to the table with the lamp next to his boss and placed the laptop there. He activated the mouse and some images splitting the screen in two began to move. Conde approached it and immediately understood that they were two takes of the hotel lobby.

"The one sitting down in the armchair is Puigventós. The same day he arrived, a person came to see him . . . We're trying to find out who he is, because neither Jorrín nor the other security guards know him. This is at six thirty in the evening, when he came down from his room and took his place in the lobby."

The man who according to Duque was Jordi Puigventós must have been around forty years old, his hair seemed white, he dressed informally and moved a small bottle of mineral water in his hands.

"That's the Catalan?" Conde asked, without being able to contain his surprise.

"Yes, that's him . . . What's wrong?"

"Damn . . . I would've said it was Richard Gere . . ."

"Richard who?" Manolo asked.

"Your lack of culture is growing, my friend . . . Richard Gere. The actor. The guy looks exactly like him . . ."

"The American actor . . . So what?" Manolo asked.

"Nothing, nothing." Conde decided to change the subject and concentrated on what they were looking at on the computer.

The background of the lobby could be normal for a place like that. In Cuban hotels in the city, more people come in and out than in a train station. Conde remembered that during his time at the university, he used to visit the Habana Libre hotel on hot afternoons to study for a while, taking advantage of the place's air-conditioning. Among those who were passing in the takes where they could see the Catalan, Conde's attention was drawn to a woman dressed in white, with a kind of long, flowy robe, who walked very close to him. The woman was wearing dark glasses and a hat that was also white on her head, pulled down almost to her eyebrows. Puigventós, when he saw her, noticed her and then followed her with his eyes. The available takes did not make it possible to see if he had smiled, although Conde thought so. For two more minutes, the clips ran and, by the way he was acting, it became obvious that the man was waiting for someone.

"It's like that the whole time. He didn't stand up, but did ask for a drink . . . I'm going to skip to seven o'clock at night," Duque informed.

The lieutenant again operated the computer and some similar images appeared on the screen. Now, all of the lights in the lobby were on and Jordi Puigventós was on the same sofa and smoking a cigar. From the side table, he reached for a small glass, from which he drank. When he returned the glass to its place, he lifted his gaze and something alarmed him, because he stood up. Then, into the two scenes came, in profile and facing forward, the figure of René Águila.

Two, three, perhaps ten times Major Palacios thought it over. And at last, he accepted. Yes, it was the best within the worst. And Lieutenant Miguel Duque had obeyed his boss, making it clear that he was not in the least excited about his superior's idea.

Behind the lights of the patrol car, the unmarked Chinese Geely driven by Duque was moving forward on the Vía Blanca toward Guanabo. With the window down, to hungrily receive the sea breeze, Mario Conde was in the passenger seat, trapped by a feeling of déjà vu. Many years before, he had made a similar trip toward the beaches to the east of Havana, only then he was much younger and the driver had been the then-squalid Manolo Palacios. The landscape, the breeze, the afternoon light, and the deep excitement of going on the hunt were the same. Even Conde's dark glasses were the same. Damn, he should start thinking about buying himself another pair.

"Why did you become a policeman?" Conde asked the young driver when they exited the tunnel under the bay and joined the highway.

"Because I like being a policeman," the other man responded.

"There are tastes that deserve a beating . . . In your case, you can see it from a mile away . . . So Manolo says you're very good . . . A star . . ."

The information slightly relaxed Duque's discomfort, and he delayed his response by a few seconds. "I do my job the best that I can . . ."

"But it's not a question of effort. Or not only of effort. In this work, there are people with skills or capacities that others don't have."

Duque nodded and didn't respond. He didn't have to or didn't want to. But Conde didn't give up and, a couple of miles later, he tried again.

"Can I ask you what you think about this whole story about the Virgin, the dead guys, the Catalan . . . ?"

"Of course, you already did," Duque responded, seemingly very intent on his job as a driver.

Conde decided to poke the lieutenant a little bit more. "Do you also think that Bobby could have had any relation . . . ?"

"I don't like to speculate. I prefer facts, details . . ." the other man said after thinking for a few moments.

It was clear that Duque had no intention of speaking of the matter, at least not with him. Conde weighed whether he should continue or not. He had always been the kind who has a problem putting on the brakes.

"Why does it bother you so much that I'm involved in this?"

Duque let out a fake laugh. "Me?!? I could give a shit . . . That's your problem. And Major Palacios's."

"You do care, Lieutenant . . . But that's okay, if you don't want to be my friend, you don't have to be. And if it bothers you too much that I'm looking for what they stole from someone whom I know, then put me in jail . . . And if it chaps your ass that your boss decided I should come with you guys, then go to hell . . . Or leave the police. Or file a complaint about your boss . . ."

Lieutenant Miguel Duque took his eyes off the road for a few moments and observed his passenger. Conde didn't even want to imagine what was going through the mind of the policeman who so wanted to be a policeman.

"Keep your eyes on the road. I don't feel like dying today," Conde warned him and focused on observing the landscape.

They spent the rest of the trip in silence and Conde regretted having caused the rupture in communication in some way. He had acted as if he did not understand the psychology of the policeman, his need to exercise some power, and his endemic lack of a sense of humor. Although, he thought that perhaps he'd gone too far.

Following Conde's indications, they turned to the right at the blinking stoplight that marked the entrance to the beach in Guanabo and took the road that went up to the lookout from which the whole coast could be seen.

While the houses closest to the highway were modest and almost all of doubtful aesthetic taste, the ones they found on the higher part of the hill exhibited other conditions. The majority were recent construction, two floors, luxurious in their way, and had been surrounded by tall walls meant to prevent entry and views by outsiders. On a street that was perpendicular to the access road, they followed a series of mansions to the end, where the developed area ended with a brusque change in the height of the hill. Who lived there, in sparkling, walled houses, so far above the noise of the world? Conde told himself that in reality, there were two invisible cities within the visible city: the frenetic anthill of the unfortunate and the shining enclaves of the politically and economically fortunate. The steps of a Black Virgin were insistent on making clear to him these distances that were beginning to be unsalvageable and more and more populated.

The wall surrounding the latest construction was even higher than that of the neighboring houses, and at the top of it were placed several bits of barbed wire and halogen lamps with motion sensors. Conde was able to make out, in the back corner, beyond the garage, the shape of what must be a surveillance camera. That was René Águila's bunker. His true nest in the mountains.

Lieutenant Duque approached the two-paneled wooden door, pressed the doorbell, and spoke through the intercom with the inside of the residence.

"Lieutenant Miguel Duque, from the Criminal Investigation Unit. Open up right now . . ."

A remote mechanism removed the sliding lock, and Duque pushed open the door. The other two policemen followed him and in the rearguard came Conde, under the tough, dispassionate gaze of the bonebreaking Black man in charge of protecting René Águila.

The good-looking *mulato* was waiting for them in the foyer and led them to what must be the music and television room of the house, where everything sparkled. There were several devices for playing music and films, all modern, efficient, gigantic, and, of course, more than shining. Four leather armchairs (also shining) turned out to be just enough to seat the owner of the house and the three policemen. As the guest of stone he was, a kind of abominable invisible man without voice or vote, Conde remained standing by the door. The place smelled like the quality leather of the armchairs and the dry perfume worn by René Águila, who, this time, was wearing an orange Lacoste shirt from his collection and, on his feet, immaculate Menorcan sandals.

"Well, what happened now? How can I help you?" René Águila asked.

Lieutenant Duque took the laptop computer one of the policemen held out to him.

"Take a look at this first," he said and operated the machine until the recording of the hotel lobby appeared on the screen. Then he turned the computer toward René Águila and patiently awaited the man's reaction.

"Yes, it's me . . . When I went to see Jordi Puigventós . . . And if you have the rest of the tapes, you'll have seen that we ate at the hotel's Italian restaurant, you'll know what we ate and, I assume, also what we talked about for two hours. Jordi wanted one table, but the waiter insisted on giving us another. The one with the microphone, right? What's the problem?"

"The problem is that Jordi Puigventós has disappeared."

René Águila shook his head, and returned the computer to Duque.

"Nothing gets lost here that doesn't want to get lost, officer . . . That Spaniard is running around out there with some *mulata* . . ."

"Catalan. And he's been missing for forty-eight hours. He left the hotel almost at your heels," Duque said. "Too much time to . . ."

Just be banging someone, Conde completed the sentence in his head. And he thought he would have said it in its entirety.

"To run around with a woman," the lieutenant finished.

"That depends on the woman," the *mulato* explained, smiling again. From where he stood, René Águila's sense of confidence reached Conde. And he thought that it must be time to correct the course of the conversation. Miguel Duque seemed to hear him.

"It's possible, everything is possible . . . Why did you go to see him?"

"Because we're going to do some business."

"May I ask what business?"

"Of course . . . You are a policeman. And since I didn't do anything illegal . . . Besides, that would be what we spoke of at the hotel." And he patted his ear to highlight his conviction that they'd been listened to or recorded. "Anyway, I got Puigventós some certificates from the Beneficencia Catalana that he had been seeking and weren't showing up anywhere.

I am capable of finding things even under the earth . . . And down there is where I found them. The original certificates from the foundation of the Beneficencia in 1848, and also more recent papers, almost all of them from the 1920s, relating to a kind of conspiracy among Catalans to create an independent state . . . I don't know if you're aware that Francesc Macià was in Havana after his crazy attempt to invade Catalonia to make it independent. And here is where the Republican Constitution project was written . . . Even the independentist Catalan flag was created in Cuba . . . They say that that's why it looks like the Cuban one, with the solitary star. There were many Catalan nationalists who thought they should follow Cuba's example and become independent from Spain. And they wanted to take advantage of the existing crisis in the country, the chaotic situation in Catalonia, even using the anarchists' methods . . . It appears that some of the nationalists met here in Havana with the anarchist Buenaventura Durruti for him to join the cause. Did you know that?"

Conde felt that Miguel Duque had been overtaken by a story of which he himself did not know the details and the absolute veracity of which he mistrusted. Anarchists and nationalists in the same room? Anything was possible, he thought, and watched Miguel Duque's face: he was almost certainly a deductive and computer genius, as Manolo said, but, with the same certainty, Conde could affirm that he had a lot of reading to do. Man does not live from computers alone, less still if that man is a police investigator. Nonetheless, he kept his silence. What René Águila was telling had a real historical background, although it could be a smoke screen. Created by him or by Puigventós? The Catalan independence plot could also be true, and that possibility protected the *mulato*.

"But the content of those documents must be in many history books . . ." Miguel Duque wanted to assume.

"Not all of it, Lieutenant. I can assure you. A while ago, I read a phrase that is applicable in this case: life is wider than history . . . There is a lot of life in these certificates: details and names that, cross-referenced with each other, could have a lot of value right now. And not just to historians."

"A mystery of the Catalans?" Miguel Duque tried to get his bearings, adding drops of irony to his question.

"Yes, a Catalan independence plot," René Águila specified. "An aspiration that began over there, came through here, crossed through the Civil War and Francoism, and still hasn't finished over there, where the matter is hotter than ever. So those papers are worth money to some people who are interested in the subject. To air them out or to make them disappear, that I don't know. This is, indeed, a mystery of the Catalans, as you say . . ."

"Those papers should be the property of the Beneficencia," Duque announced, and Conde knew that he had taken the wrong path.

"No, they're personal documents. Or copies of the originals . . . Old copies. We can ask the people at the Sociedad Catalana. But in these times of WikiLeaks . . ."

René Águila was making a gratuitous display of his skills. With his gifts and few scruples, he could cross through almost anything without falling into an abyss.

"So Puigventós came to Cuba in search of those documents?"

"Yes . . . But since his range of interests is very broad and since he's Catalan and not just any old Spaniard, I can also assume that he's trying to make the most out of this trip, right? But I don't know anything about that. Not who he was going to see or with whom he was going to go out . . . And less still where he could be right now."

"What had you both decided?" Duque took up the offense again.

"We are supposed to see each other tomorrow and seal the deal. Papers for money."

"Where?"

"He said he would come here, at eight at night. The Spaniard was going to go for a swim on the beach, and then we'd eat here and do business. I invited him to eat here because now I'm getting some marlin that are marvelous . . ."

"Can I see those papers you're going to sell him?"

"Am I obligated to do so?"

"You can view it as a courtesy," Duque said, and Conde mentally congratulated him.

The *mulato* smiled and stood up. As he left, he and Conde exchanged looks. Such an innocent look could not be that of an innocent man, thought Conde, who had to keep his reasons to himself. Besides, he had an unbearable desire to smoke. How long had it been since he lit his last cigarette?

Lieutenant Miguel Duque had made the police mistake of allowing himself to be won over by personal pride and the arrogance of power. After reading the Catalan proindependence papers and even photographing them with René Águila's permission, he decided that the visit was over. He asked the vendor of art, documents, and other miscellany to track him down immediately if he heard from Jordi Puigventós, excused himself for the time they'd taken, and collected his men.

Back in the Chinese car, Conde again contemplated René Águila's fortress. It had gotten dark and now was lit by the powerful lights that even extended to part of the street and the rocky land beyond it. Since the other man didn't say a word to him, he maintained his silence, and when the car hit the highway and was on the way to Havana, he asked Duque to leave him right there.

"I'm going to see a friend in Guanabo. I'll come back on my own and that way you'll be more comfortable," he told the policeman and left the car. Duque's abused police pride pushed him to show relief at being free of Conde's company. Without saying goodbye and at a rallying speed, Duque withdrew in his car toward the city.

Conde entered a nearby cafeteria, bought a beer, and went to sit on a wall in the place's park. He took the first swig and lit the cigarette he'd been wanting so anxiously. He was in no rush; on the contrary, he needed to let some time pass and should take advantage of it to think through his strategies before willingly going to enter the mouth of the possible wolf.

It was twenty minutes before nine when he crossed the highway and took the rising path toward Águila's nest. He took the road that led to the walled house and congratulated himself when he saw an orange light begin to blink at the edge of where the gate led to the garage. Just on time. He hurried his pace and, when the gate finished opening, the car's headlights shone on his body. Conde knew he was trying to force a lock and felt his heart beating in his chest. His only protection, he thought, was that he had already been there with some policemen and, if he turned out to be as intelligent as he seemed, René Águila would not risk stirring the hornet's nest from which, for now, he had emerged unscathed.

The *mulato* got out of the car on the passenger side. He walked toward Conde. Now he was wearing some brown loafers that matched his orange polo shirt. From the other side of the car, the shape of the bone-breaking Black man was visible.

"Today you didn't offer us the best coffee in Havana served in porcelain cups," Conde let out and lit another cigarette. He needed to seem calm.

"You didn't tell me you were a policeman," René Águila said regretfully.

"So that's true . . . The proof is that I let you tell the lieutenant that tall tale about the Catalan."

"Why do you think that the thing about the papers is a lie?" he asked, switching from the formal treatment that Conde could deserve because of his age.

"No. I know it's true and that you have authentic information, I don't know if it's valuable or not . . . But I also know that you don't lose any sleep over some papers that aren't worth too much. And I'm thinking about your standards . . ." And he directed his gaze toward the mansion. "Unless those documents are a real bomb, and I don't think so. That means that you're going to sell Puigventós something that really is worth money . . . Perhaps other papers that are not the ones you showed the star policeman . . . But, I can swear to you that as long as it's not my friend's Black Virgin or anything having to do with the death of those two guys . . . That's not my problem. I alone can't control all the taking and snatching going on in this country or give or deny the Catalans their independence . . ."

René Águila smiled sadly. "That blasted Virgin that has already caused two deaths is going to complicate our lives . . . When the police get involved in something . . ."

"It's true: that story has jumped off the tracks and is out of control. And the worst part is that it's not over . . . If something happens to that Catalan, Troy is going to burn . . . With Trojans and even Greeks inside . . . Who else was Puigventós going to see? If you tell me, I'll protect you as a source. Maybe that way, things will calm down. And in your business, calm is gold. Can you really imagine the ruckus if they kill that Catalan?"

René Águila looked over Conde's shoulder at nowhere in particular. For some reason, the former policeman was now sure that, even though he had the weapons to do so, including the bone-breaking Black man, René Águila was removed from the theft of the Virgin and the two murders. And that his most valued good was his businesses, so in need of lost calm. With the police on his heels, things could not be going well.

"The last time he was in Cuba and we talked about the Beneficencia Catalana papers, Puigventós commented to me that he needed to return to Spain because of some mess with an auction, but that he would be back at any moment because he was going to do a deal with Elizardo Soler. I really don't know what, or even if it's true, if they did it already or not . . . What I do know is that if that Catalan isn't showing up it's because he's running around after a Cuban woman. What they've all done for the last thousand years . . . When we ate at the hotel, he told me that a Cuban woman was driving him crazy. That that woman was . . . a cataclysm . . ."

Conde closed his eyes. The light of his premonitions was blinding him. "Did he say 'cataclysm'?"

"No, I'm saying it: a cataclysm . . . Chaos with a capital *C*."

"Thanks, René . . ." he said, satisfied, and gave a turn.

René Águila had told him what he needed to know and the *mulato* knew it. When Conde had taken two steps, he stopped. He went back to the garage gate at the moment in which René Águila was getting into his shiny Hyundai. Conde yelled out to him:

"René, would you give me a lift to Havana?"

When Carlos and Rabbit saw him coming, they began to applaud. Alongside the small gate at the entrance to the house, Conde bowed to his friends, who were clamoring for him from the porch, and lifted his arms: in each hand, he carried a bag. One had food and the other, drink.

"Damn, Beast, look at that, what time is it . . . Almost ten," Carlos yelled. "You were torturing us, you bastard!"

"Come on, come on," Rabbit pressured him. "I'm so thirsty and hungry!"

Conde needed distance from the strange story in which he'd gotten involved and, once he was in René Águila's Hyundai, he asked the *mulato* to do him the favor of dialing a number for him on his cell phone. Then he spoke with Skinny and asked him to track down Rabbit: he was on his way and they had belated and extraordinary catching up to do. Once he was in the city, he passed by a cafeteria and got the necessary provisions that they were now laying out on the table in the backyard, the coolest place in Skinny's house. The September heat continued beating down on Havana, which had been reverberating under a pitiless sun all day.

Before initiating their session, Conde went to the bathroom and urinated until he felt deflated. In the process, without any warning, he felt overcome by sadness: Would he lose Rabbit forever and, with him, their deep complicity and habits? Would everything end up coming apart, swallowed up by a flood? Watching how the invincible Josefina made up a bed for him, he called Tamara and told her not to wait: his work had gotten complicated and he needed to deliberate with his consiglieri. She knew all about those summits. Josefina did too, since, after giving him a kiss and saying good night, she asked that they not yell too much and that they leave Carlos lying in his bed before leaving.

"What did you bring Josefina, Conde?" Rabbit asked when he came back out to the yard.

"Some pastries and two cans of soda . . . But I already have, at home, a load of chickpeas, sausage, blood pudding, potatoes . . . Tomorrow, I'll bring them over here. She told me the other day that she felt like eating a *garbanzada*."

"At ninety years of age, in this heat! You're going to make me an orphan, Beast," Carlos protested, smiling.

"That's enough, Skinny. Your mother knows what she's doing," Rabbit interrupted. "Don't let me miss out on that stew, dammit! It has been about a decade since I've had chickpeas like that . . ."

"You're missing the pork shoulder, *Condesito*," Josefina noted from the kitchen. "Thanks for the sodas. And remember not to yell too much . . ."

"Damn, nothing is ever good enough for that old lady," Conde lowered his voice and protested, taking his first drink of the day.

"Did you know that Dulcita is coming next week?" Carlos asked his recently arrived friend.

"No . . . Not if you or Tamara haven't told me. You have me in a silo. For a while now, I'm the last one who finds out anything . . ."

Carlos's former girlfriend from their high school days, who had become widowed a few years back and had been living for many more in Miami, now divided her time between the two magnetic poles of the Florida Straits. Thanks to Dulcita and her economic help, Skinny Carlos's house had received some improvements, which included remodeling the bathroom and painting the walls. Her days in Havana, in addition, imposed a certain discipline on the savage crowd's habits. In contrast to Tamara, Skinny's regained girlfriend was capable of throwing one back with the friends, with the same frequency and intensity, but she also managed to more pleasantly break up the masculine routines with her company and, above all, with the placid intimacy she shared with Carlos behind closed doors and how much she fed the self-confidence of the man who'd been crippled for so many years. Had Dulcita also participated in Rabbit's travel plans?

"Well, that has to be celebrated, right?" proposed Rabbit, who was generally in favor of any celebration. With or without reason. So they toasted to Dulcita, to her return, to their incombustible fraternity. She had always been the best and the most complete of all of them, they admitted. So they also toasted to that.

As he had resolved, Conde told his friends about his most recent and very active detective adventures. For once, Carlos and Rabbit listened to him in silence, until he lifted his hands as if to say: that's all I've got.

"So what comes now, Beast?" Carlos asked.

"Tell Manolo what I think and throw the ball in their court. That's what the police are for, right?"

"So do you think that the business the Catalan Puigventós and Elizardo have pending has something to do with the Virgin?" Carlos continued.

"It could be, it could be," Conde pondered. "But if that was the business, then Elizardo already planned on having the Virgin, right? That could be the key to this whole mess."

"And the reason that there are two deaths now," Rabbit commented.

"The problem is that I don't know how to grab Elizardo and get what he knows or did out of him."

"What I don't understand is how no one ever knew that Virgin was here, in Cuba," Rabbit added.

"Bobby's Catalan grandfather always had Her with him, at his house," Conde said. "He didn't have Her on display, and he always said She was a Virgin of Regla . . . I don't know if Bobby himself was the one who complicated things by mixing up Yemayá with the Virgin, by showing Her to people . . . And by starting to mess around with that story of Her powers."

"Many people think that they are miracle workers, Conde," Rabbit advised him. "That they had some power of the earth, of creation . . . From what I've read, they're very rare pieces, and right now, very few are left. All were carved in the same era, more or less, and many of them are mixed up with the Crusades and the Templars . . . And you know that there's a lot of mystic speculation about them and a ton of invented or real mysteries regarding those characters. And people with the will to believe in crazy things abound in this world. In any event, there's something that is proven: those Virgins generated a special devotion. They had something . . ."

"Because they were, or are, Black?" Carlos asked.

"For starters, it appears so. And they are Black because they are associated with the earth . . . The mother of everything in many ancient cultures. The earth is the feminine recipient where the masculine seed germinates. If what I've read is true, it seems that these Black statues represent the religious thinking of several cultures: the Egyptians, the Celtic ones of pagan Europeans, and, of course, Roman and Byzantine Christendom . . . Which already come down contaminated by ancient Judaism and other local religions that were later considered to be pagan. That is why there are doubts over whether these Virgins came from Africa and the Middle East, even from Jerusalem, when the Christians regained the city at the end of the eleventh century. Or, if some were made by Venetian artists, who had also known them in the Holy Land, where there was a great Venetian, Pisan, and Genovese presence. Or whether the pagans identified the Virgin Mary with their mother goddess, the earth and nature, which are feminine . . ."

"What a mess, right?" Carlos opined and Conde nodded after taking a long drink with which he hoped to clarify his understanding.

"I already said, there are a lot of stories and real mystery and also a lot of cheap mystery surrounding these figures," Rabbit continued. "But what doesn't seem to be in doubt is that they begin to appear in Europe during what has been called the medieval Renaissance, more or less after the taking of Jerusalem. And that coincidence is historic, not coincidental. We know that the Crusades and the Templars are involved in the devotion to those Virgins and the idea that they have powers . . . Albeit only spiritual."

"He who wants to believe, sees and feels things that the nonbeliever does not see or feel," Carlos commented. "That's why I don't find it strange that if Bobby is a real believer, he is convinced that the Virgin cured him . . . Magical realism. Rulfo, García Márquez, Carpentier . . . Do you see how educated I am?"

Conde asked if he could serve himself another drink. He raised his gaze to the clear, cloudless sky, populated by stars. "So I'm supposed to believe that this Cuban story from right now has something to do with all of that in the taking of Jerusalem and the paraphernalia of the great powers of the occult? Here, in Cuba, with this heat and everything hanging on this?"

The three friends, in tacit agreement, decided that it was already too late, it was truly too hot, and that rum was too good to be complicating their lives that way. Tomorrow, they would see, and the world, that story, and time could all go to hell . . . No skin off their backs.

15.

ANTONI BARRAL, 1291

When he entered the chapel, barely affected by the morning light filtered through the portico's windowpanes and the narrow lateral skylights, brother Antoni Barral was convinced that that could be, must be, the last day of his life, the last one as well for the plaza paying the greatest price for the pride of having believed itself to be invincible, the most invulnerable. His gaze fixed forward, he advanced toward the small, white stone altar bathed by the languishing wax of burned-out candles that no one bothered to remove anymore. In the vaulted space behind the altar hung a polished wooden cross of garnet-colored cedar, as if painted with blood, under which reigned, sovereign and majestic, the magnificent and powerful image of Our Lady.

On the step that elevated the most sacred space from the rest of the temple, the knight set down his helmet, then moved the sword at his waist, and got down on his knees. With his hands united over the eight-pointed red cross displayed on his chest and his face in the direction of the effigy, he closed his eyes. He took several breaths to try to concentrate amid the subhuman shrieks of the besiegers pummeling his ears and the rhythmic commotion and penetrating infernal music, coming from the hundreds of drums, cymbals, and trumpets altering the rhythm of the beating. It was the sound and the fury of those who know they are the victors and implacably herald themselves in their proclaimed purpose, sworn on the Koran, of not stopping until they'd driven the last adept of the cross in the Prophet's beloved Holy Land to the sea.

Convinced that there would be no other opportunity for him, Antoni Barral got ready to confess all of his sins to Her, for the spiritual release to alleviate his exit from a world of which he was no longer afraid since he felt that he could qualify the days of his life as well spent, offered up to a greater good, in which he believed and for which he was going to die. He prayed and swore to the Blessed Mother that his faith had never and would never waver. He prayed and remembered all the violence committed throughout many years, guided by the cross and sword, by love and a vocation to serve, the vows of chastity and poverty, the devotion to Her, and the faith in the Anointed with which he had made an oath and in whose exercise he'd assumed as just and holy the battle with which his arms had delivered so much death that it was now impossible to count. He prayed and meditated that with his convictions, actions, and goodwill, he had not managed to make the world a better place, but rather, the opposite: perhaps because of this, his last sacrifice was necessary. He prayed, cried, asked for forgiveness for his immortal soul if he had committed excesses, when, subtly, without fanfare, at an unspecified moment of his meditation, he had ceased to listen to the shrieks and clamor as he began to notice how his body was entering a pleasant refuge, all-encompassing, an unknown physical condition that made him light, safeguarded from the surrounding events, immune to the chaos of the final moments. Just when he felt most ensconced in that refuge, with his body even levitating a few inches in the air, his forehead felt the compact and unmistakable pressure of some warm fingers capable of making him lose his balance and fall on his back, causing the resounding sound of his offensive and defensive metal wear. Lying on his back, he opened his eyes and confirmed that, before him, was only, in the same place as always, the cross and the figure of the Blessed Mother, with Her black, brilliant face, inscrutable with its shining blue eyes, almost lifelike, from which, he could have sworn, at that moment he saw two tears sprout and flow. And Antoni Barral received the vibrant premonition that he still had tasks to complete in the kingdom of this world. All he knew was that he had received new strength from a superior power and would not die on that terrible day on which the last battle would be waged before the definitive loss of what had, for decades, been the most treacherous and shining city of the known world: the city which had condemned itself through its many sins. Knowing his mission, the higher objective for which he would remain alive, the knight stood up, replaced his helmet and sword, and walked toward the altar.

A few months before, brother Antoni Barral and a few of his brothers from the Order of the Temple, hungry and ragged, had arrived at Saint Jean d'Acre. They were the survivors, perhaps escaped by sheer miracle, from the implacable fury of the Saracens of the Mamluk Sultan Qala'un, author of the siege and devastation of the very rich Tripoli. The day of his arrival, the Catalan knight was carrying on his saddle the statue of the Virgin that had been part of the goods the temple knights were fighting over with the powerful Genovese and Venetian merchants of Tripoli, the voracious and mischievous owners of the beautiful city, the same ones who with their ambitions and excesses had invoked the rage of the Mamluk sultan. Because of that dispute, ever since the statue was brought from Jerusalem along with other relics when the sacred city ended up conquered by Saladin, the statue of the Virgin, who was already said to be miraculous, had remained sadly ensconced in the church of Saint Mark, one of the city's richest, awaiting a definitive destination when the vulgar earthly debate over its ownership was resolved.

For the preservation of that wooden figure, brother Antoni had been on the verge of losing his life during Tripoli's cruel devastation, which had been carried out by the long-haired, big-shot dervishes, the most fanatical and ferocious warriors among the Islamists, men who insisted on earning their glory by slitting the throats of Christians or having their throat slit by them—it was all the same.

Following several days of battle against the besieging forces who, both in men and in weapons, greatly surpassed the Christian defenders of the city, brother Antoni and some of his other brothers from the order had understood that the plaza's fate was sealed and the only alternative was a sudden and humiliating retreat. But even amid absolute chaos, with Muslims running through the city streets, the knights had decided that they could not leave behind the order's insignias and documents. Nor could they, as brother Antoni Barral told them, leave behind the statue of Our Lady whose ownership they had always claimed, since, according to the old knights, She had been found many years before amid the foundations of what had been for more than a century the Templars' general barracks, located on the very site where the most trustworthy chronicles assured King Solomon's Temple had been and where the Ark of the Covenant had been kept. Ever since Her fabulous discovery, the miracles and prodigies attributed to that *Mater Dei*, black as the oil flowed from deep within deserts, were several, like the prayers uttered to Her by the Knights Templar, Her most loyal devotees. And it was also the Templars who, to highlight Her beauty and make tangible Her power, had asked a Venetian master carver to liven up the effigy with colors and preserving Her with the best lacquers. For Her, Antoni Barral thought, it was worth risking his life. And thus he had decided with three of his brothers, whose swords, as they carried out the rescue, had made Muslim blood flow beyond the doors of the church of Saint Mark. Tasked by his confreres with transporting the Virgin given Her heft, as he was about to leave the sacred enclosure, Antoni had to watch how the three of his companions in arms and oaths, with barely a foot on the altar, fell under a storm of lances, rocks, arrows that flew over his head and by his sides without grazing him, as if the projectiles were avoiding him, he who was tasked with carrying the Virgin. Luck or a miracle? The Templar would ask himself this repeatedly and would again ask himself during the meditations in which he engaged on the day he thought would be the last one of his life, in the chapel of the Templar fortress of the condemned Saint Jean d'Acre.

With the Virgin on his back, Antoni Barral had crossed the vineyards and fields of olive trees that surrounded Saint Jean d'Acre and deservedly felt impressed by the magnitude and scale of the city. But when he passed through the magnificent double wall, through the door of Saint Anthony, the Templar had the unsettling feeling of having fallen into the most gigantic fair in the world. In the by then already-extinct Latin kingdoms of the Holy Land, all had always pondered the vitality of that city, the most populated, cosmopolitan, and rich of the Frankish possessions in

Crusades territory, which had become the seat of the ancient kingdom of Jerusalem since the unlucky loss of the holy city. He always told himself, and Antoni Barral had the chance to confirm it with shock and surprise, that all of the riches and fantasies of the known world, all of its products and whims, any of its imaginable desires and luxuries, could be earned, purchased, or satisfied in that city and its port.

Within, above, against the majestic walls of Acre, men from a diversity of latitudes and races converged and mixed, from the pale Germanic Teutons, settled on their own street, to the very rich Genovese, Pisan, and Venetian merchants and artisans, each one of them with their own neighborhood, to the Catalan sailors, French, Lombard, and English crusaders, peoples from Byzantium, Greece, Cyprus, and even the far-off land of the Mongols, in addition to the ever-present Jewish merchants and bronze-skinned Libyan, Syrian, and Egyptian peasants, already converted to Christianity or still Muslim. Members of all religious and military orders had their general headquarters there and lived alongside dukes, counts, and even princes of possessions nearby or distant, real or fictitious, and with a high enough population of clerics destined to satisfy the demand for a cathedral, forty churches, several monasteries and hospitals, and countless internal chapels. And, of course, the city and its outskirts were also teeming with sailors, adventurers, professional warriors, scoundrels, and vagabonds, while an active army of all kinds of prostitutes, thousands of them, labored in its catacombs.

As he crossed the city, brother Antoni Barral had already perceived the vertigo of its commercial buzz and the frenetic rhythm of its peoples, clustered in the walled enclosure. From the Arab souk emanated the scent of perfumed oils mixed with myrrh, the aroma of meat roasting over the coals and sticky sweets, the stink of camel droppings, and the acidic smell of fermented milk, which neighbored the Jewish market where there shone the most coveted cloths while moneylenders, scriveners, and jewelers shouted out their professions, trying to impose their voices over the litany of their Moorish neighbors. Crowded streets led to the plaza where the also noisy Pisan and Genovese merchants offered their merchandise, sold spots on their very shiply ships toward all the ports in the Mediterranean, and even authenticated fragments of the True Cross and many bones belonging to saints and martyrs. Just across the street and in open competition with their neighbors, the always well-dressed Venetians devoted themselves to exalting the transparency of some recently imported, very fine glass cups, the quality of their mirrors, and the exclusivity of their latest products, in limited supply and also recently imported, originating in the Far East from where, they said, they had been brought by Marco Polo himself. A multitude of drunk and aggressive Lombards added to the chaos, as well as begging mutilated war veterans, Frankish soldiers stinking of lard and dried sweat, fanatics of the Torah, the Koran, and the Bible who were just as likely to announce the end of time as the arrival of the Redeemer in all of the languages escaped from the Tower of Babel.

Taken at last by the impressive fortress the order occupied in the far south of the city, close to the port's breakwaters and the Iron Tower, brother Antoni Barral and his surviving colleagues had handed over the black statue of Our Lady to the order's high chaplain. The brother, familiar with the history and majesty of the Virgin and the stories of Her miracles, had decided to give Her the best spot in the chapel, where the knights of the order usually prayed and in which, in recent years, they had carried out new initiations, old ceremonies about which envious and ill-spirited rumors had begun to propagate about indecent behaviors and heretical attitudes.

As the days passed, the initial sensation that Antoni Barral had regarding the illicit and unrestrained life in Saint Jean d'Acre went turning into a disquieting certainty. If at first he had thought that his judgment had been affected by the city's luxury and rhythm, so foreign to his crude character as a plebeian born in a remote town in the Catalan mountains and his years of a nearly monk-like life in a post of the order close to the city of Tolosa, the daily behaviors of the inhabitants of Acre confirmed his initial assessment. Perhaps because of the knowledge that they were already sentenced to losing the richest and best-fortified city in the world to the hands of Muslim armies gathered under the leadership of the sultan Qala'un, all were engaged in frenetic dealings, scheming, swindling, and hoarding, while wine, saliva, and semen ran like the lava of an erupting volcano. No one there spoke of greater missions; all that mattered was gold and lust, this life, and not the next.

The plaza's oldest inhabitants maintained that everything had been worse with the arrival of the Crusades contingent and who they called "the Italians," made up of peasants and adventurers who came from the lands in the north of the peninsula, attracted more by the high wages promised than by the pure desire to combat the infidels and save for Christendom the biblical lands participating in a crusade that would never be. The straw that broke the camel's back had been the violent inspections applied by "the Italians" to the Syrian and Libyan business owners and peasants, and almost any of the neighboring Muslims in the city. The expropriations, backed up by harassment, corporal punishment, and even several executions, had caused a rebellious attempt that forced the lax authorities to intervene and put the rabble-rousers in prison. But, in reality they were little disposed to punish some soldiers from the Church's army and had returned "the Italians" to the streets with merely a scolding and, incidentally, had created the final excuse the Mamluks needed to break the truce with the city and initiate the military campaign that would decree its end.

The exception of that generalized debauchery that yelled to be punished offered the attitude of the members of the military religious orders, on whose backs often came down the difficult task of maintaining civil peace and preparing urgent military defense. But Templars, the Hospitallers, and the Teutons were well aware that their efforts were in vain and that their military abilities, even in combination with the city's exceptional fortifications, could not withstand the already-announced massive attack. What they were not aware of, despite some veterans like Antoni Barral sensing it, was that their time in the lead and glory had passed. For them, there would be no future in Christian territories because they were arriving at the end of the days of the Latin kingdoms in the Holy Land, of the Crusades expeditions, and of the usefulness of the militias of Christ.

Among the princes, counts, dukes, maestros, bishops, and field marshals who rubbed elbows together in Saint Jean d'Acre, brother Antoni Barral met a man who, from the first encounter they maintained, seemed singular in his way of thinking, and he was dazzled by his character, which provoked both a strange feeling of empathy in him, because of how close he could seem, and of disquiet for how pragmatic and hard to grasp he also was.

The Great Captain Roger de Flor maintained he had been born in Germanic lands, but no one was convinced this was true, since at some point, they had heard him say he was a native of Brindisi, and at other points, of Barcelona. Depending on where he came from, he assumed a different name, sometimes Roger van Blume, other times Rutger Blume, but most frequently Roger de Flor. He himself talked one day about his belonging to a line of Germanic nobles, another time that his ancestors had been rich Bavarian business owners or Catalan sailors, and sometimes, he even introduced himself as the son of an Italian cardinal who was very close to Pope Gregory X. He said he knew all of the ports in the Mediterranean, and he prided himself on being the best captain and sailor that had ever navigated those seas. He was able to retell his participation in the greatest battles of the century and said he was friends with the greater part of the princes of Christianity. Since he was not yet twenty-five years old, everyone knew he was an incorrigible liar, but they enjoyed his talk and company because they also knew that amid his lies there were some great truths, like his capacities as a sailor, his very refined manners, and his ability to express himself fluently in ten different languages. There was a reason that the Great Maestro of the Order of the Temple, resolved to use what he could from the young man, had initiated him as a lay brother and had given him the title of Great Captain and the command of the greatest vessel that had ever sailed the Mediterranean: the *Falcon of the Temple*, built in Genoa and anchored in those days at the best dock of the port of Saint Jean d'Acre.

Despite the two men having such different characters, perhaps the empathy that Antoni Barral felt for the Great Captain Roger de Flor was due to the famous navigator's weakness for Catalan sailors and the rough Aragon soldiers who made up, almost entirely, the crew that led and the militia that protected the floating fortress that was the *Falcon of the Temple*. The young captain had established such a rapport with those violent warriors that he spoke with them only in Catalan (a language that, depending on the moment, he could confirm was his mother tongue), knowing himself thus more protected from possible infiltrations of the murky matters in which he always seemed to be involved.

It was during a conversation in that tongue with three of his sailors that Antoni Barral first approached Roger de Flor and spoke to him in his native language. Although they already knew each other due to the frequent councils carried out by the brotherhood's knights in light of the plaza's complicated military situation, on that occasion they maintained a long dialogue thanks to which Antoni felt for himself the snake-charming qualities of that young sailor.

The *Falcon*'s bridge was the place where, throughout the months they both lived in Acre, the Templar brother and the captain met several times. To Antoni Barral—who for the first years of his life saw only rocks, mountains, and jagged creeks, goats and wolves, poverty and rigor in that valley in the Pyrenees where he had been born—the sea always offered him a feeling of freedom and glory that he did not tire of enjoying. In addition, from the port, he had one of the best views of the city of two walls and twelve fortified towers, with its many walls of yellow rocks shining under the sun, its impassable moats, and the multicolored banners raised above the city by different military, religious, commercial, citizen, and sailing brotherhoods settled there in the most crowded chrysalis of the known world. Before them, a symbol of force and power, was the fort of the Temple knights on whose protecting walls four proud lions, painted in gold lacquer and the size of oxen, watched over the city and the sea.

Compared to young Roger de Flor's possible real life, Antoni Barral considered his own vulgar and expendable. At forty years of age, he could tell only the stories of his life as a peasant boy who, through a twist of fate, had received shelter at a Templar post in Roussillon, the neighboring area where he had arrived as a guide and assistant to two wandering knights, off to enroll themselves in a crusade and who had hired the kid's services. His mission completed, as Antoni was waiting for the end of winter to journey back through the mountains via the Coll dels Llops, the young man paid for his room by working in the post's fields, where he also had the chance to learn to read and write with a quickness that surprised everyone. His manual skills and intelligence for learning were noted by a Castilian cleric named Juan de Mendoza, and Antoni was admitted as an auxiliary brother and granted access by the post's maestro to bookish wisdom and even the diligent military training that distinguished the order. Thus, thanks to the skills he had quickly acquired, but especially to the critical situation in the Frankish cities in the Near East, and despite his plebeian origins, Antoni Barral was ordained a knight and sent to carry out his mission as a Templar in that turbulent and cosmopolitan corner of the Mediterranean where the powerful brotherhood of warrior monks had grown and fought, and where its reason for being as an institution was now at play.

The day that Antoni Barral revealed to Roger de Flor how he had left the church of Saint Mark in the lost Tripoli, carrying against his chest the statue of Our Lady who was now placed in the fort's chapel, the captain of the *Falcon* surprised him with a question that Antoni thought he had not at first understood. "Had it been worth risking your life for a wooden statue who was only that, a beautiful wooden statue of the kind they usually carved in these lands?" Antoni Barral had never questioned his actions in those terms, for him it was not only a "beautiful wooden statue," so he immediately answered that of course it had been worth it, it would always be worth it, and three of his brothers had not died in vain in that mission, since it was a very special statue of Our Lady, who was the guide and patron of the order in which they both served.

"Very heroic," Roger de Flor continued, "but you are speaking to me of two different things: of the divine being and all of Her representation. You saved a representation. Another one could always be made, right?"

Antoni smiled and said, "The representation embodies the divine, the sacred. Besides, that specific statue has been proven to possess high powers, everyone says so. In a representation, the essence of that which is represented can reside."

Roger de Flor looked toward the city and continued, "Do you know that those Muslims advancing on us now do not believe in representations, on the contrary, they forbid them? And that in the ancient scriptures, God condemned all form of representing the divine and the belief in the supposed powers of idols and effigies?" The young man continued and Antoni Barral had to admit he was right, but he did not concede:

"Our religion changed things. We are neither heretical Jews nor unfaithful Muslims . . . The statue's value lies in what it represents, and for us, She incarnates the divine Mother of God."

Roger smiled. "And was Our Lady Black?"

Now it was Antoni who smiled. "The color is not important, it's the material," he maintained. "What is decisive is faith, which is the essential."

Roger nodded: "You mix everything, brother Antoni, and you mix it because that statue that you rescued under the price of putting your life in danger is the fruit of those mixtures."

Antoni didn't understand. "What mixtures?"

Roger de Flor explained himself: "She is Black like the Osiris of the ancient Egyptians of the pharaohs, and She is Black like the Mother Earth of the old Celtic sagas of my country . . . And we, Christians, say She is Mary. All mixed in a beautiful carving of wood that could not have been buried for centuries in Solomon's Temple because Her divine power is not great enough to overcome the weaknesses of the material: She would have turned to dust, my brother."

"That is Her first miracle. Are there not incorrupt bodies? Couldn't a Virgin be one?" Antoni Barral countered, although in reality, he understood less and less. Roger de Flor's disquisitions surpassed his capacities of scholastic reasoning, but he did not stop: "What about the miracles?" Was it not enough that he and others like him believed, had faith, and received the benefits of miracles that were sometimes inexplicable? Roger watched him with his falcon's eyes.

"Do you know that the French King Louis, whom some even claim is a saint, took a dozen Black Virgins like the one you rescued from these lands?"

No, Antoni did not know.

"Well he took them to Paris because they're beautiful and because only here do they carve them so exquisitely and with such a great sense of Her power," the sailor continued. "With them, the king aimed not only to adorn the churches of his kingdom devoted to Our Lady, but also to remind posterity of his Crusades in the Holy Land, which, as you know, in reality, were a military disaster. That was why he wanted these representations, solely to feed his legend and vanity." Antoni Barral thought that perhaps the sailor was right, or partially right, but his convictions refused to accept it.

Roger de Flor retrieved a bottle of Bordeaux wine from his cabin along with two Venetian glasses. After taking the first sip, the captain pointed at Acre's walls and towers with his outstretched arm and asked, "Do you know what is really being decided with the fate of this marvelous city?"

Antoni was surprised by the turn in the conversation.

"What is being decided is the fate of the Latin kingdoms in the Levant, the Christian presence in the Holy Land," the Catalan Templar responded.

"Well, that's what the propaganda of the faith says, the public and official version," Roger de Flor began. "Remember that to satisfy that faith, another king, Richard of England, just one hundred years ago ordered the decapitation of thousands of Muslim prisoners in this same city because God gave him the license to kill infidels without homicide being a sin. And remember, by the way, that your beloved Saint Bernard was the one who offered the justification to the Lionheart, endorsed even by a pope, to promulgate that this is a holy war in which killing others does not constitute an offense against the Creator, but rather one more reason to approach glory. God save us! . . . But the truth, the truth, my friend, is that here, now, what is decided is the control of the most important commercial route in the world, the source of many riches, and that is why they are running around there with their swords and banners, those very well remunerated mercenaries of the Venetian, Genovese, and Pisan merchants. And the Church's army of the violent Lombards . . . What is being decided is the possession of these marvelous lands, of their forests and valleys planted with grapevines, olive trees, and cedars, the control of the roads for the caravans that go toward the east, the control of dozens of ports, like the one where we are . . . At play is the ownership of the riches that will spell greatness, like Alexander, like the Caesars and the pharaohs, for whomever possesses them, in the name of Jesus or of Muhammad, of God or of Allah, which is all the same . . . And knowing this, you want to fight and you were willing to die for a piece of carved wood? Do you know that too many times already, many men died for material riches thinking in good faith that they were fighting in the name of some celestial glory? Do you know that that will soon happen here, in front of and behind those magnificent walls? And that it will happen many, many times throughout the centuries in which men live on this earth? Do you have any idea how faith, the search for good, a truth that does not allow alternatives, manipulated and exacerbated, can be a covering for hate unleashed in the name of God, of a prince, or of an idea? That while we Christians kill Muslims, the Muslims will kill and kill Christians, and that both groups will soon kill each other before this city and on this land, which they say is holy, and we will continue doing so for centuries and centuries always in the name of the faith, but in reality because of its riches, because of the quest for power?"

Antoni Barral looked at the Great Captain disquietingly as he shot out his insidious questions, and when he was able to process what he had heard, he said, "You speak like a heretic. No, worse still: like a necromancer who aims to race ahead of celestial designs . . . You say upsetting things. You are dangerous, Roger de Flor. Are you really who you say you are and from where you say you come from?"

The sailor took a drink from his very fine crystal glass and turned to face the ocean, golden in the late afternoon: "I come from there, the sea. The mystery of it is my faith."

The spring brought to the plains surrounding Saint Jean d'Acre the armies of Muslim infantry and knights called upon by the young Sultan Khalil al-Ashraf, the heir to the throne of his father, the deceased Qala'un, whose mission the prince had decided to complete and whose death he wanted to avenge. For the Saracen leaders, there was no doubt that the sudden death of the great Qala'un had been the work of poisoning that the disciples of the Old Man of the Mountain did with such skill and frequency, the dissidents and mercenaries who were members of the sect of the Assassins, whose services had been bought by the nobles of Saint Jean d'Acre with the hope of thus saving the city. If they had carried out that procedure with the powerful Turkic sultan Baibars, poisoned in Damascus a few years prior, then they certainly had also carried it out with his own father, the young Khalil had said. And he, the warrior proclaimed, would very soon prove how mistaken the Christians were if they thought they would resolve their issue with a crime. A few weeks later, the sole contemplation from the Hugh, Henry, or Accursed towers of the plains inundated by the white covering of the most formidable of the Islamist armies, provoked terror and hurried a manifest destiny.

The city's defenders had, for several days, watched the spectacle of seeing the advance, like ants, of armies coming from Damas and from the country of Misir, from Hama, and the rest of Syria, also those coming with the sultan from far-off Egypt. The estimates of the most trained warriors came to be fixed at 60,000 knights and 160,000 infantry dressed in white, who surrounded the city, accompanied by one hundred war machines among which stood out the most powerful catapult ever built: named "The Furious," it required ten yoke of oxen to be moved and, as the defenders of Acre would soon find out, it had the power to launch projectiles of several quintals, with the ability to remove the most solid of walls. On April 5, 1291, the great purple tent of the Sultan al-Ashraf rose over a hill on which the crescent moon banner was already waving: the siege of the richest and most coveted Christian city on earth had begun.

On the morning following the start of the siege, Antoni Barral attended, along with all of his brothers, the mass held by the order's Grand Master Guillaume de Beaujeu in the chapel of the Templar fortress. Once the liturgical rituals were concluded and Communion was taken, the leader of the knights began his rally speech: since reinforcements were not coming from the European Christian kingdoms, King Henry was in hiding and remained in Cyprus, and the supposedly central command of the city's defense was proving itself to be incapable and generated little confidence, so they, the Templars, should assume the leadership that was theirs in principle. They would fight in the sector that had been assigned to them, to the north of the city, but they would respond without hesitation to the bastion that most needed them, which seemed to be that of the Accursed Tower, in front of the Royal Citadel, before which the procedures had placed several war machines. Enemy forces were so superior in number and weapons that the aspiration to a victory was naïve, he proclaimed. But each one of them, their oaths made on the cross and before Our Lady, should battle to the death in that holy war. There was no other mandate or decision. The order's vocation and History demanded thus.

Captain Roger de Flor and his Catalan-Aragon militia would remain posted on the *Falcon of the Temple*, the Grand Master also ordered. If military luck was against them, his mission would be to take to Cyprus or the European coast all the wounded, women, and children who had not yet been evacuated and the priests with the churches' treasures. Despite the ship being able to transport up to a thousand souls and a hundred horses, its space was going to be insufficient and, as such, the Grand Master concluded, none of the Templar brothers could escape on the ship. By their oath and honor, they must fight to their deaths to defend the bastion from the imminent attack by infidels.

The offensive siege against the city had been going on for five weeks already and, despite the many losses suffered by each group, more regrettable for the Christians, Saint Jean d'Acre was resisting. Never had those enemy armies, led by manifestations of irreconcilable fate, fought with such ardor. On the European side, as was expected, the lead had been taken by the Temple knights, under the direction of their indefatigable Grand Master and their skillful field marshal, Pierre de Servey. But the situation for the defenders was getting more and more desperate by the hour, since having just received the reinforcement of two thousand soldiers arrived from Cyprus, the city's defense had been overtaken by the aggressions of the Muslim attackers and their war machines. All of the battle's participants, on one side or the other of the wall, knew what the irrevocable ending would be.

In the battles at the foot of the wall or in some of the incursions to open land carried out by the Templars, Antoni Barral had again proven his abilities as a warrior. His sword and lance had plunged into so many Muslim bodies that it was impossible for him to make an estimate, and more than once, he thought that if all of that effort was going to be useless, wouldn't it be preferable for the heavens to at last send him to his death and thus conclude all his dealings?

On the morning of May 18 of the year of our Lord 1291, Antoni Barral had nodded off due to the exhaustion accumulated in battle and the long hours of surveillance carried out in King Hugh's tower when he was suddenly shaken awake. It was just getting light over the valleys to the east of the city, but brother Antoni could make out movement in the white mass, like a gigantic avalanche from which the beating of drums, the clanging of cymbals, and the sounding of trumpets and fifes made up the most terrifying war hymn, destined to provoke the attackers' ardor and the confusion of the besieged. In front of the Muslims went the warriors who were carrying large, tall shields, followed by those tasked with launching apocalyptic projectiles of "Greek fire," the feared ceramic containers loaded with a mixture of gas and petroleum that ignited when a wick was lit and that, upon exploding, was only possible to extinguish with vinegar. These were followed by the skilled javelin throwers and then came the squads of archers who, in a few minutes, darkened the pale sky with a cloud of arrows. Before the battalions of knights tasked with closing the offensive came the artillery units that made the already weakened city walls start shaking with the rounds of projectiles launched by the catapults. No effort seemed possible to stop the demolishing final advance: not the catapults of the besieged, or the boiling water, or the hot sand they threw from the heights of the Accursed Tower, from King Henry's tower, and from that of King Hugh. The exaltation of the Muslims was such that the big-shot dervishes, like in Tripoli, were immolating themselves to block off the city's moats with their own bodies and allow the advance of their army and the entrance to the plaza.

When the entire sector of the Saint Anthony watchtower came down, panic spread within the walls and those remaining in the city began to run toward the port, in search of the only possible escape. But the thick sea had been unleashed; perhaps the attackers had counted on it as a new ally, since it was impossible for the fugitives and the goods they did not want to abandon to board ships. Nonetheless, between the scimitars and the waves, many preferred to fight against nature and threw themselves to the sea, which voraciously swallowed them.

All seemed lost when somebody yelled that the Templar Grand Master, Guillaume de Beaujeu, was among those who fled. The only thing that prevented everyone from disbanding was the reappearance of the knight, dying on a stretcher due to an arrow wound in his left armpit. With what little strength he had left, the Grand Master managed to stand up and launched his agonizing clamor that the battle continue, since Our Lady the Mother of God would protect the faithful and reward them with an ascent to glory.

And the miracle occurred: the besieged withstood and on that afternoon the attackers, even those who had entered the city, returned to their kingdoms. For the moment, Saint Jean d'Acre, semidestroyed and licked by the inextinguishable flames of Greek fire, continued being Christian.

Before entering the chapel, on the day that, he was convinced, would be his last day on earth, Antoni Barral had climbed the wall of the Templar fortress and contemplated the city landscape. What a few months before had been a jumble of people and merchandise, all extended as protection against the rain and the sun, a lively and colorful souk like no other in the world, a brilliant city of dense glass skylights, libertine and arrogant, was just smoking ruins. The victors, dizzy with triumph and fed by their own hate, devoted themselves to destroying everything that could be destroyed, to lighting everything flammable, to profaning the sacred and the mundane, roused by the infernal rhythms of their musical instruments of war. That day in Saint Jean d'Acre, only the Templar fortress withstood as Christian territory where some two hundred brothers and several hundred terrified civilians waited for the painful denouement: in total, just about a thousand Christians from the more than 40,000 who took shelter and sinned in that city. Antoni saw behind him, at the port's mouth, at a distance that protected it from catapults and arrows, the silhouette of the *Falcon of the Temple*, weighed down with passengers and bundles to the masts, willing to take the last survivors of the desperate final resistance to any safe destination. That was if any survived, and if it was possible to rescue the coveted treasure of the Templars that, despite Roger de Flor's insistence, Marshal Pierre de Servey still refused to evacuate.

Watching the landscape of unleashed hate, vengeance, theft, fear, and pain, Antoni Barral thought in the final sense of his life. Why had Providence brought him to that place and juncture? How much had his personal decisions contributed? Or was it what some called the inevitable, luck, fate, the weight of History? If, so many years before that it seemed to have occurred in another life, he had not led those two crusading knights from the Catalan mountains to Roussillon, would his luck have been any better? In reality, Antoni Barral did not complain of the life that he been given to spend. In his land, he would have been a shepherd or a soldier under the king, like his father, his grandfather, his great-grandfather, always poor, illiterate, dead before turning forty in some battle against the Moorish armies or infected by the fever of the time. He, at least, had seen some of the most sparkling places in the known world: the city of Constantinople, rich Venice, the port of Marseille, the walls of Jerusalem, the beautiful Tripoli, the exuberant city of Acre. Only, seeing it all from this moment, which he recognized to be historic, he wondered if at some point in his life journey there existed a mistake or perhaps an unfathomable predestination to which what his fate had been was due. Ruled by that uncertainty, he got down from the castle wall and entered the deserted chapel, to kneel and pray before going out to kill and die.

With all of the delicacy and respect of which he was capable, even in that extreme circumstance, Antoni Barral kissed the Virgin's outstretched hand before hugging Her and lifting Her from the altar. She seemed heavier than on the day in which he had removed Her from the church of Saint Mark, in Tripoli, but he credited this to his weakness and accrued exhaustion. And it was at that precise moment when he had the enlightened certainty that everything in his life had been organized so that he could fulfill this specific mission. Until then, without asking his will, fate or History had led him, as it had taken him to a church in Tripoli and allowed him to leave the place without receiving a single wound, while his brothers fell one on top of the other. A greater plan, of inextricable purposes, had organized it all. And he knew that he would live, that the Black Virgin would be saved from the attackers' religious hate, and that Her celestial figure would accompany the faith of some men for many centuries.

When he left the chapel's atrium, the veteran warrior saw a scene that was the closest match possible to the Bible's descriptions of the Apocalypse: the front wall of the fortress had ceded to the Muslim sappers, and below the mountain of rocks, over which two of the magnificent sculptures of golden lions lay in agony, defenders and attackers, like in infernal vision, were bleeding out and burning, all apparently surprised by the collapse. The thundering music of the Mamluks continued, floating over the sweet smell of charred flesh. But, save for the dust and the flames sprouting from the fallen rocks and the blood that was running alongside the rocks on the ground, everything seemed frozen.

Amid that cataclysm, as if he were the last inhabitant of the city and the world, Antoni Barral walked toward the opening in the wall. Climbing over rocks and the bodies of friends and enemies, rebalancing himself to not lose his precious cargo, he searched amid the flames for an exit toward the nearby port. When he had crossed the ruins and taken the path that led to one of the still-surviving docks, the man needed to readjust the weight of the Virgin, since he could no longer hold Her with only his arms. He made an effort and managed to lift Her over his right shoulder, so She could rest there, against his neck. And when he made the first step in traveling forward again, he heard the whistle and felt the impact, but did not stop. With his left hand, he looked for the source of what had yanked him and touched the polished wood of an arrow that had sunken into the Virgin's side, precisely at the level of Her carrier's throat. Antoni Barral did not have time at that moment to think about what the confluence of actions meant: only that, due to having changed the position of the Virgin, he was still alive, fulfilling his mission. With that thought in mind, he moved forward to the end of the breakwater, from where he saw the port abandoned by vessels, although full of corpses that the tide moved, like the remains of a macabre shipwreck. And, in the distance, unreachable, the *Falcon of the Temple* with its sails already unfurled to the wind. Then he again placed the statue over his chest and, without thinking of his possibilities, Antoni Barral handed himself over to his fate: he allowed himself to fall into the sea just as a gigantic wave was breaking against the rocks that caused a shower of foam darkened by blood that was running from the devastated city. On the crest of the wave, they floated for a few moments, trapped in an embrace, a man and a representation of the Blessed Mother who, together, had to continue on a long path through the inextricable spirals of time.

16.

The Devil had not shown up, despite creating the best conditions for him. Perhaps he avoided coming around because of the Virgin, so oft invoked. But, a demon after all, his resources were infinite: and Conde confirmed it with an awakening that made him feel like he'd been mashed and submerged in sulfurous liquids. For starters, that's what he smelled like.

He started to feel some relief under the cold shower, with two aspirin in his stomach. The pot of coffee he drank and the day's first cigarette offered a little more improvement. It almost returned him to feeling like a human being, the proof that guys like him and Garbage II had to have their own lair, where the freedom of knowing there were not even any rules was the highest good.

When he was able to think, he remembered his plans for the day. He was going to earn his salary again, perhaps the last one for that work. He called Manolo and invited him over.

"Now, with all the messes we have here? That Catalan son of a bitch is still lost and . . . !"

"Listen to me, Manolo. You won't regret it."

Half an hour later, he opened the door to his former subordinate. And he saw the unmarked car, pulled up at the curb, that Manolo was now using.

"What happened to you, Conde?" Manolo Palacios asked in alarm when he saw his host's face.

"Last night, I fought with some Muslims in Saint Jean d'Acre . . . And I think I dreamed I was tangled up in the sheets with a Chinese-Cuban woman . . . But dreams themselves are only dreams . . ."

"What in the hell are you talking about? Are you going to start with all your nonsense?" Manolo asked him.

"No. Don't worry . . . And really, I'm already better, I swear it, I'm already better," Conde assured him, very proud of his capacities for recovery. He couldn't move much, or turn his head too quickly, he had to recognize that, but he was capable of speaking and even thinking, at least enough.

Manolo sat down by the kitchen table when Conde turned on the stove to brew another pot. The major was about to speak, but the other man stopped him with a gesture of the hand and the request:

"Coffee first . . ."

Listening to Manolo's fingertips drum on the table, Conde waited until the coffee was ready, sweetened it, and served two cups. A new dosage of the infusion would enliven his neurons a bit more. Manolo, who was smoking again, always without buying for himself, had a cigarette with him.

"What happened yesterday with Duque?" the officer asked. "He's raging at you."

"What's predictable happened . . . He's too much of a policeman to allow someone who's not his boss to be in his territory."

"You said something to him. I know you, Conde."

"I didn't say anything to him, Manolo. I wanted to be friendly to him . . . But your brilliant star is a proud guy. And he thinks he has a corner on the truth. Because of you, Manolo, now I found myself an enemy . . ."

Major Palacios shook his head, even when he knew Conde's assessment was right. "He's very young and—"

"A bit of a dumbass. That's why René Águila walked all over him as much as he wanted to and even fed him that mystery about an anarcho-Catalan plot."

Manolo crushed his cigarette. "Let's see, what in the hell was it that you saw?"

"René Águila told me where that lost Catalan could be."

Major Palacios knew he shouldn't be surprised. Or at least, not to make his surprise visible to him.

"Because you went back to his house?" Conde nodded. "I knew it, knew it . . . What in the hell did you go back for?"

"I had to talk to him and Duque hadn't let me."

"Talk about what? What did that guy say to you?"

"That Puigventós is the victim of a cataclysm . . ."

"Are you going to keep fucking around, buddy? Come on . . ."

"I am telling you something your Lieutenant Duque wasn't able to find out yesterday . . . That Catalan Puigventós came to Cuba with the official purpose of buying the Beneficencia Catalana papers that René Águila got for him . . . And with the unofficial purpose of taking with him a Black Virgin with whom, in principle, there should not be any further complications. Well, besides the theft . . . But, above all, he came, he comes, and whenever he can, he will come to get between the sheets with a woman named Karla Choy . . . Who's also involved in this business of buying and selling works of art, who could be tangled up in this mess about the Virgin, and who, as if that wasn't enough, or for starters, is a cataclysm, Manolo. You tell me if she isn't a cataclysm when you see her!"

To maintain his physical and mental health, Conde preferred not to accompany Manolo and his team on the expedition whose course he had set. At the end of the day, finding the lost Catalan was not his job. And if it turned out that they took a Black Virgin prisoner in that hunt, that would mean that the statue could only return to its owner's hands after a very long time, if it returned at all. All of which meant that his job, as such, would have ended as a splendid failure. Because with two murders in the way for which She was responsible, it would be best to forget about the Virgin. Conde thought about whether he should ask his friend Yoyi and, on the basis of his opinion as a businessman, go ask for the pay promised to him—or not, he concluded. Or, whether it was better to ask Yoyi to do it for him . . .

Conde knew that until Manolo called him, as he promised he would, his only choice was to wait. So, at ten in the morning, as they had decided the night before, prior to cracking open the last bottle, he left his house and met up with Rabbit in front of the old high school in La Víbora, prepared to carry out a private expedition in search of a certainty that, perhaps, at this point, would serve only to satisfy Rabbit's unleashed historical curiosity and the need for truth that obsessed Mario Conde.

To Conde's relief, Rabbit's face could compete with his own in post-alcohol devastation. It was clear that the years were passing them a bill that was becoming more and more difficult to pay, and now all of them, already sixty years old or nearly, needed more time to recover. Or be inclined to make the decision to drink less. He was relieved again when they entered the hired car that would take them to the center of Havana and a surprising and thunderous rain began to fall over the city, at first multiplying the hot humidity in the atmosphere, but then, soon after, resulting in a reduction of the reigning heat.

Taking refuge in the arcades of the Payret cinema, they decided to wait for the rain to stop in order to cover what separated them from the Avenida del Puerto and the historic Emboque de Luz. As they watched the now-deserted Parque Central, Conde decided he should use the downtime in the best possible way. Doing what he should have already done.

"Rabbit, how are things going for you?" He entered the conversation sideways, convinced he could steer it where he needed to.

"Good and bad, like always. You know . . . Why are you asking?"

"To find out . . . About your trip. And because I think I wasn't very nice to you. I'm a shitty narcissist who only thinks about myself and sometimes, I go too far . . ."

The other man smiled, displaying the teeth to which he owed his nickname. "Calm down. I know you. I knew that when you found out, you were going to get like that . . . But since I know you, I didn't wonder when you offered me the money you would earn with the Virgin so that I could travel . . ."

"That I should have earned. I think that money is fucked . . . The thing is, my brother, we're being left more and more alone . . . Everything is going to hell, everything . . ."

"You're going to tell me about being left alone? Remember that my daughter is over there and my wife only talks about how much she misses her, that she's not going to see her grandchildren grow up, that we don't have any family anymore . . ."

Conde shook his head, tossed his cigarette butt on the wet sidewalk, and looked at his friend. "Do you really think that the best thing for you would be to stay over there, as you say? It's true, your daughter is there, your family—"

"Brother, I don't know what I'm going to do . . ." Rabbit interrupted him. "I don't want to be dependent on my daughter, chasing after her, complicating her life . . . She did what she wanted and had to do. What a bunch of kids her age are doing every day. What Miki's kids did. What Rafaelito, Tamara's son, did . . . Kids who look at us and quickly come to the conclusion that they don't want to end up like us, for having done what we thought or what they told us we should do . . . But I don't want to die in poverty, either, living I-don't-know-how on the retirement that awaits us, with the few pesos that are never enough for people to have even one decent meal per day. You know that. What's fucked-up is that I don't want to die far away from here, either, suffering nostalgia over not being here . . . Why should I have to die far away after everything we've been through and done and everything that we haven't been able or allowed to do?"

Conde had an answer: We should die here because it's what belongs to us. Because we are from here. Except, at this point in the game, who would he be able to convince with that argument about belonging? What was more important: being or belonging?

"Do what you have to do," Conde said, since it was the only thing he could and should say.

"Conde, we've spent our whole lives saying that they didn't let us travel where we felt like and that we had, that we should have, the right to do so. Do you remember when we were twenty years old and you loved Hemingway so much? You always said you would have liked to go to Paris and live as Hemingway did in Paris."

"Mental masturbation of mine . . . It's very cold in Paris, there are no avocado plants there, and the rum must be very expensive."

"But you were never able to go to Paris . . . Or Alaska, either . . . Because thinking of going anywhere was just that, mental masturbation.

The country was closed under lock and key and someone else had the key, those who decided who got to travel and how, those who decided what was good and what was bad for you, what books you should or should not read, how to cut your hair, and what kind of music to listen to. For us, it has always been like that, it still is like that: someone decides for us, to take care of us and save us, right? . . . And now they've opened a little door: they let us travel, man! If you have money or not to do so is your problem, like everywhere. But we can at last do it and . . . I'm going to try it. If those damned Americans give me the visa, I want to go to Miami, to be with my daughter, see Andrés again, have a bottle there with Dulcita . . . Confirm whether the Miami airport smells like Cuban coffee and whether the people in Hialeah really live as if they were in Centro Habana, but with running water all day long . . . And then I'll see what I do."

"That sounds good, Rabbit. It sounds like the bells tolling of freedom of choice."

"Or the bells of La Demajagua . . . Carlos Manuel de Céspedes, our forefather, giving the slaves their freedom, like they taught us in our fourth-grade history class. Freedom, independence, human dignity . . ."

"It suddenly sounds amazing." Conde laughed at the historical context that Rabbit never failed to provide and added, "It's better not to speak of those bells. But go on, use your freedom, it's your right . . . And even your left . . . Well, the time for being philosophical is over . . . Let's get going, the rain stopped."

Feeling relief over the conversation he had with Rabbit, Conde subjected himself to the regulation pat down (because of their faces) that allowed them to board the little speedboat to Regla, with its prow facing the village and the hermitage of the Cubanized Black Virgin on the other side of the water.

Although they were early, they breathed easily when they learned that Father Gonzalo Rinaldi was waiting for them in the sacristy. Conde was shocked when he saw that the pastor was younger than them: until now, all the priests he had met were older than him, and in his mind, he had created an image that a priest should be a person "of a certain age." And if he was starting to be older than priests, then the problem of his old age was becoming more patent and alarming. According to his statistics, he was already older than 66 percent of the planet's inhabitants, including some priests. *That's fucked-up*, he told himself.

A steady drizzle continued to bathe the city and, beneath the sacristy's high mainstay, the atmosphere was cool and pleasant. The priest, dressed in street clothes that made him look almost youthful, offered them a pitcher of lemonade from which they both served themselves as Rabbit repeated the purpose he had mentioned on the telephone to Father Rinaldi: to learn more about medieval Black Virgins. Like the Virgin of Regla, like the one in Montserrat . . . Like the reborn Our Lady of la Vall, arrived in Cuba, seemingly, several decades before, in the hands of a young Catalan who had escaped the rage of war.

"I don't have much time anymore to spend with you, so I'm going to tell you the main thing," the priest began when the three were sitting around the small table, a higher one than normal. There, Conde esteemed, was where the Eucharist was performed prior to Communion. He was comforted by the idea of being so close to the divine. "To begin to outline the subject, I'd like to tell you that those three Virgins you've mentioned," he addressed Rabbit, "are different . . . The Virgin of Regla of Chipiona, in which ours is inspired, has a whole legend about Her origins that places Her in Hippo, in North Africa, in the fourth century. They even say that Saint Augustine himself carved Her and that his disciples brought Her to what today is Spain in the fifth century. But all of that is a myth. The original statue must be from the fourteenth century; in other words, post-Romanesque, although what remains of her was also carved in black wood. Meanwhile, the one from Montserrat is not black: She is of a color known as white lead that has blackened with the years, something different."

"So la Moreneta isn't really *morena*?" Conde smiled. "Given the whole thing the Catalans have about that . . ."

"Well, she's not black, perhaps because she is a European carving, although she is medieval, Romanesque, of the same school and time as Our Lady of la Vall. And from what you can see in the photos, the Virgin you're looking for is Romanesque, black, and it's very possible that she came from North Africa in the twelfth century with the Crusades and

Templars that were in Jerusalem in that era and in other cities of the so-called Frankish states. The best proof of the North African origins of those Virgins is a historical document, not a story or a myth. There is a French Chronicle from 1255, in which it is commented that, the year before, the French King Louis IX, Saint Louis, returned from his incursion in Jerusalem during the Sixth Crusade and brought back several statues of Black Virgins that he had obtained in the Holy Land . . . There's no reason to question that detail, first of all, because it does not mythologize anything or glorify anyone and, secondly, because it refers to an event very close in time. It is just that, news, that offers a certainty: in North Africa, these Black Virgins existed in sufficient quantities for the French king to make off with a whole load of them."

"Why from the Holy Land, why Black, why so many Virgins?" Rabbit went on, and the priest raised his hands, asking for clemency.

"That's what's complicated about the story . . . The problem is that there are many answers, too much invention and mysticism, but I'm going to tell you the most important ones. Or, the most well-founded. Just at the time of the Crusades, the cult of the Virgin Mary was at its apogee. Two or three centuries before, there had not existed such a strong devotion for the Mother of Jesus. But in the twelfth century, it did exist and the person who pushed it the most in Europe was Bernard of Clairvaux, Saint Bernard, of whom it was said that he was the man who best represented the medieval Renaissance of the twelfth century. Among other things, he was the founder of the monastic order of Cîteaux, as well as promoted the existence of the order of the Templars, already in its definitive form. He also defended the idea of a holy war in which, for the faith, even the act of killing another human being was endorsed if he was an infidel, a heretic, a pagan enemy of the Holy Church . . ."

"None of this turning the other cheek if you get smacked," Rabbit noted.

"No, no . . . Well, more or less . . . The fact is that Saint Bernard himself had a very peculiar story with the Virgin: he said that when he was young, before an altar where Our Lady was worshipped, from the breast of the statue, fell three drops of milk to his lips . . . And the miraculous Virgin was Black . . ."

"That seems too similar to the story of my friend who had the Virgin . . ." Conde recalled. "He says that he saw Her crying or sweating . . ."

"The important thing is that at the time, thanks to Saint Bernard and other devotees, even the term *Our Lady* became popular and so extensive back then that they began to dedicate chapels, churches, even cathedrals to Her . . . The great Gothic cathedrals. That is why several of them are dedicated to Notre Dame, right? And if some of those mothers of the Lord who presided over cathedrals, parishes, chapels, were Black and came from the Holy Land, it is due, I believe, to there being in North Africa at the time artists who were more qualified, as they say now, than in medieval Europe. Those artists were the heirs of a high culture that goes back to the times of the Egypt of the pharaohs and Greco-Latin greatness, which was preserved more in that part of the world than in medieval Europe. An area where having black or copper-colored skin was much more common . . ."

The priest took a long sip of lemonade and ramped up.

"On the other hand, as you know, Christianity was the result of several traditions that mixed, crystallizing in a time and space of many cultural convergences. As a religion, it is the offspring of a tradition, of a historic time. Among its antecedents, there appears to be, without a doubt, the Egyptian influence of venerating the mother goddess, who in that culture was Isis, the daughter of the god of the earth, wife and simultaneously sister of Osiris, the judge of the dead, and the mother of Horace, who reigned over the day. Isis was the divinity considered to be the center of the universe. So Isis was represented with dark features . . . That mother goddess was the generator of life, and life is related to the earth, with its fertility . . . With its black color. These are the key numbers in the equation through which Black Virgins began to appear in North Africa and medieval Europe and, since they became fashionable, for lack of a better word, they were reproduced in great quantities by European makers, seemingly Venetian maestros in particular, the most knowledgeable, progressive, and enterprising of the time and everything related to art, navigation, business . . . No one better than them to obtain the black wood brought from the interior of Africa or the Middle East, where ebony abounds along with other kinds of textures and similar colors . . ."

"So how do the Templars come into this story, Father?" Conde asked.

"So, in that entire cultural process, it has been proven that the knights of the Order of the Temple, the Templars, played an important role. It is no coincidence that the boom of those Virgins coincided with the order's two-hundred-year history and with the devotion to Our Lady that they practiced and propagated thanks to spreading out through a good part of Europe with their posts, where they usually had at least a chapel . . . These were especially numerous in the South of France, in the north of Spain. In these regions, not coincidentally, you can find, for centuries and even today, the majority of the Black Virgins in conservation, who must be just a small part of the ones that existed and disappeared, due to natural or human effects, like fires, which were so frequent in those centuries . . . In sum, as you can imagine, being the parish priest of the church in which a Black Virgin is venerated, I've had to study the subject in depth, in which there are still many historical mysteries awaiting a well-founded response. And mystical mysteries which will always be mysteries . . ."

Conde and Rabbit were nodding and processing. The light of the priest's words was clearing away the final shadows.

"Historical and mystical mysteries such as what, Father?" Rabbit asked.

"Like the sphere that some Black Virgins or the baby Jesus hold in Their hands. The sphere is perfection, that is true. But it is also the earth, the world, the kingdom of God . . . The mother is the earth. Or the earth is the planet . . . But, in the twelfth century, some madmen dared to think that the world was a sphere . . . Mysteries such as how many of the chapels dedicated to these Virgins are in places that for the European Celts, who adored the Mother Earth in a special way, had a telluric power. Mysteries like Their relation to the Camino de Santiago, the route of the stars, the Milky Way. Milk and the mother, the earth and fertility, the route toward the West . . . In sum."

"So what about what they say regarding the powers of those Virgins?" Conde then interrupted.

Father Gonzalo Rinaldi smiled. "Are you both believers?"

Conde and Rabbit looked at each other before starting to move their heads. No, they were not.

"So it's difficult for you to understand me . . . To believe, faith is necessary. And, until now, I've been speaking to you with reason, telling you a story . . . A historical one. But with faith or without it, I think the thing about the power these Virgins have is very clear. Because it's real . . . To those who have placed their devotion in them. There is a lot of talk of miracles, like the one regarding Saint Bernard that I told you about and hundreds, perhaps thousands more. The one that is most often repeated is that of making women fertile who had believed themselves to be sterile, or of reviving dead children . . . I, as a priest, testify that miracles exist, although not all the ones that present as such are as miraculous. As the rational being that I also am, I consider that many extraordinary or inexplicable events, which we call miracles, occur because our thoughts and subconscious have the power, and even this you both must admit, right? And since you admitted, then you must also accept that that power is real for those who invoke it sincerely. That is the key to everything . . ."

"The power of faith and of the mind," Conde summed up.

"Yes, a power of which science still does not know the true proportions and capabilities . . . What it does know is that the need to believe turns out to be something that supersedes us. It is the response before a mystery. And everything tends to be projected through a figure that constitutes a symbol, the representation of an idea . . . Like a flag, for example. Are there not people who immolate themselves with a flag or for a flag? I know it's not the same, but the act reveals to us the power of symbols. The need for symbols, I would say. And those statues that represent Our Lady, the Mother of God, the generic mother . . . Adam was born of clay, from the earth . . ."

The two friends nodded. Some details offered by the priest were new and revealing for them. Not the essential: that, they already knew. Only now, they had the conviction of how tangible the Black Virgin's power could be for Bobby and how valuable Her possession could be. Because of Her mystical powers and because of real history. The price of that statue could be incalculable, and, because of it, there were now two more victims in what was probably a long and populated list of men sacrificed on the altar of the powerful statue, perhaps brought by some anonymous

Templar or a sanctified king from Jerusalem's mythical hills, the Holy Land for which three religions had fought and killed, and continued to fight and kill, when curiously, they believed in the same God.

Suddenly, it seemed that something as unusual as autumn had arrived on the island. The rain had stopped, but the sky continued to be low and dark, and the atmosphere was charged with an affectionate, although ephemeral thickness. According to Father Gonzalo Rinaldi, it was the presence of a trough, which had positioned itself over Cuba's extreme western part, from where it would keep moving until it undid the charm of the season.

Like on every occasion that he heard that meteorological explanation, Conde asked himself how long those things called "troughs" had existed. When he was a boy, everything was simpler: there existed, in descending order, hurricanes, bad weather, summer rainstorms, and winter drizzles. Because he confused a several-days-long memorable stretch of bad weather with some temporary winter drizzles, the grandfather of a friend was called by the name of that meteorological event for the rest of his life. But now everything was resolved as a trough . . .

When the speedboat returning them to Havana docked at Emboque de Luz, they found that Manolo was waiting for them in the jail-like shed. At the mere sight of his expression, the former policeman had an idea of what happened.

"The Catalan didn't show up?" was his first question.

"Let's go, we'll talk out there," Manolo proposed. "It stinks in here . . ."

"Can I stay with you?" Rabbit asked, who was always more discreet.

"Yes, let's go . . ." the policeman accepted and pointed at Conde. "After all, this moron's going to tell you everything anyway."

Conde and Rabbit looked at each other and followed the officer. They left the shed and walked toward the recently restored walk on the Alameda de Paula, the city's oldest. Since the sun had yet to appear, they sat down on one of the low walls that served as benches, facing the bay's dark waters.

"Okay, shoot," demanded Conde, who needed to know.

Manolo sighed. "Well, we went to the cataclysm's house . . . And she really is. What a woman!"

"Damn, I'm the only one who hasn't seen her," Rabbit protested. "Is she really Chinese? Incidentally, in the eleventh century, when they brought the Chinese from Canton and they came here to the port, they took them—"

"Stop telling stories, Rabbit," Conde told him. "Go on, Manolo, talk . . ."

"Well anyway . . . She says she hasn't seen Puigventós and, of course, that he has not been to her house. She knew the Catalan was in Cuba, she confessed that she also knows him, but since she doesn't have any pending business with him, it didn't interest her."

Conde considered the information and concluded:

"She's lying. Karla saw him. I'm sure of it . . ."

"So where does she have him, under her skirt?" Manolo asked.

"It wouldn't be a bad place to hide, actually," Conde opined. "But if he's not there, he's close . . ."

"I spoke to her for a while, put the screws to her as best I could, but I couldn't do anything else . . . So we went to see the other character who could know something, Elizardo Soler. He was leaving his house. And he also swears up and down that he has not seen Puigventós and that he doesn't know where he could be. But he did reiterate the Catalan's fondness for our female compatriots . . ."

"This was also pulling one over on us. He knows something . . ."

"Why are you so sure? One of your premonitions? Don't fuck around, Conde, not with this . . ."

Rabbit was on the verge of intervening, but Conde's look stopped him.

"It's more than a premonition, Manolo. It's something I know . . . But that I don't know. Something I saw, but that I lost . . . I'm convinced . . . Seriously. And what I am sure of is that all of those clever cats are lying or hiding something. All of them, including my friend Bobby . . ."

Conde took out his cigarettes and offered one to Manolo, who accepted.

"Are you going to go on and on about what you see and don't see? Because of you, I'm smoking again," Major Palacios protested as he lit his cigarette. "And because of that Catalan and the Black Virgin and . . . Conde, Puigventós has been missing for three days already. It's too much time. I had to send Duque to the hotel to ask the Spanish manager, Puigventós's friend, not to make a formal report. Because we are already looking for him and when there's a report, it has to be communicated to the Spanish consulate, to the Foreign Ministry, to those gentlemen in the Special Police Corps for Foreigners . . . And then things will be a big fucking mess. I don't even want to imagine it."

Conde heard an alarm coming from a dark corner in his memory.

"Does State Security have something to do with this?"

"No, of course not," Manolo assured him. "Why are you so insistent on State Security?"

"It's just that I remembered right now that Ramiro told me someone from State Security had gone to see him."

"No, I don't think so. I would know," Major Palacios reaffirmed.

Carefully, from his place, Rabbit raised his hand as if asking permission to speak. And without anyone's authorization, he said, "I only wanted to tell you that the Chinese who came from Canton were taken to some rooms that were over there, in Regla . . . And to ask a question: What comes now?"

Conde and Manolo looked at Rabbit, and then looked at each other.

"We keep looking for Jordi Puigventós," Manolo responded. "I just don't know where he is."

"Puigventós is wherever the Virgin is. Or nearby. And the Virgin is with whoever killed Raydel and Ramiro. That's the unifying thread," Conde opined.

Manolo took another drag from his cigarette and tossed the butt in the air. "I've already got Immigration breathing down my neck. I also asked them to stay calm. They gave me until today. I'm desperate . . ."

Conde knew the pressure his former subordinate must be under. "Manolo, take me home, I need to think. And to go to the bathroom, too . . ."

Major Palacios stood up and looked around. "It's looking nice here, right," and he pointed at the old boulevard and its restored surroundings. At one point, the area had been one of the centers of the city that depended on the bay and its port activities. As the years passed, its degradation had been complete, out of control, and it was encouraging to enjoy its renaissance.

"All of nineteenth-century Havana came through here," Conde called to mind. "Martí, Casal, Villaverde . . . Here Heredia, Varela, Domingo del Monte, Saco came to sit and talk . . ."

"And?" Manolo admonished him.

"And . . . Well, that between them all, they invented Cuba. At this point, I don't know if it was a good or bad invention. What do you think, Rabbit?"

"That's enough already, buddy," the policeman protested. "I don't have all day and . . ." Manolo scratched his head. "So, sitting right here, those characters invented Cuba? Stop fucking around, Conde . . . Well, forget about that. Let's go," Manolo cut off the nationalist and foundational reflections. "Besides, look, it's going to rain again."

From the sea, the violent clouds of the presumed trough advanced toward the city, crossing over Regla and Casablanca.

"So let it rain. Let the city, the country, the world be flooded. Let the thunder, lightning, and sparks come. Let the hail and snow fall. Let there be wind, gales, whirlwinds, and even troughs," Conde said, giving free rein to his apocalyptic propensity before the two other men's condescending stares: they knew him too well to be alarmed by his inclinations. "Damn! Let the hurricane come! Let there be a cataclysm! That's what we need, a cataclysm! Or at least a miracle," he concluded and hurried up to reach Rabbit and Major Manuel Palacios, who were no longer listening to him because they were running to the car, frightened by the first large drops of the new rainfall brought by the supposed trough.

The rain benefited the city all afternoon. The deficient or inexistent practical prevision of the apocalyptic Conde prevented him, as almost always, from preparing himself for the circumstance. So, when hunger arose, he had to content himself with making an omelet with the only two eggs he'd stored in his refrigerator and cutting the avocado that, taking advantage of their being locked away due to the rain, he stole from his neighbors, the happy owners of a generous tree. He shared the omelet with Garbage II and, with the help of coffee and cigarettes, resolved to think. To better do so, Conde sometimes used sheets of paper on which he placed names, details, general ideas he tried to relate to one another. He had learned that practice from the deceased Captain Jorrín himself.

For the time being, he knew, and noted it with initials and arrows, that among Karla Choy, Jordi Puigventós, Elizardo Soler, René Águila, and his friend Bobby, there were several links, but they now all went through the existence of the Black Virgin (he signaled Her with the initials BV and placed them within a circle at the center of the page) and Her unknown whereabouts. The Virgin should also link all of them, or at least several of them, to Yúnior-Raydel and Ramiro the Cloak, the deaths in the equation. The Virgin, in and of Herself, opened two powerful lines that could even cross: the mystical one—Her powers—and the earthly one—money—a pragmatic and cash-based version of power. Which of those lines had been activated in the relation among the characters and between the characters and the BV? Conde began to draw new circles around the words he had written and more lines that moved out from them, like escape chutes with no known destination. He felt incapable of making the key connection and asked himself how much his abilities may have declined in the years since he left his job as an investigator. And how much they decayed with the progressive hardening (or softening) of his aging neurons. He thought that at some point he should call Tamara, although he decided to wait an hour longer, to be sure that she would return home. The image of the woman, the house, peace, placid love, enveloped him with the feeling of calm that turned into drowsiness.

Listening to the monotonous beat of the rain and enjoying the cooled-off atmosphere, he went to bed with one of his old volumes of poetry by José María Heredia. Having evoked him as he walked on the Alameda de Paula, almost two hundred years before, had revived in Conde the cyclical necessity of going over his verses charged with telluric force, exalted passions, communication with nature. Had Heredia been as apocalyptic as him? In reality, better than him: the nth lecture of his verses was enough to confirm it.

> *Lord of the winds! I feel thee nigh,*
> *I know thy breath in the burning sky!*
> *And I wait, with a thrill in every vein,*
> *For the coming of the hurricane!*

When he awoke, it had gotten dark and stopped raining. He could not specify whether he had dreamed again. Only the image was there. Like the dinosaur. And now he could see it.

An hour later, when he opened the door, he was face-to-face with Manolo's exhausted visage. Behind him, he saw the less friendly face of Lieutenant Miguel Duque, whom Conde nodded at briefly, convinced that he'd have time enough to tear him up at his leisure. In the back, in the twilight and under the persistent rain now falling, was the vulgar Chinese Geely in which the police had traveled from headquarters.

Before greeting him, Manolo reprimanded him. "Make sure this is not another case of your clowning around! What's this about a dinosaur?"

"The shortest story in the world. And the best," Conde responded. "Do you want me to tell it to you?"

"'When he awoke, the dinosaur was there,'" Miguel Duque quoted. "Augusto Monterroso."

Manolo turned around to look at his subordinate, and Conde, despite himself, smiled. Had he been wrong about that Duque and it turned out that he was actually an educated policeman? With faith, miracles do happen, as Carlos had told him and as Father Rinaldi had confirmed.

"I'm surrounded!" Manolo concluded.

Conde invited them into the dining room. He confirmed that Duque was carrying the laptop in his hands and asked them if they wanted coffee. "I just made it," he added. But both declined the offer.

"I can't fit another coffee in this body," Manolo commented. The other man did not explain his no. It was obvious that he did not want anything from Conde: not even coffee.

Each one sat down and Conde was the first to speak. "This afternoon, I told you I had seen something and that I didn't know what it was . . ."

"Yes, so did you see it already? In your dreams?"

"No, in a movie . . . Rather, in two, and I think we all saw it," said Conde, who was enjoying his melodramatic manipulation of the information. "The first movie we saw in the theater or on TV and the main character is an actor called Richard Gere . . . who does what he does in that movie and every movie he acts in because women think he's a good-looking guy, although he is a worse actor than I am a baseball player."

"What are you talking about, buddy?"

"About a guy who likes women, Richard Gere . . . And about movies. Like one that's there, on the computer. Lieutenant Duque, can I humbly ask something of you?"

"Conde, Conde . . ." Manolo scolded him.

"What do you want?"

Conde, with the same seriousness, continued:

"First of all, I'd like to congratulate you for your literary knowledge, but I'd like to remind you that the story you cited is much longer: 'When he awoke, the dinosaur was *still* there.' And then, I'd like to ask if you would be so kind as to turn on that digital device and look for the first film we saw yesterday of Puigventós in the hotel lobby . . ."

The lieutenant let out a loud sigh. He knew Conde was poking at him, only in a way that was disarming. He immediately opened the laptop and turned it on. Manolo was now looking at Conde and the lieutenant, expectantly. He knew that something important could be revealed by the Jurassic image that Conde had had, and that was why he was *still* there. Like the dinosaur, right?

Duque looked for the recording and pressed play. He moved the device on the table and Conde brought it closer to himself, touching it only with the tips of his fingers, as if it were contagious. For a few minutes, they were all silent. At a given moment, Conde nodded, moving his head slowly.

"Lieutenant, do me a favor, play that part of the tape again . . . And both of you, watch it."

Duque pulled the device back, did some maneuvering, and returned it to the side of the table occupied by Conde. Manolo and Duque stood behind their host.

On the screen of the computer, the hotel lobby came to life again. Puigventós was sitting on the sofa and drinking from his little bottle of water. People passed beside him, in one direction and another.

"What is it, Conde?" Manolo demanded, and with his hand, Conde requested patience. The images were moving just as the three of them had seen several times, until the shots showed, front and profile, the woman in white with a hat and glasses who was crossing near Jordi Puigventós.

"Stop there, Duque," Conde told the lieutenant, who pressed the key and froze the image. Conde concentrated on the still image. "No, you can never see the face well, but . . ."

"The woman dressed in white? What's wrong with her?"

"She appears to be a young woman," Conde proposed without really responding.

"She is young. You can tell by the way she walks," Manolo stated.

"Manolo, although you can't see her face, I think I know who she is and why she was in the hotel, and besides, on top of that, I think I even know why Jordi Puigventós isn't showing up . . . That woman is Karla Choy and it's no coincidence that she is there and dressed that way. I think this is the damned unifying thread . . ."

This time, Conde decided to accompany them. He didn't want to miss the presumed climactic scene of the show for anything.

When the Geely in which they were traveling stopped in front of Karla Choy's house-gallery, two patrol cars came out of nowhere and parked next to the Chinese car. One of the policemen, whom the others called Calixto, dressed in a uniform and with sergeant's bars, approached Manolo and held out a piece of paper to him. Manolo moved under the light of a nearby lamppost to read the document and confirmed that he was within the law: they could search Karla Choy's house, he said, and Calixto confirmed that he had placed two men at the back of the mansion, to prevent a possible surreptitious exit.

When the woman who could pride herself on being amid Havana's most desirable opened the door, a look of exhaustion came over her face.

"Again!" she protested.

"Yes, Karla, again, but different," Manolo said and handed over the search warrant. The young woman read it and returned it to the major.

"What do you want to see? Sketches for paintings?"

"First we want you to see something on this computer." He pointed at the device Miguel Duque was carrying. "Where do we sit down?"

The woman made a gesture for them to follow her and walked toward the glassed-in dining room in the back. Conde placed himself at the head of those following her to be the first to enjoy the harmonious movement of the cataclysmic young woman's body and no longer had any doubt: Karla Choy was the woman in white. Thank you, Wilkie Collins.

"Rey, you tricked me," the young woman then said.

"Not at all . . . I was passing by and got in on this story. I'm really not a cop . . ."

Karla and Duque occupied the seats Manolo pointed at, while he placed himself behind them. Conde, on his end, took advantage to disappear behind the four policemen who had begun to search the house, accompanied by two neighbors who'd been called in to serve as witnesses to the police work. The goal was to find any clue capable of revealing Jordi Puigventós's presence there.

A few minutes later, when he returned to the dining room, Conde saw that the images from the hotel lobby were running on the screen. At just the right moment, Conde alerted Duque.

"Stop."

The four of them watched the two frames occupied in the middle by Jordi Puigventós and the woman in white.

"What do you have to say, Karla?" Manolo asked.

"About what, Major?"

"About that woman who's there." Manolo pointed at the screen.

Karla studied the image. She looked at Manolo and shook her head.

"I don't know who she is, you can't see her face . . ."

"But right now, we can reconstruct that woman, Karla. With a wide-brimmed hat and everything," Conde said, and when the others turned around, they saw the former policeman, with the movements of a magician, was extracting from a large bag with the Emporio Armani symbol emblazoned on it, a long dress, a wide-brimmed hat, and a foulard, all white. Exactly like those worn by the woman frozen on the computer screen, the woman whom the dumbstruck Jordi Puigventós could not stop looking at.

Havana, so torrid, humid, tropical, and prone to troughs and the like, had come to have a difficult relationship with rain. Eight or ten hours of ordinary summer downpours with the aspiration to be autumnal turned the city into a deplorable version of Venice: a puddle with houses. The streets, with their sewers full of earth and shit, had become lakes and rivers depending on their inclination. The sidewalks, full of potholes, bumps, and cracks accumulated by years of abandonment, turned into traps capable of devouring any living being who risked crossing them. The electric and telephone lines crackled on their posts until they exploded, fell, leaving citizens in the dark and cut off from communication for time that was immeasurable. The roofs of the houses, worn away by the relentless beating of the sun on them for years, whimpered under the sky's downpours, soaking them up and transferring the precipitation indoors. In the "settlements" that had popped up on the periphery, the scene had to be terrible: mudslides, overflowing ditches, busted ceilings and walls, conquered or broken by the humidity and the weight of water. Shadows and desperation.

Pushed by his triumph and pride, Conde did not accept Lieutenant Duque's invitation to take him back home or wherever he wanted to go. Like the policeman he once was, he knew that his role in the recent staging had ended with his key scene of showing the proof of an undeniable relationship. Now, it was the real policemen's turn and, despite what some people thought, in reality, Conde no longer was one and protocol could not be broken for him. Thanks and goodbye. The others would continue the work.

When the uniformed policemen had left with Karla Choy toward headquarters, Manolo approached his former colleague, who was getting ready to leave. The rain had stopped at that moment, but, beneath the tree that covered them, above their bodies, the flooded leaves cried down onto their bodies.

"What do you think of all this, Conde?" Manolo asked him as he gestured for a cigarette.

"That's what I always ask you . . ."

"When I was lost," the other man recalled.

"But now, we're not. There's a connection between Karla and the Catalan, she herself already admitted. Pull on that thread and . . ."

"The costume you found proves that she was at the hotel . . . But a woman with the intelligence and long-term vision that Karla has, why wouldn't she have made that proof disappear if she knew we were coming after her? No, she couldn't be such an idiot, Conde . . . What if what she told us is true? That she only had an amorous relationship with Puigventós? What if it's true that she hasn't seen him for two days and that she doesn't know where the hell he is? What if she didn't tell us anything this morning because she didn't want to get caught up in a problem that's not hers?"

"Too many conditionals, Manolo . . . She knows something. If, as you say, another conditional, she is not involved in the theft of the Virgin, perhaps she knows with whom her Catalan boyfriend was going to do business. Elizardo and René Águila could be the ones with the biggest bucks . . . Well, you know how to crack that nut . . . Even the toughest guys go soft at headquarters. And that girl is not going to be the exception."

"But, if she's not involved in anything serious . . . Why doesn't she tell us what she knows and get out of this?"

Conde thought. "Because she's frightened?"

Manolo looked at him questioningly. "Frightened of what? Or by what?"

"Couldn't it be of whom?"

"Yes . . . Of someone who is capable of killing two kids to keep the Virgin?"

"It's not a bad option. I would also be afraid of a guy like that . . . Or she could be afraid because of Puigventós, who is lost . . ."

"What in the hell could have happened to that Catalan?" Manolo asked himself aloud and tossed the cigarette butt toward the street.

Conde took two more drags of his cigarette and imitated Manolo. Then he raised his gaze to the foliage from which the drops kept falling on his head and shoulders. He felt fuzzy and swampy, like Havana.

"If you don't find Puigventós today, you're going to have quite a situation with the Spanish consulate and with the Foreign Ministry."

"Why in the hell are you reminding me of this, Conde? I know it and . . ."

"I'm thinking, Manolo, wait . . . Just talking out loud."

"And what are you thinking?"

Conde thought a little more and finally responded, "Nothing . . . I'm not thinking anything. And do you know why? Because, there's something irrational in this whole mess."

"You already told me that . . . So what? I'm leaving. Let's see what we can get out of Karla . . . with how tired I am. This shitty job . . ."

"Manolo," he called out when the other man was walking away. "Can you imagine the party the dykes are gonna have when a bonbon like Karla Choy shows up in the women's prison?"

"I can imagine, I can imagine . . . You're always thinking of shit, man."

"Tell her . . . An idea like that will soften her up more than a pressure cooker . . ."

Still muttering his protests, Major Manuel Palacios walked away toward where Lieutenant Duque was waiting for him, alongside the Chinese Geely. Conde saw them leave and immediately knew that euphoria and pride were usually bad advisors. It was raining again and he had no idea how to get out of that residential neighborhood to arrive at Tamara's house. He remembered that at some point, buses used to pass by there that could get him closer. Extinguished bus lines, like so many other things. Like the dinosaurs.

An hour later, dripping water, in the vicinity of where he'd chosen to spend the night, Conde was still pondering the poor relationship between the city and the rain, between Cubans and urban transportation, between troughs and downpours, trying even to discern whether the invention of Heredia, Varela, Saco, and del Monte, Martí's dream, had worked or not in the best way. Luckily for him, he was not obliged to return to his house, since, before he went out with Manolo and Duque, his neighbors with the avocados had stopped by his yard with a bag of leftovers of rice and chicken for Garbage II. It smelled so good and he was so hungry that Conde was envious of his dog, for whom he placed an exaggerated ration of food in his bowl so that he would become strong and hold out until the next arrival of reinforcements.

When he opened the door to Tamara's house, where he presumed a healthy, frugal meal would be awaiting him, he was hit by a strong aroma and had the pleasant sensation of having returned to a sweet home. And, immediately, he suffered the rebellion of his awakened gastric juices. Because Tamara's house smelled like sofrito of olive oil, garlic, and onion, like cumin and bay leaf, like delicious things, like food . . . *Carne estofada?* Havana-style picadillo with olives and capers? Dutch-style fillet? Was he before a miracle of nature, history, and the most stubborn memory?

Silently, as he liked to do, he prepared himself to respond to the gastronomic surprise that Tamara was preparing by acting dramatically. He began in the very foyer by removing his flooded shoes, dripping shirt, and pants, and since he was at it, he removed his underwear. *Surprise for surprise*, he said to himself, and walked toward the kitchen wearing just his damp socks. In the room, he saw the woman, her back to him, stirring the fragrant food with a large wooden spoon as it cooked in a gigantic pan. Then he spoke:

"What time is dinner?"

The woman turned around, alarmed by the voice, and Conde immediately felt his scrotum wrinkling and his penis shrinking up into itself like a pinched accordion.

"Aymara!" he exclaimed when he discovered that the cook was not Tamara, but her twin sister.

"Oh Conde, but you . . . !" the woman began, surprised at the recently arrived man's nudity, but her expression quickly changed to a smile as she yelled, "Tamara, your husband has gone crazy!"

17.

Night swallowed up the rainy clouds and the morning arrived clear, with a sparkling transparency. From the bed, Conde looked at the shine of the trees in the yard, washed by the rain, and enjoyed the feeling of relaxation. A morning without calendars, without physical or existential anguish, and even without troughs? He had to enjoy it . . . He gave a half-turn over himself and contemplated Tamara's relaxed face and the silver reflection of drool running from the edge of her mouth. He wanted to imbibe that liquid that nourished him so much, but he refrained. No one had the right to disturb someone else's slumber, he told himself, he, a veritable warehouse of broken dreams.

Carefully, he stood up and went to the bathroom to empty his bladder. As he urinated, he smiled when he remembered his thunderous theatrical entrance from the night before and the pleasant dinner he had with Tamara and her sister, Aymara, who'd arrived unannounced from Italy with her nephew, Rafael, Tamara's son whom she had taken in to her Lombardy home several years before. The first reason for the trip, the twins had explained when they were already settled, drinking a respectable Montalcino, nibbling at pieces of Parmesan, slices of prosciutto, and black olives from Crete, had been nostalgia, which was always lying in wait, the sticky sensation of belonging that could reveal itself even at the calmest and most satisfactory moments, a love-hate relationship with what is yours that distance allowed hibernate and maintain alive. The second and better reason was the announcement, postponed until it could be delivered in person, face-to-face, that Rafael Junior and his Italian wife, Cristina Belleza, were going to be parents and, as such, would make a grandmother out of Tamara, whose eyes welled up with happiness and who was simultaneously worried over the fact of entering grand-parenthood, and with an Italian grandchild! The third, because this time there were reasons enough, was that of both being present for Conde's upcoming sixtieth birthday party that Carlos and Dulcita were already organizing, an occasion that Aymara and Rafael Junior would not miss for anything in the world: sixty, sixty, they repeated the horrible cipher, and affirmed that sixty is not just any age. More than the bewilderment caused by being reminded of his birthday or the disquiet that in a few months he would be the lover of a woman who would become a grand-mother, had been confirming that Tamara's son, perhaps softened by im-minent fatherhood and overcome by a now long-standing habit, seemed to have decided to suddenly change his attitude toward Conde and accept him as he had been for the last twenty-five years and still was and appar-ently would be: the love of his mother's life. Even if his dick was a little short, the uncontainable Aymara had added, still amused by the theatri-cal entrance.

He decided to return the dinner prepared by his sister-in-law in kind by making a breakfast that was possible thanks to the powerful reinforce-ments arrived from the Italian great beyond. After drinking several doses of Kimbo coffee, his favorite among all those sold in the world, in a porce-lain cup, and placing the plates and silverware on the table, he confirmed that it was already past eight in the morning and that those slumbering had no intentions of altering their state, exhausted by jet lag and the previous evening's emotions.

He entered the study armed with another cup of coffee and closed the door. He dialed the number to Manolo's office, and the major's secretary asked him to hold on the line. Conde had time to savor his Kimbo with its Neapolitan flavor and to light a cigarette, from which he took two drags before hearing Manolo's voice.

"Thank goodness you're awake already . . . Outside Tamara's house, Duque is waiting for you . . . Get yourself over here right now . . ."

Conde was alarmed by Manolo's cautionary request.

"What the hell happened, Manolo?"

"Madness . . . But I'll tell you when you get here . . . Oh, and do me the favor of not fighting with Duque on the way, huh, Conde?"

asked you to come here because now I'm really lost."

"Are you going to drop the mystery and tell me what the hell happened?"

Manolo pointed at the chair in front of his desk and fell into his own soft-backed chair.

"First I need to remind you of something . . . If someone up there finds out that I'm allowing you any part in this, I'll be the next guy to show up dead. Remember that . . ."

"But why would they find out? Aren't you in charge of this whole operation now? Could your brightest star report you?

"No, Duque wouldn't do that . . . But I have to be careful, you know . . . There's always someone around here who wants to fuck over someone else . . . Or have you forgotten what happened to Rangel?"

"Of course I didn't forget . . . But let's stop all this bellyaching . . . Go ahead and talk already and stop beating around the bush, buddy . . ."

"The Catalan showed up," Manolo let out.

Conde received the news like a beating and took a moment to process.

"Did Karla say where he was?"

"No, he literally showed up. As if he had returned from the dead, because he nearly did . . . They found him yesterday night at the provincial hospital in Matanzas, and from there, they sent him here, to headquarters . . ."

"What the hell are you saying to me, Manolo?"

"What you just heard . . . Duque was working Karla when they called me from the Matanzas police to tell me they found the foreigner you are looking for. Jordi Puigventós Batet. They had admitted him several hours before, but he was unconscious and didn't have any ID on him. And since whatever word he said was in Catalan, the hospital police reported him as a Frenchman, not a Spaniard . . ."

Conde scratched his arms. Now he was the one who was lost. "Unconscious? What happened to him?"

"He says he was jumped in Matanzas. Close to the Catalan Hermitage . . . That they took everything from him . . . But that he thought they wanted to kill him, like Raydel and Ramiro. He's shitting his pants. And I took advantage of that to make him sing . . ."

"What the hell was he doing in Matanzas?"

"Looking for the Virgin, Conde! That blasted Virgin!"

Conde scratched more furiously.

"Let's see, Manolo, rewind and explain to me so that I can understand . . . He was looking for the Virgin in the Catalan Hermitage?"

"If you could just let me speak, buddy! Let's see, let's start from the top, huh?" Conde agreed and the other man sighed before speaking. "Puigventós told me that, as we thought, the day he arrived in Cuba, after having dinner with René Águila, he went to Karla's house. They had, have, a relationship, and she, as part of the game I didn't want to find out more about, would disguise herself for him . . . That is why she showed up like that at the hotel. Well, you know how that is . . ."

"No, I don't know. But I can and want to imagine it. Karla disguised as a nudist, for example. The cataclysm . . ."

"What disguise . . . Stop bullshitting, buddy . . ."

"What shit to be sixty years old! Can you imagine that I didn't even try to flirt with that woman?" Conde lamented. "Come on, go on . . ."

"Well, he went to her house and was there for two days until they called him the day before yesterday on his cell phone to tell him they could do the deal with the Virgin."

"They called him? Who called him? He confessed that he came in search of the Virgin?"

"He found out through René Águila that the Virgin had been stolen. And he asked René, Elizardo, and Karla to try to find out who could have Her because he wanted to buy Her, at whatever price . . . And the three of them told him that the best thing for him to do was to come here and search for Her as well . . . But, as he finished up some business in Spain, things got complicated here. Raydel showed up dead and they killed Ramiro."

"So he didn't know Raydel?"

"He says he might have seen him once, but he had no relationship with him . . . If he's not telling the truth and Puigventós encouraged him to steal the Virgin, what's sure is that he's not the one who killed him. Or Ramiro . . . Because he was still in Spain."

"So who called him to go to Matanzas?"

"Someone who identified himself as Roger Flor . . . That name must be made-up."

"Yes, although it sounds familiar. I've heard it somewhere . . ."

"Well, that Roger Flor told him he knew that Puigventós was interested in buying the Black Virgin from Bobby and that Bobby hadn't wanted to sell Her . . . But that they could talk about the matter. And the Catalan thought that was his opportunity to take the loot for even less money than he had previously thought."

"Aha. Go on, keep going, let me see if I understand. This is kind of crazy . . . Roger Flor? Yeah, that name sounds familiar, so familiar . . . But, who could that character be who knew Puigventós had wanted to buy the Virgin from Bobby? Bobby didn't display his Virgin, She wasn't for sale . . . I myself didn't know they had ever talked about the subject."

"Puigventós found out that Bobby had the Virgin just a few months ago. He found out through Karla, who found out from Elizardo Soler. It was before Bobby traveled to Miami, when he spoke with him about his interest in buying Her."

Conde focused. Something was beginning to make sense. Or too much sense.

"So what happened after Roger Flor's phone call?"

"They agreed to meet in Matanzas. At the Catalan Hermitage. He was supposed to go alone, not say anything to Karla, not mention the business to anyone, or there would be no deal. The Virgin was red-hot, he says they told him. So he went to the bus terminal and grabbed one of those vans that go to Matanzas. With all the money he must have and he didn't hire a taxi! In Matanzas, he got another van until he was close to the chapel. When he was walking along the street that goes up to Montserrat Hill, he got hit on the head and wasn't aware of anything else until he woke up at the hospital and found out he'd been jumped and that some kids had picked him up on the street."

Conde closed his eyes for a few moments. "Do you believe him? That he, of all people, was mugged? On his way to the place where he had been told to meet someone?"

"It's all very strange . . . With the number of tourists running around Varadero and Matanzas, that they would mug Puigventós just when he was going to do the deal with the Virgin?"

"If it wasn't a mugging, Manolo . . . Then what did they want? No one can think that Puigventós was going around with I-don't-know-how-much money on him to buy that Virgin in the middle of the street, right? But they didn't want to kill him, either, like the other two, because whoever hit him, if he had wanted to take him out of the game, could have knocked him off and there would end any trail of Puigventós and what he knew about the Virgin and Bobby, Soler, Karla, René . . . Anyone else?"

"Yes, the story is strange. We thought that he was lost because he was the loose end . . ."

"But he *is* the loose end, Manolo! Because whoever is behind all of this was not thinking that Puigventós would arrive in Cuba after he'd already had to kill two people for the Virgin. What that person had planned was a deal without any greater complications . . . With Puigventós or without him, although better with him . . . Things went sideways in the worst way. Because of that, if the person, or people, who called him to Matanzas wanted to silence him but the Catalan remains alive . . . Then, he really was mugged! The muggers got there first and saved him, Manolo!"

"You think?" Major Palacios did not seem convinced of Conde's hypothesis.

"But that doesn't matter now, or it matters less . . . The fact is that the man showed up, alive."

"Incidentally, that Catalan may look a lot like that actor you say is very good-looking and whom all the women like, but his pits stink badly enough to make you dizzy . . . I don't know how a woman like Karla . . ."

Conde shook his head and continued. "So now we know he came to Cuba in search of the Virgin, and it seems that Karla is not involved in any dark part of the story and that she likes to dress up to spice things up . . .

Can you imagine Karla . . . ? Damn, Manolo, now this thread leads to Bobby and his friend Elizardo. Or am I going crazy?"

Through the two-way mirror, Conde watched as Bobby and Elizardo entered the interrogation room at headquarters. Each one did so in his own way: Bobby, shitting himself him in fear, and Elizardo with confidence and arrogance. Behavior so resounding that it made him consider for a moment that his assumptions, premonitions, and theories could be wrong. But he was convinced of something: those two characters were the only possible path to the truth and the Black Virgin. A few minutes later, he saw Manolo and Duque enter: one with a notebook, the other with a laptop.

Conde felt his temples beating, pure adrenaline. He'd been forced to accept Manolo's condition: his presence in the enclosure could invalidate the procedure, so he would watch the conversation (as the police insisted on calling it) behind the mirror and, if necessary, he would note anything to Major Palacios through the wireless earpiece the policeman wore. While he was waiting for the interrogation to be prepared, Conde, who felt a buzz in his ear, called Rabbit and asked him if the name Roger Flor sounded familiar.

"Of course, *viejo* . . . That guy was a character. Roger de Flor, *Ro-yer*, without an accent over the *o* . . . He was the captain of the largest ship there was in the Mediterranean in the thirteenth century: the *Falcon of the Temple*. And then he became a pirate or a corsair, with some criminals who called themselves the Catalan Company. I think they killed him in an ambush . . . Oh, and it was suspected that he robbed a part of the Templars' treasure . . . Those same Templars who worshipped Our Lady when Black Virgins were in vogue, as Father Rinaldi told us yesterday . . ."

"Thanks, Rabbit . . . You see, what the hell am I gonna do when you're not here?"

"You'll be fucked. Or you'll look it up on the internet. It's easier . . ."

"Is everything really on the internet?"

"And then some . . ."

"Well, that's good . . . Thanks, buddy."

A half hour before they brought in Bobby and Elizardo, Miguel Duque had returned from the art vendor's mansion with the frustrating news that, following the authorized and carried out search, nothing had shown up that would allow them to connect the house's owner with the Black Virgin or the crimes committed surrounding Her, although among the thousands of things found were much-sought-after pieces such as several funerary sculptures stolen from the cemetery, some pornographic movies made in Cuba, and other merchandise that was even as compromising as several pieces of frozen beef, worthy in and of themselves of earning him a long prison stay for the crime of receiving stolen goods, since according to the country's laws, you could earn a longer sentence for stealing and dismembering a cow than for killing a human being. To everyone's bewilderment, no great amount of money or jewelry or valuable paintings showed up, either. Their only possible chance, as such, continued to be carrying out an interrogation from which, manipulating the interests and characters of those interviewed, some spark could emerge and ignite a whole fire of clarity.

As they had agreed, Manolo allowed Duque to begin the attack. The most promising subjects were Bobby and Elizardo's relationship with Jordi Puigventós given the light shed by the Catalan's statement and the attack he'd suffered in Matanzas, which seemed to have saved him from a worse fate.

Conde had to admit that Duque was good at his job. He moved like a predator on the prowl, sniffing out his victims' weaknesses and distractions, before taking them to the edge from which he could throw them. He asked them for information and simultaneously gave them details, to prove how much he knew about them. But he didn't manage to make way. When he asked Bobby, he said what they already knew. When he addressed Elizardo Soler, the man repeated the story that had already been revealed. Neither admitted to having seen Jordi Puigventós in the last two days. Regarding Karla Choy and René Águila, on whose respective ambitions, ills, and lack of scruples both dwelled, they had only seen them to find out if they had any news about the Virgin stolen by Raydel and to alert them about Her possible entry to the market. Nonetheless,

Lieutenant Duque repeated questions, demanded details, tried to confront them, in search of a crack to enter and move forward.

From his forced position of spectator, Conde followed the dialogue, watched in turn by Sergeant Calixto, who was stuck to him like a flea. A growing unease invaded him as the interrogation went on without any notable advances. He thought that perhaps neither Bobby nor Elizardo Soler knew more than they had already admitted, but his conviction that the two were unrepentant tricksters would not leave him and much less, his premonition that both, or at least one of them, knew or had done much more than he was confessing. At one point in the conversation, Conde had hope that something would come to light: Manolo, gathering strength from the exhaustion of two nights spent almost completely awake, entered the round with his usual rage. No one was leaving there, he warned, until the truth was known. There was a face-off between everyone implied, including the Catalan Puigventós, Karla Choy, and René Águila. He would order new search warrants for each one's houses and properties. He would search everything down to their cavity fillings . . . Did any of them know Roger Flor? But he didn't manage to nudge the interrogated: Bobby sobbed and Elizardo denied, they didn't know anything about anything, less still about Roger Flor.

Conde had the certainty that they were not on the best path to reach solid ground and, through his microphone, he whispered to Manolo to stop the offense and take a break. Perhaps, he proposed, he should interrogate them separately, with different strategies. In the room, Manolo nodded and looked at his guests.

"I know that you, both of you or one of the two of you, is up to your neck in shit," Manolo began, "and we're going to find out . . . If one of you is not guilty of anything, then reconsider now and think that the other one wanted to fuck him over . . . We're going to take a coffee break and will be back in a bit. I regret not being able to invite you, but our budget has been cut. You know how things are . . ."

"How long are you going to have us here?" Eli asked, without losing his confidence and composure.

"Until I decide . . . And I'm slow at making decisions, you know? The law gives me seventy-two hours . . . And it doesn't matter who you're the son of or who your friends are or if you are or aren't the Cuban James Bond. So get comfortable . . ."

Bobby was shaking his head, on the verge of bursting into tears. Elizardo, meanwhile, smiled sarcastically, nearly in satisfaction. Manolo tapped Duque's forearm and they both stood up and headed for the exit.

"Can I smoke?" Elizardo asked, and Manolo turned around with a dour expression, as he raised his arm, ready to say no, to go off on a rant, but he immediately had to take it to his ear as he received Conde yelling:

"Let him smoke! I have a hunch!"

Manolo stopped his movements and gave a half turn. Before leaving, he said:

"Yes, smoke. And think . . ."

Through the glass, Conde saw Manolo and Duque exit, and noticed that Elizardo was smiling very discreetly, since he knew he was being watched. Without looking at Bobby, who was sobbing again, he removed the lighter and the pack of cigarettes he carried in his pocket. Elizardo's left hand covered the pack of cigarettes from which, with his right, he extracted a filtered cigarette that he took to his mouth. When he flicked on the lighter and drew it toward the cigarette, Conde discovered a slight shaking in his hand, which could be normal for someone in his situation. At that moment, Manolo reached his side.

"Why in the hell do we have to let him smoke?"

"Because no one is perfect, Manolo . . . Wait, be quiet . . ."

Conde watched Elizardo Soler smoke and focused on mining the recesses of his brain with a dizzying speed, looking for something to rest on, until he thought he found it when he remembered the results of the house's search.

"Manolo, go in there again and tell me if Elizardo's cigarettes smell a lot like American cigarettes . . ."

Manolo looked at his former boss and a light shone in his eyes.

"And if it's a blond American cigarette, ask him what he did with the Portocarrero he had in his office . . . Go on . . ."

Conde got closer to the glass to watch Manolo's return to the interrogation room. At ease, as if he had no rush, the officer pulled his chair out and sat down.

"The coffee was good . . . Just brewed . . . Would you give me a cigarette?" he asked Elizardo, and the man, as if it were of no importance, moved the box toward Manolo with his left hand. When the major took it, he made a gesture of disgust. "Chesterfield . . . No thank you, I can't stand blond American tobacco. It tastes sweet . . . And stinks."

Elizardo shrugged his shoulders and took back the box Manolo was returning to him. Outside, Conde sweat.

"Elizardo . . . So, what happened to the big Portocarrero painting that was in your office?"

A very slight movement in the man confirmed to Conde that his premonition had not been mistaken.

"I sold it a few days ago . . ."

"To whom?" Conde whispered, and Manolo, like a replicant, asked Elizardo the question.

"An American who was in Cuba. Jerry Carlson's the name."

"For how much?" Conde asked. Manolo continued in his role.

Elizardo thought for a moment. He looked at Bobby, who had stopped sobbing and was following the dialogue with interest.

"Forty thousand . . ." Elizardo said at last.

"Cheap, no?" Conde and Manolo said.

"That depends . . ."

"Yes, on how rushed one is to sell a painting like that . . . Which is surely worth more. So, what about the money, where's the money? In your house, we didn't find . . ." Conde continued, dragging along Manolo who seemed like a ventriloquist's doll.

Elizardo thought again, just for a few moments. Enough for Conde to know that he was forging a lie.

"The American hasn't paid me yet . . . He couldn't come to Cuba with that money in hand. The U.S. embargo, you know . . ."

"Yes, the embargo . . . That's very trusting of you," Conde said, Manolo repeated after him, and the former policeman, changing his tone of voice, whispered to Major Palacios. "Tell them you're going to confirm that Jerry

Carlson was in Cuba and two or three other things and let them go. Let them go!"

Without worrying about what was happening in the interrogation room, Conde approached Lieutenant Duque.

"Don't waste time in fighting with me or resenting me . . . Put a tail on both of them, but especially Elizardo Soler . . . If I'm not mistaken, tonight, we'll recover the Virgin . . . Make sure the surveillance on Elizardo is very discreet; he knows we're going to follow him . . . That guy tells people that he's from State Security and sometimes they really believe he's an agent! Do it now!" he yelled as he saw Manolo taking leave of his guests. Without paying attention to what he was doing, Conde wiped the palms of his hands on his pant legs. They were sweating and his heart was beating quickly. It was obvious that he could still think and act like the cop he had once been. Elizardo Soler had been right in his preliminary diagnostic. And Conde would soon know that he had been as well: a psychopath marks everything with his irrationality.

With the rest of the convertible pesos he still had, Conde invited Manolo to eat at a private restaurant close to headquarters. The place was neither elegant nor expensive, but it was efficient and served good portions. He had to nourish himself, and then Manolo could rest, until the moment came for him to act. Now, all they could do was spend their time waiting, like hunters lying in wait.

As they ate, Conde examined Manolo's cell phone two or three times to make sure the device was working. They were supposed to call them on that electronic contraption if there was any movement. To keep the line free, he went out onto the street for a few minutes and made several phone calls from a pay phone: to Tamara, to tell her not to wait for him and to have the best time possible with her sister and her son; to Carlos, to chew him out for organizing a party behind his back for a birthday he didn't want to celebrate and to tell him that he was missing in action because things with Bobby's Virgin had gotten complicated, but he missed him, he loved him, and he couldn't live without him, despite still, *still* not being homosexual; and last to Yoyi, to ask what he thought about the possibility of getting paid what was agreed upon for the Black Virgin's recovery if, as he thought, She showed up but the police temporarily or definitively kept Her, and he received the expected response from his business partner: "You make sure She shows up and I'll make sure you get paid . . . Let's see if I give you that money on the day of your birthday party, it's going to be great." Conde told him to go to hell and hung up with a pleasant feeling: when so many things were turning to shit, he had the privilege of counting on friends who loved him and whom he loved.

Relieved of responsibilities, he returned to the restaurant, ordered his coffee, paid for what they had consumed, and tried to organize the rest of the afternoon. He knew that Manolo would have preferred to have him far away at this stage of the process, but he could not miss the final act of the show he had been following since Bobby called him and raised the curtain.

They returned to headquarters and took refuge in Manolo's office after the major ordered his secretary to bother him only if Lieutenant Duque or Sergeant Calixto called, or, of course, if a cataclysm occurred. Within the compound, with the air-conditioning on full force, Manolo recognized that Conde was an unrepentant opportunist and immediately admitted to his exhaustion and settled in on a sofa placed against the wall. Conde, meanwhile, took the visitor's armchair, from which a notable extension of the seemingly calm city could be seen. It was not long before Manolo was snoring.

At nine at night, when they no longer expected to receive the alarm-bell call, Manolo's cell phone rang and Miguel Duque's name appeared on the screen: the eagle had left the nest. Elizardo Soler had left driving a car that was not his, seemingly alone, and heading east, possibly toward the Malecón and the tunnel under the bay.

"He's leaving the country," Conde said when he finished listening to the lieutenant.

"That's what he thinks," Manolo retorted, and they left the office in search of the waiting car in the headquarters' parking lot.

The communication between Duque and Manolo was reestablished through their car radios. Duque informed them that they had crossed the tunnel and continued on east, toward the beaches, the northern coast, the city of Matanzas as the last foreseeable destination: fifty miles of coastline from which clandestine exits from the island frequently occurred. Meanwhile, Sergeant Calixto, tasked with following Bobby's surveillance, confirmed that his objective was still inside his house.

When the car Manolo was driving took the highway east, Conde refused to think of his déjà vu. Life was this: circles, turns, roundabouts from which a powerful line escapes one day and changes everything in a few minutes or, even, you go to Hell. Or to nothing.

"Conde, we're running around in circles here . . . Where could the Virgin be?" Manolo asked, and the other man understood that in their excitement, neither of them had asked the award-winning question. "After the search we did at his house, I don't think it was there . . . And if Elizardo is leaving because of everything that happened with the Virgin . . . Is he going to leave without Her? That's a guaranteed three million . . ."

Conde lit a cigarette. He did not have any halfway decent response to give Manolo. "Or he has Her very well hidden and can leave Her in Cuba until someone takes Her out, or goes to get Her before going to the point of departure," he speculated without the least idea of how close he could be to the target. "But he knows that we're closing in on him and his greatest problem right now is to escape . . ."

"So did he have his exit prepared already or did he take care of it just today after we spoke with him?" Manolo continued, with his implacable police logic.

"As far as I'm concerned, he had prepared for it ever since the story got more tangled with the missing Catalan . . ." Conde surmised. "That's why they didn't find much at his house. Besides, it's not easy to prepare an exit from one minute to another . . ."

"It depends on what you're willing to pay, Conde . . . A speedboat can get here in mere hours . . ."

"Yes, and Elizardo can pay . . . I still don't believe that a guy like him, with everything he had, would have complicated himself with that Virgin . . ."

"Money, Conde, money . . ." Manolo declared.

"Or power, Manolo . . . Which is worth more than money and is addictive. You know that . . . Many people here know that, right?"

"You said it, I didn't." Manolo smiled.

"Either way, it's still hard for me to believe that this Elizardo is the one who killed the two kids. Too much violence for his type. Too much risk for a man who moves the kind of money he does and lives like he lives. The guy was even preparing himself for what could happen in the future. He didn't want to be left out of the game that's going to be played . . ."

"But you know, Conde . . ."

"Yes, I know . . . The unfathomable human soul and . . . A twisted mind. If I try to impose order on what happened, with two dead guys, a statue of the Virgin whom they say performs miracles, some characters who always live to the max, someone who plays at something they believe is a sure thing, all added up, it has a whiff of madness. Damn, that would be good . . . !" Conde stopped his reasoning when the car radio required Manolo's attention. It was Sergeant Calixto.

"Yes, Calixto, proceed . . ."

"The objective has visitors . . . Karla Choy and the Catalan just arrived . . ."

Conde and Manolo looked at each other. What the hell was going on?

"Keep the surveillance. Wait and see if something happens . . . Ask for reinforcements to follow Karla and Puigventós when they leave. And search them if they're carrying a package," Manolo improvised at this unexpected juncture, and cut off. "What could those two be looking for with your friend Bobby, Conde?"

"They're going around in search of the Virgin, Manolo. What else could it be? The damned Virgin . . ."

"You see, Conde . . . If you stayed behind like I told you to, now I could be sending you to Bobby's house and . . . But if Bobby had the Virgin, why is Elizardo the one who wants to leave Cuba?"

"I don't know, but don't worry too much about it, either, Manolo. There is time for Bobby and the others. But with Elizardo, if he's going to do what we think, then we have only one swing . . . And if we don't hit the ball, we're done . . . And if he's just on a stroll through Havana, then we wave to him if we pass by him . . . Oh, and I was going to tell you that it would be good—"

The car radio crackled again. Now it was Lieutenant Duque speaking, with an alarmed voice.

"Yes, speak, what's happening?"

"Elizardo left the highway! He took the old road to Guanabacoa . . . He's not leaving the country . . ."

"Follow him, we're already practically behind you," Manolo said to him.

"But the thing is, I lost him! The guy got away from me!" Duque exclaimed, practically weeping.

Manolo sped up the car and Conde closed his eyes. He made a mental map of the city. The highway, the old road to Guanabacoa, the south and the east of Havana, and then he yelled.

"San Miguel del Padrón . . . He's going to the 'settlement,' Manolo. I knew it, man, I knew it! The Virgin is still there!"

"But what . . . ?"

"Go on, speed up, put on your lights . . . Let's take the Vía Blanca and see if we get there before him. Tell Duque . . . I knew it, dammit, I knew it! The Virgin remains there . . . And what I wanted to say was that it would be good to know if Elizardo was ever really an undercover agent or if he was ever admitted to Havana's psychiatric hospital . . . Watch it or you'll kill us, dammit!"

Night in the "settlement" made the landscape of poverty even more dismal. The previous day's rains had turned the irregular interior paths to mud and, on more than one occasion, Conde and Manolo nearly fell to the ground. A few lights, coming from some of the improvised houses, slightly illuminated some of the paths that couldn't even dream of benefiting from asphalt or public utilities. In contrast, ever since they began their advance, the sound of one or of different reggaeton songs (he would never be capable of distinguishing between the unity or diversity of the works, to apply some name to that noise) would accompany them with its monotonous, percussive beat, like the anthem of a Maasai warrior.

Manolo had parked the car on a side street close to the "settlement," which was dark like the whole neighborhood. Before entering the area, he was able to confirm with Duque that Elizardo Soler's car, which he had been able to track down again, seemed to be headed there after taking the main highway. From that moment on, they would communicate via cell phone, which Manolo put on vibrate. They were betting everything on one card.

In front of the houses, rooms, mud cabins, and sheds where immigrants from within the nation lived, Conde and Manolo saw children, young people, adults, and old people devoted to the art of allowing time to flow with the confidence, or without it, that something would change . . . Or not. The looks they received were hostile but contained: their trained senses in such situations warned those in the "settlement" that the two nocturnal visitors could not be anything but policemen and they avoided any possible confrontation, since they knew that against power, they, the pariahs of the earth, would be on the losing side. On a street corner, Conde had the confirmation that he and Manolo had been tagged: following a long whistle, which floated even over the reggaeton, at the next intersection, there was an immediate dispersion of shadows. For a moment, it worried him that some inhabitants of the "settlement" could warn Elizardo Soler of the presence of policemen in the area, but the unusual fact of the agents going ahead and the pursued man being behind them, gave him peace: no one would realize the equation and Elizardo would be taken for another policeman and the cautious silence would remain intact. At the end of the day, what was happening, until now, did not involve them and they would not mix themselves up in it, nor did they care, as the laws of the jungle stipulated.

When they took the rising path that led to the deceased Ramiro's room, Conde slipped in the mud and fell. He cursed himself, the wet earth, Elizardo Soler's mother, being an old fart who falls wherever, and warned Manolo that if he laughed, he would kick him in the ass. Without too much surprise, they observed how Ramiro's room, cordoned off a few days before as the site of a crime, had been revolutionarily reclaimed by a family who, instead of listening to reggaeton, seemed to be watching some recorded television program, almost certainly one made in Miami, in which they were talking about an imminent liberating invasion of the island destroyed by a dictatorial regime for fifty-five years.

Conde led Manolo to the edge of the territory occupied by the "settlement," beyond Ramiro's room, and, using the police flashlight for the first time, they crossed the barbed-wire fence and looked for an appropriate surveillance point between some trees whose foliage was falling to the ground. From there, they would have visual access to the path, to Ramiro's room, and to a good part of the wire fence that marked off the vacant land. Then, Manolo removed his vibrating cell phone, studied the screen, and, following the pronouncement of an almost inaudible "yes," listened for a few seconds and repeated the affirmation in the same tone and volume. In the darkness, he nodded at his partner in the hunt.

A few minutes later, they saw the silhouette, barely lit by the clarity that escaped through one of the back windows of Ramiro's room. The man crossed the fence just behind the room and remained still. He must have been observing the landscape, perhaps getting his bearings. A ray of concentrated light, coming from a small but powerful source, better marked the man's position, who chose a possible path between the trees and the aggressive marabú bushes. This could be another voyage to the Inferno.

Guided by the firefly light that led to the recently arrived man, Conde and Manolo followed the path marked with rigorous precautions. More than once, they heard the pursued man's muffled exclamations, the same ones they themselves could have let out with each pinch of the marabú's knifelike needles. On two or three occasions, the man stopped, getting his bearings. Conde and Manolo barely breathed. They knew that without the Virgin in his hands, everything they had or could have against Elizardo Soler could be circumstantial and they needed to surprise him in possession of the divine object of desire.

A few feet ahead, Elizardo stopped. In the darkness, Conde could make out the large trunk of a tree, perhaps a ficus, from which two branches emerged in the strange shape of the cross. Surrounding the tree, the leaves on the bushes hid the upper part of Elizardo's body and, for a few moments, the beam of light that must have been coming from his cell phone. Conde remembered at that moment that, according to Father Gonzalo Rinaldi, many of the Black Virgins brought along with them the legend of having appeared in caves, wells, and the trunks of trees! He didn't think twice: with one swipe of the hand, he took Manolo's flashlight and, without protecting himself from the marabú's attack, ran toward Elizardo Soler's shadow, and when he pushed aside the foliage hiding him, he turned on the flashlight at the very moment in which the man, raised on a piece of wood leaning against the rough trunk, was extracting from the hollow that reached the heart of the tree the brilliant statue of a majestic Black Virgin.

From that moment on, everything went into fast-forward: Conde saw how Elizardo Soler turned around and, without transition, from his left hand came a flash that blinded him. At the same time that he heard the detonation resounding on the arid, empty land, Conde felt that hit to his torso capable of pushing him against the vegetable claws of the raging marabú. His back hurt more than his chest, he managed to think before losing consciousness and regretting that everything would end before he turned the obscene sum of sixty years. Too young to die? Mario Conde asked himself when he heard a second and, immediately, a third detonation. And he suddenly felt himself plunged into pain as silence took over. Because, always, everything else is silence.

18.

N*egro* . . . can I have a drink already?"

Doctor Francisco Galarraga looked at his patient and pointed an admonishing finger at him that looked more like a Bantu sword. In simple opposition, on his dark face, his eyes looked like two searchlights that scanned, as if it were a foreign body, the speaker's physiognomy.

It had been Doctor Galarraga, a surgeon, who had received the man, wounded by a bullet three days prior, in the emergency room. Transported on a gurney pushed by a lame nurse who crashed into walls and seats, the wounded man had been taken to the vestibule of the operation room, and when he saw the jet-black face lean over him from which those luminous eyes observed him, he thought that he had earned his assent to the heavens because of his life's good acts and that the Black angel of an old friend was awaiting him alongside Saint Peter.

"What in the hell are you doing here?" he asked the doctor at that moment, his very dark skin suddenly turned ashen. "Negro, did I die already?" inquired the patient, who was really worried.

"I'll tell you in a minute," the doctor responded and began to study the wound as he said, "Yes, the world truly is small . . . Conde in person . . . How in the hell . . ."

"Hold on, Negro, it hurts, it hurts . . ." the man on the gurney protested when the surgeon touched the edges of the wound on the upper-left part of his thorax.

"Keep still, buddy," the doctor scolded him. "Don't be such a jackass."

"Yes, I am . . . I'm gonna pass out, man. They shot me, dammit! Am I dying?"

Doctor Galarraga smiled. His teeth, of horselike proportions, were also shining and white.

"Only the good die young . . . The bullet went through you and it seems there are no affected organs or bones . . . It might have nicked your clavicle . . . Either way, I'm going to have to do an X-ray. So I'm going to clean you up, and if there's no bigger problem, I'll do a small operation and sew you up . . . Shall I use a bit of anesthesia?"

"Yes, of course. Better if it's general, Negro."

"Go wash your own ass, Conde."

The doctor and patient had met many years before. It was practically inevitable that they had met in high school at La Víbora and, besides, on the school's baseball team, for which Pancho Galarraga, alias "El Negro," played second base. Conde and his other classmates had given him the nickname of "El Negro" because, among the many Black students with whom they shared classrooms, Galarraga managed to stand out due to the resounding darkness of his skin. His former classmates still of sound mind continued to remember how, thanks to El Negro's enormous home run, the school's team had reached the finals of a provincial championship . . . That it later lost.

"Negro, let Tamara and Carlos know . . . Tell them it's serious, go on."

"Let me finish up with the wound first . . . I'll call them, but . . . You're going to make things complicated for me, Conde!"

The doctor had been right, since by midnight, when he'd already been sewn up and bandaged, with his left arm immobilized, the wounded man's provisional bed looked like a beehive. Tamara and Aymara had been the first to arrive. Soon after, the recently landed Dulcita showed up, pushing Carlos's wheelchair. Yoyi, Rabbit, and Candito arrived a little later, and the parade was closed out by Major Palacios and Lieutenant Duque, whose face looked like a poorly made tiger: some orange stripes crossed his cheeks and forehead in several directions.

When he saw Manolo, Conde asked him:

"What the hell happened?"

"I'm not really sure, buddy . . . We have to reconstruct the events and—"

"What about Elizardo?"

"I had to shoot him," Manolo said.

"What do you mean . . . ?"

"I killed him, Conde," Major Palacios whispered and looked off toward the window that overlooked the hospital garden.

It was at that moment that Doctor Galarraga decided to cut off the summit.

"Well, now everyone knows that Conde is not going to die from this one . . . I'm going to take him for observation. I have to leave him here for two or three days. There's always the danger of internal hemorrhage or an infection and I want to keep him close. Someone can stay the night with him . . ."

"I'll stay," Tamara leaped, imposing her unquestioned priority.

"Me, too," Carlos said, firmly.

"Only one can stay," the doctor warned.

"Negro, Tamara's staying and so am I . . ." Carlos said. "Or do you want me to get up from here and smack you a couple of times? Or tell this whole hospital that you are nothing but a thief who used to steal cans of meat with me from the warehouse when they sent us to school in the countryside?"

"So it was with El Negro that you used to steal the cans of Russian meat!" Candito was surprised.

The doctor threw up his hands, giving up, but was insistent on taking the wounded man for observation.

The following night, Conde's hospital room again turned into a solidarity meeting. All that was missing was the Creedence Clearwater Revival music and some bottles of rum for the "activity," as someone called the meeting, to reach its best form. At eight o'clock, when established visiting hours were over, Doctor Galarraga and the head nurse tried to impose order and sanity, but Conde's friends, gathered around the bed, refused to leave the room. Major Palacios had announced his visit and none of them wanted to leave there without learning the details of the story that nearly cost Conde his life and had ended in the death of one Elizardo Soler. El Negro Galarraga, convinced that the rebellion in course was uncontrollable, negotiated with the mutineers that they remain in the hospital for one more hour or he would call the police. "I'll really call them, dammit," he insisted.

The doctor did not have to send for them, since the policemen Manuel Palacios and Miguel Duque arrived about twenty minutes later, and they asked the surgeon to forgive them for being late. Major Palacios then took the preferential chair they had reserved for him alongside the convalescent's bed.

"How do you feel?"

"Fine, Manolo, thanks . . . But come on and talk already, buddy! What was the deal with Elizardo?"

"Conde, Conde, calm down," El Negro Galarraga, who was also seated, reprimanded him. Already in so deep, the doctor was not going to miss the best part of the show. The head nurse, of course, remained to listen to the story.

"My thought is that Elizardo went crazy," Manolo began to narrate. "When he saw that you had discovered him with the Virgin in his hands, he fired the first shot at you, and I think what saved you was that you passed out . . ."

"Anyone would pass out after a shot!" Conde advised. "There are people who even die and everything . . ."

"The problem is that I couldn't see anything, because you had taken the flashlight, and besides, there were those thick bushes that didn't let me see what was happening on the other side, where the tree with the hiding place was. But, Elizardo shot at you a second time. Based on the trajectory of the shot that nicked the bushes, we think the bullet went over your head because you were already falling to the ground . . ."

"That son of a bitch shot at me again?"

"And he was always shooting to kill. He was desperate, out of control. But that shot was the one that cost him his life. I had already taken out my gun with the first shot, and when I saw the second explosion, I fired two times in that direction and heard him yell . . . Since I didn't know what happened, I approached him by making a circle, guided by the light coming from the flashlight lying on the ground, next to you. When I got to where both of you were, I saw that I had hit Elizardo twice. Once in the chest, another time in the neck . . . He was dying. And when I saw you immobile, with your chest full of blood, I thought that he had fucked you up . . ."

"So, what did you think? Poor Conde?"

"No, I thought, look at what happened to Conde for being an idiot, because right away, you started moaning and I knew you were alive, although I had no idea whether you were in serious condition . . . Two minutes later, Duque and his people arrived and we ran out of there with you . . . Duque took you out of there over his shoulder . . . Look at his face . . ."

Conde and the other listeners looked over at the lieutenant. Like the night before, his face looked like that of the last Mohican or the Lion King: the orange lines of disinfectant crossed in all directions.

"Duque picked you up and carried you out. The marabú needles nearly ripped him to pieces . . . They had to bathe his wounds in thimerosal and give him a tetanus shot."

"Thank you, Lieutenant," Conde said.

"There's no reason to thank me," Duque responded coarsely, almost as a reflex.

"Today, Sergeant Calixto was able to find some of Elizardo's medical records . . . He has a psychiatric file that could serve as the basis for a doctoral thesis."

"I knew it," Conde muttered. "The guy was an explosive mix of mad and son of a bitch."

"I wouldn't have wanted to kill him," Manolo muttered. "I shot as a reflex . . . I thought he had killed you . . ."

"I would have done the same, Manolo," Conde tried to console him. "And the son of a bitch really did try to kill me . . ."

"In any event, there will be an investigation. The prosecutors love to sit us in a chair and dig into the dirt . . . I'm sure they're going to call on you to make a declaration and—"

"What about the Virgin?" Carlos then interrupted, with his usual gesture of waving his hands to make way. "What the hell happened to the Virgin?"

"We have Her at headquarters. And we know what we know," Manolo said, Socratically. "Raydel stole Her and gave Her to Ramiro for safekeeping or hid Her himself. Perhaps, they had thought of leaving Cuba together . . . But we can't ask either one if Elizardo was behind the theft. I would say he was . . ."

"So would I," Conde remarked. "Raydel lived like a prince at Bobby's side and stole the Virgin because someone proposed buying Her from him, thinking that the kid was easy to trick. And that had to have been Elizardo . . . Although it doesn't make much sense to me that a guy who lived like Elizardo did, who had everything he had, would get involved in organizing this theft. No matter how mad he was . . ."

"Experts say that the Virgin is medieval and authentic and that She's worth . . . between two and three million euros," Lieutenant Miguel Duque advised them.

"Daaaaamn!" the Pigeon let loose. "That's real money to Elizardo, and to anyone . . ."

"Well, three million . . . would drive even the sanest person crazy," Conde surmised. "And Eli wanted to be rich like his grandfather Sarrá . . . He stole the family sculptures from the cemetery . . ."

"The logical thing would be for Raydel to steal the Virgin and for Elizardo to pay him some money and then get him out of Cuba. That must've been the agreement. When Raydel already had the Virgin, Elizardo put together the show of the purchase and the clandestine exit via the coast . . . But he thought he could recover the Virgin with very little or no money and fuck over Raydel in the meantime. All of this got tangled up when the kid showed up without the Virgin and almost certainly asked for more money because he had known what She could be worth for a while . . . And that was when Elizardo went crazy, as Conde says . . ."

"The crazy son of a bitch," the wounded man added. "He tortured Ray to get out of him where he was keeping the Virgin, the kid told him Ramiro the Cloak had Her, and then he killed him. He waited a few days, to see what was happening, or because he became afraid . . . And when he finally went to take Her or buy Her from Ramiro, I arrived . . ."

Manolo nodded. "I imagine that when he knocked you out with the blow to the head, he got the detail out of Ramiro about where the Virgin was and killed him. It's a miracle he didn't kill you that day as well."

"What a fucking guy!" Carlos exclaimed. "So why do you think he didn't knock off Conde, too?"

"Because Super Pigeon arrived!" Yoyi said, carrying out the gesture of opening his shirt and showing off his prominent sternum.

"I imagine that's it," Manolo admitted. "He didn't have time . . . Or he got scared. Or he thought that Conde was still a policeman, and killing a policeman always complicates things much more . . ."

"What doesn't click for me is that he preferred to leave the Virgin where She was hiding," Candito commented. "You could have found Her . . ."

"I'm sure he thought that was the best hiding place," Manolo proposed. "And that if someone, us or Conde, found Her, he would not even have touched Her. He would lose the Virgin, but be saved from anything else . . . Two dead guys changed everything . . . No, it wasn't a bad idea to leave Her there. Worst case, he merely lost what he had never had . . ."

"Yes, that could be," Conde commented. "That possibility sounds good . . . Which means he wasn't crazy at all. He left it in that tree, but things got difficult and he decided to pick Her up and leave with Her . . . What stirred up the wasp's nest was the arrival of the Catalan Puigventós . . . Did Elizardo really mean to kill him as well?"

"If it was Elizardo who called him to the Catalan Hermitage in Matanzas . . . It was to kill him as well. And I can't think of any other person besides Elizardo who could have called the Catalan to go to Matanzas, and have him go running so happily there. Maybe that story about a certain Roger Flor calling him was something he made up."

"So, what about the rest of them, Manolo? Bobby, Karla, René Águila, Puigventós?"

"They're a bunch of liars and thieves, but we let them go already. If any of them was in cahoots with Elizardo Soler in any part of this story, I don't think we'll be able to find out. Luckily for them, Elizardo took all of this shit to his grave . . . And none of them is going to accuse themselves of having any role in the story."

"So what happens with the Virgin now?" Conde continued.

"She's the only one who remains in prison."

"You're not going to return Her to Bobby?"

"That's not up to the police anymore, Conde. And you know that . . ." Manolo made the gesture of pointing up, in search of the highest stratosphere. "Now the folks in the Foreign Ministry are in touch with the ones from Spanish Patrimony. Since it seems that the Virgin disappeared in Spain during the Civil War, they had assumed She'd been destroyed and they're looking for documentation . . . I can't imagine what comes next. If he's very lucky, after this whole story is investigated, your friend Bobby could end up recovering Her, but I don't think so . . ."

"Are you listening, Yoyi?" Conde said to his business partner.

"Well, the party's over . . ." Doctor Galarraga interrupted after looking at his watch. "Conde has to rest. Tomorrow morning, I'll evaluate him and see if I can release him . . . Who is staying with him today?"

"I am." Yoyi the Pigeon leaped forward, without giving the rest of them a chance. "Conde and I have to talk. And that way, I'll take him early tomorrow if you release him . . . We've got to save gas, right?"

The farewell process lasted half an hour, in the best Cuban style. When they were finally alone, Conde merely looked at Yoyi.

"I already told you I would take care of Bobby . . . You found the Virgin. Mission accomplished."

"You think?" Conde asked, who didn't believe it. No, not when they were dealing with Bobby.

When he performed the clinical exam the following morning, Doctor Galarraga decided that the wounded man could leave, under the condition of continuing to take antibiotics and under strict orders to rest for the next seven days, when he would evaluate him again. Tamara, who had come to listen to the diagnostic, and Yoyi, awaiting the medical judgment to take Conde in his Chevy Bel Air, nodded at the surgeon's request. Then they heard the question about alcohol that Conde was posing to his former classmate. With his finger raised, his eyes shining in his very black face, Doctor Galarraga proclaimed:

"Not one, Conde, not even one drink . . . You're taking antibiotics . . . You cannot drink until . . . Until," the doctor was thinking. "Until your birthday. On October ninth, I will lift the prohibition. Is that clear?"

19.

ANTONI BARRAL, OCTOBER 8, 2014

You amass, organize, bind the pages on which, throughout several weeks and many hours of forced solitude, painful effort, and incisive doubts, you've been recording letters, syllables, words, phrases, sentences, paragraphs saved or later discarded and conceived of again, always with effort, besieged by all kinds of uncertainty. You have waged an unequal battle with your abilities through which you have tried to find and express some sense, at least a trace of sense, to the most burning mystery of existence: How do you make a life, or, in reality, how do you undo it, pluck the leaves away, trampled, dragged by the gales of the irrevocable, tyrannical circumstances?

As the pages run through your hands, in the somewhat mechanical exercise of numbering them, you are surprised by a feeling of distance, almost of remoteness, capable of causing you a sharp uneasiness that you can't quite explain. You even suffer a strange reaction in your skin toward the fibrous texture of the rough paper, worn down by so much handling throughout these days. You understand that now nothing, not even matter, survives the feeling of belonging, of unfolding and revelation that accompanied you the whole time you were typing with the prehistoric Underwood you inherited from your father, and later when you struck through what you had typed, noted, cursed your impotence on those same papers.

Nothing remains anymore of the acrobatic searches and the possible meetings that cornered you when you tried to turn into a recovered present the acts and thoughts of past and carried out lives of someone you baptized with the same name repeatedly. Again and again the same name, although it was another Man to whom you had granted the slippery gift of reincarnation or return or reoccurrence or just the lucky possibility of the confluence of the atavistic fragments of lives sentenced to be attracted by History's powerful magnet, earthly powers, and the unappealable reign of time. Again and again, a being born of your obsessions, to whom you had given attitudes, precise thoughts, so close to your own real and written life in that the borders between what was created and what was lived became confused for you in a jumble of properties that at some point struck you as an unfaithful albeit innocuous replacement of which, nonetheless, you could not and did not fully want. Because its quality as a lie constitutes its saving and inalienable condition, its essence as creation, its value as possible truth, many times even more accurate than the possible truth or truths. From within yourself, you molded that historic and atemporal being. Clinging to the present, you wrote the past until you lost all notion of the limits of the permanent and the transpired. But, in the process of creation, you never lost the remaining consciousness that while you were converting the past into the present, what was written immediately became part of that same past: something irreversible, fleeting, purely irrecoverable, that ran between your fingers and that you took leave of by the magnificent fact of fixing it and later seeing it go off into the distance, like a ghost ship, an apparition whose shapes got mixed up for you as if you were watching History and time through the transparent veil of a teardrop.

You had arrived together at that point, from which each one would continue alone. That is the point of cleaving that makes you suffer the curse of the demiurge that has consumed itself, rib by rib, to cut out new postures and discovers how, in the end, it is merely an inert trunk lying in some corner of time. Although, you are almost surprised, your feet remain, and feet are the path.

It comforts you to recall, in contrast, that as you were shaping the story of the live wanderings of the character whom you decided to name Antoni Barral, the act of creation of those other lives, one and several simultaneously, had offered you a pleasant feeling of power. When writing, at the very least, you could choose, shape, save, or discard, with the power that in your real and possible life you had never been given, with the capacity to decide, in the past and the future, that you had been able to get much enjoyment from. The existences of Antoni Barral, if in reality he had them on that plane of physical and historic events that is known as reality, in his ways of manifesting himself and carrying himself perhaps had not seemed like the probable creation they now were, although you are convinced that they would have functioned under the same rules. Because nothing or almost nothing would have depended on an individual power of selection, of free will exercised freely, and less still on a conscious and voluntary construction. You know well that in the reality of the possible lives of one or several bodily Antonis, other forces, remote, powerful, and castrating, would have been the ones in charge of leading them and sculpting their real existences, if they had been real. As yours has been shaped: from above and from outside, with a perverse reduction in your freedom of decision, without any margin for error and rectification. With the overwhelming lack of space to redo what has been done and program what is to be done.

The conviction that only from writing comes the possibility of building others on the basis of what you have been and are served causes you to try to distance yourself from yourself, see yourself from the perspective that ended up being revealing, simultaneously pleasant and painful. Because your questionable imaginative capacity is informed by your lived experiences and what you've experienced through books, limited and recurring, and, as such, contaminated. Because of that, at the same time you move forward, you amassed pages, read, had gone perceiving this clarifying distance, because you were turning into someone else, freeing yourself from yourself and in some way, completing yourself through these others. Gaining freedom. Is that writing? Trends fading into one another? Giving up yourself in favor of what is created? Trying to recompose what has no possibility for restoration? Manipulating the clumsy spectacle of a lived life, without any possible previous design, and transforming it into a more benevolent and logical creation, in some way less human and as such, more satisfactory? Playing at being free? Even, being free?

20.

OCTOBER 9, 2014, BIRTHDAY

He opened his eyes, under the cover of the pages typed over several days, tangled up with an old dog who was in need of a bath again, warmed by the impertinent and resounding light of dawn in the tropics: the same light as always, filtered through the window, that inundated the room and fell like a reflector projecting against the wall from which, as his first action of the day, he would rip and scribble—he ripped and scribbled—the calendar that, with its twelve squares distributed in four rows, had pursued him for nine months, nine days, and nine hours since the interactive calendar: 9-9-9. He was already sixty years old. He had crossed into old age.

In the last three weeks, several times he came to feel he was on the verge of exploding. He managed to fulfill with the prisonlike discipline the medical orders of not drinking for the infinite number of days demanded and, in such terrifying and lucid sobriety, he had had to put down his weapons and also follow the various dispositions, orders, and agreements issued by the Organizing Commission for the Sixtieth Birthday of *Compañero* Mario Conde, as Aymara denominated the preparation committee, with the unanimous approval of everyone else implied in the process. In the midst of so much obedience and so many rules, he had managed to raise, nonetheless, a miserable demand that he considered nonnegotiable: the night before, the last day before he became old, he wanted to spend at his house, alone with his own company and that of

Garbage II, and to sleep in his bed, where he would awaken—and he did awake—on the day of the foreseen celebration.

In too many ways, the final days of his previous age had been the strangest and most impersonal of his life, and, at the same time, the calmest and most productive. The former policeman could not help but see them as a period that was even more confusing than the one he lived through just after having received Elizardo Soler's gunshot, when he thought he would die and confirmed with his own flesh—such appropriate words—how simple that journey could be, how easily one could cross over the line of to be or not to be, which had always been and would be the question.

When he settled into Tamara's lair to spend his convalescence and, incidentally, to be under permanent watch, they had considered the problem of Garbage II's care. Since no other solution was possible, the dog had been rescued by Rabbit and Candito and taken to his owner's recovery home, where Tamara would welcome him. From the initial negotiations, complex as any peace treaty and agreement based on mutual understanding, the hostess had established one unappealable condition: the dog must be bathed and would not sleep in the bed with her and Conde. The convalescent and the dog accepted both clauses and promised each other to behave as decently as their respective natures allowed, and they swore, besides, to do everything possible not to piss against the side of some armchair.

While two women who were almost identical but so different, Tamara and Aymara, took turns to care for him and cure him, Conde, perhaps unsettled by the lead that had gone through him, or by the impossibility of living his usual bad life, saw himself pressed to fulfill an incisive need that ended up rising up within him. As such, every morning, after he had an abundant dose of Kimbo coffee for breakfast, smoked his first cigarette of the day, and walked a couple of blocks around the neighborhood with Garbage II, he returned to the house and occupied the generous mahogany desk that, many years before, Ambassador Valdemira had acquired from a French antiquarian. Writing became a challenge, born of an unfathomable calling, from an indomitable urge. Relying on the well-populated library, which he himself had continued nourishing with some jewels that fell in his hands as a dealer of old books, Conde had begun to sketch a story—that aimed to be squalid and moving—of the incarnations of a historic figure without a past who, across History, lived some fictious and novelized lives, although in many ways similar to his own life.

The return to writing had been a comforting and simultaneously agonizing exercise, to which he had been able to hand himself over with greater intensity and effort ever since Bobby, pushed by the Pigeon, had shown up at the twins' house with the purpose of settling an outstanding bill for Conde's work and the past, and had freed him from an uncomfortable burden.

As soon as he arrived, his former classmate started asking for every manner of forgiveness. In many ways, he said on the verge of tears, he felt responsible for the bad experience his friend had gone through, a situation that had almost cost him his life. Every day that passed, he added, the health of Mario Conde had been in his prayers and supplications, without a doubt heard by their addressees. Old Bobby only regretted that that entire murky journey, which carried along with it three dead, including the infamous and treacherous Elizardo Soler, could also imply the possibility of having lost forever his powerful Virgin of Regla who was not really a Virgin of Regla, but without a doubt powerful and, to him, without any possible discussion, his saving mother Yemayá. But Conde was not in any way responsibile for the outcome in which he himself had landed, Bobby recognized. Because the weaving of the plot had begun long before when, to impress Elizardo and, if possible, take him to bed, he broke the veil of secrecy over the Black Virgin maintained by his near-grandfather, that Josep Maria Bonet, who wasn't really called Josep Maria Bonet. With his betrayal, Bobby had ended up awakening the maddest and most morose ambitions. That was why he vehemently insisted on paying his friend for his work, as he had agreed with Yoyi the Pigeon. As it should be, he stated.

When Bobby went to give him the $2,000 agreed upon for finding the Virgin, Conde had already decided that, if he was trying to be fair, he should reject the money, and he said so to his former classmate. While the Virgin had appeared, Bobby had not recovered Her, perhaps he never would recover Her, and both men regretted it. Purely speaking, he had not fulfilled his job, Conde went on, with an inevitable regret: "Given how much I could use that cash . . ."

"Conde, I know what you are thinking . . . Please, take the money. You earned it," Bobby assured him, holding out the prized envelope toward the hands of his former classmate. "I don't have my Virgin and you know that pains me . . . But you found Her and the money is not a problem," he added, looked around, and lowered his voice before continuing. "Amid the madness that went on and with Eli dead, no one found out that I kept several of his paintings, among them that Portocarrero that you went nuts for the day you saw it . . . And . . . I sent it all to Israel and"—Bobby further lowered the volume and leaned forward—"do you know how much the Portocarrero sold for in Miami?"

The eyes of the man who had once been a shy and repressed classmate were shining, the edges of his lips were moving into a smile, and at that moment, Conde felt that Bobby was delivering another gunshot, just like that, point-blank, and he reacted quickly.

"No, I don't want to know," he said, as he took the envelope of cash. This type of cultural bloodletting, all the more frequent, pierced him, and the fact of feeling himself close to another one of Bobby's tricks, in some way spurred by his own actions in search of the lost Virgin, was not pleasant. But, he also thought, he had worked and he had to survive: so, he took out four hundred-dollar bills and returned the rest of the money to Bobby. "Take the envelope. You owed me for three days of work and expenses, nothing else."

"But, Conde . . ."

"'But, Conde' nothing, man . . ."

"My brother," he started to say. "I don't understand you . . ."

"Of course you don't understand me, Bobby . . . You can't understand me . . . When you went to see me and we talked about the past, I wanted to believe the tale that you were seeking me out so I could help you because we were friends. I don't know if you were always like that or if we all made you like that, but you've become a bad person who doesn't respect even the most sacred things. You tricked me I don't know how many times. You told me whatever you felt like. You used me, Bobby, because I thought we really were friends . . . And at this point I don't know if the

Catalan Puigventós was interested in the Virgin because you yourself wanted to sell Her to him and the others beat you to it—"

"How can you think that? I swear to you that I—"

"Don't swear on anything or anyone . . . Those are all your problems. What I do know is that I don't want something that doesn't belong to me and that, because you are as you are, shouldn't belong to you, either. That I'm a complete moron? I've known that for years . . . What I don't know, Bobby, what I can't understand is how a man like you, who swears he believes in the Virgin, in Yemayá, in God and the angels and archangels, who prays and beseeches the heavens, could be so immoral . . . Is that what you get out of your faith?"

"Damn, Conde . . . I didn't—"

"You did, Bobby. You used me several times and after they shot me and nearly fucked me up, you just told me that you took advantage of what was going on to keep the Portocarrero painting and other things that I don't know or want to know how you got out of Elizardo's house. You are a bandit . . . And what gets me the most is that I believed in you . . . So go now, Bobby . . ."

The other man stood up. He looked like he was about to cry, and Conde, despite himself, without being able to avoid it, began to feel compassion for him.

"Are you going to report me?" Bobby asked, with the rest of his money in his hands and fear showing on his face.

"No, although I should . . . For being a thief and a son of a bitch . . . I was really mistaken about you. You moved me with your stories of fear and repression, with your cancer and your faith . . . But this is something else . . . So go, disappear. I cannot say it was a pleasure to have seen you again. Besides, now I know that it is true that you also took fake paintings out of Cuba to sell them in Miami . . . Dammit, Bobby . . . Get the hell out of here already!" he yelled and felt a twinge in the wound in his shoulder and the wound in his soul.

When he was left alone, Conde noticed that his hands were shaking, but he immediately felt tangible relief running through him. He was at peace with himself and with History: whatever happened now with

Roberto Roque Rosell, alias Bobby, and the statue of Our Lady of la Vall was not his business.

Later, the wave of those literary, emotional, and pleasant days without alcohol, in reality too pleasant and too little alcohol, so strange, went washing over him like dead weight and had ended up annoying him, as if the confluence of beneficial presences and absences, instead of a prize, were part of a plot against his spirit and personality. He needed to return to his disastrous real life, that, as greater compensation, had the stamp of his ownership: it was *his* bad life, *his*. The other one he was inhabiting seemed like an impostor, like Bobby's lives. Because of that, with Tamara's understanding consent, and as a part of the signed agreements, the day before his birthday he had returned to his house, with his dog, his disorder, his obsessions, his routine, and some typed pages full of additions and crossings out. On the way, he topped off his load of possessions with a bottle of rum.

After taking down and tearing up the calendar where he had noted the much-feared date that he had just begun to live, Conde brewed the first coffee of his advanced age and, the cup in one hand and cigarettes in the other, went to the rooftop. A pressing and unexplored need pushed him to take advantage of the pleasant October morning, and once on the roof, he settled down on the cement block that served as his watchtower: at his feet was the neighborhood he had known for sixty years of life, of his parents' and grandparents' lives, almost certainly that of his great-grandfather and perhaps even that of his great-great-grandfather. Many lives and years in a small and deteriorated physical space that, because of the time that had passed and the maintained permanence, belonged to him and to which he belonged, for the tranquility of his spirit, which was always in tormented conflict. He calmly breathed in the air in which the colorful aroma of a flamboyant tree mixed with the dark car exhaust and the undefinable smell of the recently baked buns made from the dubious flour of the present that didn't remind one at all of the aroma of the baguettes that, at some point, in a nearly perfect past, had come out from the insides of the same bread-baking oven. A lost and affectionate odor that only remained in his stubborn sentimental memory.

He lit the first cigarette as a sixty-year-old without making any promises of abstaining from nicotine and thought about what awaited him that night: the farewell party to an age and the welcoming (welcoming?) of another. It would be an unequivocal celebration in which, to please his boundless friends, he would have to act as if he were happy, when in reality, he was not. Not even the fact of knowing that, in his house, were the sheets conceived during the days of controlled convalescence, some papers that returned him to one of his most worn aspirations, served to calm down the overwhelming feeling of loss, of fatigue. His now turned out to be an almost bodily void that he never expected to feel, at least not in such a precise and chronologically exact way: because he had never believed in birthdays or closed dates and had lived his existence like an unstoppable flow through which you toss your best belonging over your shoulders. You leave time behind, your time, and you peer out, every day, at the unforeseeable: a future of which you do not know how it will be or how long it will last, if it will get twisted or flow monotonously and pleasantly. And right there, in the unfathomable, arose the most dismal void: in the tomorrow, not in the yesterday.

Then he saw him. He was walking on the sidewalk with his decided step and his usual bad appearance, grimy and dirty: like someone for whom the past and the future were the same thing or, worse still, didn't mean anything, since its edges had faded in the circularity. Now, instead of bags, he wore on his feet the already-tattered shoes that, three or four weeks before, Mario Conde had given him, and God knew how many miles the wanderer had made them cover.

He smiled when he saw him and was surprised when the man with the bags on his feet, who, for the moment, was no longer walking with bags on his feet, stopped in place, lifted his head, and looked toward the heights where Conde was hunkered down. The poor man moved his hand, in a gesture of greeting that was returned with a similar one, and raised his voice only as much as necessary to be heard by the man posted on the roof.

"I haven't seen you for days . . . I'm glad that you're already well . . . Oh, and happy birthday!"

When he heard him, Conde shuddered. He had expected to hear anything except a birthday greeting expressed by that man, at times invisible, whom he only knew for having given him the shoes he now wore. He was so confused and dumbstruck, that he asked the poor man, "What did you say?"

"I wished you a happy birthday. Sixty is a good age. To continue living or to die."

Conde could not shake his surprise. Was this engineered by Carlos and Rabbit? No, it couldn't be . . . He had congratulated him on arriving at sixty!

"And how do you know . . ."

"There are things I know . . . But many others that I don't know . . . Things that no one will ever manage to know . . . Although one has returned to where he never was . . . Have a good one," the man concluded, made a gesture of goodbye with his hand, and continued on his way, marked by God knows what compass, until he got lost among the people, the smoke from the cars, the blinding October light, the absence of the smell of baking bread. The man had disappeared, as he usually did, and Mario Conde again asked himself, despite the evidence of the shoes he was wearing, the same ones that he had worn until the moment in which he donated them, whether that character was real or merely a reflection of his fears, obsessions, and painful meditations. Or a trick of time.

EPILOGUE

He awoke with the premonition that something would happen. He couldn't know what; he was incapable of imagining it. Only that that day something would happen. Large, small, medium: something singular would occur. Nor did he have any idea why that enlightened certainty would come to him as he opened his eyes and received the always impertinent light that penetrated his window. Annoyed, he set aside the invasive feeling as much as he could and, like any other morning of his life, he resolved to face the day. He brewed coffee, smoked cigarettes, fed Garbage II. He got ready to hit the streets in search of books, earning his living how he could. He remembered, due to some subconscious whim, or perhaps because of his recent relationship with the feast days, that it was December 17, Saint Lazarus's Day. The leprous saint surrounded by dogs, the Babalú Ayé of the Yorubas: a day for fulfilling promises or awaiting miracles. Perhaps he would be surprised by one and that would be what could happen: it would be welcome, for example, to find a good library for sale whose books would help him come out of the recurrent poverty in which he seemed to live. That would be an acceptable miracle. Although he was fed up with the same circumstances, and continued without believing in the intangible, he now knew better than if one has enough faith, a miracle can happen. But faith, precisely, was what Mario Conde most lacked and would lack. He also lacked coffee. Real coffee.

And dreams. And hopes. And years to think that it was or would be possible to begin again, if such a miracle were practicable. Luckily, other things abounded. Premonitions for example. And he had the certainty that some of them would even become true.

MANTILLA, DECEMBER 17, 2014–AUGUST 10, 2017

AUTHOR'S NOTE

The Transparency of Time is a novel and should be read as such. Its present and past realities are anchored in real historical scenes and contexts, but all crafted for the purpose of its writing and use as a novel. As we say now: it is inspired by (see the dictionary) real events.

The chapters of the novel that take place in the past are completely fictitious re-creations of characters and scenes rooted in several documented historical moments. I have, as always, respected the essence of those periods and situations in a fictionalization that begins with thorough historical research. The hamlet of la Vall de Sant Jaume is the product of my imagination, and, through its structure and landscapes, I try to re-create any other small hamlet in the Catalan Garrotxa. The Black Virgin, Our Lady of la Vall, is also fictitious, but like many other Romanesque Black Virgins that exist or existed and disappeared or were destroyed, Her history and origins could have been as I've created them.

The episodes in the Cuban present, however, are based on living knowledge and the exploration of a reality that is part of my own experience, although the investigative process in the crime drama in which Mario Conde participates is pure fiction.

As always, I'd like to express my gratitude to a group of friends, my loyal readers and willing collaborators. To my friend and translator to the French, Elena Zayas, for her active efforts in searching for historical, written, and graphic information and for her patient and critical appraisal of my initial drafts. To my dear Lourdes Gómez for reading and for seeking out bibliographies that were beyond my reach in Cuba. To my editor Juan Cerezo, for his close evaluation and for being my first guide to discovering the physical landscape and life in the Garrotxa during a memorable journey. To Carme Simón, the director of Olot's Municipal Library, for her revelatory tour of the most remote and characteristic places in the Catalan Pyrenees. To Alejandro Ramírez Anderson, for opening the doors to the "settlement" for me. To my friend and editor Vivian Lechuga, for her patience and willingness.

I cannot help but thank the following reader friends for the time and critiques they offered: José Antonio Michelena, Rafael Grillo, Miguel Katrib, Rafael Acosta.

And, as expected, once again, I thank Lucía. For reading my work, for serving as the brakes, for knowing to ignore me on the days that the writing didn't flow, for always supporting me (in the broadest sense of the word): in times of peace and especially in times of war, that gunfire amid which life, history, and geography have made me live and write, before and after any miracle.

A NOTE ABOUT THE AUTHOR

Leonardo Padura was born in Havana, Cuba, in 1955. He is the author of *The Man Who Loved Dogs*, *Heretics*, and the genre-bending Mario Conde detective novels, which have been translated into numerous languages and are the basis for the Netflix miniseries *Four Seasons in Havana*. He is the recipient of many awards, including the esteemed Princess of Asturias Award, and has been called "Cuba's greatest living writer."

A NOTE ABOUT THE TRANSLATOR

Anna Kushner, the daughter of Cuban exiles, was born in Philadelphia and has been traveling to Cuba since 1999. She has translated the novels of Norberto Fuentes, Marcial Gala, Guillermo Rosales, and Gonçalo M. Tavares, as well as two collections of nonfiction by Mario Vargas Llosa.